D1392299

The Secret Supper

JAVIER SIERRA

TRANSLATED BY

ALBERTO MANGUEL

ATRIA BOOKS

New York   London   Toronto   Sydney

ATRIA BOOKS
1230 Avenue of the Americas
New York, NY 10020

This book is a work of fiction. Names, characters, places and incidents are products of the author's imagination or are used fictitiously. Any resemblance to actual events or locales or persons, living or dead, is entirely coincidental.

Copyright © 2004 by Javier Sierra
Copyright © 2004 by Random House Mondadori, S.A.

English translation © 2006 by Simon & Schuster, Inc.
Originally published in Spanish in 2004 as *La cena secreta* by Plaza & Janés

ISBN-13: 978-1-4165-4381-7
ISBN-10:   1-4165-4381-3

This Atria Books export edition March 2007

10 9 8 7 6 5 4 3 2 1

ATRIA BOOKS is a trademark of Simon & Schuster, Inc.

Manufactured in the United States of America

For information regarding special discounts for bulk purchases, please contact Simon & Schuster Special Sales at 1-800-456-6798 or business@simonandschuster.com

To Eva,
who has illuminated the path of this traveler

The Secret Supper

No one took any notice.

None of the merchants, moneylenders or friars strolling by in the twilight around San Francesco il Grande noticed the slovenly, ill-dressed man who hurried into the Franciscan church. It was the eve of a holiday, a market day, and the inhabitants of Milan were busy gathering provisions for the coming days of official mourning. Under such circumstances, it was only natural that the presence of yet another beggar left them unconcerned.

But the fools were once again mistaken. The beggar who entered San Francesco was not an ordinary man.

Without giving himself a moment's respite, the ragged man left behind him the double row of benches that lined the nave and hurried on toward the main altar. There was not a soul to be seen inside the church. At last he had been permitted to see a painting, *The Virgin of the Rocks*, that few in Milan knew by its real name: the *Maestà*.

He approached the altar cautiously. His heart beat faster. There, utterly alone in the church, the pilgrim warily stretched out his hand, as if he might be forever united to the sacred scene. As he cast his eyes on the celebrated painting, suddenly a detail caught his attention. How strange! The pilgrim was overcome by a vertiginous feeling of horror. Someone had meddled with the *Maestà*.

The pilgrim did not dare move a muscle but remained frozen to the spot at the sound of the dry, deep voice behind him. He hadn't heard the door of the church creak open, so the intruder must have been watching him for a fair while now.

"I can tell you're like all the others. For some dark reason you heretics come in droves to this House of God. Its light attracts you, but you are incapable of recognizing that."

The pilgrim's pulse was racing. His hour had come. He felt dazed and angry, cheated in having risked his life to kneel before a fraud. The painting he was looking at was not the *Opus Magnum*.

"It can't be—" he whispered. The intruder laughed out loud.

"It is easy enough to understand. I'll grant you the mercy of knowledge before sending you to burn in hell. Don't you realize that Leonardo has betrayed you?"

Was it possible that Leonardo had actually betrayed his brethren?

The pilgrim realized that something was terribly wrong. He heard behind him a metallic scraping, like that of a sword being unsheathed.

"Am I to die as well?"

"The Soothsayer will do away with all of the wicked."

Architectural plan of the convent and church of Santa Maria delle Grazie in present-day Milan.

1. Tribunal
2. Refectory
3. Leonardo da Vinci, *The Last Supper*

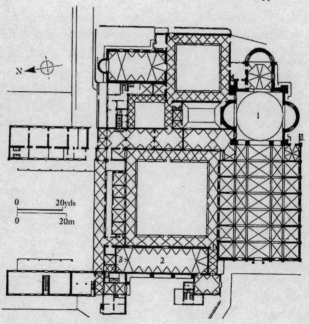

A cast of characters appears on pages 387 to 394.

PREFACE

In the Middle Ages and the Renaissance, Europe still held intact its gift for understanding ancestral images and symbols. Its people knew how and when to interpret the design on a column, a particular figure in a painting or a simple sign on the road, even though only a minority had, in those days, learned to read and write.

With the arrival of the Age of Reason, the gift for interpreting such languages was lost, and with it, a good part of the richness bequeathed to us by our ancestors.

This book makes use of many of those symbols as they were conceived once upon a time. But it also intends to restore to the modern reader the ability both to understand them and to benefit from their infinite wisdom.

1

I cannot recall a more dangerous and tangled puzzle than the one I was called upon to solve in the New Year of 1497, when the duchy of Ludovico il Moro lay in its painful death throes, while the Papal States watched on.

The world was then a dangerous, fast-changing place, a hellish quicksand in which fifteen centuries of faith and culture threatened to collapse under the onslaught of new ideas imported from the Far East. Suddenly, from one day to the next, Plato's Greece, Cleopatra's Egypt and even the extravagant curiosities of the Chinese Empire that Marco Polo had discovered seemed to deserve greater praise than our own Scriptural stories.

Those were troubled days for Christendom. We were ruled by a simoniac Pope (a Spanish devil crowned under the name of Alexander VI who had shamelessly bought his own tiara at the latest conclave), governed by several princes seduced by the beauty of all things pagan, and threatened by Turkish hordes armed to the teeth, waiting for an opportunity to invade the Western Mediterranean and convert us to the faith of Islam. In all truth, it can be said that never before, in almost fifteen hundred years of history, had our own faith stood so utterly defenseless.

And there, in the midst of it all, was this servant in

God, Agostino Leyre, the very same who is writing to you now. I found myself at the threshold of a century of transformation, an epoch in which the world was shifting its borders daily and demanding from us all an unprecedented effort to adapt. It was as if, with every passing hour, the Earth became larger and larger, constantly obliging us to update our store of geographical knowledge. We, men of the cloth, had already begun to realize that there would no longer be enough of us to preach to a world peopled by millions of souls who had never heard of Christ, and the more skeptical among us foresaw a period of imminent chaos that would bring into Europe a whole new tide of pagans.

In spite of such terrible things, those were exciting years. Years that I look upon now with a certain nostalgia, today, in my old age, from this miserable exile that slowly devours both my health and my memories. My hands barely obey me, my eyes grow dim, the burning sun of southern Egypt melts my brain and only in the hours before dawn am I capable of ordering my thoughts and reflecting on the curious fate that led me to this place—a fate from which neither Plato, nor Alexander VI, nor even the pagans were excluded.

But I must not run ahead of my story.

Suffice it to say that now, at last, I'm alone. Of the secretaries I once had, not a single one remains, and today only Abdul, a youngster who doesn't speak my tongue and who believes I am an eccentric holy man who has come to die in his land, looks after my most basic needs. I eke out my life in an ancient tomb hollowed in the rocks, surrounded by sand and dust, threatened by scorpions and almost prevented from walking by my two weak legs. Every day, faithful Abdul brings into my cubicle some unleavened bread and whatever leftovers he finds at home. He is like the raven that for sixty years would carry in his beak half an ounce of bread to Paul the Hermit, who died in these same lands, more than a hundred years old. Unlike that ominous bird, Abdul smiles when he delivers his burden, without quite knowing what else to do. It is enough. For someone who has sinned as much as I have, every moment of contemplation becomes an unexpected gift from the Creator Himself.

But, as much as solitude, pity too has come to gnaw away at my soul. I'm sorry that Abdul will never learn what brought me to his village. I would not know how to explain it to him by signs. Nor will he ever be able to read these lines, and even in the remote eventuality that he might find them after my death and sell them to some camel driver, I doubt whether they will serve any purpose other than fueling a bonfire on a cold desert night. No one here understands Latin nor any of the romance languages. And every time that Abdul finds me in front of my pages, he shrugs in astonishment, knowing full well that he is missing something important.

Day after day, this thought fills me with anguish. The intimate certainty that no Christian will ever read what I am writing clouds my mind and brings tears to my eyes. When I finish these pages, I will ask that they be buried with my remains, hoping that the Angel of Death will remember to collect them, and carry them to Our Everlasting Father when the time comes for my soul to be brought to Judgment. It is a sad story. But then, the greatest secrets are those that never see the light.

Will mine manage to do so?

I doubt it.

Here, in the caves they call Yabal al-Tarif, a few steps away from the great Nile that blesses with its waters an inhospitable and empty desert, I only pray God that He give me enough time to justify my deeds in writing. I am so far removed from the privileges I once enjoyed in Rome that, even if the new Pope were to forgive me, I know I would be unable to return to God's fold. I would find it unbearable to hear no longer the distant cries of the muezzins in their minarets. And the longing for this land that has so generously welcomed me would slowly torture my final days.

My consolation lies in setting down those past events exactly in the order in which they took place. Some I suffered in my own flesh. Others, however, I only heard of long after they had happened. And yet, told one after the other, they will give you, hypothetical reader, an idea of the enormity of the puzzle that changed my life forever.

No. I cannot continue to turn my back on my fate. Now that I have reflected on all that which my eyes have seen, I feel irrevocably compelled to tell everything . . . even if the telling will serve nobody's purpose.

2

The puzzle begins on a January night in the year 1497, far, very far from Egypt. That winter, three decades ago, was one of the coldest that the chronicles record. It had snowed copiously and all of Lombardy was covered in a thick white mantle. The monasteries of San Ambrogio, San Lorenzo and San Eustorgio, and even the pinnacles of the cathedral, had all vanished under the snow. The wagons laden with wood were the only things still moving in the streets, and most of Milan slumbered, wrapped in a silence that seemed to have settled in many centuries ago.

It happened at about eleven o'clock at night on the second day of the year. A woman's heartrending howl broke the frozen peace of the Sforza palace. The howl was followed by sobs and the sobs by the piercing cries of the court's professional mourners. The last stirring of the *serenissima* Beatrice d'Este, a woman in the flower of life, the beautiful wife of the Duke of Milan, had forever shattered the kingdom's dreams of glory. Dear God! The duchess had died with her eyes wide open, furious, cursing Christ and all his saints for having taken her so soon to His side, clutching, with what strength she had, the habit of her horrified confessor.

Yes, that is when everything started.

I was forty-five years old when I read for the first time the report of what happened that day. It was a terrifying story. The Order of Bethany, as was its custom, had requested the report secretly from Ludovico il Moro's chaplain, who had sent it down to Rome without delay. That is how the Papal States worked in those days: more swiftly and efficiently than any other state, so that, long before the official announcement of the duchess's death had arrived at the Holy Father's diplomatic office, our brethren already knew all the details of the story.

At the time, my responsibility within the complex structure of Bethany was to attend to the Master General of the Order of Saint Dominic. Our organization survived within the narrow margins of strict confidentiality. In an age characterized by palace intrigues, murders by poison and family treason, the Church required an information service that would allow it to know exactly where it could tread safely. We were a secret order, faithful to none other than the Pope and the visible head of the Dominicans. That is why, in the outside world, almost no one had ever heard of us. We hid behind the ample cloak of the Secretariat of Keys of the Papal States, a marginal, neutral organism of scarce public visibility and very limited competence. However, behind the walls, we functioned as a secret congregation, a sort of permanent commission set up to examine government matters that might allow the Holy Father to foretell the movements of his many enemies. Any scrap of news, however minuscule, that might affect the status quo of the Church would immediately pass into our hands, where it would be weighed and transmitted to the pertinent authority. That was our sole mission.

In this context, I became familiar with the report on the death of our adversary, Donna Beatrice d'Este. I can still see the faces of our brothers celebrating the news. Fools! They thought that Nature had saved us the trouble of having to kill her. Their enthusiasm showed how simply their minds worked, always resorting to the gallows, to the verdict of the Holy Office or to the hands of a paid cutthroat. But that was not the case with me. Unlike the rest of the brethren, I was far from certain that the departure of the Duchess of Milan meant the end of a long chain of irregularities, conspiracies and threats against the faith that had seemed to lurk in Ludovico il Moro's court and had for months caused unease among our network of informants.

Certainly, it was enough to mention her name at one of the general chapter gatherings of Bethany for rumors to overrun the rest of the debates. Everyone knew her. Everyone knew of her un-Christian activities, but no one had ever dared denounce her. Such was the terror that Donna Beatrice inspired in Rome, that not even the report we received from the duke's chaplain—who was also the loyal prior of our new monastery of Santa Maria delle Grazie—had referred in any way to her unorthodox doings. The Father Prior Vicenzo Bandello, reputed theologian and learned leader of the Milanese Dominicans, merely described to us the event that had taken place and kept a safe distance from any political question that might have compromised him.

Nor did anyone in Rome reproach him for his prudence.

According to the report signed by the Father Prior, everything had seemed quite normal until the day before the tragedy. Up to that date, the young Beatrice was said to possess everything a woman might want: a powerful husband, an overflowing vitality and an infant about to be born who would perpetuate its father's noble name. Drunk with happiness, she had spent her last afternoon nearly dancing from room to room and chattering with her favorite lady-in-waiting in the Rochetta Palace. The duchess lived unconcerned by the worries that would have troubled any other mother in her land. She had decided that she would not even feed her child so as to keep unspoiled her small, delicate breasts: a carefully selected nurse would be in charge of overseeing the child's upbringing, would teach it to eat and to walk, would rise with the dawn to lift it out of its cot, wash it and wrap it in warm cloths. Both baby and nurse would live in the Rochetta, in a room that Donna Beatrice had decorated with care. For Beatrice d'Este, maternity was to be a delightful and unexpected game, free of responsibilities and concern.

But it was precisely there, in the small paradise she had imagined for her scion, that tragedy overtook her. According to the Father Prior, just before the Eve of Saint Basil, Donna Beatrice fainted on one of the couches of the palace. When she awoke, she felt ill. Her head was turning, and her stomach fought to empty itself with long and fruitless retchings. Not knowing what sickness had overcome her, the strong cramps in her bowels following the vomiting led her to fear the worst. Ludovico il Moro's child had decided to advance its arrival in the world without anyone foreseeing such a contingency. For the first time in her life, Beatrice was frightened.

The doctors took longer than expected to reach the palace that day. The midwife had to be fetched from outside the city walls, and when all the staff needed to assist the duchess finally congregated at her side, it was too late. The umbilical cord that fed the future Leon Maria Sforza had wrapped itself around the baby's fragile neck. Little by little, neat as a rope, it tightened until it throttled him. Immediately, Beatrice noticed that something was amiss. It seemed to her as if the baby, who seconds earlier had been pushing vigorously to emerge from her belly, had all of a sudden stopped his attempts to come into the world. First he trembled violently and then, as if the effort had drained him, he lost all strength and became stone still. Seeing this, the doctors cut the mother open from side to side, while she writhed in anguish, biting into a vinegar-soaked cloth. But their gesture was useless. Horrified, they discovered a bluish, lifeless baby, his eyes glassy, hideously strangled in his mother's womb.

And that is how, in terrible pain, without even a moment to come to terms with the loss, Beatrice herself breathed her last a few hours later.

In his report the Father Prior said that he arrived in time to see her agony. Bloody, with her innards exposed and drenched in an unbearable pestilence, she seemed delirious with the torment, crying out for confession and extreme unction. Fortunately for our brethren, Beatrice d'Este died before receiving the sacraments.

I say "fortunately" advisedly.

The duchess was barely twenty-two years old when she left our world. Bethany was well aware that she had led a sinful life. Since the days of Pope Innocent VIII, I myself had had occasion to study and store a number of documents concerning her debauchery. The thousand eyes of the Secretariat of Keys of the Papal States knew well the kind of person the Duke of Ferrara's daughter had been. Within the walls of our general quarters on Mount Aventino, we could boast that no important document issued from the European courts was unknown to our institution. In the House of Truth, dozens of readers examined daily missives in all languages, some of them encrypted by means of the most abstruse devices. We would decipher them, classify them according to their importance and store them in the archives. Not all, however. Those which referred to Beatrice d'Este had long held a priority in our duties and were kept in a room to which few of us were allowed access. These irreproachable documents showed that Beatrice d'Este was possessed by the demon of occult science. And, worse still, many alluded to her as the principal instigator of the magic arts practiced in Ludovico il Moro's court. In a country traditionally prone to the most sinister heresies, this piece of information should have been weighed very carefully. But no one did so at the time.

The Dominicans of Milan—among them, the Father Prior—had several times held in their hands proof that

Donna Beatrice, as well as her sister Isabella in Mantua, collected amulets and pagan idols, and that both women professed an immoderate passion toward the prophecies of astrologers and dissemblers of every kind. But the Dominicans never did anything about it. The teaching that Isabella received from those deceivers was so wicked that the poor woman spent her last days convinced that our Holy Mother Church would soon disappear forever. Often she would say that the Papal Court would be dragged to the Last Judgment and there, among archangels, saints and pure men, the Eternal Father would condemn us all with no pity.

No one in Rome was more aware than I of the activities of the Duchess of Milan. Reading the reports that arrived concerning her, I learned how devious women can be, and I discovered to what extent, in barely four years of marriage, Donna Beatrice had changed the behavior and the aims of her powerful husband. Her personality began to fascinate me. Superstitious, addicted to profane literature and seduced by whatever exotic notion circulated in her fiefdom, her obsession was to bring to Milan the former splendor of Florence under the Medici.

I believe it was this that put me on my guard. Though the Church had managed gradually to undermine the pillars of that powerful Florentine family, weakening the support they lent to thinkers and artists fond of unorthodox notions, the Vatican was not prepared to face a resurgence of such ideas in the great northern city of Milan. The Medici villas, the memory of the Academy that Cosimo the Elder had founded to rescue the wisdom of the ancient Greeks, the exaggerated protection he had given to architects, painters and sculptors, filled not only the fertile imagination of the duchess but mine as well. Except that she allowed these things to guide her own beliefs and infect the duke himself with their poisonous allure.

Since the day when Alexander VI ascended to Peter's throne, in 1492, I kept sending messages to my superiors to warn them of what might happen. No one paid any attention to my advice. Milan, so close to the French frontier and with a political tradition of rebellion against Rome, was the perfect candidate to nurse what might become an important schism within the Church. Nor did Bethany believe me. And the Pope, lukewarm toward heretics (barely a year after having donned the tiara, he had already begged forgiveness for having hounded such kabbalists as Pico della Mirandola), lent deaf ears to my warnings.

"That friar, Agostino Leyre," my brothers in the Secretariat of Keys used to say about me, "pays too much heed to the messages from the Soothsayer. He's bound to end up just as mad."

3

The Soothsayer.

He is the only piece missing to finish the puzzle.

His presence merits an explanation. The fact is that, besides my own warnings to the Holy Father and to the highest powers in the Dominican Order concerning the Duchy of Milan's errant path, there were others that issued from a quite different source, thereby confirming my worst fears. He was an anonymous witness, well informed, who every week would send to our House of Truth minutely detailed letters denouncing the beginnings of a vast sorcerer's operation in the lands of Ludovico il Moro.

His letters started arriving in autumn of 1496, four months before the death of Donna Beatrice. They were addressed to our order's seat in Rome, at the monastery of Santa Maria sopra Minerva, where they were read and put away as the work of a poor devil obsessed with the presumed doctrinal strayings of the Sforza family. I do not blame them. We were living then in times of madness, and the letters of yet another fanatic did not overly worry any of our father superiors.

Except for one.

It was the archivist who, at Bethany's latest general

chapter meeting, spoke to me of the writings of this new prophet.

"You should read them," he said. "As soon as I saw them I thought of you."

"Indeed?"

I remember the archivist's owlish eyes, blinking feverishly.

"They are a very curious thing. They have been written by someone who shares your same fears, Father Agostino. A prophet of the Apocalypse, cultivated, well versed in grammar, such a man as the Christian world has not seen since the times of Friar Tanchelmo de Amberes."

"Friar Tanchelmo?"

"Yes. A crazy old man from the twelfth century who denounced the Church for having turned itself into a brothel, and who accused the priests of living in constant sin. Our Soothsayer does not go so far as that, even if, by the tone of his letters, I suspect he won't be long in getting there."

Leaning forward, the archivist added in a wheezing voice:

"Do you know what makes him different from other madmen?"

I shook my head.

"That he seems better informed than any of us. This Soothsayer is a fiend for the exact detail. He knows everything!"

The friar was right. The Soothsayer's fine, bone-colored sheets of parchment, written in perfect calligraphy and now piled up in a wooden box sealed with the word *riservato*, referred with obsessive insistence to a secret plan to turn Milan into a new Athens. I had been suspecting something like this for a long time. Ludovico il Moro, like the Medici before him, was among those superstitious leaders who believed that the ancients had a knowledge of the world far more advanced than ours. He believed in a timeworn story according to which, before God punished the world with the Flood, humanity had enjoyed a prosperous Golden Age that first the Florentines—and now the Duke of Milan—wished to bring back at all costs. And to achieve this, these people would not hesitate to cast aside the Bible and the Church's tenets, since, they argued, in those past days of glory, God had not yet created an institution to represent Him.

But there was more: the Soothsayer's letters insisted that the cornerstone of the project was being laid down before our very noses. If what the Soothsayer had written was true, Ludovico il Moro's cunning was beyond measure. His plan to convert his domain into the capital of this rebirth of the philosophy and science of the ancients was to rest on an astonishing foundation: on no less a place than our new monastery in Milan.

The Soothsayer had managed to surprise me. Whoever the man hiding behind such revelations might be, he had delved much further into the matter than I would have ever dared. As the archivist now warned me, he seemed to have eyes everywhere, not only in Milan but also in Rome, since several of his latest missives carried the disconcerting heading *Augur dixit*—"the Soothsayer hath spoken." What kind of informer were we dealing with? Who, except someone well placed within the Curia, would know what name had been given to him by the clerks of Bethany?

Neither of us knew whom to accuse.

In those days, the monastery referred to in his messages—Santa Maria delle Grazie—was in the process of being built. The Duke of Milan had appointed the best architects of the day to work on it: Bramante was in charge of the church's gallery, Cristoforo Solari of the interior, and not a single ducat was spared to pay the finest artists for the decoration of every one of its walls. Ludovico il Moro wished to turn our temple into a mausoleum for his family, a place of eternal repose that would render his memory immortal for centuries to come.

And yet, what was for the Dominicans a privilege was for the author of these letters a terrible curse. He foresaw terrible calamities for the papacy if no one put a stop to the project, and he predicted a dark and fatal time for the whole of Italy. It was indeed in all fairness that the anonymous author of these messages had earned for himself the title of Soothsayer. His vision of Christendom could not have been bleaker.

4

No one paid any heed to the poor anonymous devil until the morning on which his fifteenth letter arrived.

On that day, Brother Giovanni Gozzoli, my assistant at Bethany, burst noisily into the scriptorium. He was waving in the air a new message from the Soothsayer, and oblivious to the reproachful glances of the studious monks, he walked straight up to my desk.

"Father Agostino, you must see this! You must read it at once!"

I had never seen Brother Giovanni so distraught. The young man waved the letter before my eyes and, in a strangled voice, whispered: "It's incredible, Father. Incredible."

"What is so incredible, Giovanni?"

Brother Giovanni took a deep breath.

"The letter—this letter—the Soothsayer—Master Torriani asked that you read it at once."

"Master Torriani?"

The pious Gioacchino Torriani, thirty-fifth successor of Saint Dominic de Guzmán on Earth and the highest authority of our order, had never before taken any of these anonymous messages seriously. He had disposed of them with indifference, and once or twice he had even scolded me for wasting my time on such nonsense. Why had he changed his attitude? Why did he send me this new letter, begging me to study it immediately?

"The Soothsayer—" Brother Giovanni gulped.

"Yes?"

"The Soothsayer has uncovered the plan."

"What plan?"

Brother Giovanni was still holding the message, trembling with the strain. The letter, consisting of three sheets with the wax seal broken, fell softly onto my desk.

"Ludovico il Moro's plan," my secretary whispered, as if freeing himself from a heavy load. "Don't you understand, Father Agostino? It explains what he really wants to do at Santa Maria delle Grazie. He wants to perform magic!"

"Magic?" I asked, astonished.

"Read it!"

I delved into the letter on the spot. There was no doubt that whoever had written it was the same person responsible for the previous ones: the headings and the handwriting betrayed a common author.

"Father, please read it!" he insisted.

I soon understood his urgency. The Soothsayer was bringing to light once again something that everyone had thought long buried and forgotten, an event that had taken place almost sixty years ago, in the days of Pope Eugene IV, when the Patriarch of Florence, Cosimo de' Medici, later known as the Elder, decided to finance a council that, had it succeeded, might have changed forever the course of Christendom. It was an old story. It appears that Cosimo had arranged for a gathering, which lasted several years and proved to be fruitless, between opposing diplomatic delegations, with the intention of reuniting the Eastern Church and that of Rome. The Turks were then threatening to extend their influence over the whole of the Mediterranean, and they had to be stopped at whatever cost. Cosimo, the old banker, had the wild idea of uniting all Christians under the same banner in order to face the enemy with the strength of a common faith. But his plan was unsuccessful.

Or perhaps not entirely.

What the Soothsayer revealed in his message was the existence of a secret purpose behind the council, a hidden objective whose consequences could still be felt in Milan six decades later. According to the Soothsayer, Cosimo de' Medici, in addition to engaging in the political debates of his day, had spent much of his time negotiating with delegations from Greece and Constantinople for the purchase of old books, optical instruments and even manuscripts attributed to Aristotle and Plato, which had been thought long lost and which he ordered to be translated. In these ancient texts, Cosimo learned astonishing things. He discovered that already in Athens, people believed in the immortality of the soul and knew that the heavens were responsible for everything that moved on Earth. However, let it be understood: the Athenians did not believe in God, but in the influence of the heavenly bodies. According to those infamous treatises, the stars cast their influence on earthly matter through a "spiritual heat" similar to that which unites body and soul in human beings.

Aristotle spoke of this "heat" after having studied the chronicles of the Golden Age, and Cosimo fell under the charm of the philosopher's teaching.

According to the Soothsayer, the old banker had founded an academy, in the style of the Greek ones, whose sole purpose was to teach these secrets to artists. Through his studies, Cosimo became convinced that the design of works of art was an exact science, and a work created in accordance with certain subtle codes would come to reflect the cosmic forces and might thus be used to protect or to destroy its owner.

"Well? Have you seen, Father Agostino?" Giovanni's question brought me out of my thoughts. "The Soothsayer says that art can be employed as a weapon!"

Indeed. One paragraph further on, the letter spoke of the power of geometry. Numbers, harmony, sound—all were elements that could be employed in a work of art so as to make it emanate beneficial influences. Pythagoras, one of the Greeks who admired the Golden Age and who had so dazzled Cosimo de' Medici, had declared that "numbers are the only verifiable gods." The Soothsayer cursed them all.

"A weapon," I hissed. "A weapon that Ludovico wants to conceal inside Santa Maria delle Grazie."

"Exactly!" Giovanni seemed full of pride. "That is precisely what he says. Can it be possible?"

I was beginning to understand the sudden interest of Master General Torriani in the matter. Years ago, our beloved superior had condemned the work of the artist Sandro Botticelli because of a similar suspicion. Torriani accused him of using images inspired by pagan cults to illustrate works destined for the Church. But his denunciation also contained more serious matter. Thanks to Bethany's informers, Torriani had learned that Botticelli had, in the Medici's Villa di Castello, depicted the arrival of spring using a "magic" technique. The dancing nymphs had been placed in the painting like the sections of a gigantic talisman. Later, Torriani discovered that Lorenzo di Pierfrancesco, Botticelli's patron, had requested an amulet against aging, and the resulting painting was the magical remedy. In fact, Botticelli's picture concealed an entire treatise against the onslaught of time which included half the divinities of Olympus dancing against the advance of Chronos. And they had pretended to pass off a work like this as something devout, proposing it as a decoration for a Florentine chapel!

Our Master General had managed to discover the infamy in time. His clue was Chloris, one of the *Primavera* nymphs, painted with a sprig of bindweed sprouting from her mouth. This was the unmistakable symbol of the "green tongue" of the alchemists, those searchers of eternal youth, drunk with false ideas that the Holy Office was obliged to persecute wherever they emerged. Even though we in Bethany never managed to decipher the details of that mysterious language, the suspicion was enough for the painting never to be displayed within the walls of a church.

But now, if the Soothsayer was right, the story was threatening to repeat itself in Milan.

"Tell me, Brother Giovanni, do you know why Master Torriani asks me to study this message?"

My assistant had sat down at a nearby desk and was leafing through a recently illuminated book of hours. He made a grimace as if he had not understood my question.

"What? Have you not read the letter to the end?"

I once again turned my eyes to the pages. In the final paragraph, the Soothsayer spoke of Beatrice d'Este's death and how this would speed up the success of Ludovico il Moro's magic plan.

"I see nothing particular here, dear Giovannino," I protested.

"Does it not surprise you that he refers to the duchess's death in such explicit terms?"

"Why should that surprise me?"

Brother Giovanni sniggered:

"Because the Soothsayer dated and sent this letter off on December thirtieth. Three days before Donna Beatrice's stillbirth."

5

"So you're willing to swear that you've hidden a secret in this wall?"

Perplexed, Marco d'Oggiono stood scratching his chin, as he once again cast his eyes over the mural the Master was painting. Leonardo da Vinci amused himself with such games. When he was in a good humor (and on that day his humor was excellent), it was hard to see in him the celebrated artist, inventor, builder of musical instruments and engineer, favorite of Ludovico il Moro and the toast of half of Italy. On that cold morning, the Master bore the expression of a mischievous child. Knowing full well that his behavior upset the friars, he had taken advantage of the strained calm that had settled on Milan after the death of the duchess to inspect his work in the refectory of the Dominican fathers. He stood high above, content among his apostles, upon a six-meter scaffolding, leaping from board to board like a young boy.

"Of course there's a secret!" he cried. His contagious laughter echoed in the empty vaults of Santa Maria delle Grazie. "You need only look at my work attentively and take into account the numbers. Count them! Go ahead, count!" He laughed.

"But, Master—"

"All right." Leonardo shook his head condescendingly, stretching out the last word in protest. "I see that it will be difficult to teach you. Why don't you pick up the Bible there below, next to the box with brushes, and read out John 13, beginning with the twenty-first verse? Perhaps you'll find illumination."

Marco, one of the young, handsome apprentices of Leonardo, ran in search of the holy book. He lifted it from the lectern in a corner by the door and held it in the palm of his hand. It must have weighed at least several pounds. With an effort, Marco leafed through the volume printed in Venice and bound in the blackest leather with copper corners, until the Gospel According to John lay before him. It was a beautiful edition, with large black Gothic letters and floral engravings in each incipit.

"When Jesus had thus said," he read out, "he was troubled in spirit, and testified, and said, Verily, verily, I say unto you, that one of you shall betray me. Then the disciples looked one on another, doubting of whom he spake. Now there was leaning on Jesus' bosom one of his disciples, whom Jesus loved. Simon Peter therefore beckoned to him, that he should ask who it should be of whom he spake."

"Enough! Quite enough!" thundered Leonardo from high up on the scaffolding. "Now look up here and tell me: have you not yet unraveled my secret?"

The disciple shook his head. Marco knew that the Master had a trick up his sleeve.

"Master Leonardo," he said, lending a tone of clear

disappointment to his reproach, "I know that you are working on this passage in the Gospels. You teach me nothing new instructing me to read the Bible. What I want to know is the truth."

"The truth? What truth, Marco?"

"It is rumored in the city that you are taking so long to finish this work because you want to hide in it something important. You have abandoned the fresco technique and have chosen instead another one, much slower. And why? I'll tell you why: so you can reflect at your leisure on that which you want to transmit."

Leonardo remained impassive.

"They know all about your taste for mysteries, Master, and I too wish I could learn them all! Three years by your side, preparing concoctions and assisting your hands in tracing the sketches and cartoons. That should give me some advantage over those outsiders, don't you think?"

"Of course, of course. But who is saying all these things, if one may know?"

"Who, Master? Everyone! Even the monks in this holy place often stop your apprentices and question them."

"And what do they say, Marco?" he bellowed again from on high, with growing amusement.

"That maybe your Twelve are not the true portraits of the Apostles, like Filippo Lippi or Crivelli would have painted them, that maybe they depict the twelve constellations of the zodiac, that you may have hidden in the gestures of their hands the notes of one of your musical compositions for Ludovico il Moro . . . They say all sorts of things, Master."

"And you?"

"Me?"

"Yes, indeed, you." Another mischievous smile lit up Leonardo's face. "Having me so close by, working every day in such a splendid room, what conclusions have you reached?"

Marco lifted his eyes toward the northern wall where Leonardo was giving a few last touches with a brush of very fine hairs. On that wall was depicted the most extraordinary Last Supper Marco had ever seen. There was Jesus, present in the flesh, in the exact center of the composition. His look was languorous and his arms outstretched, as if he were watching from the corners of his eyes the reactions of his disciples to the revelation he had just made to them. Close by his side was John, the beloved, listening to Peter's urgent whisper. If one sharpened one's senses, one could almost see them move their lips, they looked so real.

But John was no longer leaning on Jesus' bosom, as the Gospel said. Indeed, he gave the impression of never having done so. On the other side of Christ, Philip, the giant, was standing with his hands digging into his chest. He seemed to be asking the Messiah: "Am I the traitor, Lord?" Or James the Elder, puffing up his chest like a bodyguard, swearing everlasting loyalty. "None will harm you while I am near," he seemed to boast.

"Well then, Marco. You have not yet answered me."

"I don't know, Master . . ." He hesitated. "This work of yours has something that bewilders me. It is so, so—"

"So?"

"So close, so human, that it leaves me speechless."

"Good!" Leonardo applauded, then dried his hands on

his apron. "You see? Without knowing, you are already closer to my secret."

"I don't understand you, Master."

"And perhaps you never will." He smiled. "But listen to what I'm about to tell you: everything in Nature holds a mystery of some kind. The birds hide from us the clues to their flight, the water has locked away the cause of its extraordinary strength. And if we ever succeeded to make painting a mirror of that nature, would it not be right to have it embody that same vast capability of guarding information? Every time you admire a painting, remember that you are entering the most sublime of all arts. Never remain on the surface: enter the scene, move among its elements, uncover its unknown details, prowl its recesses—and in that way you'll grasp its true meaning. But let me warn you: you need courage for the task. Many times, what we find in a mural like this one is far removed from what we expected to find. Bear that in mind."

6

Without delay, Brother Giovanni fulfilled the second part of the mission entrusted to him by the Master General.

After our conversation, having shown me the Soothsayer's latest letter, he returned to the Order's Mother House, leaving Bethany before sunset. Torriani had ordered him to return and apprise him of my reaction. In particular, he wanted to know my opinion regarding the rumors about the serious irregularities in the renovation of Santa Maria delle Grazie. My assistant must have given him my message, which was brief and clear: if my old fears were finally taken into account, and if, in addition, the revelations of the Soothsayer were to be considered credible, then he had to be found in Milan, and he had to tell us, from his own lips, the extent of the duke's secret plans for the monastery.

"In particular," I had insisted to Giovanni, "the work of Leonardo da Vinci must be examined closely. Already in Bethany, we were well aware of his fondness for hiding heterodox ideas in paintings apparently pious. Leonardo worked in Florence for many years and was acquainted with the descendants of Cosimo the Elder. Among all the artists working at Santa Maria, he is the one most likely to share the ideas of Ludovico il Moro."

Giovanni added my one other serious concern to his report to Master Torriani: I had insisted on the need to open an investigation into the death of Donna Beatrice. The Soothsayer's exact forecast suggested the existence of a sinister occult plan, conjured up by Duke Ludovico or by one of his wicked advisors, in order to install a pagan republic in the very heart of Italy. Even though it made little sense for the duke to order the assassination of his wife and one of his future heirs, the mind of those steeped in the occult sciences often follow unpredictable paths. It was not the first time that I'd heard of the need to sacrifice a noteworthy victim before a great undertaking. The ancients, barbarians of the Golden Age, did so often.

I believe that Torriani was roused by my conclusions.

The Master General alerted Brother Giovanni of his intentions, and on the following morning, while snow was still falling over Rome, he left his rooms in the Monastery of Santa Maria sopra Minerva set upon attacking the very root of the problem.

Defiantly riding a mule up the snow-laden roads leading out of the Eternal City, Torriani reached the headquarters of Bethany and asked to see me as soon as possible. I never learned what terms Brother Giovanni had employed to inform him of my concerns, but it was obvious that they had impressed him. I had never seen our Master in such a state. Two bruised bags hung under his gray eyes, extinguishing all light; his back seemed bowed under the weight of the bleak responsibility that now stifled his joyful character and made his shoulders drop despondently. Torriani, my mentor, guide and old friend, was hastening toward the end of his life with all marks of disillusionment on his face. And yet, a faint glimmer in his look betrayed a sense of urgency.

"Can you attend to a servant a God, drenched and sick?" he asked as soon as he saw me in the atrium of Bethany.

I was surprised to see him there at such an early hour. He had ridden up alone, without a retinue, a blanket flung over his habit and his sandals covered in rabbit skins. For the superior of the Order of Saint Dominic to have abandoned in such a state our Mother House and his parish, and crossed the city in a storm in order to meet with the head of his intelligence service, the matter had to be of utmost gravity. And even though his somber features invited immediate discussion, I dared not ask any questions. I waited for him to divest himself of his humble wraps and to drink the glass of hot wine that was offered him. We climbed up to my small study, a dark room full of boxes and manuscripts, from which all of Rome could be seen, and as soon as the door was closed, Father Torriani confirmed my worst fears:

"Of course I've come about those blessed letters!" he cried, arching his white eyebrows. "And you ask me who I think is the author? Precisely you ask me that, Father Agostino?"

Torriani took a deep breath. His wizened body struggled for warmth, aided by the wine. Outside, the snow continued to fall heavily on the valley.

"My impression," he continued, "is that our man must be someone in the duke's service or, if not, a brother in the new monastery of Santa Maria delle Grazie. It must be someone well familiar with our customs, someone who knows into whose hands these letters are delivered. And yet—"

"And yet?"

"You see, Father Agostino, since I read the letter I sent to you yesterday, I have not slept a wink. Out there is someone warning us of a serious act of treason against the Church. The matter is of greatest urgency, especially if, as I fear, our informant belongs to the community of Santa Maria—"

"You believe the Soothsayer to be a Dominican, Father?"

"I am almost certain. Someone from within, witness to Ludovico's advances, who doesn't dare denounce him for fear of retaliation."

"And I suppose you've already examined the lives of all those friars in search of your candidate. Am I mistaken?"

Torriani smiled with satisfaction.

"All. With no exception. And most of them come from good Lombard families. They are men of the cloth loyal to both Ludovico and the Church, men not inclined to fantasies or conspiracies. In a word, good Dominicans. I can't imagine which of them might be the Soothsayer."

"If it truly is one of them."

"Of course."

"Let me remind you, Master Torriani, that Lombardy has always been a land of heretics . . ."

The Master General, shivering, stifled a sneeze before responding. "That was long ago, Father Agostino. For the past two hundred years, there hasn't been a trace of the Cathar heresy in the whole area. It is true that those cursed souls who inspired our beloved Saint Dominic to create the Holy Inquisition took refuge there after the Albigensian Crusade, but they all perished without having been able to spread the contagion of their ideas to others."

"And yet, Master, we cannot dismiss the possibility that their blasphemous notions appealed to the Milanese mind. Otherwise, why are they so open to heterodox ideas? Why would the duke accept pagan beliefs if he himself had not grown up in an atmosphere inclined to them? And why," I continued, "would a Dominican, loyal to Rome, hide behind anonymous messages, if he himself did not take part in the heresy he now denounces?"

"Fabrications, Father Agostino! The Soothsayer is not a Cathar. On the contrary: he is concerned with maintaining orthodoxy with greater zeal than the General Inquisitor of Carcassonne himself."

"This morning, before your arrival, I once again went over all his letters. And the Soothsayer is clear about his goal from the very first message he sent us: he wants us to send someone to stop Ludovico il Moro's plans for Santa Maria delle Grazie. It is as if whatever the duke does with the rest of Milan—the piazzas, the navigation channels, the locks—were of no importance to him. And that lends weight to your theory."

Torriani nodded with satisfaction.

"But, Master," I ventured to contradict him, "before

taking action we should decide whether his request does not hold a trap."

"What? Do you propose to leave the Soothsayer to his own devices in spite of the proofs he has offered us? But you yourself have for some time now denounced the doctrinal strayings of the duke's late wife!"

"Precisely. They are a cunning family. That man, whoever he is, asks for our help, which we can no longer deny him. Furthermore, with the assistance of Cardinal Ascanio, brother of the duke, I've corroborated even the smallest detail in his reports. And believe me, they are exact.

"Exact," I repeated, while attempting to place my thoughts in order. "But what surprises me most in this affair, Master, is your own change of attitude."

"There has been no such change," he protested. "I set aside the Soothsayer's letters until I had solid proofs to back them. Had I not believed in them, I would have destroyed them, don't you think?"

"Well then, Master Torriani, if our informer is supported by truth, if he is indeed a Dominican worried about the future of his new monastery, why then does he mask his identity when he writes to you?"

Master Torriani shrugged his shoulders in perplexity.

"I wish I knew, Father Agostino. It worries me. The more time goes by without our finding answers, the more disturbed I become. These days the breaches in our order are many, and to open yet another wound within the bosom of the Church means bleeding Her with no hope for cure. That is why it is time for action. We cannot allow for the events in Florence to be repeated in Milan. It would be disastrous!"

Yet another wound. I hesitated to bring up the subject, but Torriani's silence left me no alternative.

"I imagine that you're referring to Father Savonarola—"

"Who else?" The old man took a deep breath before continuing. "The Holy Father's patience is at an end, and he is considering excommunication. Savonarola's sermons against the papal opulence are becoming more and more acrimonious, and furthermore, his prophecies regarding the end of the House of Medici have been fulfilled. Now, with a crowd in tow, he announced the Lord's dire punishments against the Papal States. He says that Rome must suffer to purge its sins, and the wicked man rejoices in his prediction. And the worst about it is that every day he has more followers. If by chance the Duke of Milan were to join in his apocalyptic ideas, no one would be able to stop the discredit to our institution."

In confusion, I crossed myself at the bleak prospect outlined by the Master General.

In those days, Father Girolamo Savonarola was, as all of Rome knew, Torriani's most worrisome problem. Everyone spoke of him. A persistent reader of the Book of Revelation, this Dominican of brilliant tongue and great seductive power had recently established a theocratic republic in Florence to fill the gap left by the flight of the Medici. From the vantage of his new pulpit, he raged against the excesses of Pope Alexander VI. Savonarola was a madman or, even worse, a fearless rogue. He lent deaf ears to the calls to order from his superiors, and he deliberately ignored canonical legislation. The *Dictatus Papae*, which, from the eleventh century, exempted the Pope and his court from all possibility of error, filled him with outrage, and challenging even the nineteenth sentence ("No one may judge the Pope"), he shouted from the altar that His Holiness must be stopped in the name of God Himself.

Our Master General had been driven to despair. Not only had he been unable to stifle that madcap's dreams of grandeur, but he had been helpless to prevent Savonarola's attitude from compromising the entire order in the eyes of His Holiness. The rebel, proud as Samson before the Philistines, had rejected the cardinal's hat offered to him to silence his criticism, and had even refused to abandon his tribune in the Florentine monastery of San Marco, alleging that he had a more important divine mission to accomplish. For this reason alone Master Torriani did not want the loyalty of the Dominican preachers questioned in Milan. If the Soothsayer was a Dominican and he was correct in his warnings against Ludovico il Moro's pagan plans for our new house in the city, then our order itself would once again be called into question.

"I've reached a decision, Father Agostino," the Master General declared with severity, after a moment's reflection. "We must abolish any shadow of a doubt from the works at Santa Maria delle Grazie, even appealing to the Holy Inquisition, if need be."

"Master, you are not thinking of bringing the Duke of Milan before a court?"

"Only if necessary. You know full well that nothing pleases the princes of this world more than to uncover the weaknesses of our Church and use them against us. That is why we are obliged to forestall their movements. Another scandal like that of Savonarola, and our House would be left in very bad standing in the eyes of the Papal States. You understand that, don't you?"

"And how, if I may ask, do you intend to reach the Soothsayer, confirm his denunciations and gather the necessary information to judge him, all without raising suspicion?"

"I've given the matter much thought, my dear Father Agostino," he muttered enigmatically. "You know better than I do that if I sent one of our inquisitors at the wrong time, the Milan tribunal would ask too many questions and thereby destroy the discretion demanded in this case. And if such a far-reaching plot does indeed exist, the accomplices of Ludovico il Moro would quickly hide its evidence."

"And so?"

Without answering, Torriani opened the study door and went down the stairs to the entrance gate. He entered the stables courtyard and sought out his mule: the emergency meeting was at an end. Outside, the storm was still blowing strongly.

"Tell me, what are you planning to do?" I insisted.

"Ludovico il Moro has decreed that the duchess's state funeral should take place in ten days' time," he answered at last. "There will be envoys from everywhere coming to Milan, and then it will be easy to enter Santa Maria and make the pertinent inquiries to find the

Soothsayer. However," he added, "we can't send any simple friar. It must be someone discerning, knowledgeable in laws, heresies and secret codes. His mission will be to find the Soothsayer, to confirm his accusations one by one and to stop the heresy. And it must be a man from this house. From Bethany."

The Master General cast a wary glance at the road he was about to take. With luck, the ride would take him an hour, and if his mule did not slip on a sheet of ice, he would reach his home with the midday sun.

"The man we need," he said as if announcing something of momentous importance, "is you, Father Agostino. None other would solve the matter with greater efficacy."

"I?" I was astonished. He had pronounced my name with morbid delectation while searching for something in his saddlebags. "But you are aware of the fact that I have work to do here, commitments—"

"None like this one!"

And pulling out a thick wad of documents sealed with his personal ring, he handed it over to me with one last command:

"You will leave for Milan without delay. Even today, if possible. And with that"—he looked toward the wad I now held in my hands—"you will identify our informer, find out what truth lies in this new danger and attempt to discover a remedy for it."

The Master General pointed to a sheet of parchment placed on top of the wad. On it, in large characters written in red ink, was the puzzle with the signature of our correspondent. I had seen the signature many times, since it appeared in Latin at the end of each of the Soothsayer's letters, but until now I had given it little attention.

I felt my eyes cloud over as they fell on those seven lines, which would henceforth become my principal concern.

They read:

Oculos ējus dinumera,
sed noli voltum ādspicere.
In latere nominis
mei notam rinvenies.
Contemplari et contemplata
aliis tradere.

Veritas

Though the text itself was simple, I had no idea what it meant.

Count its eyes
but look not on its face.
The number of my name
you shall find on its side.
Observe and give to others
the result of your observation.

Truth.

Of course, I obeyed. What else could I have done?

I arrived in Milan after Twelfth Night. It was one of those January mornings in which the glitter of the snow blinds the eyes and the clean air freezes the innards without pity. To reach my destination, I had ridden almost without stopping, except for three or four hours of sleep in filthy inns, and I was stiff and wet after a three-day journey in the midst of the cruelest winter in memory. But all that was of no importance. Milan, capital of Lombardy, the hub of court intrigues and of territorial squabbles with France and the neighboring counties, the city I had so thoroughly studied, lay now before me.

It was an impressive metropolis. The city of the Sforza, the largest south of the Alps, occupied twice the space of Rome; eight large gates guarded an impenetrable wall around a circular plan that, seen from above, must have resembled the shield of a giant warrior. And yet it was not its defenses that awed me but its newness and cleanliness that gave the city a profound sense of order. Its citizens did not relieve themselves in every corner, as they did in Rome, nor were visitors incessantly assailed by prostitutes. Here, every angle, every house, every public building seemed conceived for some superior function. Even its proud cathedral—in appearance fragile and skeletal, in contrast with the massive bulks of those in the south—poured its soothing influences over the entire valley. Seen from the hills, Milan looked like the last place on earth to breed sin and disorder.

Some distance before reaching Porta Ticinese, the city's noblest entrance, a kind merchant offered to accompany me to the Tower of Filarete, the main gate into Ludovico il Moro's fortress. Built on one of the corners of the urban shield, the Sforza castle seemed like a miniature replica of the city walls. The merchant laughed at the look of surprise on my face. He said he was a tanner from Cremona, and a good Catholic, to boot, who would gladly accompany me into the fortress in exchange for a blessing for himself and his family. I accepted the bargain.

The good man left me by the duke's castle exactly at the ninth hour. The site was even more magnificent than I had supposed. Banners with the terrible arms of the Sforzas—a sort of giant serpent devouring a poor soul—dropped from the battlements. Thin blue flags waved in the wind while, from somewhere inside the fortress, half a dozen huge chimneys belched big puffs of thick black smoke. The Filarete entrance consisted of a menacing portcullis and two gates studded with bronze. No fewer than fifteen men kept watch, poking with their pikes the bags of grain that were being unloaded from carts in the vicinity of the kitchens.

One of the soldiers showed me the way. I was to walk to the west end of the tower inside the fortress itself and ask for the visitors' reception area and the "mourning offices" that had been set up to receive the delegations for the funeral of Donna Beatrice. My Cremona guide had already warned me that the whole city would come to a halt on that day. And indeed, there was not much activity going on, considering the hour. I was surprised that Ludovico's secretary, a lanky courtier with an expressionless face, received me almost without delay. His name was Marchesino Stanga, and he apologized for being unable to conduct this servant of God unto his master. Even so, he examined my letter of introduction with a skeptical eye, making certain that the pontifical seal was authentic, and returned it to me with a gesture of regret.

"I'm sorry, Father Leyre," said the courtier, apologizing profusely. "You must understand that my lord is seeing no one after the death of his lady wife. I imagine you realize what a difficult moment we are going through, and the duke's need to be left alone."

"Of course," I agreed with feigned courtesy.

"However," he added, "when the mourning period is over, I will acquaint him with the fact of your presence in the city."

I would have liked to look Ludovico in the eye to discover, as in the many interrogations I had witnessed, whether or not he hid sinister intentions of heresy or crime. But the clerk, dressed in a velvet doublet and a scarlet robe trimmed with fur, and speaking in a tone of petty superiority, was bent on preventing me from doing so.

"Nor can we provide you with lodging, as is our custom," he said dryly. "The castle is closed and we are not admitting visitors. I beg you, Father, to pray for the soul of Donna Beatrice and to return after the funeral. Then we will welcome you as you deserve."

"*Requiescat in pace*," I muttered as I crossed myself. "I will do so. And I will also pray for you."

I was in a peculiar situation. Without being able to set myself up in the vicinity of the duke and his family, and thus prevented from wandering, as I had intended, more or less freely through the castle, my first investigations would be delayed. I had to find discreet lodgings that would grant me a place to study in peace. With Torriani's documents burning a hole in my bags, I would need a quiet atmosphere, three hot meals a day and a good deal of luck to decipher the secret. Since it was not sensible for a monk to seek a room among the laity, my choices were soon reduced to two: either the venerable monastery of San Eustorgio or the very new one of Santa Maria delle Grazie, where the possibility of crossing paths with the Soothsayer fired my imagination. Then, the question of lodging settled, I would have time enough to concentrate on the clue that Master Torriani had put into my hands in Bethany.

I admit that Divine Providence aided me in this matter. San Eustorgio soon revealed itself to be the worse of the two options. Lying very close to the Cathedral, next to the main market, it was usually full of busybodies who would soon be asking themselves what kind of business could bring a Roman inquisitor to this place. Even though its location would afford me a certain perspective on the Soothsayer's activities, saving me from the risk of meeting him face-to-face without knowing his identity, it nevertheless offered me more inconveniences than advantages.

As to my other choice, Santa Maria delle Grazie—besides being the presumed hiding place of my quarry—presented a small but solvable disadvantage: that was where the crowded obsequies of Donna Beatrice would take place. Its chapel, recently renovated by Bramante, was about to become the center of everyone's attention.

Otherwise, Santa Maria had everything I required. Its well-stocked library, lodged on the second story of one of the buildings that opened onto the so-called Cloister of the Dead, held volumes by Suetonius, Philostratus, Plotinus, Xenophon and even Plato himself, purchased in the days of Cosimo the Elder. It stood near the duke's fortress and at not too great a distance from the Porta Vercellina. It possessed an excellent kitchen, a splendid pastry oven, a well, a vegetable garden, a tailor's shop and a hospital. And above all, its greatest advantage was this: that, unless Master Torriani was much mistaken, the Soothsayer might well appear to me in one of its corridors without my having the need to solve any riddle whatsoever.

I was naïve.

Except in this latter respect, Providence did its work well. There was one cell still vacant at Santa Maria, which was immediately put at my disposal. It was a tiny room, barely a few feet long, holding a cot with no mattress and a small table set under a window overlooking the street called Magenta. The monks asked no questions. They perused my credentials with the same look of distrust as that of the duke's secretary, but they relaxed once I assured them that I had come to their house in search of peace for my troubled soul. "Even an inquisitor needs time for recollection," I explained. They understood.

One single condition was imposed on me. The sexton, a monk with bulging eyes and a strange accent, warned me very sternly:

"Never enter the refectory without permission. Master Leonardo doesn't want anyone interrupting his work, and the Abbot wishes to please him in every way possible. Do you understand?"

I nodded my assent.

8

The first place I visited was the library of Santa Maria. I was very curious about it. Built over the disputed and now restricted refectory that the Soothsayer had branded the focal point of all evil, it was a vast room with rectangular windows, lined by a dozen small reading tables and the librarian's large desk. Immediately behind it, protected by a thick locked door, was where the books were kept. What especially drew my attention was the heating: a boiler on the ground floor fed steam into a series of copper pipes that lent warmth to the floor tiles.

"It's not for the readers," the monk responsible for the place hastened to explain, seeing me interested in the ingenious contraption. "It's for the books. We keep volumes that are too valuable to allow them to be ruined by the cold."

I think that Father Alessandro Trivulzio, the guardian and custodian of the library, was the first monk to regard me not with suspicion but rather with shameless curiosity. Tall, bony, extremely pale and exquisitely mannered, he seemed delighted to see a new face in his realm.

"Not many people come here," he admitted. "Much less all the way from Rome!"

"Ah. So you've already found out I'm Roman?"

"News has wings, Father. Santa Maria is still a small community. I doubt that by now there's anyone in the community who is not aware of the arrival of an inquisitor in our house."

The monk winked conspiratorially.

"I'm not here on official business," I lied. "I'm here because of personal matters."

"It makes no difference. Inquisitors are men of letters, scholars. And here most of the brothers have difficulties reading or writing. If you stay for a time among us, I think we'll enjoy each other's company."

Then he added:

"Is it true that in Rome you work in the Secretariat of Keys?"

"Yes," I said doubtfully.

"Wonderful, Father. That's wonderful. We'll have much to talk about. I think you've chosen the best place in the world to spend some time."

I found Alessandro agreeable. He was close to fifty years old and appeared wholly at ease, with a hooked nose and the sharpest chin I had ever seen, while his Adam's apple seemed ready to pop out of his throat. On his desk he kept a pair of thick spectacles, no doubt to magnify the print in those extensive volumes, and the sleeves of his habit bore several impressive ink stains. Though I did not confide in him at once (in fact, I tried not to look at him too closely so as not to become bewitched by his ungainly face), I will say that a heartfelt current of affection flowed immediately between us. It was he who insisted on attending to my needs personally during my stay at the monastery, and he even offered to show me around that splendid building in which everything seemed so new. Furthermore, he promised to protect my peace and quiet so as to allow me to concentrate on my work.

"If your example caught on and more brothers came to our house to study," he complained, not able to hold back his tongue, "we might soon be able to transform it into a House of General Studies like those in Rome, or even perhaps into a university—"

"Don't other monks come here to study?"

"Very few for what this place can offer. Even though our library might seem modest to you, it holds one of the most important collections of ancient texts in the entire dukedom."

"Indeed?"

"Forgive me if I commit the sin of immodesty, but I've been working here for a long time now. Perhaps, to a cultured Roman such as yourself, it might seem poor compared to the Vatican Library, but please believe me if I say that we hold books here that even the librarians of His Holiness could not imagine—"

"In that case," I answered courteously, "it will be a privilege to consult them."

Father Alessandro bowed his head as if accepting the compliment, and started shuffling his papers around, as if looking for something important.

"First, I need a small favor." He laughed between his teeth. "In fact, you are a gift from Heaven. For someone like yourself, trained to decipher messages at the Secretariat of Keys, a riddle like this will be child's play."

The Dominican extended toward me a piece of paper

with a few scrawls. It was a simple drawing. A rough musical scale interrupted by a single misplaced note ("za") and a hook. Like this:

"Well?" he asked impatiently. "Do you understand the thing? I've spent three days trying to solve it in vain."

"And what are you supposed to be able to read here?"

"A sentence in the Romance tongue."

I studied the riddle without being able to divine its meaning. Obviously, the clue had to be in that misplaced "za." Things that were not in their right place always held an answer, but what of the hook? I placed the elements in order in my head, beginning with the scale, and I grinned with amusement.

"It's a sentence, certainly," I said at last. "And very simple."

"Simple?"

"All that's required is to be able to read, Father Alessandro. See here: if you begin by translating the hook into Romance, that is to say, *'amo,'* the rest of the drawing becomes clear at once."

"I don't understand."

"It's easy. Read *amo* and then the notes."

Dubiously, the monk followed the drawing with his finger:

"L'amo . . . re . . . mi . . . fa . . . sol . . . la . . . 'za' . . . re . . . *L'amore mi fa sollazare!*" he leapt up. " 'Love gives me pleasure.' That Leonardo is a scamp! He'd better not let me catch him! To play like this with musical notes—*Maledetto!*"

"Leonardo?"

The mention of that name brought me back to reality. I had come to the library seeking a quiet place to decipher the Soothsayer's enigma. A clue that, unless we were much mistaken, closely concerned Leonardo, the forbidden refectory and the work he was there engaged in.

"Ah!" the librarian exclaimed, still euphoric with the discovery. "You have not yet met him?"

I shook my head.

"He is another lover of riddles. He challenges the monks of Santa Maria with one every week. This was one of the hardest ones."

"Leonardo da Vinci?"

"Who else?"

"I thought . . . ," I said hesitatingly, "that he seldom spoke with the monks."

"That is only true when he's working. But as he lives nearby, he often comes to supervise the work and jokes with us in the cloisters. He loves wordplay and puns, and he makes us laugh with his witticisms."

The monk's answer, instead of amusing me, filled me with unease. I was here to decipher a message that had baffled all the cryptographers of Bethany. A text bearing no resemblance to the ribald phrase disguised by Leonardo in a musical staff. A text on whose resolution several affairs of state depended. Why was I wasting time on inconsequential chatter?

"At least," I said somewhat brusquely, "your friend Leonardo and I have something in common: we both like to work alone. Could you show me to a table and make sure that no one disturbs me?"

Father Alessandro understood that I was not requesting a favor. He wiped the winning smile from his lean face and obediently assented.

"Make yourself at home. No one will interrupt your studies."

That afternoon, the librarian kept his word. The hours I passed brooding over the seven lines that Master Torriani had given me in Bethany were some of the most solitary I spent in Milan. I knew that, more than any previous task, this one required absolute seclusion. I read the verses once again:

> *Oculos ejus dinumera,*
> *sed noli voltum adspicere.*
> *In latere nominis*
> *mei notam rinvenies.*
> *Contemplari et contemplata*
> *aliis tradere.*

> Veritas

It would all be a question of patience.

Just as I had learned in the workshops of Bethany, I applied to those nonsensical lines the techniques of the admirable Father Leon Battista Alberti. Father Alberti would have loved the challenge: not only was there a hidden message to be disentangled behind a common text, but the message would probably lead me to a work of art that held a worthy mystery locked within it. Father Alberti was the first scholar to write about the art of perspective; he was also a lover of art, a poet, a philosopher, the composer of a funeral dirge for his dog and the designer of Rome's Trevi Fountain. Our praiseworthy teacher, whom God summoned prematurely to His side, used to say that in order to solve any puzzle, no matter what its type or its origin, one had to go from the apparent to the latent. That is to say, to identify first what is obvious—the "za"—in order to then seek its hidden meaning. And he set forth yet another useful law: riddles are always solved without hurry, attending to minute details and allowing them to settle in our memory.

In this case, the obvious, the very obvious fact was that the verses contained a name. Torriani was certain of it, and I too; the more I read them, the more certain I became. We both believed that the Soothsayer had left us this clue in the hope that the Secretariat of Keys would solve it and communicate with him, so there had to exist an unequivocal way of reading it. Of course, if our anonymous informer was as cautious as he seemed, only the eyes of a shrewd observer would identify it.

Something else that attracted my attention in those lines was the occurrence of the number seven. Numbers are usually important in this type of enigma. The poem consisted of seven lines. Its strange, irregular metrics had to mean something, like Leonardo's hook. And if that "something" was the identity I was after, the text warned me that I would find it only by counting the eyes of someone whose face I was not allowed to see. The paradox disarmed me. How could I count the eyes of someone without looking him in the face?

The text resisted my advances. What did the mysterious allusion to the eyes mean? Perhaps something related to the seven eyes of the Lord described by Zechariah, or the seven horns and seven eyes of the slain lamb of the Apocalypse? And if so, what kind of a name might be found behind a number? The middle line was eloquent enough: "The number of my name you shall find on its side." What number? A seven perhaps? Might it refer to a numeral, the seventh in an order? Like the Antipope, Clement VII of Avignon, for example? I quickly discarded that possibility. It was unlikely that our anonymous scribe was worthy of a number after his name. What then? And furthermore, how should I interpret the strange error I discovered in the fourth verse? Why, instead of *invenies*, had the cryptographer written *rinvenies*?

Oddities piled up on oddities.

My first day's labor at Santa Maria offered me only a single fact: the last two phrases of the "signature" were, with utter certainty, formulas typical of a Dominican. Torriani's instinct had not failed him. *"Contemplari et contemplata aliis tradere"* was a famous dictum of Saint Thomas, taken from the *Summa theologica* and accepted as one of our order's best-known sayings: "To contemplate and to offer to others the fruit of your contemplation." The second one, *"Veritas,"* or "Truth," besides being another common Dominican motto, used to appear on our coat of arms. It is true that I had never seen both phrases together but, read one after the other, they seemed to say that in order to reach the truth, one needed to remain vigilant. At least, the advice was good. Father Alberti would have applauded.

But what about the two previous sentences? What name or number did they conceal?

9

"Have you heard anything about the new guest at the monastery of Santa Maria?"

Leonardo used to spend the last hours of daylight scrutinizing his Last Supper. The rays of the setting sun transformed the figures at the table first into reddish shadows and then into dark and sinister silhouettes. He frequently visited the monastery of Santa Maria in order to cast his eyes on his favorite work and to seek distraction from his daily occupations. The duke was pushing him to finish the colossal equestrian statue in honor of Francesco Sforza, and during the day, Leonardo allowed himself to be obsessed with the monumental horse. And yet, even Ludovico was aware that the artist's true passion was in the refectory of Santa Maria. Almost sixteen by thirty feet, the painting was the largest he had ever undertaken. Only God knew when he would finish it, but that was a detail that did not concern him. So abstracted was Leonardo in the contemplation of his magical scene that Marco d'Oggiono, the most inquisitive of his apprentices, was forced to repeat his question:

"Truly you haven't heard of him?"

Absentmindedly the Master shook his head. Marco discovered him sitting on a wooden crate in the middle of the refectory, his blond mane unkempt, as he often appeared at the end of his working day.

"No, I haven't," he answered. "Is he someone interesting, *caro*?"

"He's an inquisitor, Master Leonardo."

"A terrible occupation."

"The fact is, Master, that he too seems very much interested in your secrets."

Leonardo glanced away from his *Cenacolo* and sought out the blue eyes of his disciple. He looked serious, as if the proximity of a member of the Holy Inquisition had stirred a deep-rooted fear in his soul.

"My secrets? You ask about them again, Marco? They are all here. I told you so yesterday. Visible to all. Years ago, I learned that if you wish to hide something from the stupidity of humans, the best place to do so is there where everyone can see it. You understand that, don't you?"

Marco nodded without much conviction. The Master's good humor from the previous day had entirely vanished.

"I've given much thought to what you told me, Master. And I think I've understood something about this place."

"Have you, now?"

"In spite of working on hallowed ground and under the supervision of men of God, you didn't intend to depict Christ's first Mass in your Last Supper, did you?"

The Master arched his thick blond eyebrows in astonishment. Marco d'Oggiono went on:

"Don't pretend to be surprised. Jesus is not holding up

the Host in his hand, nor is he instituting the Eucharist, and his disciples are neither eating nor drinking. They are not even receiving His blessing."

"Well, well," Leonardo exclaimed. "You're on the right path."

"What I don't understand, Master, is why you've painted that knot at the far end of the table. The wine and the bread are mentioned in the Scriptures; the fish, even though none of the evangelists mention it, can be understood as a symbol of Christ Himself. But who ever heard of a knot in the tablecloth of the Last Supper?"

Leonardo extended a hand toward Marco, calling him to his side.

"I see that you've tried to penetrate the mural. Well done."

"And yet, I'm still far from your secret, am I not?"

"The arrival should not matter to you, Marco. Concern yourself with traveling the path."

Marco opened his eyes wide.

"Haven't you heard me, Master? Aren't you worried that an inquisitor should have come to this monastery asking about your Last Supper?"

"No."

"And that is all?"

"What should I say to you? I have more important things to worry about. Like finishing this Last Supper—and its secret." Leonardo stroked his beard with an amused gesture before continuing. "You know something, Marco? When at last you discover the secret I'm painting and are able to read it for the very first time, you'll never be able to stop seeing it. And you'll ask yourself how you could have been so blind. These, and no others, are the best-guarded secrets: the ones that stare us in the face and which we are unable to see."

"And how will I learn to read your work, Master?"

"Following the example of the great men of our time. Like the geographer Toscanelli, who has finished designing his own secret under the eyes of the whole of Florence."

The disciple had never heard of Leonardo's old friend. In Florence, they called him "the Physician" because, even though he had spent years earning his living drawing his maps and was a passionate reader of the writings of Marco Polo, he had long ago been a medical doctor.

"But I'm sure you know nothing of all that." Leonardo shook his head. "So that you don't accuse me again of not teaching you to read secrets, today I'll tell you of the one Toscanelli left in the Cathedral of Florence."

"Truly?" asked Marco, eagerly.

"When you return to that city, don't forget to pay a visit to the enormous dome that Filippo Brunelleschi built for the Duomo. Walk quietly under it and fix your eyes on the small opening in one of its sides. On the feasts of Saint John the Baptist and of Saint John the Evangelist, in June and in December, the midday sun streams through that hole from more than two hundred sixty feet above ground and lights up a strip of marble that my friend Toscanelli carefully placed on the floor."

"And why did he do that, Master?"

"Don't you understand? It's a calendar. The solstices marked there signal the beginning of winter and of summer. Julius Caesar was the first to note this and to establish the duration of a year as 365 days and a quarter. He also invented the leap year. And all by observing the sun's progress along a strip like that one. Toscanelli, therefore, decided to dedicate the device to him. Do you know how?"

Marco shrugged his shoulders.

"Placing at the beginning of his marble meridian, in an unusual order, the signs of Capricorn, of Scorpio—and of Aries."

"And what is the relationship between the signs of the zodiac and the dedication to Caesar, Master?"

Leonardo smiled.

"Therein lies the secret. If you take the first two letters of the Latin name of each of those signs, in the order he gave them, that is to say, CA-ES-AR, you'll have the hidden name we're looking for."

"Ca-es-ar . . . Clear as water! Perfect!"

"Indeed."

"And something like that is hidden in your *Cenacolo*, Master?"

"Something like that. But I doubt that this inquisitor, whom you so much fear, will ever discover it."

"But—"

"And, yes," Leonardo interrupted him, "the knot is one of the many symbols accompanying Mary Magdalene. One of these days I'll tell you all about it."

10

I must have fallen asleep at my desk.

When Father Alessandro shook me toward three in the morning, just after matins, a painful stiffness had taken over my whole body.

"Father, Father!" the librarian was clamoring. "Are you all right?"

I must have answered something, because between shakings the librarian said a few words that all of a sudden had me wide awake.

"You speak in your dreams." He laughed, as if still mocking my inability to solve riddles. "Matteo, the prior's nephew, heard you mutter some strange phrases in Latin and came into the church to let me know. He thought you were possessed!"

Alessandro was watching me with a look partly amused and partly worried, snorting through that hooked nose of his with which he seemed to threaten me.

"It's nothing," I apologized with a yawn.

"Father, you have been working for a very long time. You have hardly eaten anything since you arrived, and my concern for you goes unheeded. Are you certain that I can't help you in your labors?"

"No, it won't be necessary. Please believe me." The

librarian's maladroitness regarding the clue of the hook did not promise great assistance.

"And what was that about *Oculos ejus dinumera*? You repeated the words again and again."

"Is that what I was saying?"

I turned pale.

"Yes. And something about a place called Bethany. Do you often dream of Biblical places, of Lazarus and his resurrection, and things like that? Because Lazarus came from Bethany, didn't he?"

I smiled. Father Alessandro's innocence seemed limitless.

"I doubt you'd understand, my brother."

"Try me," he said, rocking on his feet to the rhythm of his words. The librarian was standing barely a hand's width away, observing me with growing interest, his large Adam's apple rising and falling in his throat. "After all, I'm the monastery's man of letters . . ."

I promised to satisfy his curiosity in exchange for something to eat. I had only just realized that I had not even gone down to supper on my first night at Santa Maria. My stomach was making noises under my habit. With solicitude, the librarian led me to the kitchen and managed to rustle up a few scraps from suppertime. Outside the night was pitch-black, while the pale flicker of a candle lit the indoors.

"It's *panzanella*, Father," he explained, helping me to a still-warm bowl that heated my freezing hands.

"*Panzanella?*"

"Eat. It's a bread soup, made with cucumber and onion. It will please you."

The thick and aromatic gruel slid like silk down my innards. I also devoured an excellent nougat confection called *torrone*, as well as a couple of dried figs. Then, with my stomach satisfied, my reflexes began to respond once again.

"Won't you eat, Father Alessandro?"

"Oh, no." The tall man smiled. "The fast forbids me. I've been fasting since before you arrived."

"I understand."

The truth is that I paid his words no more attention.

So I fell asleep repeating the first verses of the Soothsayer's message, I reproached myself. It was not surprising. While thanking Father Alessandro for his care and praising the deserved reputation of the kitchen, I remembered that already in Bethany, I had been able to assert that those lines did not belong to any quotation from the Gospels. In fact, neither did they belong to any text by Plato or other known classical authors, nor to the epistles of the Church fathers or to the articles of canonical law. These seven lines disobeyed the most elementary cipher codes employed by cardinals, bishops and abbots, who in those days encrypted almost all their communications with the Papal States, for fear of being spied upon. Rarely were their writings legible: they were translated from official Latin into a jumble of consonants and numbers, thanks to very elaborate substitution charts, cast in bronze by my much admired teacher Father Alberti. In general, these charts consisted of a series of superimposed wheels along whose rims were printed the letters of the alphabet. With skill and a few minimum instructions, the letters on the outside wheel were substituted by those on the inside wheel, turning any message into a cipher.

So much precaution had its reasons. For the papal court, the nightmare of being discovered by noblemen whom they hated or courtiers against whom they plotted had, in a very short time, multiplied the labors of Bethany a hundredfold and had turned us into an indispensable tool for the administration of the Church. But how was I to explain all this to the kind Alessandro? How was I to confess that the clue that tormented me escaped all known methods of encoding and, for that very reason, had become my obsession?

No: *Oculos ejus dinumera* was not the sort of message that one could simply explain to someone uninstructed in secret codes.

"May I ask what you're thinking, Father Agostino? I'm beginning to believe that you pay me no attention whatsoever."

Father Alessandro took hold of my sleeve to lead me back to the dormitories through the dark corridors of the monastery.

"Now that you've eaten," he said in a fatherly tone, without however losing the mocking smile he had worn since our first encounter, "it would be best if you rested until the office of lauds. I'll come and wake you shortly before dawn and you can let me know your business then. Agreed?"

Against my will, I said yes.

At that hour, the cell was frozen, and the very idea of stripping off my habit and slipping into a hard, damp bed terrified me more than staying awake. I asked the librarian to light the candle on the night table, and we agreed to meet at dawn and stroll through the cloister to clarify matters. And yet the idea of sharing details of my work with someone else was far from appealing. In fact, I had not yet paid my respects to the prior of Santa Maria, but something told me that Father Alessandro, in spite of his lack of skill in ciphers, would be of some use to me in this puzzle.

Fully dressed, I lay down on the bed and covered myself with the only blanket at my disposal. In this position, letting my eyes stray over a ceiling of whitewashed beams, I went over once again the problem of the encrypted verses. I had the impression of having overlooked something, an absurd but fundamental "za." And so, with my eyes wide open, I recalled all I knew about the origin of the lines. If I was not mistaken in my judgment, and the coming dawn was not fogging up my wits, it seemed quite clear that the name of our anonymous informant—or at the very least his number—was hidden in the first two verses.

It was a curious game. As with certain Hebrew words, there are some that, besides their usual sense, carry a determinative particle that complements their meaning. The two Dominican mottoes indicated that our man was a preacher: of this I was almost certain. But what about the preceding lines?

> *Count its eyes*
> *but look not on its face.*
> *The number of my name*
> *you shall find on its side.*

Eyes, face, name, side . . .

In the gloom, utterly exhausted, I came upon the answer. Perhaps it was another impasse, but all of a sudden the number of the name no longer seemed absurd. I remembered that the Jews call *gematria* the discipline that consists of assigning to each letter of the alphabet a numerical value. John, in his Book of Revelation, employed it in a masterly fashion when he wrote, "Let him that hath understanding count the number of the beast: for it is the number of a man; and his number is Six hundred threescore and six." And that 666 corresponded, indeed, to the cruelest man of his time, Nero Caesar, the sum of whose letters added up to the terrible triple number. And if the Soothsayer were a converted Jew? And if, fearing punishment, he had hidden his identity for that very reason? How many monks at Santa Maria would know that Saint John had been initiated to the *gematria* and had accused Nero in his book without putting his own life at risk?

Had the Soothsayer done likewise?

Before falling asleep, I feverishly transposed that idea to the Roman alphabet. Considering that A (the Hebrew *aleph*) was equivalent to 1, B (*beth*) to 2, and so on, it would not be difficult to translate into numbers any given word. Now all I had to do was add up the numbers obtained and the resulting sum would give me the definitive numerical value of the elected name. The number. The Jews, for instance, calculated that the secret and full name of Yahweh added up to the number 72. The kabbalists, those magicians who worked with Hebrew numbers, complicated matters even more by seeking numbers for the 72 names of God. In Bethany, we often made fun of them.

In our case, unfortunately, the question was much bleaker, because we were ignorant even of the numerical value of our correspondent's name—that is, if he had one. Unless, following point by point the instructions in his verses, we might be able to find it on the side of someone with eyes into whose face we couldn't look.

And with that riddle worthy of the Sphinx, I allowed myself to be lulled to sleep.

11

Shortly before lauds, Father Alessandro came punctually to my cell, smiling happily like a newly arrived novice. He must have thought that it wasn't every day that a doctor from Rome was willing to share with him an important secret, and he was preparing to enjoy his moment of glory. And yet he gave me the impression that he wished to proceed gradually, as if fearing that the "revelation" would end too soon and leave him unsatisfied. Therefore, either for reasons of courtesy or in order to prolong the pleasure of having me to himself, the librarian explained that dawn would be a good time to go to confession: that is, after introducing me to the other members of his community.

The clock on Bramante's dome sounded the hour of five as the librarian began to lead me, pulling me along through fog, toward the church. The building, at the opposite side of the cells, stood close to the library and the refectory, and consisted of a rectangular nave of modest dimensions. Its barrel vault was held up by granite columns stripped from a Roman mausoleum and was covered from foot to ceiling by geometrically designed frescoes, spiked wheels and suns. The ensemble seemed a little overburdened for my taste.

We arrived late. Clustered around the main altar, the brothers of Santa Maria were already chanting the Te Deum under the tenuous light of two enormous candelabra. It was freezing cold, and the misty breath of the friars blurred their faces like a thick and mysterious fog. Alessandro and I stood by one of the church pilasters and watched them from a comfortable distance.

"The one in the corner," whispered the librarian, pointing toward a puny monk of narrow eyes and curly white hair, "is the Father Prior Vicenzo Bandello. In spite of his frail figure, he's a scholar among scholars. For years he has been fighting against the Franciscans and their notions about the Virgin's Immaculate Conception. Even though, to tell the truth, many believe he will lose the battle."

"Is he a doctor of theology?"

"Of course," he firmly assented. "The swarthy young man to his right, with the long neck, is his nephew, Matteo."

"Yes, I've met him."

"Everyone believes that one day he will become a celebrated author. And a little further back, next to the door of the sacristy, are the brothers Andrea, Giuseppe, Luca and Jacopo. They are not only brothers in Christ; they are also sons of the same mother."

I looked at their faces one by one, trying to memorize their names.

"You told me that only a few are capable of reading and writing fluently. Is that right?" I asked.

Father Alessandro was not able to guess the reason for my question. If he could answer me precisely, I might be able to discard at once a fair number of suspects. The Soothsayer's profile corresponded to a cultured man, learned in many disciplines and well placed in the duke's entourage. At that point, I still believed that the probability of failing to unravel the enigma was high (I was still smarting from the clumsiness with which I had first examined Leonardo's musical riddle) and that, if everything else failed, I would have to resort to mere deduction in order to identify the Soothsayer. Or to entrust myself to luck.

The librarian cast a glance over the congregation, trying to recall their skill with words.

"Let's see," he muttered. "Brother Guglielmo, the cook, reads and recites poetry. Benedetto, the one-eyed monk, worked for many years as a scribe. The good man lost an eye trying to escape from an assault on his previous monastery, in Castelnuovo, while protecting a copy of the Book of Hours. Since then, he's always in a foul humor. He complains about everything, and nothing we do for him seems satisfactory."

"And the boy?"

"Matteo, as I told you, writes like an angel. He's only twelve years old, but he's a very alert and curious youngster . . . And now, let me see." The librarian hesitated once more. "Adriano, Stefano, Nicola and Giorgio learned to read with me. Andrea and Giuseppe as well."

In barely a few seconds, the list of candidates had grown to enormous proportions. I had to attempt another strategy.

"And tell me, who is that handsome friar, that tall, strong fellow on the left?" I asked with great curiosity.

"Ah! That is Mauro Sforza, the gravedigger. He's always hiding behind one of the brothers, as if he were afraid of being recognized."

"Sforza?"

"Well, he's a distant cousin of Ludovico. Some time ago the duke asked us, as a favor, to admit him into the monastery and treat him as one of us. He almost never speaks a word. That frightened look is always on his face, and wicked tongues say that it's because of what happened to his maternal uncle Gian Galeazzo."

I started. "Gian Galeazzo Sforza?"

"Yes, the legitimate Duke of Milan, who died three years ago. The same one whom Ludovico poisoned in order to gain the throne. Poor Brother Mauro was in charge of looking after Gian Galeazzo before being sent here to us, and no doubt it was his hand that served the beverage of hot milk, wine, beer and arsenic that burned up his uncle's stomach and killed him after three days of agony."

"He killed him?"

"Let us say that he was the instrument of the crime. But that," he said blowing through his teeth, happy for having surprised me, "is a secret of the confessional. You understand."

Guardedly, I observed Mauro Sforza and took pity on his melancholy fate. To be forced to abandon court life in exchange for one in which his only possessions were a cloak of coarse wool and a pair of sandals must have been for the youngster a hard blow to take.

"And he writes?"

Alessandro gave no answer. Shivering with cold, he

pushed me toward the congregation, not only to take part in the prayers but also to benefit from the body warmth of the group. As soon as he saw me, the Father Prior, beaked as an eagle and quite as vigilant, welcomed me with a nod and carried on with his devotions, which lasted until the first ray of the sun flooded through the rose window of brick and glass above the main entrance. I cannot say that my arrival caused any excitement in the community since, other than the prior, I doubt whether any of the brothers took heed of my presence. I did notice, however, that the Father Prior gestured sternly toward my guide, who then awkwardly moved to the other side.

Not only that: as soon as the prior had given us his benediction, Father Alessandro urged me to leave the company and follow him into the hospital ward.

In those early hours, the few sick who had spent the night there were still asleep, lending the red brick court-yard a lugubrious aspect.

"Yesterday you said that you knew Master Leonardo quite well . . . ," I began. I was certain that the truce he had allowed me before showering me with questions was about to come to an end.

"And who doesn't know him here! That man is a prodigy. A strange prodigy, God's most singular crea-ture."

"Strange?"

"Well, let us say that his behavior is somewhat anar-chic. You never know if he's coming or going, if he's going to paint in the refectory or if he merely wishes to reflect on his work and look for new cracks in the over-lay, or errors in the features of his characters. He spends the day carrying his small notebooks everywhere, making observations of everything."

"A meticulous man—"

"Not at all. He's disorganized and unpredictable, but he possesses an insatiable curiosity. Even as he's working in the refectory, he's imagining all sorts of crazy devices to better the daily life in the monastery: automatic spades to dig the garden, water pipes leading to the cells, self-cleaning pigeon towers—"

"The painting he's working on is a Last Supper, is it not?" I interrupted.

The librarian stepped up to the magnificent granite water well that adorned the center of the hospital cloister and looked at me as though I had just fallen from the skies:

"You haven't seen it yet, have you?" He smiled, as if well aware of my answer and pitying my condition. "What Master Leonardo is finishing in the refectory is not a Last Supper, it is *the* Last Supper, Father Agostino. You'll understand what I mean when you see it with your own eyes."

"So he's a strange but virtuous soul."

"You see," he corrected, "when Master Leonardo arrived at this house three years ago and began his preparations for the *Cenacolo*, the prior didn't feel that he could be trusted. In fact, in my role as archivist of Santa Maria and as the person responsible for our future scriptorium, he ordered me to write to Florence to find out if Leonardo was an artist one could trust, someone who kept his deadlines and was meticulous in his work, or whether he was one of those fortune seekers who leave everything half finished and whom one must bring to court to get them to complete what they have started."

"And yet, if I'm not mistaken, he had come recommended by the duke himself."

"That is true. But, for our prior, that was not enough of a guarantee."

"I see. Pray continue. What did you discover? Was he precise in his work or was he careless?"

"Both!"

I made a gesture to indicate my puzzlement.

"Did I not tell you he was a strange man? As a painter, he's no doubt the most extraordinary we've ever seen, but he is also the most rebellious. He finds it enormously hard to finish a project on time; in fact, he's never done so. And what is worse, he cares nothing for the instructions of his patrons. He always paints according to his whim."

"That isn't possible."

"It is, Father. The brothers of San Donato's monastery in Scopeto, close to Florence, commissioned from him a Nativity fifteen years ago—and he has still to finish it! And do you know what's even worse? Leonardo made alterations in the scene to the very limits of what can be tolerated. Instead of painting an ordinary Adoration of the Shepherds, come to make homage to the Christ Child, Leonardo started painting something he called *The Adoration of the Magi* and filled it with twisted characters, horses and men gesticulating grotesquely toward the heavens, things that are nowhere described in the Gospels."

I held back a shiver.

"Are you certain of this?"

"I never lie," he said curtly. "But that is nothing compared to the rest."

Nothing? If Father Alessandro's insinuations proved themselves to be true, the Soothsayer had fallen short in his fears: that devil from Vinci had landed in Milan, leaving behind a trail of serious pictorial distortions. Some of the lapidary phrases I had read in the anonymous letters began to echo in my mind like thunder before a storm. I allowed him to continue:

"That was no ordinary Adoration. It didn't even have a Star of Bethlehem! Don't you think that is odd?"

"What does it tell you?"

"Me?" Father Alessandro's cold, pale cheeks acquired a warm peach color. It made him blush that a learned man from Rome should ask him, with undisguised interest, his sincere opinion of something. "The truth is that I don't know. Leonardo, as I've told you, is an unusual creature. I'm not surprised that the Inquisition should be interested in him—"

"The Inquisition?"

I felt another stab in my guts. In the short time we had known each other, Father Alessandro had developed an uncanny ability to surprise me. Or perhaps I had become more susceptible? His mention of the Holy Office made me feel guilty. How was it that I hadn't thought of it earlier? Why had I not consulted the general archives of the *Sacra Congregazione* before traveling to Milan?

"Let me tell you about it," he said with enthusiasm, as if he enjoyed searching his memory for this kind of thing.

"After leaving his Adoration of the Magi unfinished, Leonardo moved to Milan, where he was engaged by the Fraternity of the Immaculate Conception, which, as you know, belongs to the Franciscans of San Francesco il Grande and with whom our prior is in constant conflict. And there, Leonardo fell into the same trouble he had encountered in Florence."

"Again?"

"Of course. Master Leonardo was supposed to paint a triptych for the fraternity's chapel, with the assistance of the brothers Ambrogio and Evangelista de'Predis. Between the three, they received two hundred scudi in advance for the work to come, and each of them set himself to a section of the altarpiece. The Tuscan took charge of the central panel. His task was to paint a Virgin surrounded by the prophets, while the side panels would depict a chorus of mystical angels."

"No need to continue: he never finished his work—"

"No, not at all. This time Master Leonardo finished his part but didn't deliver what had been asked of him. In his painting there wasn't a single prophet to be found. Instead, he'd painted a portrait of Our Lady in a cave, with the Child Jesus and Saint John the Baptist. The impudent scoundrel assured the brothers that his painting depicted the encounter of the two infants during the Flight to Egypt. But that too is a story absent from all four Gospels!"

"And so they denounced him to the Inquisition."

"Yes. But not for the reasons you imagine. Ludovico intervened to impede the trial, and thereby freed him from certain condemnation."

I doubted whether I should proceed with my questioning. After all, it was he who wanted me to tell him about the riddles. But I couldn't deny that his explanations intrigued me.

"What, then, was the accusation they made before the Inquisition?"

"That Leonardo had sought inspiration for his work in the *Apocalipsis Nova*."

"I never heard of such a book."

"It's a heretical text written by an old friend of his, a Menorite Franciscan called João Mendes da Silva, also known as Amadeo of Portugal, who died in Milan in the same year that Leonardo finished his painting. This Amadeo published a tract in which he dared to suggest that the Virgin and Saint John the Baptist were the true protagonists of the New Testament, and not Christ."

Apocalipsis Nova. I made a mental note of this information to add it to the future file I might open on Leonardo, accusing him of heresy.

"And how did the brothers figure out the relationship between the *Apocalipsis Nova* and Leonardo's painting?"

The librarian smiled.

"It was obvious. The painting showed the Virgin next to the Child Jesus and the angel Uriel next to John the Baptist. In normal circumstances, Jesus should appear blessing his cousin, but the painting depicted the exact opposite! And the Virgin, instead of embracing her Son, was stretching her arms in a protective gesture toward the Baptist. You understand now? Leonardo had portrayed Saint John not only as receiving legitimate acknowledgment from Our Lady but also as blessing Christ Himself, thereby showing his superiority over the Messiah."

I congratulated Father Alessandro enthusiastically.

"You're a very keen observer," I said. "You have shed light on the intelligence of this humble servant of God. I am in your debt, my brother."

"If you ask, I shall answer. It is a promise I always keep."

"Like fasting?"

"Yes, like fasting."

"I admire you, Father Alessandro. I do indeed."

The librarian beamed like a peacock, and as the light began to dissolve the shadows in the cloister, illuminating the shrouded bas-reliefs and ornaments, he dared break a certain period of reserve that, I believe, he had imposed upon himself.

"In that case, will you allow me to help you with your puzzles?"

Caught in the moment, I knew not what to answer.

12

In the following days, the other friar with whom I frequently spoke, besides Father Alessandro, was the prior's nephew, Matteo. He was still a child but more alert and curious than others of his age. Perhaps for that reason, young Matteo had been unable to resist the temptation of approaching me and asking what life was like in Rome. The great city of Rome.

I don't know how he imagined the pontifical palaces and the endless avenues of churches and monasteries, but in exchange for my detailed descriptions he shared with me a number of confidences that made me wary of the librarian's good intentions.

Laughing, he told me the only thing that made his uncle, the prior, lose his temper.

"And what might that be?" I asked, intrigued.

"To find Father Alessandro and Leonardo with their sleeves rolled up, chopping lettuce in Brother Guglielmo's kitchen."

"Leonardo goes into the kitchen?"

My surprise puzzled him.

"He does it all the time! When my uncle wants to find him, he knows that the kitchen is his favorite hiding place. He might not dip a brush in paint for days, but he can't stop himself from visiting us and spending hours by the hearth. Didn't you know that Leonardo ran a tavern in Florence, where he used to be the cook?"

"No."

"He told me so himself. It was called At the Sign of the Three Frogs, and the owners were Sandro and Leonardo."

"Is that true?"

"Of course! He explained that he had set it up with another painter friend, Sandro Botticelli."

"And what came of it?"

"Nothing! His customers didn't like his vegetable stews, his anchovies wrapped around cabbage buds, or a dish they used to make out of cucumbers and lettuce leaves in the shape of frogs."

"Does he do the same thing here?"

Matteo smiled. "My uncle won't let him. Since he arrived at the monastery, what he likes most is trying out things with the stuff in our pantry. He says he's looking for the menu for the Last Supper. And that the food placed on that table is as important as the portraits of the apostles . . . and for the past weeks, the scoundrel has been bringing his apprentices and friends to eat at a large table he laid out in the refectory, while he empties the cellars of the monastery."

"And Father Alessandro helps him?"

"Father Alessandro?" he echoed. "He's one of the ones who sit at the table and eat! Leonardo says he takes advantage of the situation to study their profiles and reflect on how he'll paint what they're eating, but no one has seen him do anything other than gorging himself on our food!"

Matteo laughed with amusement.

"The truth is," he added, "that my uncle has written several times to the duke complaining about Leonardo's abuses, but the duke has paid no attention to him. If this goes on, Leonardo will leave us with none of our harvest."

13

Friday the thirteenth was never a favorite day among the Milanese. More susceptible to French superstitions than other Latin races, the day that linked the fifth day of the week with the ominous place occupied by Judas at the Last Supper table evoked for them traumatic anniversaries. Almost two centuries earlier, it was on a Friday the thirteenth, in the year 1307, that the Knights Templar were arrested in France under the orders of Philip IV, nicknamed the Fair. They were then accused of denying Christ, of spitting on His crucifix, of exchanging obscene kisses in places of worship and of adoring an extravagant idol called Baphomet. The order of the knights of the white mantles fell into such a state of disgrace that from that day onward every Friday the thirteenth was held to be a day of evil omen.

The thirteenth day of January, 1497, was no exception.

At midday, a small crowd gathered at the doors of the monastery of Santa Marta. Most of the merchants had already closed their shops of silk wares, perfumes or woolen cloths on the Piazza del Verzaro, behind the cathedral, so as not to miss the sign. They seemed impatient. The announcement that had brought them there was singularly precise: before the setting of the sun, the servant of God Veronica da Benasco would render her soul unto the Lord. She herself had prophesied it with the same assurance with which she had prophesied so many other calamities. Admitted into the presence of princes and popes, held to be a living saint by many, her latest accomplishment had been to secure her own expulsion from Ludovico il Moro's palace barely two months ago. Gossip had it that she asked to be received by Donna Beatrice d'Este to tell her of her fatal destiny and that the duchess, in a fit of fury, ordered that she be locked up in a monastery so as never to set eyes on her again.

Marco d'Oggiono, Master Leonardo's favorite disciple, had known her well. He had often seen Leonardo deep in conversation with her, since Leonardo enjoyed discussing with the nun her strange visions of the Virgin. Not only did he take notes of what she said but many times Marco had surprised him sketching a feature of her angelic face, her sweet gestures and her painful demeanor, which he would later attempt to transpose onto his paintings. Unfortunately, unless Sister Veronica was much mistaken, these confidences would come to an end that very Friday. Before lunchtime, Marco dragged his master to the deathbed of the nun, aware that there was very little time left.

"Thank you for agreeing to come. Sister Veronica will be happy to see you one last time," whispered the disciple to his teacher.

Leonardo, aware of the scent of incense and oils in the small cell, admiringly observed the saintly woman's marble face. The poor thing could hardly open her eyes.

"I don't think there's anything I can do for her," he said.

"I know, Master. It was she who insisted on seeing you."

Leonardo bent his head until it was close to the dying woman's lips, which kept trembling as if muttering a painfully inaudible litany. The parish priest of Santa Marta, who had already anointed Sister Veronica with the holy oils of Extreme Unction and was reciting the Rosary by her side, allowed the visitor to come even closer.

"Do you still have twins in your paintings?"

The Master was taken aback. The nun had recognized him without even opening her eyes.

"I paint what I know, Sister."

"Ah, Leonardo!" she whispered. "Don't think I haven't realized who you are. I know it well. Even though at this point in my life, it isn't worth arguing with you any longer."

Sister Veronica spoke haltingly, in a low tone of voice that made it difficult for Leonardo to understand her.

"I saw your altarpiece in the Church of San Francesco, your *Madonna*."

"Did you like it?"

"The Virgin, yes. You are a very gifted artist. But the twins, no. Tell me, did you change them?"

"Yes, Sister. Just as the Franciscan brothers asked me to."

"You have a reputation for being stubborn, Leonardo.

Today I was told that you've painted twins again, this time in the Dominican refectory. Is it true?"

Leonardo drew himself up in astonishment.

"You've seen the *Cenacolo*, Sister?"

"No. But everyone talks about your work. You should know that."

"As I said before, Sister Veronica, I only paint that of which I'm certain."

"Then why do you insist on including twins in your paintings for the Church?"

"Because they existed. Andrew and Simon were brothers. Saint Augustine and other theologians tell us so. James the Less was often mistaken for Jesus because of their close resemblance. I've made none of it up. It's written in the Scriptures."

The nun stopped whispering and raised her voice to a cry: "Leonardo! Don't make the same mistake you made in San Francesco! An artist's mission is not to confuse the faithful but to show them clearly the characters that have been entrusted to him."

"Mistake?" Leonardo had raised his voice involuntarily. "What mistake?" Marco, the priest and the two nuns attending at the deathbed turned toward him.

"Come, come, Master Leonardo," the dying woman muttered. "Did they not accuse you of confusing Saint John with our Lord Jesus in your painting? Did you not depict them as alike as two drops of water? Did they not have the same curly hair, the same chubby cheeks and almost the same gesture? Did your painting not lead one to a perverse confusion between John and Christ?"

"It won't happen this time, Sister. Not in the *Cenacolo*."

"But I've been told that you've already painted James with the same face as Jesus!"

Everyone heard Sister Veronica's complaint. Marco, still dreaming of being able to show his teacher that he was capable of deciphering the secrets of his work, paid close attention.

"There's no possible confusion," Leonardo answered. "Jesus is the axis of my new work. He's an enormous A in the middle of the mural. A gigantic alpha. The origin of my entire composition."

Marco stroked his chin thoughtfully. How was it that he hadn't seen it before? As he conjured up the Last Supper in his mind, it was true that Jesus resembled a large capital A.

"An A?" Sister Veronica lowered her voice again. Leonardo's words had surprised her. "And may I know what it is that you've inscribed in your work this time around?"

"Nothing that true believers can't read."

"Most good Christians are unable to read, Master Leonardo."

"That is why I paint for them."

"And has that given you the right to include yourself among the Twelve Apostles?"

"I portray the most humble of them all, Sister Veronica. I portray Judas Thaddeus, almost at the very end of the table, just as Omega comes at the very end of the line begun by Alpha."

"Omega? You? Careful, Leonardo. You are extremely proud, and pride might cause you to lose your soul."

"Is that a prophecy?" he asked ironically.

"Don't mock this old woman. Pay attention to what I'm about to tell you. God has given me a clear vision of that which is to come. You must know, Leonardo, that today I will not be the only one whose soul will ascend unto the Eternal Father," she said. "Some of those others whom you call the true faithful will accompany me into the Halls of Judgment. And I am very afraid that they will not enjoy the Lord's divine mercy."

Marco d'Oggiono, much impressed, saw that Sister Veronica was panting with the effort of speaking.

"But you, on the other hand, have time left to repent and to save your soul."

14

I will never be able to thank Father Alessandro sufficiently for his help on the days following our walk.
Other than himself and young Matteo, who sometimes
would sneak into the library to see what the reclusive
monk from Rome was doing, I barely exchanged a word
with anyone. The rest of the monks I would see only at
mealtimes in the improvised refectory that had been
installed next to the so-called Large Cloister, and sometimes in church during prayers. But in both places the
rule of silence was imposed and it was therefore not easy
to engage one of them in conversation.

In the library, however, everything was different.
Father Alessandro would lose the stiffness he showed
among his brethren and would loosen his tongue, which
was so stifled at other moments of his monastic life. The
librarian's hometown was Riccio, on Lake Trasimeno,
closer to Rome than to Milan, which in a certain way
explained his isolation from the rest of the friars and his
perception of me as a somewhat disadvantaged country-
man in need of protection. Though I never saw a morsel
of food pass his lips, every day he brought me water, a
certain wheat pasta dark as pebbles (a specialty of
Brother Guglielmo that he would procure for me in

secret) and even clean oil for my lamp when it threatened to go out. All this (I later learned) in order not to leave me, in the hope that his unexpected guest would feel the need to unburden himself on someone and thus reveal to him new details of his "secret." I believe that with every passing hour, Alessandro imagined this secret to be more and more colossal. I admonished him, saying that the imagination was not a useful ally for someone bent on deciphering mysteries, but he would merely smile, certain that his abilities would someday prove useful.

One aspect of his personality never gave me cause for complaint: his humanity. Father Alessandro soon became a dear friend. Whenever I needed him, he was near. He would console me when I would fling my pen to the ground, in despair at the lack of results, and he would encourage me to continue trying to solve the devilish riddle. But *Oculos ejus dinumera* seemed to resist all my efforts. Even applying numerical value to its letters yielded nothing but confusion. After three days of disillusionment and sleepless efforts, Father Alessandro, having seen the verses and having learned them by heart, was playing with them himself, attempting with a frown to break the code. Every time he thought he had found a glimmer of light in the tangle, his face would light up with satisfaction, as if suddenly his lean features had become softer and his sharp-angled face transformed into that of an enthusiastic child. On one of those occasions, I learned that his favorite conundrums were those made up of numbers and letters. After reading Ramon Llull, inventor of the *Ars Magna* of secret codes, he had devoted his whole life to them. My book-owl friend was an inexhaustible source of surprises. He seemed to know everything, every important work on the art of cryptography, every kabbalistic treatise, every biblical essay. And yet, all this theoretical preparation finally did not seem to be of much use to us.

"Well now," Alessandro muttered on one of those afternoons in which the whole community was bursting with activity in preparation for Donna Beatrice's funeral. "Do you think that maybe we should count the number of eyes on one of the images in the monastery to find the solution to our problem? Could it be as simple as that?"

I patted his hand affectionately even as I shrugged. What was I supposed to answer? That his suggestion was now all that was left to try? The librarian watched me with his owlish eyes, his hand on his pointed chin. But, like myself, he did not put much hope in the proposal, and with reason. If the number of the name was to be sought in the number of eyes on an image, whether that of the Virgin, of Saint Dominic or Saint Anne, the result would lead us into an impasse. It would be impossible to find a name of only one or two letters, which was the obvious conclusion we would reach by counting the eyes of any of the images in Santa Maria. Furthermore, none of the brethren had such a short name or nickname. There was no Io, Eo or Au lodged here. Not even a three-lettered name such as Job would be of any use to us. In Santa Maria, there were no Jobs, nor any Gads or Lots, and even if there were, on the face of what image would we find the three eyes that would allow us to identify the author of the letters?

All of a sudden, I realized something. What if the riddle did not refer to a human being? If it referred to a dragon, a seven-headed hydra with fourteen eyes or some other kind of monster painted on the margins of one of the rooms?

"But there are no such monsters anywhere in Santa Maria," protested Father Alessandro.

"In that case, we're probably mistaken. Perhaps the figure whose eyes must be counted is not in the monastery, but in some other building. In a tower, a palace, another church nearby—"

"That's it, Father Agostino! We have it!" The librarian's eyes were flashing with excitement. "Don't you see? The text doesn't refer to a person or an animal, but to a building!"

"A building?"

"Of course! My God, how slow-witted we've been! It's clear as crystal! *Oculos* means 'eyes,' but it also means 'windows.' Round windows. And the church of Santa Maria is full of them!"

The librarian scribbled something on a piece of paper. It was a quick alternate translation, and he passed it on to me in the hopes that I would approve it. If he was right, we had had the solution in front of our very eyes all the time. According to my book owl's version, our "Count its eyes but look not on its face" could also mean "Count its windows but look not on its façade."

It could not be denied. Though somewhat forced, the new text had an overwhelming sense.

The exterior of the church of Santa Maria was, indeed, full of a kind of oculus, of round windows designed by a certain Guiniforte Solari according to that pure Lombard style so dear to Ludovico il Moro. They were everywhere, even within the perimeter of the brand-new Bramante dome beneath which I had been praying for a whole week. Could the solution be that simple? Father Alessandro had no doubts about it.

"You see? On the lateral façade, Father Agostino!" he insisted. "The second part confirms it: *In latere nominis mei notam rinvenies*. We must seek the number of the name on its side! We must count the windows on the only side that has them, other than the main façade! That's where you'll find your number!"

It was the happiest moment of my sojourn in Milan.

15

No one took any notice.

None of the merchants, moneylenders or friars strolling by in the twilight around San Francesco il Grande noticed the slovenly, ill-dressed man who hurried into the Franciscan church. It was the eve of a holiday, a market day, and the inhabitants of Milan were busy gathering provisions for the coming days of official mourning. Besides, news of the death of Sister Veronica had spread like wildfire through the city, occupying most of the conversations and unleashing a passionate debate on the true powers of the visionary.

Under such circumstances, it was only natural that the presence of yet another beggar left them unconcerned.

But the fools were once again mistaken. The beggar who entered San Francesco was not an ordinary man. His knees were bruised from hours of penance, and his scalp had been devotedly tonsured. He was a man fearful of God, a man pure of heart, and as he crossed the main threshold into the church, he trembled, certain that one of the superstitious neighbors, perhaps impressed by Sister Veronica's auguries, would sooner or later betray him.

He had no trouble imagining the sequence of events

that would unfold. Very soon, someone would run to tell the sexton that there was yet another beggar in the church. The sexton would tell the deacon who, without delay, would tell the executioner. For weeks, this is what had been happening and nobody seemed to care. The false beggars who had reached the church before him had all vanished without a trace. That is why he was certain that he would not leave this place alive. And yet, it was a price he was gladly willing to pay . . .

Without giving himself a moment's respite, the ragged man left behind him the double row of benches that lined the nave and hurried on toward the main altar. There was not a soul to be seen inside the church. Better this way. In fact, he could already almost feel the presence of the saint. He had never known himself to be so close to God. The Holy One was near. How else could one explain that at that very hour the light filtering through the stained-glass windows was exactly the right one to appreciate all the details of the "miracle"? The pilgrim had waited so long to reach this altarpiece and give homage to the *Opus Magnum* that his tears began to flow with the emotion. And rightly so. At last he had been permitted to see a painting, *The Virgin of the Rocks*, that few in Milan knew under its real name: the *Maestà*.

Was this the end of the road?

The false beggar intuited it was so.

He approached the altar cautiously. He had heard the work described so many times that the voices of those who instructed him in its hidden details, in the true key to its reading, clustered now in his mind, clouding his reason. The painting—which at 189 by 120 centimeters perfectly fit the opening in the altar intended for it—was unequivocal. In it, two infant boys had their eyes fixed on each other, while a woman of serene features raised her protective arms over them, and the solemn angel Uriel pointed toward the Father's elect with an accusing and steady finger. "When you see the gesture, you'll be confirmed in the truth that has been revealed to you," he thought he could still hear. "The angel's look will tell you that you're right."

His heart beat faster. There, utterly alone in the church, the pilgrim warily stretched out his hand, as if he might be forever united to the sacred scene. It was true. As true as the blessings of his faith. Those who had traveled here before him had not lied. None of them. This work of Master Leonardo held the clues that would allow them to end the millenary quest for the true religion.

As he cast his eyes once more on the celebrated painting, suddenly a detail caught his attention. How strange! Who had painted halos over the three heads of the evangelical characters? Had his brothers not told him that this superfluous adornment, the fruit of backward minds thirsty for wonders, had been deliberately omitted by the masterly painter? Why, then, were they there? The false beggar felt frightened. The halos were not the only thing that had been altered in the *Opus Magnum*. Where was Uriel's finger, pointing toward the true Messiah? Why was his hand on his lap, instead of identifying the authentic Son of God? And why was the angel no longer fixing his eyes on the viewer?

The pilgrim was overcome by a vertiginous feeling of horror. Someone had meddled with the *Maestà*.

"You doubt, do you not?"

The pilgrim did not dare move a muscle but remained frozen to the spot at the sound of the dry, deep voice behind him. He hadn't heard the door of the church creak open, so the intruder must have been watching him for a fair while now.

"I can tell you're like all the others. For some dark reason you heretics come in droves to this House of God. Its light attracts you, but you are incapable of recognizing that."

"Heretics?" he asked in a whisper, without stirring.

"Come now! Did you really think we wouldn't notice?"

The pilgrim was unable to speak another word.

"At least this time you won't have the consolation of praying to your despicable image."

The pilgrim's pulse was racing. His hour had come. He felt dazed and angry, cheated in having risked his life to kneel before a fraud. The painting he was looking at was not the *Opus Magnum*. It was not the promised *Maestà*.

"It can't be—" he whispered. The intruder laughed out loud.

"It is easy enough to understand. I'll grant you the mercy of knowledge before sending you to burn in hell. Leonardo painted your *Maestà* in 1483, some fourteen years ago already. As you might suppose, the Franciscans were not much pleased with it. They had expected a painting that would reinforce their belief in the Immaculate Conception and that might serve to illuminate the altar. Instead, he offered them a scene that is not described in any of the Gospels and that brings together Saint John and Christ in a pause during the Flight to Egypt."

"The Mother of God, John, Jesus and the angel Uriel. The same one who warned Noah of the Flood. What wrong can you see in it?"

"You are all the same," the voice replied with bitterness. "Leonardo agreed to make changes in that first version and eliminate the insolent details."

"Why insolent?"

"How else would you refer to a work in which you cannot distinguish Saint John from Jesus Christ, and in which neither the Virgin nor Her Child are crowned with the halo of sainthood that belongs to them by rights? What are we to make of the fact that both holy infants are identical to one another? What kind of blasphemy is this that seeks to confound believers?"

A sudden feeling of relief allowed the pilgrim to breathe deeply for the first time. The executioner—because he was certain it was he to whom he was speaking—had not understood anything. The brothers who had preceded the pilgrim and who had never returned must have died at the hands of the executioner without revealing the motives for their discreet worship, and he himself was resolved to maintain his vow of silence even at the cost of his own blood.

"I won't be the one to clarify your doubts," he said serenely, without daring to face the voice.

"A pity. A real pity. Don't you realize that Leonardo has betrayed you? If you look closely you'll see that he's painted a new version of the *Maestà*. In the painting before you, you can see that both infants are now clearly distinguishable from one another. The one next to the Virgin is Saint John. He carries his long-stemmed cross and prays, while receiving the blessing of the other infant, the Christ Child. Uriel is no longer pointing his finger at anyone, and it is clear at last who is the awaited Messiah."

Was it possible that Leonardo had betrayed his brethren?

The pilgrim once again stretched his hand toward the painting. He had arrived here protected by the crowds who were streaming into Milan to attend the funeral of Donna Beatrice d'Este, his protector. Had she too given them up? Was it possible that everything for which they had struggled for so long was now collapsing?

"In fact, I don't need you to clarify anything," the voice continued, defiantly. "We already know who inspired this wickedness of Leonardo's, and, thanks be to God, that miserable creature has long ago gone to the grave. Do not doubt it: God will rightly punish Amadeo of Portugal and his *Apocalipsis Nova*. And with him, his notion of the Virgin, not as Mother of Christ, but as symbol of wisdom."

"And yet, it is a beautiful symbol," the pilgrim protested. "An ideal shared by many. Or are you planning to condemn all those who paint the Virgin with the Child Jesus and Saint John?"

"If they lead to confusion in the souls of the believers, yes, we will."

"And do you really think they will allow you to lay

your hands on Leonardo, on his apprentices or on Master Luini?"

"Bernardino de Lupino? The one also called Lovinus or Luini?"

"Do you know him?" the pilgrim asked.

"I know his work. He's a young imitator of Leonardo who obviously commits his same mistakes. But have no fear, he'll fall as well."

"What are you thinking of doing? Killing him?"

The pilgrim realized that something was terribly wrong. He heard behind him a metallic scraping, like that of a sword being unsheathed. His vows forbade him to carry weapons, so he mouthed a prayer to the false *Maestà*, begging for counsel.

"Am I to die as well?"

"The Soothsayer will do away with all of the wicked."

"The Soothsayer—?"

He had not finished asking his question when a strange convulsion shook his innards. The sharp blade of a huge steel sword pierced his back. The pilgrim let out a terrible groan. The metal sliced through his heart. The keen sensation, brief as lightning, made him open his eyes wide with terror. The false beggar felt no pain, only an icy coldness, a frozen embrace that made him stagger over the altar and fall on his bruised knees.

It was the one and only time he saw his assailant.

The Soothsayer was a sturdy shadow, black as charcoal and expressionless.

Night was falling in the church. Everything was growing dark and still. Even time seemed to be strangely slowing down. As he slumped to the altar pavement, the bundle the pilgrim carried on his back became undone, and a few pieces of bread and several cards printed with curious effigies tumbled onto the floor. The first corresponded to a woman wearing the Franciscan habit, a triple crown on her head, a cross like that of Saint John the Baptist in her right hand and a closed book in her left.

"Cursed heretic!" said the Soothsayer when he saw it.

The pilgrim returned a cynical smile, as he watched the Soothsayer pick up the card and dip a pen in his blood to jot down something on the back.

"You'll never . . . open . . . the priestess's . . . book," the pilgrim said.

From his hunched position, his heart pumping streams of blood onto the paving stones, he managed to see something that he had up to now overlooked. Even though Uriel was no longer pointing at John the Baptist as in the true *Opus Magnum*, his open eyes spoke volumes. The "fire of God" was pointing with his sideways look toward the wise man of the Jordan, as the true Savior of the world.

Leonardo, he consoled himself by thinking, before falling into the eternal darkness, had not betrayed them after all. The Soothsayer had lied.

16

We waited for the first light of Saturday the fourteenth of January to abandon the interior of the monastery and explore at ease the brick façade of Santa Maria delle Grazie. Father Alessandro, who had proven to possess a certain natural ability for solving riddles, was once again exultant. It was as if the frost that, hours earlier, had frozen this part of the city were no concern of his. At half past six, immediately after the service, the librarian and I were ready to go out into the street. It was to be a simple operation that would take us no longer than a couple of minutes, but which, however, troubled me deeply.

Father Alessandro took notice and decided to remain silent.

He knew full well that, whatever the "number of the name" that we would obtain by counting the round windows on the façade, we would still not have solved the problem itself. We'd have a number, perhaps the number rendered by the name of our anonymous informer, though we could not even be sure of that. What if it were the sum total of the letters of his family name? Or of the number of his cell? Or—?

"I'd forgotten to tell you something," he said at last.

"What is it, Father?"

"It's something that may console you. Once we've obtained that blessed number, we'll still have much work ahead if we want to get to the bottom of this puzzle."

"That is so."

"Well, then you should know that Santa Maria houses a community of monks who are the most ingenious in solving riddles in the whole of Italy."

I smiled. The librarian, like so many other servants of God, had never heard of Bethany. So much the better. But Father Alessandro insisted on explaining the reasons for his proud assertion. He assured me that the favorite pastime of these thirty select Dominicans was, precisely, to solve riddles. A number excelled in the art; not a few amused themselves by composing riddles for the others.

"The woods bear sons who later lay them low. Who are they?" the librarian recited in a singsong voice, in spite of my disinclination to include games in our mission. "The handles of the ax!"

Father Alessandro spared me no details. Of everything he said, what most drew my attention was to learn that riddles at Santa Maria were not used only for recreational purposes. Often the monks could use them in their sermons, turning them into instruments of indoctrination. If what the librarian was saying was not an exaggeration, within these walls was the largest training camp for riddle makers in the whole of Christendom, not counting Bethany. Therefore, if the Soothsayer had sprung from somewhere, this was the perfect place.

"Follow my advice, Father Agostino," said the librarian, anticipating my thoughts. "When you have the number and if you don't know what to do with it, consult any of our brothers. The person you least imagine may give you your solution."

"Anyone, you say?"

The librarian made a gesture.

"Of course! Anyone! I'm certain that the brother in charge of the stables will know more about riddles than a Roman like you. Don't be afraid to ask the prior, the cook, the pantry keepers, the scribes, any one of them! One thing, however: make certain you don't speak too loudly or you'll be admonished for breaking the vow of silence that every monk must keep."

And with these words, he lifted the bar that blocked the main entrance to the monastery.

A small avalanche of snow fell from the roof, crashing with a dull sound at our feet. To be candid, I had not expected that something as banal as exploring the façade of a church at dawn would prove to be such a delicate exercise. The intense coldness of the morning had turned the snow into a dangerous sheet of ice. Everything was white, deserted and wrapped in an intimidating silence. The very idea of approaching Maestro Solari's brick wall and skirting the enclosure of the third cloister would have put fear in the heart of the bravest of men. An ill-timed slip might break our necks or leave us lame for the rest of our days. Not to mention the difficulty of having to explain to the monks what we were doing at that time of dawn so far from our prayers, risking our lives beyond the monastery walls.

We gave the matter no further thought. Cautiously, trying not to get our sandals more wet than necessary, we advanced slowly between the chunks of ice toward the center of the façade, parallel to the street. We crossed it almost on all fours and, once Father Alessandro and I saw that we were at a proper distance, with a perspective on the ensemble of the building, we observed the windows with great care. A feeble interior light made them sparkle like the eyes of a dragon. There they were, in front of us, a series of round windows that adorned the church along its entire length. The main façade was now around the corner, barely a few steps beyond, its "face" turned away from us.

"Look not on its face," I whispered through chattering teeth.

Frozen, hiding my hands in the sleeves of my woolen cloak, I counted: one, two, three . . . seven.

That seven disconcerted me. Seven verses, seven round windows . . . There was no doubt now that the number of the anonymous correspondent was that recurrent, blasted seven.

"But seven what?" asked the librarian.

All I could do was shrug.

What happened later that day showed me the way to proceed.

"So you are the Roman father who has sought lodgings in our house?"

Father Prior Vicenzo Bandello of Santa Maria delle Grazie scrutinized me with great severity before inviting me to enter the sacristy. At last I was meeting the man who had written the report on the death of Beatrice d'Este for Bethany.

"Father Alessandro has spoken much about you," he continued. "Apparently, you are a scholarly man. A meticulous intellectual, with strong willpower, someone who may enrich our community during his stay among us. What did you say your name was?"

"Agostino Leyre, Father Prior."

The prior had finished the office of terce as the insufficient sun hovered over the Valley of Padana. He was about to withdraw to prepare his sermon for Donna Beatrice's funeral when I accosted him. Only partly was it an impulsive act on my part. Hadn't Father Alessandro insisted that I ask any of the brethren about my riddle? Had he not assured me that the least expected among the monks might grant me the correct answer?

And who was less expected than the Father Prior himself?

I made my decision shortly after returning frozen from our adventure, in search of warmth inside the monastery. Luck had it that as I ventured into the sacristy I happened to come upon the Father Prior. The librarian had left me, with the excuse that he needed to get food in the kitchen for our next working session, and I seized the opportunity.

Father Prior Vicenzo Bandello was a little over sixty, with a face creased like an old sail, a strong chin and a surprising tendency to allow his gestures to betray every one of his emotions. He was even smaller than I thought the night I'd seen him in the church. He was moving nervously between the painted doors of the sacristy cupboards, uncertain as to which to close first.

"Tell me, Father Agostino," he said while putting away the chalice and paten from the previous Mass. "I'm curious. What exactly do you do in Rome?"

"I'm appointed to the Holy Office."

"I see, I see . . . And, if I understand correctly, in the spare time left by your duties, you delight in solving puzzles. That's splendid." He smiled. "I'm certain we'll get along well."

"It is precisely that subject about which I'd like to speak to you."

"Is that so?"

I nodded. If the Father Prior was the eminence that the librarian had vaunted, it was probable that the presence of the Soothsayer in Milan would not have escaped his notice. But I had to exercise caution. Perhaps he himself was the author of the letters and was afraid of disclosing his identity until he was sure of my true intentions. Even worse, perhaps he was not aware of the Soothsayer's existence, but if I revealed it to him, who could prevent him from alerting Ludovico of our plans?

"Tell me this, Father Agostino. As someone who delights in uncovering secrets, you must have heard of the art of memory?"

The Father Prior asked the question nonchalantly while I was trying in vain to determine to what degree he might be involved in the matter of the anonymous correspondence. Perhaps I was being too zealous. It seemed as if every new monk I encountered at Santa Maria became part of my list of suspects. The Father Prior was to be no exception. The truth is that, of all possible alternatives, of the close to thirty friars who lived within these walls, the Father Prior was the man whose profile best fit that of the Soothsayer. I can't imagine how we did not realize it back in Bethany. Even his first name, Vicenzo, consisted of seven letters, like the seven lines of the infernal *Oculos ejus dinumera* or the seven windows of the southern façade of the church. It came to me as I watched him opening and closing cupboard doors and secreting away a large bunch of keys under his habit. The Father Prior was one of the few who had access to the budgets and plans of the duke for Santa Maria, and likely the only one who would make use of a safe official courier to send his letters to Rome.

"Well?" he asked, amused to see me so lost in

thought. "Have you or have you not heard of this art?"

I shook my head while searching his features for something that would confirm my suspicion.

"That's too bad!" he continued. "Few are aware that our order boasts several great scholars in this worthy discipline."

"I never heard of it."

"And, of course, neither will you have heard that Cicero himself mentions this art in his *De Oratore,* or that an even earlier treatise, *Ad Herennium,* describes it in detail and offers us a precise formula to recall whatever we wish—"

"Offers us? The Dominicans?"

"Of course! For the past thirty or forty years, Father Agostino, many of our brethren have been studying this art. You yourself, who work every day with complicated files and documents, have you never dreamt of being able to store away in your mind a text, an image, a name, without having to go over it again because you can be certain it will stay with you forever?"

"Of course. But only the most gifted can—"

"And needing it in your work," he cut me off, "have you never tried to find the best method to achieve such a miracle? The ancients, who did not possess the same ability to copy books as we have, invented a masterly device: they imagined 'palaces of memory' in which to store their knowledge. You haven't heard of them either, have you?"

I shook my head, astonished into silence.

"The Greeks, for instance, conceived of a large building full of sumptuous galleries and rooms, and then

would assign to each window, arch, column, stairs or hall
a different meaning. In the entrance they'd 'store' their
knowledge of grammar, in the main hall that of rhetoric,
in the kitchen, oratory. And in order to remember something they'd put away there, all they had to do was go
into that corner of their palace with their imagination
and extract it in the inverse order in which it had been
placed there. Ingenious, isn't it?"

I looked at the Father Prior without knowing what to
say. Was he offering me a clue permitting me to ask him
about the letters we had received in Rome? Should I follow Father Alessandro's advice and consult him about
the puzzle without any further hesitation? Fearful of losing his early confidence, I gave him a subtle hint:

"Tell me, Father Prior. And if instead of a 'palace of
memory' we were to use a 'church of memory'? Could we,
for example, conceal a person's name in a church of brick
and stone?"

"I see that you're clever, Father Agostino." He
winked at me sarcastically. "And practical. What the
Greeks applied to imaginary palaces, the Romans and
even the Egyptians tried out on real buildings. If those
who entered them knew the precise 'memory code,' they
could wander through the rooms and at the same time
receive valuable information."

"And using a church?" I insisted.

"Yes, a church could also be used," he conceded. "But
before explaining how one of these mechanisms would
work, allow me first to show you something. As I mentioned, in the past few years, Dominican brothers from
Ravenna, Florence, Basel, Milan and Freiburg have been

working on a mnemonic method based on images or architectural structures especially designed for this purpose."

"Designed?"

"Yes. Adapted, retouched, embellished with decorative details that seem superfluous to the profane eye but are essential for those who know the secret vocabulary behind them. You'll understand if I give you an example, Father Agostino."

The Father Prior produced from inside his habit a sheet of paper that he smoothed out on the offering table. It was no larger than the palm of his hand, white, with wax seal stains on one corner. Someone had printed on it a female figure with her left foot resting on a ladder. She was surrounded by birds and bore on her breast a number of strange objects. At her feet, an inscription in Latin that identified her clearly as "Lady Grammar." Her eyes were fixed on no place in particular and had an absent look.

"We are currently putting the finishing touches on one of these images, which, from here onward, will help us recall the different parts of the art of grammar. Here it is," he said, pointing at the extravagant figure. "Do you wish to see how it works?"

I nodded.

"Look carefully," the Father Prior urged me. "If someone were to ask us at this very moment what are the terms on which grammar is based, and we happened to have this print before us, we'd be able to answer without the slightest hesitation."

"Truly?"

The Father Prior enjoyed my disbelief.

"Our answer would be precise: *praedicatio, applicatio* and *continentia*. And do you know why? In all simplicity: because I've 'read' it in this image."

The Father Prior bent over the page and drew imaginary circles with his finger around different parts of the image.

"See here: *praedicatio*, or 'preaching,' is indicated by the bird in her right hand, which in Latin, *passer*, begins with the letter *P*, and also by the banner in her left hand in the shape of that same letter. Preaching is grammar's most important attribute, which is why it's indicated with two elements. Also, it's the mark of our order. After all, we are all preachers, aren't we?"

I observed the graceful banner that Lady Grammar

was holding, folded over itself in the shape of the letter P, just as the Father Prior had described.

"The next attribute," he continued, "*applicatio*, or 'dedication,' is represented by *aquila*, the eagle, which Grammar bears on her arm. *Aquila*, like *applicatio*, begins with the letter *A*, so that the mind of someone initiated in the *Ars Memoriae* will establish the connection immediately. And as to *continentia*, 'containment,' you'll see it written on the woman's breast. If you look at the shape of those objects—the bow, the wheel, the plow and the hammer—as if they were the shape of letters, you'd read at once the word: c-o-n-t . . . *continentia*!"

It was amazing. In a seemingly innocent image, someone had managed to enclose a complete theory of grammar. Suddenly it occurred to me that the books being printed by the hundreds in workshops in Venice, Rome or Turin included engraved frontispieces that might hide secret messages that we scholars were incapable of seeing. At the Secretariat of Keys, we had never been taught anything like it.

"And what about the objects that the birds are holding? Do they also have a meaning?" I wondered, still astonished at the unexpected revelation.

"My dear brother: everything, absolutely everything, has a meaning. In these times in which every lord, every prince, every cardinal has so many things to hide from the others, every one of his actions, as well as the works of art for which he pays or the writings he patronizes, has a hidden meaning."

The Father Prior concluded with an enigmatic smile. I seized on the opportunity.

"And you?" I asked. "Are you hiding something too?"

The Father Prior looked at me with the same ironic expression. He passed a hand over his perfect tonsure and distractedly smoothed the hair around it.

"A prior also has his secrets, indeed."

"And would he hide them in a church that has already been built?" I pressed.

"Oh!" he said, startled. "That would be very easy. First, I'd count everything in it: walls, windows, towers, bells . . . The numbers are what's most important! Then, once the whole church is reduced to numbers, I'd see which of them can be paired with the appropriate letters or words. And I'd compare both the number of letters in a word and the value of that word when translated into numbers."

"That is *gematria*, Father Prior! The secret science of the Jews!"

"It is *gematria*, yes. But it is not a negligible branch of knowledge, as your scandalized attitude seems to assume. Christ was a Jew and he learned *gematria* in the temple. How else would we know that 'Abraham' and 'Mercy' are two numerically twinned words? Or that 'Jacob's ladder' and 'Mount Sinai' when added up, in Hebrew, are 130, which tells us that they're both places by which to ascend to God's chosen heavens?"

"That is to say," I interrupted, "that if you had to hide your Christian name, Vicenzo, in the Church of Santa Maria, you'd find a particular characteristic of the building that would add up to seven, like the seven letters in your name."

"Exactly."

"Like, for example . . . seven windows?"

"That would be a good choice. Though I'd probably choose one of the frescoes that decorate the church. It would allow me to add more nuances than a simple succession of windows. The more elements you add to a given space, the more versatility you grant the art of memory. And, truthfully, the façade of Santa Maria is somewhat too simple for such a purpose."

"Do you think so?"

"Yes, I do. Also, seven is a number subject to too many interpretations. It is the sacred number above all others. The Bible makes use of it constantly. I don't think I'd choose such an ambiguous number to conceal my name."

The Father Prior seemed sincere.

"Let's make an agreement," he said all of a sudden. "I'll let you have the puzzle our community is now working on, and you let me have yours. I'm certain that we'll be able to help one another."

Naturally, I accepted.

18

Delighted, the Father Prior asked me to accompany him to the far end of the monastery. He wanted to show me something. At once.

Quickly we passed the central altar, leaving behind the choir and the gallery, which were receiving the finishing touches for Donna Beatrice's funeral, and entered the long passageway that led to the Cloister of the Dead. The monastery was a place of great sobriety, with visible brick walls and granite columns in impeccable order set along carefully paved corridors. On the way to our mysterious destination, the Father Prior nodded to Brother Benedetto, the one-eyed scribe whose custom it was to stroll aimlessly under the arches, his single eye lost in a breviary that I was not able to identify.

"Well?" he growled, feeling himself addressed by his superior. "Once again going to visit the *Opus Diaboli*? It would be better if you buried it under a load of quicklime!"

"Brother, please! I need you to come with us," the Father Prior commanded. "Our guest needs someone who can tell him the stories related to this place, and there's no one better suited than you. You're the oldest friar in our community, older still than the walls of this house."

"Stories, eh?"

The old man's single eye glittered with emotion at my interest. I myself was bewitched by the sight of this man who seemed to enjoy showing his wound to the world, as if boasting of the scar the missing eye had left on his face.

"Many stories are told in this house, of course. For instance, you don't know why we call this courtyard the Cloister of the Dead?" he asked as he joined us on our excursion. "That is easy: because here is where we bury our brethren so that they return to the earth in the same way they arrived, with no commemoratory plaques or honors. No vanity here. Only the habit of our order. The day will come when the entire courtyard will be full of bones."

"Is this your cemetery?"

"Much more than a cemetery. It is our waiting room before entering Heaven."

The Father Prior had reached a large double-paneled door. It was a sturdy-looking piece of wood with a strong iron lock into which he fitted one of the keys he was carrying. Brother Benedetto and I looked at each other. My pulse quickened: I guessed what it was that the Father Prior wanted to show me. Father Alessandro had intimated as much, and naturally I had prepared myself for the grand moment. There, in a large room exactly below the library, was the famous refectory of Santa Maria delle Grazie to which Leonardo had restricted the monks' access. Unless I was mistaken, this was the true reason for my presence in Milan and why the Soothsayer had written his threatening letters to Bethany.

A new idea occurred to me: Did the Father Prior and I share the same riddle without knowing it?

"If this place were already consecrated"—the Father Prior's face lit up as he pushed the heavy door—"we'd all wash our hands and you two would wait outside until I gave you leave to enter—"

"But it hasn't been!" screeched the scribe.

"No. Not yet. But that will not prevent its holy atmosphere to soak into our souls."

"Holy atmosphere! Rubbish!"

And with these words, we entered.

As I had supposed, I had stepped into the monastery's future refectory. It was dark and cold, lined with huge cartons resting against the walls among the jumble. Ropes, bricks, screens, boxes and, most curious of all, a table set for dinner and covered with a large cotton cloth; all filled a room that seemed to have fallen into oblivion a long time ago. The table was the thing that most drew my attention, since it seemed to be the only trace of order amidst the chaos. Nothing suggested that it had been put to use. The plates were empty and, like the crockery, were covered by a fine coat of dust, as if untouched for weeks.

"I beg you not to be alarmed by the sorry state of our dining room," said the Father Prior as he rolled up the sleeves of his habit and made his way through the sea of wooden planks. "This will be our refectory. It's been like this for three years now, can you imagine? The brothers are barely allowed to enter, by order of Leonardo himself, who keeps it locked up until his work is finished. In the meantime, our furniture lies molding in that corner there, among the dirt and the detestable smell of paint."

"It's a veritable hell, did I not say so? A hell with its very own devil—"

"Brother Benedetto, in God's name!"

"Don't worry," I said. "In Rome we're always under construction; the atmosphere is familiar."

Separated from the rest of the stuff by wooden screens, in one of the side wings of the immense room, one could make out a board cut out in the shape of a U, on which were piled up long benches painted in black varnish, as well as the remains of an exquisite wooden canopy, rotting with mold. As we made our way through the discarded furniture, the Father Prior commented:

"None of the decoration work in the monastery is on time. But the worst delays are in this room. It seems impossible to reach the point at which it will all be finished."

"It's Leonardo's fault," Brother Benedetto growled again. "He's been toying with us for months. Let's finish with him, once and for all!"

"Please be silent. Let me explain our problem to Father Agostino."

The Father Prior looked both ways, as if to ascertain that there was no one else listening. The precaution seemed absurd: since we had left the church, we had not met anyone except the one-eyed monk, and it was hardly likely that there'd be someone hiding there instead of preparing for the funeral or attending to daily duties. And yet the Father Prior seemed uncertain, afraid. Perhaps that is why he lowered his voice to a whisper as he bent over my ear:

"You'll soon understand my precaution."

"Indeed?"

The Father Prior nodded nervously.

"Master Leonardo is said to be a very influential man and might have me removed if he knew that I've allowed you to enter without his permission."

"Leonardo da Vinci?"

"Don't say his name so loud!" he whispered. "Does it surprise you? The duke himself called on him four years ago to help him decorate this monastery. Ludovico il Moro wants the Sforza family pantheon to be placed beneath the apse of the church and he requires magnificent, unimpeachable surroundings to justify his decision in the eyes of his relatives. That is why he contracted Leonardo. And believe me when I say that since the duke embarked on this project, there hasn't been a single day of peace under this roof."

"Not one," Brother Benedetto confirmed. "And you know why? Because this Master who always wears white, whom you'll never see eating meat or killing an animal, is in truth an evil soul. He's introduced a sinister heresy in his paintings for our community and has defied us to find it before he finishes them. And Ludovico il Moro lends him his support!"

"But Leonardo is not—"

"A heretic?" he interrupted me. "No, of course not. At a first glance, he doesn't appear to be one. He won't hurt a fly, he spends his days meditating or jotting down things in his notebooks, and gives every appearance of being a wise man. But I'm certain that the Master is not a good Christian."

"May I ask something?"

The Father Prior nodded in assent.

"Is it true that you ordered all available information to be gathered on Leonardo's past? Why have you never trusted him? The brother librarian told me so."

"You see, it was just after he launched his challenge. As you can understand, we were forced to dig into his past to find out what kind of man we were dealing with. You'd have done the same had he challenged the Holy Office."

"I suppose so."

"I did indeed put Father Alessandro in charge of drawing out a profile of his work, in order to be a step ahead of his plans. That was how we found out that the Franciscans in Milan had already been plagued by serious problems because of Master Leonardo. Apparently, he used pagan sources to document his paintings, leading the faithful into dangerous misinterpretations."

"Father Alessandro told me about that too, and about a heretical book by a certain Amadeo."

"The *Apocalipsis Nova*."

"Exactly."

"But that book is only a small sample of what was discovered. Didn't he tell you anything about Leonardo's scruples regarding certain biblical scenes?"

"Scruples?"

"Very revealing scruples. Until this very day, we haven't been able to find a single work by Leonardo depicting the Crucifixion. Not one. Nor any that show scenes from Our Lord's Passion."

"Perhaps he was never commissioned to paint one."

"No, Father Agostino. The Tuscan has avoided painting these scriptural episodes for some obscure reason. At first we thought he might be a Jew, but later we discovered that he wasn't. He didn't keep the rules of Sabbath nor any of the Hebrew customs."

"So, then?"

"Well . . . I believe that anomaly is somehow related to the problem that concerns us."

"Tell me about Leonardo. Father Alessandro never mentioned that he had ever challenged you."

"The librarian wasn't present when it took place. And, in our community, barely half a dozen brothers are aware of the facts. It all started during one of the courtesy visits that Donna Beatrice paid Leonardo, a couple of years ago. The Master had finished painting Saint Thomas in the Last Supper. He had depicted him as a bearded man, lifting his index finger, seated close to Christ."

"I imagine that the finger is the one he'll later put in Christ's wound, once Our Lord was resurrected, isn't that right?"

"That is what I thought and that is what I said to Her Grace. But Leonardo laughed at my interpretation. He said that we priests had no idea of symbolism, and that if he wished he could portray Mahomet himself without any of us noticing."

"He said that?"

"Donna Beatrice and the Master burst out laughing, and we felt very offended. But what could we do? To quarrel with the duke's wife and with his favorite painter? If we did, no doubt Leonardo would have blamed us for the delays in his Last Supper."

The Father Prior continued.

"In truth, it was I who provoked him. I wanted to show him that I wasn't as thickheaded in interpreting symbols as he made me out to be, but in doing so, I entered a field into which I never should have ventured."

"What do you mean, Father Prior?"

"In those days, I used to visit the Rochetta Palace in order to inform the duke of the progress of the work at Santa Maria. And on several occasions I came upon Donna Beatrice playing in the throne room with a deck of cards. The figures on these cards were strangely attractive, painted in lively colors. They depicted hanged men, women holding stars, fauns, popes, blindfolded angels, devils. Very soon, I learned that these cards were an old family heirloom. They had been designed by the old Duke of Milan, Filippo Maria Visconti, with the assistance of the *condottiere* Francesco Sforza, in 1441. Later, when Sforza gained control over the dukedom, he offered the deck to his children, and a copy eventually ended up in the hands of Ludovico il Moro."

"What happened then?"

"You'll see. One of these cards showed a woman dressed as a Franciscan, holding a closed book in her hand. It drew my attention because the woman was wearing a man's habit, and she seemed to be pregnant. Can you imagine? A pregnant woman in a Franciscan habit? The whole thing seemed a mockery. Well, I don't know why, I recalled that card during the discussion with Leonardo, and I decided to show off. 'I know what the Franciscan woman on the card means,' I said. Donna

Beatrice became very serious. 'What can you know?' she sneered. 'It's a symbol that refers to you, Your Grace,' I said. She became interested. 'The Franciscan woman is a crowned maiden, which means she has your same honored position. And she is pregnant, which proclaims the same state of grace for you. That card is a warning of what fate has in store for you.' "

"And the book?" I asked.

"That was what offended me most. I told her that the Franciscan woman kept the book closed in order to hide the fact that it was a forbidden text. 'And what text might that be?' Master Leonardo questioned me. 'Perhaps the *Apocalipsis Nova*, with which you are so familiar,' I replied with a touch of scorn. This was when Leonardo mustered up his courage and proposed the challenge. 'You have no idea,' he said. 'Obviously it's an important book. As important as the Bible, even more so, but your theologian's pride will prevent you from ever knowing it.' And he added: 'When the future son of Her Grace is born, I will have finished incorporating its secrets into my *Cenacolo*. And I assure you that, even though they'll be in front of your very noses, you won't ever be able to read them. That will be the greatness of my riddle. And also the proof of your foolishness.' "

19

"When might I see *The Last Supper?*" I asked the Father Prior.

He smiled.

"Now, if you wish," he said. "There it is, in front of you. All you need to do is open your eyes."

At first, I did not know where to look. The only painting I was able to make out in the dark refectory, which stank of damp and dust, was a Mary Magdalene hanging on the southern wall of the room. She was grasping the feet of Christ on the Cross and weeping under the ecstatic look of Saint Dominic. She was kneeling on a rectangular stone on which I could read a name I had not heard before: "Io Donatvs Montorfanv P."

"That's a work by Master Montorfano," the Father Prior explained. "A pious, praiseworthy piece, which he finished a couple of years ago. But it isn't the one you wish to see."

The Father Prior then made a gesture toward the opposite wall. The story of the card and the secret book had distracted me to the point that I could barely make out what my eyes were seeing. A mountain of planks filled a fair section of the refectory's northern corner, and yet the feeble light that lit that particular area allowed me to perceive something that froze me to the spot. Indeed: beyond the barrier of boxes and cartons, in between the spaces left by the great wood scaffolding that crossed the wall from one side to the other, another room could be seen! It took me a moment to understand that this was an illusion. But what an illusion! Sitting at a rectangular banquet table identical to the one that had attracted my attention upon entering, thirteen human figures with lifelike attitudes and gestures seemed to be acting out some theatrical work for our eyes only. But it was no comedy, God forgive me the thought! They were the most realistic and moving portraits I had ever seen of Our Lord Jesus Christ and His disciples. It is true that a few of the faces still needed more definition, among them that of Christ Himself, but the composition was almost finished—and it breathed life.

"Can you see it? Can you make out what's behind it?"

I swallowed hard before nodding.

Brother Benedetto, oddly satisfied, gave me a light tap on the shoulder, inviting me to draw nearer to the magical wall.

"Come closer, it won't bite you. It's the *Opus Diaboli* of which I warned you. Seductive as the serpent in Eden, and quite as poisonous."

It is impossible to put into words what I felt at that moment. I had the impression of seeing a forbidden scene, the frozen image of something that had taken place fifteen centuries ago and that Leonardo had managed to immortalize with inconceivable realism. I could not understand then why Brother Benedetto called it "the work of the Devil" when it seemed to be a gift of the angels themselves. As in a trance, I walked toward it, without looking to see where I put my feet. The closer I got, the more alive the wall seemed to become. Dear God! Suddenly I understood the function of that table laid out beneath the scaffolding: cloth, crockery, jugs and crystal glasses, and even porcelain dishes were set out in identical fashion on the wall six feet above it, as real as those below. But who were those disciples? Whose features had he borrowed for the portraits? Where had he found inspiration for their clothing?

"If you like, Father Agostino, we can climb onto the scaffolding to take a closer look. I don't think Master Leonardo will be around today to supervise his work."

Of course I'd like to, I thought.

"You will soon discover that, however close you get, you won't appreciate it more. What happens here is the contrary of what happens in an ordinary painting: if you approach the work too closely, you become dizzy and incapable of finding a single brushstroke to help you better understand it."

"A further proof of his heresy!" Brother Benedetto growled again. "The man is a sorcerer!"

I was dumbfounded. For a few seconds, maybe minutes, I was incapable of tearing my eyes from the most marvelous figures I had ever seen in my entire life. There, indeed, were no traces, outlines or erasures, nor smudges of charcoal pencils. What did it matter? Even in its unfinished state, with two of the apostles barely sketched onto the wall, with the face of Our Lord still devoid of expression and the outside borders of three other figures waiting to be colored in, the painting allowed the viewer to roam freely through the sacred feast. The Father Prior, aware of the time, made an effort to return me to reality.

"Tell me, Father Agostino, with that intelligence with which you so impressed Brother Alessandro, have you noticed nothing unusual about this work?"

"I—I don't know what you mean, Father Prior."

"Come, Father. Don't disappoint us. You've agreed to help us solve our riddle. If we succeed in associating the anomalies in this painting with the contents of one of the forbidden books, we'd be able to seize Leonardo and accuse him of seeking inspiration in apocryphal sources. It would mean his end."

The Father Prior paused before continuing.

"I'll give you a clue. Have you not noticed that none of the apostles, not even Christ Himself, has a halo? You can't say that's normal in a Christian work of art!"

My dear God! The Father Prior was right! My stupidity knew no limits. I had been so taken aback by the extraordinary realism of the characters that I had not noticed this all-important absence.

"And what of the Eucharist?" interjected the scribe. "If this is, as he claims, the Last Supper, why does Christ not have before him the bread and the wine to consecrate? Where is the cup of the Holy Grail that will receive His precious blood of redemption? And why is His dish empty? A heretic, that's what Leonardo is! A heretic!"

"What are you suggesting? That Master Leonardo wasn't following the biblical text when he painted this scene?"

I thought I could still hear Father Alessandro's explanations regarding the Virgin's portrait that Leonardo had painted for the monks of San Francesco il Grande. On that occasion as well, Leonardo had disregarded not only the scriptural indications but also the instructions of his patrons. My question, therefore, must have seemed to them puerile:

"Did you ask him why he's done this?"

"Of course!" the Father Prior answered. "And he laughed in our faces, calling us fools once again. He said it wasn't up to him to help us interpret his Last Supper. Can you believe it? The cunning fox comes here every other afternoon, gives one of the apostles a brushstroke, sits for hours contemplating his work and then he barely deigns to speak with the brethren to explain the oddities of his composition—"

"At least he's bound to justify himself by quoting a passage from the Scriptures . . . ," I ventured, knowing full well the answer.

"From one of the Gospels?" The scribe's question sounded full of sarcasm. "You know the texts as well as I do, so tell me, which one describes Peter holding a dagger at the table, or Judas and Christ dipping their hands into the same dish? No, you won't find those scenes anywhere. Nowhere at all."

"You must demand that he explain himself!"

"He slips away. He says he's only accountable to the duke, who's the one who pays his wages."

"You mean to say he comes and goes here as he pleases?"

"And accompanied by whomever he chooses. Sometimes, even by court ladies whom he wishes to impress."

"Forgive me the boldness, Brother Benedetto, but even with the unpleasantness of being treated in such a manner, these are not arguments that would allow you to accuse him of heresy."

"Why not? Isn't all this enough? Is it not sufficient to have a Christ without his attributes, a Last Supper with no Eucharist, a Saint Peter hiding a dagger to attack God-knows-whom?"

Brother Benedetto wrinkled his red nose in anger, muttering under his breath. The Father Prior tried to soothe him by saying to me:

"You don't understand, do you?"

"No," I answered.

"What Brother Benedetto has tried to explain is that, even though to you this is only a marvelous representation of the Last Supper scene, it might not be that entirely. I've seen many painters work on similar commissions, no doubt less ambitious, but I'm at a loss to understand what it is that Leonardo wishes to display in my house," said the Father Prior, emphasizing the possessive to show how troubled he was by the matter. He then caught me by the sleeve of my habit and continued in a gloomy tone of voice:

"We are very much afraid that the duke's painter is trying to ridicule our faith and our religion, and that if we don't find the key to read his work, his affront will remain here forever, in eternal mockery of our stupidity. That is why we need your help, Father Agostino."

The Father Prior's last words echoed through the vast refectory.

Then the one-eyed scribe pushed me toward another spot beneath the scaffolding, from which several of the guests at the *Cenacolo* could be clearly seen.

"You want more proofs? I'll give you yet another to help you burn that impostor!"

I followed him.

"You see?" he shouted. "Look well!"

"What am I supposed to see, Brother Benedetto?"

"Leonardo, that's whom! Don't you recognize him? The bastard has portrayed himself among the apostles. He's the second figure from the right. No doubt about it: his same eyes, his big and powerful hands, even his blond mane. He says it's Judas Thaddeus, but the figure has all his own features!"

"But truly, Brother Benedetto, I see nothing wrong with that either," I answered. "Ghiberti too portrayed himself on the bronze doors of the Baptistery in Florence, and nothing happened. It's very much a Tuscan custom."

"Is it, indeed? And why is Leonardo the only character at the table, together with Saint Matthew the Apostle, who appears with his back to Our Lord? Do you really believe he means nothing by it? Not even Judas Iscariot has such an insolent attitude! You must know this," he added in a threatening tone. "Everything that devil Leonardo does follows a secret plan, a purpose."

"But Brother, if Leonardo is Judas Thaddeus, then who is the real Matthew, who also turns his back on the Lord?"

"That is what we are hoping you will tell us! That you'll identify the disciples, that you'll reveal to us the truth about this cursed Last Supper!"

I tried to calm the enraged old man.

"Father Prior, Brother Benedetto," I said, addressing them both. "In order to put my brain at the service of your riddle, I need to know on what do you base your accusation against Master Leonardo. If you're seeking to make a case against him, if you wish to put a stop to his work with solid arguments, we must have irrefutable proofs, not mere suspicions. I don't need to remind you that Leonardo is under the protection of the Duke of Milan."

"We'll tell you what you want to know. But first answer one more thing . . ."

I was thankful to hear once again the calm voice of the Father Prior, who now stepped back a few paces in order to examine *The Last Supper* in its entirety.

"Can you tell, simply by looking at it, what *exactly* is depicted by this scene?"

His emphasis made me hesitate.

"You tell me please, Father Prior."

"I will. To all appearances, it seems to be the moment described in the Gospel according to John, when Jesus announces to His disciples that one among them will betray Him. Ludovico il Moro and Leonardo chose the passage very carefully."

"*Amen dico vobis quia unus ex vobis tradet me,*" I recited from memory.

" 'Verily, verily, I say unto you, that one of you shall betray me.' Exactly."

"And what do you think is strange in the choice?"

"Two things," he answered. "First, that unlike the traditional Last Suppers, they did not choose for this one the institution of the Eucharist, the consecration of the bread and the wine. And second"—he paused as if in doubt—"here the traitor doesn't seem to be Judas."

"No?"

"Look at the mural, for Heaven's sake!" Brother Benedetto insisted. "I only have one eye left, but I can see quite clearly that the one who's going to betray Jesus, to kill him even, is Saint Peter."

"Saint Peter? Are you certain?"

"Yes, Simon Peter, the very one there," Brother Benedetto insisted, pointing him out among the dozen faces. "Can't you see how he's hiding his dagger behind his back and prepares to strike Christ Himself? Can't you see how he's threatening John with a hand on his neck?"

The old man muttered his accusations vehemently, as if he had been examining the disposition of the figures for a long time, working secretly, and had reached conclusions hidden from the rest of us common mortals. The Father Prior assented somewhat hesitatingly.

"And precisely, what do you think of *that* John the Apostle?" His emphasis alerted me. "Have you seen how he's been painted? No beard, with delicate, manicured hands, with a face like that of a Madonna. In fact, he looks like a woman!"

I shook my head in disbelief. John's face wasn't finished. One could only discern the sketch of soft, rounded, almost adolescent features.

"A woman? Are you sure? No woman sat at the Supper described in the Gospels—"

"I see you're beginning to see the light," the Father Prior answered more calmly. "That is why it's so urgent that we solve this riddle. Leonardo's work holds far too many misunderstandings. Too many veiled allusions. God knows how much I enjoy puzzles, the art of concealing information in real or painted places, but the solution to this one escapes me."

I noticed that the Father Prior was making an effort to restrain himself.

"Of course," he continued without waiting for a response, "it's still early for you to appreciate all the aspects of this problem. Come back whenever you like. Take advantage of Leonardo's absences. Sit down and admire his work, and try to decipher it in sections, just as we have been trying to do. In a few days' time you'll feel the same discouragement that we feel now. This mural will become your obsession."

After saying this, the Father Prior proceeded to hunt through his bundle of keys. He produced a large heavy one, made of iron, with three wards in the shape of a Latin cross.

"Keep it. There are only three copies in existence. Leonardo has one, and frequently lends it to his apprentices. I hold the other, and the third one is now in your hands. And come to Brother Benedetto or to me if you require any information."

"No doubt," said Brother Benedetto, "we'll be of more use to you than the brother librarian."

"But may I ask what you expect from this humble inquisitor who is now at your service?"

"That you find a complete and convincing explanation of this Last Supper. That you identify, if it exists, the book on which he said it was based. That you determine whether that book is or is not a heretical text like the *Apocalipsis Nova*. And if it is, that you detain him."

"In exchange," the Father Prior continued, smiling, "we will help you with your riddle. Even though, in fact, you haven't yet told us what it is."

"I'm looking for the man who wrote these verses."

And I showed them a copy of *Oculos ejus dinumera*.

20

Bernardino Luini hardly dared cast his eyes beyond the easel. Even though he was a man of over thirty, with his adolescence long behind him, this kind of work always upset him. He had never known a woman—in fact, he was perhaps the only one in the guild who never had—and he had sworn to God that he never would. He had also promised it to his father, just after turning fourteen, and before that to his master when, as an apprentice, he entered the most prestigious *bottega* in Milan in order to learn the artist's craft. Now, however, he regretted it. The fact was that Crivelli's daughter had, for the past two weeks, put his weak nature to the test. Naked, with her golden locks falling down either side of her body, sitting on the edge of the bench with her blue eyes fixed on the ceiling, the little sixteen-year-old countess was the living image of desire. Every time she dropped her angelic posture and glanced at him, Bernardino felt as if he were dying.

"Master Luini," Donna Lucrezia's voice sounded softly, as if it too were tempting him, "when do you think the child's portrait will be ready?"

"Very soon, my lady. Very soon."

"Remember that the deadline for our contract is next week," she insisted.

"I know that well, my lady. Of no other date am I so fully aware."

The young Venus's mother often attended the modeling sessions. It was not that she distrusted Bernardino Luini, a man of irreproachable reputation who was rarely seen working outside a monastery, but she had heard so many stories about the voracity of the clergy and even of that of the Pope himself, that she did not think it superfluous to oversee these encounters. Luini was a very handsome man, though perhaps somewhat effeminate, and yet he was the only gentleman whom her husband allowed unescorted into their house without fearing for her honor. Because the count certainly had reasons to be concerned: rumors of a relationship between his very beautiful wife and the Duke of Milan were on everybody's lips. Lucrezia was a much-desired woman, a free woman for whom every novelty was a source of excitement. And Elena, their daughter, already appeared to be her mother's worthy successor.

"Isn't she beautiful?" the countess observed proudly. "Those apples she has for breasts, so firm, so hard . . . You can't imagine, Master Luini, how many men have been driven wild at the sight of them."

Wild? The painter barely managed to keep his brush from trembling violently. His canvas already depicted almost all of the details of Elena's body, though he had imagined her hair darker and longer, covering her belly and hiding from sight that source of all pleasures which he had long ago renounced.

"What I don't understand is why you've chosen the subject of Mary Magdalene to portray my daughter, and precisely at this moment. It's as if you wished to draw the attention of the Holy Inquisition. And all Magdalenes are sad, miserable women. And I don't know what to think of that horrible skull in her hands . . ."

Luini put down the brush on his palette and turned toward Donna Lucrezia. The afternoon light was falling on her couch, outlining the forms now vaguely familiar: the blond tresses identical to those of Elena, the highly delineated cheekbones, the same moist, fleshy lips. And the same breasts, rising and falling under a tight bodice of Dutch cloth. Seeing her reclining there, he fully understood the extravagant passion of Ludovico for such beauty, and barely paid attention to her comments about the Inquisition.

"My lady," he said. "I must remind you that you yourself gave Master Leonardo permission to choose the subject and send you the disciple of his choice."

"Yes, I know. It's too bad that he himself is still so busy with that blessed *Cenacolo* of his."

"What can I tell you? Master Leonardo asked me to paint a Magdalene, and that is what I'm doing. And, coming from him, the choice should make your family proud."

"Proud? Wasn't Mary Magdalene a whore?" she exclaimed. "Why could he not have ordered a simple portrait of my daughter, like the one your master painted of me? Why insist on disgracing my family with an unpleasant story that has been pursuing us for centuries?"

Bernardino Luini said nothing. The Crivelli family

was from a Venetian clan that had seen better days and that now, thanks to the skills of Leonardo's workshop, hoped to find a good match for their daughter by means of a portrait that would sing her virtues. And with a Magdalene like this one, it would not be difficult to achieve their purpose. In fact, it had been their lean purse and not their spoken wishes that had allowed the Master the freedom of choice. Leonardo had not wasted his chance, and Luini made an effort not to smile as he recalled Leonardo's cunning. Donna Lucrezia had been modeling for years in Leonardo's *bottega* on Corso Magenta, lending life to some of his most notable work. If he had now decided to have Elena painted as Christ's favorite, it was because he soon expected to initiate her in his mysteries.

Lucrezia was the last exponent of a long line of women who were thought to be the heirs of the real Mary Magdalene, a bloodline of soft-featured females who, generation after generation, inspired poets and painters, and who were not always aware of the inheritance they passed on.

Luini applied a few more brushstrokes, trying to avoid Elena's contagious smile. After a while, he broodingly picked up the conversation.

"I think you are somewhat rash in your judgment, my lady. Mary Magdalene, Saint Mary Magdalene," he corrected himself, "was a woman braver than most. She was named the *casta meretrix*, the chaste prostitute, and, unlike the disciples who, with the exception of John, fled Jerusalem when Our Lord was crucified, she accompanied Him to the very top of Golgotha. Therein lies, my lady, the reason for the skull in your daughter's hands. Also, it was to Mary Magdalene that Christ first appeared after His resurrection, thereby showing the deep love He felt for her."

"And why do you think He did it?"

Luini smiled with satisfaction.

"To reward her for her courage, of course. Many of us believe that it was then that the Resurrected Christ entrusted her with a great secret. Mary Magdalene had proved to Him that she was worthy of such a distinction and we artists, every time we paint her, try to come a little closer to what was then revealed."

"Now that you say so, I believe I too have heard Master Leonardo speak of that secret, even though he avoided giving a great deal of explanations. Your master is certainly a man full of mystery."

"Many people, my lady, consider intelligence itself to be a mystery. Perhaps one day he'll tell us all. Or perhaps he'll choose your daughter as his confidante—"

"Anything is possible with that man. I have known him since he arrived in Milan in 1482, and his intrigues have never ceased to surprise me. He is so unpredictable—"

Lucrezia stopped in midsentence, as if recalling old memories. Then she asked with great curiosity:

"You yourself, by chance, would not know the secret of Mary Magdalene?"

Luini looked back at his painting.

"Consider this, my lady: the true teachings of Christ to mankind could only reach us after Our Lord overcame the ordeal of His Passion and underwent His Resurrection with the help of God the Father. Only then did He become fully certain of the existence of the Kingdom of Heaven. And when He returned from the dead, whom did He first encounter? Mary Magdalene, the only one who had the strength to await His return, disobeying the orders of both the Sanhedrin and the Roman officials."

"We women have always been braver than you men, Master Luini."

"Or more imprudent."

Elena remained silent, listening with amusement to the conversation, enjoying the warmth of the fire emanating from the chimney place behind her.

"I admire the tenacity of women as much as you do, my lady," Luini said, picking up his brush once more. "That is why you should know that, from that revelation on, Mary Magdalene displayed virtues even more remarkable."

"Did she?"

"If one day they are disclosed to you, you'll see how faithfully they are reflected in your Elena's face. Then you'll be more than satisfied with this portrait."

"Master Leonardo never spoke to me of these virtues."

"Master Leonardo is very cautious, my lady. The virtues of Mary Magdalene are a delicate matter. They even frightened the disciples at the time of Our Lord. Not even the evangelists wished to tell us much about them!"

The countess's eyes flashed maliciously.

"Of course! Because she was a whore!"

"Mary never wrote a single line. Women in her time

didn't," Master Luini continued, ignoring the countess's taunts. "Therefore, whoever wants to know more about her must follow in John's footsteps. As I've told you, John the Beloved was the only one who behaved properly when Christ was crucified. Whoever admires Mary Magdalene must also admire John and hold his Gospel to be the most beautiful of the four."

"Forgive me for insisting, but in what measure was Mary Magdalene special in the eyes of Christ, Master Luini?"

"In that He kissed her on the lips in front of His disciples."

Donna Lucrezia gave a start.

"What are you saying?"

"Ask Leonardo. He knows the books in which these secrets are revealed. Only he knows the true features of John, of Peter, of Matthew . . . even of Mary Magdalene. Have you not yet seen his wonderful work at Santa Maria?"

"Yes, of course I've seen it," she answered angrily, recalling once again that because of the *Cenacolo* it was not Leonardo who was here, in her house. "I was there a few months ago. The duke wanted to show me the progress in the work of his favorite painter, and I was dazzled by the magnificent mural. I remember that several of the faces of the apostles were not yet finished, but no one at the monastery was able to tell us when they'd be ready."

"No one knows, that's true," Luini agreed. "Master Leonardo can't find the models he wants for some of the apostles. If even with the many sinister faces at the court it's difficult to portray the evil of Judas, imagine how complicated it is to find a pure and charismatic face like John's. You can't begin to guess how many faces the Master has had to examine, trying to find the right one for the Beloved Disciple! Leonardo suffers greatly every time he comes across an obstacle like this and is inevitably delayed."

"Take my daughter to him!" the countess laughed. "Let him sit Mary Magdalene at the table in John's place!"

Laughing, Countess Crivelli lifted herself from her couch in a cloud of scent. Majestically she approached the painter and laid a delicate hand on his shoulder.

"Enough talk for today, Master Luini. Finish the portrait as soon as possible and you'll receive the rest of your payment. You have at least two more hours of light before sunset. Use them well."

"Yes, my lady."

The heels of Donna Lucrezia's shoes resounded on the tiles and then vanished. Elena remained still, without blinking. Magnificent, her clean pink skin recently shaven by her handmaidens, she lay there for a moment and then, when she was sure that her mother had left the rooms, she jumped onto the couch.

"Yes, yes, Master Luini!" She clapped her hands, dropping the skull, which rolled down to the fireplace. "Do it! Introduce me to Leonardo! Let me meet him!"

Luini observed her from behind the canvas.

"Do you really want to meet him?" he whispered, applying a few more strokes of paint, unable to feign indifference.

"Of course I want to! You yourself said that maybe he'd reveal to me his secret—"

"I warn you, Elena: you may not at all like what you find out. He's a man of powerful character. He seems absorbed in other things, but in fact he can see everything with a keen jeweler's eye. He can tell how many petals are on a flower at which he has only glanced, and he studies everything in minutest detail, to the great despair of his assistants."

The little countess would not be dissuaded.

"I like that, Master Luini. A man who cares about details!"

"Yes, yes, Elena. But, to tell you the truth, he's not overly fond of women—"

"Oh!" A disappointed tone colored her voice. "That seems to be common among artists, isn't that right, Master Luini?"

The painter hunched even further behind the canvas as his model stood up and displayed her beauty in full. A stifling warmth flushed his face and dried his throat.

"Why . . . why do you say that, Elena?"

She climbed back onto the couch and peered at him behind his easel.

"Because you've been painting me naked for ten days now, you and I locked up in this room, and you have made no attempt to come closer. My ladies-in-waiting tell me that it isn't normal, and the wicked vixens are asking themselves whether you may not be a *castratus*."

Luini found no words to answer. He lifted his eyes to meet hers and found himself at barely a breath's distance from her face, inhaling the scent of jasmine, his whole skin prickling. He was never able to explain what happened afterward: the room began to spin around him, and an irresistible strange force gripped him from inside and overcame him completely. He threw the brush and paints aside and drew the little countess to him. The touch of her young body aroused him powerfully.

"Are you . . ." He hesitated.

She laughed.

"Not any longer."

She bent over him and kissed him.

21

Just as the Father Prior had foreseen, *The Last Supper* soon became my obsession. That Saturday afternoon alone, key in hand, I visited it four times before sunset, after having ascertained that the place was empty. I believe, in fact, that it was on that day that the community began to call me Father Trottola, which means "spinning-top." They had their reasons. Every time a monk crossed my path, he would find me as if dazed, wandering close to the refectory, a single repeated question on my lips: "Has anyone seen Master Leonardo?"

I suppose I arrived at the monastery at the very worst moment to see him. The preparation for the funeral had altered the daily habits of the city, especially those of Santa Maria delle Grazie. While Father Alessandro and I were hard at work trying to solve the Soothsayer's riddle, the rest of the brethren were spending their time getting ready for the following day. The duchess had been dead for twelve days now and her body lay embalmed in an acacia coffin in the castle's family chapel. Ambassadors from the kingdoms invited to the funeral strolled impatiently through the monastery and the duke's fortress in search of information about the ceremony.

The truth be told, I remained ignorant of all this

coming and going until Sunday morning, January the fifteenth, which was the feast of Saint Mauro. Donna
Beatrice was to be buried in the recently finished Sforza
pantheon, beneath Santa Maria's main altar, and it was
probable that the Soothsayer, who had so many times
warned us against her, might decide to be present. I
thanked Heaven for the morning bells that woke me. I
had slept badly. I had dreamed of the twelve men of the
Cenacolo chattering and moving around the Messiah. I
could almost guess their dark intentions, but I felt that
time was against me to unveil their secrets.

After early morning prayers, I headed toward the
refectory. No doubt, this would be the only moment I
would have to enjoy its comfortable solitude. I would
lose myself again in Leonardo's brightly colored brushstrokes and allow myself to imagine that his mysterious
task was not to paint a wall but to rescue from it, bit by
bit, with a surgeon's precision, a magical scene carved in
the plaster by the angels themselves.

I was immersed in these thoughts when, upon turning
west in the Cloister of the Dead, I saw that the door protecting the refectory had been left wide open. Two men
whom I had never seen before were talking at the
threshold.

"Have you heard about the librarian?" I heard the one
closest to me ask. He was dressed in red breeches, a
striped yellow-and-white doublet, and had the face of a
cherub with golden curls. At the mention of Father
Alessandro, I pulled my hood over my head and, pretend-
ing to be occupied with something else, listened from a
safe distance.

"The Master mentioned something," the other man answered. He was a slim, dark youth, handsome and of an athletic build. "They say he's very worried, and everyone fears he'll do something rash."

"It doesn't surprise me. He's been fasting too long. I think he's losing his mind."

"From fasting?"

"The lack of food must be giving him hallucinations. He's obsessed about being discovered and taken away from his books. You should have seen him trembling with fear last night. He looked like a reed in the wind."

The athletic youth cast a glance in my direction, forcing me to move on if I did not want to be discovered. I managed to hear a few last words.

"I doubt they'd dare take him away from his books. He's carried out his obligations too well to deserve such a punishment."

"Then you agree with me?"

"Of course. The fast will end up killing him."

The conversation I had heard made me wary. That something as intimate, as private as Father Alessandro's fast should be bandied about by a pair of lay youngsters from outside the community was far from normal. I later learned that the man in red breeches was Andrea Salaino, Leonardo's favorite disciple and protégé, and that the darker one was a nobleman who was hoping to become a painter and whose name was Marco d'Oggiono. As the Father Prior had warned me, they often made use of the refectory. They would open it in order to prepare the paint mixtures for their master or to lay out his tools. But what were they doing there on a Sunday, just before Donna Beatrice's funeral and ceremonially dressed? How was it that they spoke of Father Alessandro in such terms and so knowledgeably of his customs? And why did they seem so worried? Intrigued, I passed by them, as if headed toward the library stairs, trying not to attract their attention.

My mind kept pouring out questions: Where had the librarian been on the previous night? Had he truly met with Master Leonardo? And what for? Had he not openly criticized the Master in our conversations? How did it happen that they were now such friends?

A shiver ran down my spine. The last time I had spoken with Father Alessandro was the day before, at vespers. He had shown me the manuscripts that Leonardo had consulted in the monastery library, while I attempted to find which one of them might be the closed book of Donna Beatrice's card. The truth is that I had not perceived any change in his mood. I had, however, felt a certain pity for him. This monk who had welcomed me to Santa Maria, who had assisted me from the very first day I set foot in the monastery, was one of the few unaware of what was being plotted under his roof.

Out of guilt, that very afternoon I ended up telling him all I knew about Leonardo and his challenge to decipher the *Cenacolo*. I owed it to him.

"What I'm about to tell you," I warned him, "must never pass your lips."

The librarian looked at me, puzzled.

"Well, do you swear?"

"In Christ's name."

I nodded, satisfied.

"Good. The Father Prior believes that Leonardo has hidden a secret message in the refectory mural."

"In *The Last Supper?*"

"Exactly. The Father Prior suspects it's something that may hurt the doctrine of Holy Mother the Church. Something that Master Leonardo may have taken from one of the books you found for him."

"Which one?" he asked impatiently.

"I thought you might know."

"I? The Master asked for many titles in our library."

"Which ones?"

"There were so many . . ." He sounded doubtful. "I don't know. Maybe he was especially interested in *De Secretis Artis et Naturae Operibus.*"

"*De Secretis Artis?*"

"It's a rare Franciscan manuscript. If I'm not mistaken, I think Leonardo heard Amadeo of Portugal refer to it. You know him?"

"He's the author of *Apocalipsis Nova.*"

"The same. In this book, an English monk called Roger Bacon, a celebrated writer and a heretic imprisoned by the Holy Office, explained the twelve ways in which one can hide a message in a work of art."

"Is it a religious text?"

"No, rather a technical one."

"And what other book might have served him as inspiration?" I insisted.

Father Alessandro stroked his chin as he reflected. He seemed neither nervous nor uneasy with my questioning. He was as helpful as ever, as if my confidences about Leonardo had not affected him in the least.

"Let me think," he said. "Perhaps he made use of the lives of saints compiled by Jacobus de Voragine . . . the book known as *The Golden Legend*. Yes, perhaps there you may find what you're looking for."

"In the book by the celebrated Bishop of Genoa?" I asked, astonished.

"That was his title, more than three hundred years ago."

"And what possible connection could there be between *The Golden Legend* and the message hidden in the *Cenacolo*?"

"If such a message exists, perhaps his book might hold the key to it," Father Alessandro said, shutting his eyes as if seeking deeper concentration. "Friar Jacobus de Voragine, a Dominican like us, gathered in the East as much information as he could on the lives of the early saints, as well as on Our Lord's disciples. His discoveries filled Master Leonardo with enthusiasm."

"He gathered information in the East?" I said, somewhat skeptically.

"Don't be surprised, Father Agostino. The facts in his book are not precisely canonical. The Church would never accept his argument of the close blood ties between the Twelve Apostles. Did you know, for example, that Simon and Andrew were brothers? Perhaps that is why Leonardo painted them as twins on the refectory wall."

"Truly?"

"And do you know that Jacobus states that, during his life, many people mistook James the Less for Jesus? And have you noticed the great resemblance between them in the *Cenacolo*?"

"Then Leonardo must have read his book," I said, though still uncertain.

"More than that. He must have studied it in depth. And from what you suggest, it seems as if he's studied it with more interest than Bacon's book. Believe me."

And with that, Father Alessandro broke up our last conversation. It was for this reason that, hearing the apprentices say that the librarian had met with Leonardo that same night, I felt suddenly afraid. Their indiscretion confirmed not only that Father Alessandro had hidden from me something as important as his friendship with Leonardo but also that the man I believed to be my only friend in Santa Maria had in all probability betrayed me.

But why?

22

I looked everywhere for the librarian. On his desk lay the two volumes of Bishop Jacobus de Voragine, which Father Alessandro had shown me on the previous afternoon. In large embossed letters, they displayed the name of the author and the Italian title of the book: *Legendi di Sancti Vulgari Storiado*. Of the other book, of Father Bacon's treatise on the secret arts, there was no trace. If Father Alessandro had it in his collection, he must have kept it somewhere safely inaccessible.

Was I imagining things, or had the librarian tried to steer my attention away from that book? And if so, why?

The questions kept piling up. I needed Father Alessandro to explain certain things. But even though I asked for him in the church, the kitchens and the dormitory, no one could tell me where to find him. Nor could I insist too much. In the growing tide of visitors to Santa Maria to see the funeral procession from close quarters, it was easy to lose sight of an elderly librarian. I knew that sooner or later I would run into him and he would then inform me what in Heaven's name was going on.

At about ten in the morning, the square in front of the church and the entire length of the road from

Santa Maria to the castle were full of a silent crowd. All the people were wearing their finest garments and they carried candles and dry palm leaves to wave as the duchess's coffin went by. There was hardly room to breathe. In the church, however, only the ambassadors and selected visitors were allowed, by express orders of the duke himself. Beneath the gallery, a platform had been erected, covered in velvet and crossed with tasseled ropes of gold, from which Ludovico il Moro and his closest men would say their prayers. The whole area was under the protection of the duke's private guards and only we, the monks of Santa Maria, enjoyed a certain freedom of movement to enter and leave the church.

I headed toward the nave of the church, not so much with the hope of coming across Father Alessandro as with the notion of meeting Leonardo for the first time. If his helpers had opened the refectory that morning, it was likely that their master would not be too far away.

My instinct failed me.

At the stroke of eleven, a sudden turmoil broke the peace of Santa Maria. The main door, beneath the largest round window, opened with a great noise. The trumpets outside sounded to announce the arrival of Ludovico il Moro and his retinue. The announcement drew the silent attention of the faithful who had been allowed in. It was then that a dozen men with somber faces and vacant looks, their garments covered in long cloaks trimmed with black fur, entered the church with a martial step in the direction of the tribune. And that is when I saw him. Even though he was the last in the procession, Leonardo stood out like Goliath among the Philistines. But it was not only his stature that attracted my notice. Instead of the embroidered silk and precious stones that adorned the other men's garments, Leonardo was dressed from head to foot in white. His blond beard, carefully trimmed, fell straight down over his breast, and he walked turning from side to side, as if looking for familiar faces in the audience. He gave the impression of being a ghost from the past, in stark contrast with the duke himself, who, several steps ahead of the procession, wore his black hair cut round in the modern style, as a frame for his dark features. All eyes were on Leonardo. Even the pages and standard-bearers from the several various households attending the funeral noticed his presence before that of the duke. Leonardo, however, seemed aloof from it all.

"Welcome to the House of the Lord," the Father Prior exclaimed when they reached the altar. He was surrounded by the brethren, who were dressed as befitted the occasion, and accompanied by the Archbishop of Milan, the head of the Franciscan Order and a dozen court clerics.

Ludovico il Moro and his retinue crossed themselves and occupied the places reserved for them. At the same time, a group of musicians displaying the Sforza coat of arms entered the church announcing the arrival of the coffin.

Master Leonardo, standing in the third row of the platform, kept a keen eye on everything and, from time

to time, scribbled mysterious jottings in one of the notebooks he always carried with him. It seemed to me that
he paid the same attention to the faces in the crowd as
he did to the sound of Santa Maria's organ, or to flutter-
ing banners of the different groups in attendance. Someone had told me that the previous afternoon he had
fallen into ecstatic contemplation over the flight of four
hundred pigeons released in the Piazza del Duomo, and
that he had listened with rapt delight to the cannon
blasts from the city walls that the papal nuncio had
ordered in honor of the late duchess. For Leonardo,
everything merited attention, everything held within
itself traces of the secret science of life.

Of course, I was not the only one to watch his movements during the ceremony. All around me, Leonardo
was the main subject of conversation. The more I
observed his blue eyes and his majestic demeanor the
more I felt the need to know him. The Soothsayer first,
and then the Father Prior had provoked in me what was
now a burning thirst.

The guests at the ceremony did nothing to extinguish
it. They whispered like lovebirds, commenting on the
Tuscan's latest eccentricity: the completion of a treatise
on painting in which he maligned most other artists in
order to sing his own praises. His privileged mind was
employed in myriad endeavors, from easing the duke's
sorrow with ingenious entertainments to designing
impossible drawbridges, assault towers that would move
without the aid of horses, and cranes to help unload
woolsacks from the ships in the canals.

Leonardo, lost in thought, seemed unaware of the

passions he provoked. Now he was sketching in his notebook the strange costume the duke was wearing: a cape of beautiful black silk, ripped open in various places, as if the widower himself had torn it with his bare hands.

Little did I suspect how close I was to speaking with the Master.

It was Brother Giberto, Santa Maria's sexton, who gave me the chance of first meeting the painter, during an occasion both dramatic and unexpected.

It happened while the Father Prior was pronouncing words of the consecration. The young man from the North, all pink cheeks and carrot-colored hair, walked up to me from behind and pulled roughly at my cloak.

"Father Agostino! Listen!" he cried with an anguished voice, his bloodshot eyes opened wide. "Something terrible has happened in the city! You must know at once!"

"Something terrible?"

Brother Giberto's hands trembled.

"It's God's punishment! God's punishment to those who dare defy Him!"

The sexton was not allowed to finish. Brother Benedetto, the one-eyed monk, and Father Andrea de Inveruno, with his delicate manners, approached us with urgent gestures.

"We must go at once! Quickly!"

"Will you come with us, Father Agostino?" the sexton asked, panting for breath. "I think we'll need as much help as we can get."

Their urgency convinced me. I did not know where I was to accompany them nor why; but when I saw one of the duke's pages approach Leonardo to whisper in his ear and a look of alarm spread over Leonardo's face, I hastily accepted. Something strange had taken place. Something serious. And I wanted to know what it was.

23

The duke's two men could hardly believe their eyes. Dangling in front of them from a portico in the Piazza Mercanti, a thick rope fastened tightly about his neck, was the lifeless body of a monk.

The captain of the guard, Andrea Rho, had not yet had his breakfast. In fact, he had only just finished buttoning up his uniform when the news came to break the peace of his Sunday morning. His white hair disheveled, his belly uncovered, his whole body reeking like a newly awakened bear, Captain Rho approached the scene reluctantly to see what had happened. There was little he could do. The poor soul's skin was cold and bluish, the veins in the face were swollen, the open eyes dry. The terror apparent in their look suggested a cruel and painful death. The man had suffered a long agony before breathing his last. The arms fell limp at both sides of the Dominican habit; the well-cared-for hands, thin and stiff, were barely visible beneath the sleeves. A soft stench of death reached the captain's nostrils.

"Well?" The captain cast a long glance over the sensation-seeking crowd. Many were on their way back home, frustrated because they had not managed to catch a glimpse of the duchess's sumptuous funeral carriage, and the sudden commotion now promised them some sort of compensation. The captain distrusted them all. He looked for a guilty face, a glint of murderous pride.

"What have we here?" he asked.

"A priest, sir. A friar," his companion answered respectfully as he tried to keep the crowd at bay with his arms spread out and his pike stuck in the ground.

"I can see that, Massimo. I was awakened with the news."

"Well, sir." The soldier hesitated. "It seems like the man must have been hanged this very morning. And as no shops or stores are open today, no one seems to have seen anything."

"Have you searched him?"

"Not yet."

"Why not? Then you can't tell if they robbed him before killing him?"

Massimo shook his head warily. It was obvious that he had never before touched a corpse. The captain gave him a scornful look before turning his attention to the crowd.

"No one knows anything, eh?" he shouted at them. "You're a bunch of cowards! Vermin is what you are!"

No one moved. The crowd watched, entranced by the subtle pendular movement of the body, asking themselves in low whispers what had happened. God knew that men of the cloth never carried fat purses and that thieves hardly ever profit from attacking them. And if it wasn't thieves, then who had murdered this monk? And why had he been hanged in this manner, leaving him in full sight in a public place?

Andrea Rho walked a couple of times around the corpse before questioning his subordinate once again.

"All right, Massimo. Let's be clever about this. What would you say happened here? Has he been killed or did he hang himself?"

The young man, shoulders hunched and eyes on the ground, reflected hard for a moment on the question, as if his promotion depended on the answer. He measured his words carefully, and when he was about to reply, he stopped short. A loud and powerful voice rose from among the crowd.

"He's taken his own life!" someone shouted from far back. "He's killed himself! There's no doubt about it, Captain!"

It was a man's voice, gruff and strong, that almost made the market pillars tremble. The crowd was impressed.

"Also," the voice continued, "I know his name! It's Father Alessandro Trivulzio, librarian of Santa Maria! May God take pity on his soul!"

The speaker then stepped forward, making his way through the throng. The captain stood watching him in astonishment. He was an extraordinary individual, tall, robust, impeccably dressed in a cotton gown that reached down to his feet, and a mass of hair untidily bunched under a woolen hat. He was accompanied by a timorous-looking youngster, not more than twelve or thirteen years old, obviously fearful at the proximity of death.

"I see! At last, a brave man! And who are you, may I

ask?" said the captain. "How can you be so sure of what you're saying?"

The giant looked the captain in the eye before answering.

"That's easy, Captain. If you pay attention to the body, you'll notice that there're no signs of violence on it except the bruising on the neck. Had he fought against his murderer or had he been attacked, his habit would be dirty, or even torn and bloody. And it isn't so. This monk accepted death willingly. And if you look even closer, you'll see the barrel that served him as scaffold in order to reach the beam and tie the rope."

"You are very knowledgeable about death, sir," the captain said ironically.

"I've seen more than you can imagine, and from close at hand. Studying the dead is one of my interests. I have even opened them up to explore their entrails scientifically." The giant stressed these words, as if anticipating the horrified murmur that ran through the crowd. "Had you seen as many hanged men as I have, Captain, you'd have noticed something else."

"And what is that?"

"The fact that this body has been hanging here for several hours."

"Is that so?"

"No doubt about it. All you need to do is observe the cloud of flies buzzing around it. This particular kind, small and restless, wait two or three hours before descending on a corpse. Can you see how they flutter around it in search of nourishment? Isn't that extraordinary?"

"You have still not told me who you are."

"My name is Leonardo, my captain. And I'm a servant of the duke just as you are."

"I've never seen you before."

"The duke's domains are vast," Leonardo answered, stifling a laugh, improper under the circumstances. "I'm an artist and I work on several of his projects, one of them in Santa Maria delle Grazie. That is how I knew this poor soul. He was a good friend."

As he crossed himself, the captain cast a curious eye on the stranger and felt satisfied that he was indeed someone of note in the city. Along with everyone else in Milan, he had heard of a certain wise man called Leonardo and of his extraordinary powers. He tried to remember what he had heard: that not only was he capable of trapping the human soul on canvas or creating the largest equestrian statue ever seen—in honor of the late Francesco Sforza, Ludovico il Moro's father—but that he also had medical skills that verged on the miraculous. This man fitted the picture rather well.

"Tell me then, Master Leonardo. According to you, why would a monk from Santa Maria delle Grazie decide to hang himself here, in this place?"

"That I don't know, my captain," Leonardo answered in a gentler tone. "Even though I can easily interpret the external signs, the will of men is often more difficult to fathom. And yet, perhaps the answer is a simple one. Just as I often come to this marketplace to buy canvas and paints, he may have come here to buy something he needed. Afterward, a dark thought may have crossed his mind, and he decided that this was the right moment to die. Don't you think?"

"On a Sunday?" The captain sounded skeptical. "And with the duchess's funeral being celebrated in his own monastery? No. I don't think so."

Leonardo shrugged.

"Only God knows what may cross the mind of one of His servants—"

"Just so."

"Perhaps if you brought down the corpse and searched it carefully, you might find a clue as to what it was that brought him to this marketplace. And if you think it may be useful, I put at your disposal my medical knowledge and my full collaboration, in order to discover the time and cause of his death. All you have to do is send the body to my study at—"

The Master never finished his sentence. At that very moment Brothers Andrea, Giberto and Benedetto, and I, reached the group of onlookers. The one-eyed monk was at the lead, silent, a look on his face like that of a beast about to pounce. When he saw Leonardo's white gown close to Father Alessandro's body, he grew pale.

"Don't you dare desecrate the body of a servant of Saint Dominic, Master Leonardo!" he shouted out, advancing toward him.

Leonardo turned his head to us and immediately greeted us with a bow and his condolences.

"I'm sorry, Brother Benedetto. I feel this death as much as you."

The one-eyed monk cast a glance at Father Alessandro's body and seemed to tremble at the sight. But he was not as distraught as I was. I held the librarian's cold, stiff hands, unable to believe that he was really dead. And what was I to think of Leonardo? What was our master painter doing there, showing such sorrow for Father Alessandro? Did this not confirm my fears that both men had maintained a close relationship? I crossed myself and swore that I would solve this matter.

"May God welcome him into His Eternal Kingdom," Leonardo said.

"What is it to you?" shouted Brother Benedetto with sudden fury. "After all, he was nothing in your eyes but a useful fool! Admit it now, while his body is still present!"

"You always underestimated him, Brother Benedetto."

"Not as much as you did, Master Leonardo! And what is more, I'm surprised that you should be ready to pronounce upon his death so quickly. It's hardly worthy of your scholarly fame. Our librarian was fond of life. Why would he think of parting with it?"

I waited for Leonardo to answer, but he did not open his mouth. Perhaps he guessed what Brother Benedetto's game was. The monks at Santa Maria would try to convince the police that Father Alessandro had fallen into an ambush. To accept the theory of suicide would have meant dishonor for the dead priest and would make it impossible for him to be buried in hallowed ground.

Carefully, we brought the body down from its improvised gallows. The librarian's face was frozen in a curious grimace that made him look as if he were almost mischievously smiling, in harsh contrast with his terrified, wide-open eyes. Leonardo, with a compassionate gesture that no one expected, approached the dead man, lowered his eyelids and whispered something in his ear.

"Do you also speak with the dead, Master Leonardo?"

Captain Rho, standing close to the painter, laughed at the thought.

"Yes, I do, my captain. I've told you we were good friends."

So saying, he reached for the hand of his young blond companion and walked off in the direction of the Vicolo del Gallo.

24

Even now, I can't explain my reaction.

Seeing Master Leonardo walk away among the crowd, I remembered Father Alessandro's advice: "The person you least imagine may give you your solution." And if the riddle of the Soothsayer's identity were in the hands of his worst enemy? What could I lose by consulting him? Would my sleuthing be affected by exchanging a few words with the blue-eyed giant dressed in white?

I decided to give it a try.

I left Brothers Andrea, Giberto and Benedetto, who were rolling up their sleeves and carrying away the mortal remains of Father Alessandro. After making my poor excuses I hastened toward the alley where I had observed Leonardo disappear. But when I turned into it, I could no longer see him and proceeded to run up the steep cobbled street.

"You take great pains to overtake a poor artist." It was the Master's deep voice, coming from somewhere behind me. He had stopped to scrutinize a vegetable stand and I had passed by him without noticing his presence.

Leonardo and the youth both grinned at me, their pale eyes and their smiles identical.

"Let me see if I can clarify," Leonardo continued, as

he examined some garlic. "The Father Prior's lackey—
the one-eyed Benedetto—sends you to ask me if I know
anything about the librarian's death. Am I mistaken?"

"I'm afraid you are, Master," I answered, approaching
him. "It isn't Brother Benedetto who sends me, but my
own curiosity."

"Your curiosity?"

I felt my stomach muscles tighten. From close by,
Leonardo was far more handsome than he had seemed up
on the platform. His forthright features declared him a
man of principle. He had thick, strong hands, capable,
no doubt, of ripping out a tooth if necessary or of lending
life to a wall with his magical designs. When he looked
at me, I had the impression that it would be impossible
to lie to him.

"Allow me to introduce myself," I said, somewhat out
of breath. "The truth is, I don't belong to the community
of Santa Maria. I'm only a guest there. My name is
Agostino Leyre. Father Agostino Leyre."

"And why are you here?"

"I'm in Milan for only a short time. But I didn't want
to let the occasion pass without telling you how much I
admire your work in the refectory. I would have liked to
see you under more auspicious circumstances, but God
provides as He will."

"The refectory, indeed." Leonardo cast his eyes down.
"Too bad that not all the brothers share your point of
view."

"Father Alessandro admired you."

"I know, Father, I know. The father librarian helped
me during several difficult phases of my work."

"Was that what Brother Benedetto meant when he said that he'd been your useful fool?"

Leonardo observed me closely, as if deciding what language to use with the man standing before him. Perhaps he had not yet identified me as the inquisitor of whom no doubt his apprentices had already spoken. Or if he did, he tried not to let me know.

"Maybe you're unaware, Father, but the librarian helped me greatly in achieving one of the most important characters of my *Cenacolo*. And he was generous and unselfish enough to model for me without accepting anything in exchange, except the hardships he had to endure as a result of his gesture."

"Hardships?" I asked. "What hardships?"

Leonardo raised his eyebrows at my astonishment. I suppose he could not understand my overlooking a detail of such importance. And in a remarkably calm voice he deigned to enlighten me.

"An artist's work is harder than what people imagine," he said in all seriousness. "For months, we roam about searching for a certain gesture, a profile, a face that will fit our idea of a subject and serve as our model. I needed a Judas. A man with evil stamped on his face, but not any evil. I needed an ugliness both intelligent and awake, that would reflect the internal struggle of Judas to fulfill the mission God Himself entrusted to him. Because you'll agree that without Judas's treason, Christ would have never achieved his destiny."

"And did you find him?"

Leonardo drew back in surprise. "Don't you understand? Father Alessandro was my model for Judas! His face had all the features I was after. He was an intelligent but tormented man, and his hard, sharp traits were almost offensive to look at."

"And he allowed himself to be portrayed as Judas?" I asked, astonished.

"Very willingly, Father Agostino. And he was not the only one. Other monks in this community sat for my composition. But I chose only those with the purest features."

"But Judas—" I protested.

"I understand your astonishment, Father. And yet, you should know that our librarian knew exactly what he was risking. He was aware that no one in his community would ever look at him in the same way again after he'd lent himself to something like this."

"Understandably so."

Leonardo paused as if debating whether to continue the conversation. Taking once again the boy's hand in his, he added, as an afterthought:

"What I couldn't foresee, and far less, wish, was that Father Alessandro was to end his days just like Judas himself: hanging from the neck and all alone, far from his brethren and despised by them all. Or had you not noticed that strange coincidence, Father?"

"Not until you mentioned it."

"You'll soon learn, Father Agostino, that in this city nothing happens just by chance. Don't ever forget it. All appearances here are deceiving. And truth lies where you least expect to find it."

I did not have the courage to ask him about his conversation with Father Alessandro on the night of his death, nor whether he had heard of a certain fierce enemy of his that some of us knew as the Soothsayer. Uneasily, I watched him walk away and disappear uphill.

25

Luini wanted very much to run away, but his willpower failed him once again. Even though his conscience was loudly begging him to escape from the clutches of the girl, his flesh was already enjoying the advances of Donna Elena. What do I care about conscience? he thought, and regretted the thought a moment later.

Never before had the master painter found himself in such a fix. One of the most desirable young women in the duchy was leading him down the path of passion without his having had even to open his mouth. Crivelli's daughter was a beauty, a Magdalene with certainly the most angelic face he had ever seen. And yet Luini could not avoid feeling as Adam had felt, dragged to his perdition by the hand of a lustful Eve. He had the impression of digging his teeth into a poisonous apple whose juices made him lose his zealously guarded innocence. For, strange as it may seem, Master Bernardino Luini counted himself among the few who still believed that the Tree of Knowledge of Good and Evil had been hidden by God between a woman's thighs, and that eating from its fruit, even once, meant eternal damnation.

"*Miserere, Domine . . .* ," he prayed in despair.

If Donna Elena had given him then a moment's

respite, the painter would have burst into tears. But no: blushing red as a cardinal's hat, he gave in to all the young countess's whims and listened in horror as she, straddling him with a laugh, asked him to tell her all about Mary Magdalene's virtues.

"Tell me everything!" she said mockingly. "Explain your interest in her! Let me into Leonardo's secret!"

Luini, short of breath, his breeches at his feet, sitting on the same couch occupied moments earlier by Countess Lucrezia, was trying hard not to stammer.

"Elena, please, I can't."

"Promise you'll tell!"

Luini kept silent.

"Promise!"

Finally, the master sinner gave in.

When it was all over and he had caught his breath, the painter stood up slowly and got dressed. He felt full of confusion and embarrassment. Master Leonardo had warned him of the dangers of the daughters of Eve, telling him that to give in to them was to betray the highest obligation of every artist, the sacred precept of solitary creation. "Only if you keep yourself away from wife or mistress will you be able to dedicate body and soul to the supreme art of creation," he had written. "If, on the contrary, you go with a woman, you'll divide your gifts in two, and in three if you have a child, and if you bring two or three children into this world, you'll lose your gifts entirely." Leonardo's threats surfaced now in his mind and made him feel weak and unworthy. He had sinned. In barely a few minutes, his reputation as a man of perfection had been wrecked. He had become a hideous parody of his old self. The evil done was irreversible.

Donna Elena, still sprawled on the couch, looked at her painter without understanding why he had suddenly grown cold.

"Are you all right?" she asked softly.

Once again, Luini kept silent.

"Have I not pleased you?"

Luini, holding back a grimace with moist eyes, tried to repress the feeling of remorse. What could he say to this creature? How could she understand the sense of failure, of helplessness in the face of temptation, that he now felt? And worse: Had he not promised her, with the Lord as his witness, that he would reveal to her the secret she so much wished to know? And how would he fulfill his promise? Did he not wish to know it too, just as much as Elena did? Turning his back to her, he cursed the weakness of his flesh. What was he to do? Was he to sin twice in the same afternoon, breaking his vow of chastity first, and then his word?

"You're sad, my love," Elena whispered, caressing his shoulders.

The painter closed his eyes, still without saying a word.

"But me, you've filled me with happiness. Do you feel guilty for having given me what I was crying out for? Are you sorry that you've carried out a lady's wishes?"

Guessing the reasons for his melancholy, she tried to set his mind at ease.

"Don't blame yourself for anything, Master Luini. There are those, like Friar Filippo Lippi, who take advantage of their work in convents to seduce the young novices. And Friar Lippi was a man of the cloth!"

"What are you saying?"

"Oh!" she said, laughing to see him so startled. "You should know all about him, Master Luini. Friar Lippi died not more than thirty years ago. I'm sure your Leonardo must have known him in Florence. He was a very famous painter."

"Are you accusing Friar Lippi—?"

"Of course," she said, pulling him toward her. "In the convent of Santa Lucia, when he was supposed to be finishing several paintings, he seduced a certain Lucrezia Buti and left her with child. Didn't you know? Well, then. Many believe that the Buti family, feeling themselves dishonored, sent him to his grave with a good dose of arsenic. Don't you see? You, you're not guilty of anything! You've not forced me to break a holy vow! You've simply given love to one who was asking you for it!"

Master Luini felt uncertain. But even in his doubts, he could see that the beautiful Elena was trying to help him. Moved in spite of himself, he made an effort to utter a few intelligible words:

"Elena . . . If you still wish it, if you still desire to know the secret that so intrigues you, the inspiration for this portrait of yours, I'll tell you what I know about the mystery of Mary Magdalene."

The little countess watched him curiously. Luini was making a great effort to pronounce each of the words.

"You're a man of honor," she said. "I know you'll keep your promise."

"Yes. But you must promise me now that never again

will you touch me. And that you'll never breathe a word of what I'm about to tell you."

"Will that secret let me know the reason for your melancholy, Master Luini?"

The painter looked the little countess in the eyes but found it hard to sustain her gaze. Elena's concern for his well-being disarmed him. He recalled what he had heard Leonardo say about the race of Mary Magdalene: that their eyes were capable of melting any man's heart, thanks to the powerful charm of their love. The troubadours had not lied. How could such a creature be denied the knowledge of her own origins? Would he be such an insensitive monster as not to show her the path?

Forcing himself to smile, Bernardino Luini agreed at last to fulfill her heart's desire.

26

"Listen then," Luini said.

"I had just turned thirteen when Master Leonardo accepted me as an apprentice in his *bottega* in Florence. My father, a soldier of fortune who, thanks to the Visconti of Milan, had managed to set aside a fair amount of money, thought it convenient that I should be instructed in the art of painting before giving myself over to the monastic life or, at the very least, to a secular existence ruled by the laws of God. His purpose was clearer than mine at the time: he wished to keep me away from the horrors of war and grant me protection under the thick mantle of the Church. And as, in his opinion, there was no artist's workshop in Milan that was good enough for me, he assigned me an annual allowance and sent me to Florence, which was then still governed by Lorenzo de' Medici.

"That is where it all started.

"Master Leonardo da Vinci set me up in a large dilapidated house. The outside was all black and looked fearful. The inside, on the contrary, was well lit and had almost no walls to divide it. Its rooms had been pulled down in order to create a vast space full of the strangest devices imaginable. On the ground floor, close to the entrance, were nurseries for plants, seeded flowerpots and cages full of larks, pheasants and even falcons. Next to them were molds in the shapes of heads, horses' feet and tritons' bodies, to be cast in molten bronze. There were mirrors everywhere, and candles. To reach the kitchen, you had to make your way along a corridor lined with wooden skeletons and strange wheels, enough to terrify anyone. Just to think of what the Master might be hiding in the attic filled me with panic.

"Other apprentices of Leonardo lived also in the house. They were all older than I was, so that, after the taunts of the first days, I found myself in a more or less comfortable position and was able to begin to adapt myself to my new life. I believe that Leonardo took a fancy to me. He taught me to read and to write in Latin and Greek, and explained to me that without this schooling it would be useless to teach me another form of writing known as 'the science of images.'

"Can you imagine, Elena? My duties were doubled or tripled. They included such peculiar things as learning botany or astrology. In those years, the Master's motto was '*Lege, lege, relege, ora, labora et invenies,*' that is to say, 'Read, read, reread, pray, work and thou shalt find.' His favorite texts—and consequently mine as well—were the lives of saints by Jacobus de Voragine, the book known as *The Golden Legend.*

"Tommasso, Renzo and the other apprentices hated those readings, but for me they were a marvelous discovery. In those pages, I learned incredible things: dozens of curious anecdotes, miracles and adventures of the saints and the apostles, which I would never have otherwise imagined. For example, I read there that James the Less was known as 'the Lord's brother' because he resembled Him as one drop of water resembles another. When Judas agreed with the Sanhedrin to identify Our Lord by kissing him, it was because they were afraid He'd be confused with James.

"Of course, there's not a word about this in the Gospels.

"I also enjoyed the adventures of the Apostle Bartholomew. This disciple who was built like a gladiator had the other eleven in awe because of his ability to tell the future. Alas, such foresight did not help him much: he was unable to see that he'd be skinned alive in India.

"These revelations took root in me, granting me a unique talent to imagine the faces and characters of the men and women who've played such important roles in the history of our faith. This was what Leonardo was after: to stimulate our imagination of the sacred stories and to provide us with the special gift of transferring them onto our canvases. He gave me then a list of apostolic virtues drawn from Jacobus de Voragine, which I still have. Look here: he called Bartholomew *Mirabilis*, 'He Who Is Miraculous,' because of his talent for telling the future. Jesus' twin brother, James, he called *Venustus*, 'He Who Is Full of Grace.' "

Elena, amused by the respectful veneration with which Luini unfolded the piece of paper he had taken out of his pocket, tore it from his hands and, without understanding much of it, proceeded to read:

Bartholomew	*Mirabilis*	He Who Is Miraculous
James the Less	*Venustus*	He Who Is Full of Grace
Andrew	*Temperator*	He Who Prevents
Judas Iscariot	*Nefandus*	The Abominable One
Peter	*Exosus*	He Who Hates
John	*Mysticus*	He Who Knows the Mystery
Thomas	*Litator*	He Who Placates the Gods
James the Elder	*Oboediens*	He Who Obeys
Philip	*Sapiens*	He Who Loves High Matters
Matthew	*Navus*	He Who Is Diligent
Judas Thaddeus	*Occultator*	He Who Conceals
Simon	*Confector*	He Who Fulfills

"And you've kept this all these years?" Elena asked, playing with the brittle piece of paper.

"Yes. I remember it as one of Leonardo's most important lessons."

"Well, now you'll never see it again." She laughed.

Elena lifted the paper over her head, expecting the painter to try and retrieve it. Luini pretended not to notice. He had seen the list so many times, he had studied it with such intense devotion, trying to express the qualities of the Twelve Apostles, that he no longer had any real need for it. He knew it, in every sense, by heart.

"And what about Mary Magdalene?" the little countess asked in a disappointed tone of voice. "Her name is not among these. When will you tell me her secret?"

Master Luini, his eyes fixed on the crackling logs in the fireplace, took up his story.

"As I said, I was profoundly affected by Jacobus de Voragine's book, *The Golden Legend*. Now, so many years later, I realize that the passage that marked me most was the one concerning Mary Magdalene. For some strange reason, Master Leonardo wanted me to study it with particular attention. And I obeyed.

"In those days, the revelations with which the Master completed his lessons on Bishop Jacobus did not horrify me in the least. At thirteen, I made no distinction between orthodoxy and heterodoxy, between what the Church found acceptable and what it found inadmissible. Maybe that's why the first thing that I learned was the meaning of her name. 'Mary Magdalene' means 'Bitter Sea,' 'She Who Sheds Light' and also 'The Enlightened One.' About the first, the bishop wrote that it referred to the sea of tears she wept throughout her life. She loved the Son of God with all her heart, but He had come into the world with a mission that precluded their union, and Mary Magdalene had to learn to love Him in a different way. Leonardo explained to me that the symbol best suited to show her virtues was the knot. Already in Egyptian times, the knot was associated with the magic arts of the goddess Isis and—Leonardo explained—Isis had helped the god Osiris resurrect. The method she employed was based on the art of untying knots, a bitter art, since who isn't made bitter by the prospect of disentangling a well-tied knot? 'Whenever you see a knot clearly depicted in a painting, you'll know that it has been dedicated to Saint Mary Magdalene,' were the Master's words.

"Regarding the two other meanings of the name,

deeper and even more mysterious, they are related to a notion dear to Leonardo and about which he often spoke to us: the notion of light. According to him, light is God's only resting place. God the Father is light, the heavens are light, everything, deep down, is light. That is why he kept repeating that if man succeeded in mastering light, he'd be able to summon forth God and speak to Him whenever he needed to.

"What we then didn't know was that this notion of light as the medium by which we can speak to God had arrived in Europe precisely through Mary Magdalene.

"I'll also tell you this: after Christ's death on Golgotha, Mary Magdalene, Joseph of Arimathea, John His Beloved Disciple and a small number of the Messiah's most faithful followers fled to Alexandria to save themselves from the repression that had fallen upon them. Several remained in Egypt and founded there the first and wisest Christian communities that are known to us, but Mary Magdalene, keeper of the greatest secrets of her Beloved, didn't feel safe in a land so close to the city of Jerusalem. That's why she ended up seeking refuge in France."

"What were those secrets?"

The little countess's question brought Luini back sharply to the present.

"Important secrets, Elena. So important, that since that time only a few select mortals have had access to them."

The young woman opened her eyes wide.

"Do you mean the secrets He revealed to her after rising from the dead?"

Luini nodded.

"The very same ones. But they have not yet been revealed to me."

Master Luini picked up the thread of his tale.

"Mary Magdalene, also known as Mary of Bethany, set foot in the south of France, in a small town that ever since carries the name of Les Saintes-Maries de la Mer, because there were several Marys who sought refuge there. She preached the good word of Jesus and initiated people into the 'secret of light' that several heretics made theirs, such as the Cathars and the Albigensians, and ended up becoming the new patron saint of France, Our Lady of the Light.

"But the time of peaceful revelations soon came to an end. The Church realized that these ideas meant a threat to the hegemony of Rome and put an end to their dissemination. From its point of view such a conclusion was only to be expected. How could the Pope tolerate the existence of Christian communities that had no need of a clergy in order to address themselves to God? How could Christ's representative on Earth consider himself inferior, or even equal, to Mary Magdalene? The Church therefore declared her anathema, and degraded and insulted the woman who had loved Jesus and who, like no other mortal, knew of His human condition.

"And, dear Elena, let me explain something else.

"One day, early in 1479, while Florence was still reeling from the attack on our venerated Lorenzo de' Medici, Master Leonardo received a strange visitor in his *bottega*. He was in his fifties, dressed impeccably in black with blond curly hair and, in spite of his age, bearing a resemblance to the cherubs we had been struggling to paint on our canvases. The stranger, who had arrived without being announced, showed polite manners and wandered through the Master's house as if it were his own. He even took the liberty of commenting on our works one by one. Mine was by chance a portrait of Mary Magdalene holding an alabaster vase in her hands, a detail which, when the stranger saw it, seemed to delight him immensely. 'I see that Master Leonardo teaches you in the proper manner,' he said approvingly. 'Your sketch has great possibilities. Continue.' I confess I felt flattered.

" 'And tell me,' he said, 'do you know the meaning of the vase that your Magdalene is holding?'

"I shook my head.

" 'It's in the fourteenth chapter of Mark, my boy! That woman came 'with an alabaster box of ointment of spikenard very precious, and she broke the box and poured it on Jesus' head,' just like a priestess would do with a true king . . . a mortal king, of flesh and bone.'

"The Master arrived at that very moment. To everyone's surprise, he did not seem at all upset to find a stranger in his *bottega*, but rather, delighted. The two men embraced fondly and began, then and there, to discuss all sorts of high matters, divine and human. That was how I first heard something I'd never imagined about the real Mary Magdalene.

" 'Work seems to be progressing apace, my dear Leonardo,' the man said proudly. 'Even if, since Cosimo's death, I feel that our efforts might soon come to nothing.

The Republic of Florence is to face terrible trials in the near future.'

"The Master took the delicate hands of the visitor in his, large as those of a blacksmith.

" 'To nothing, you say?' he bellowed in his deep voice. 'But your Academy is a temple of knowledge as solid as the pyramids of Egypt! Isn't it true that in the past few years it has become a place of pilgrimage for young men who want to learn more about our brilliant ancestors? You've successfully translated the works of Plotinus, of Dionysius, of Proclus and even those of Hermes Trismegistus himself, and you've given us Latin versions of the secrets of the ancient pharaohs. How could all this work be lost? You're the most remarkable thinker in all of Florence, my friend!'

"The man in black blushed gracefully.

" 'Your words are kind, Leonardo, my friend. However, our struggle to regain the knowledge that humanity lost in its mythical Golden Age is at its lowest ebb. That is why I've come to see you.'

" 'You speak of defeat? You?'

" 'You know that which obsesses me since I translated Plato for old Cosimo, don't you?'

" 'Of course! Your old idea about the immortality of the soul! The whole world will honor your name after such a discovery! I can almost see it, sculpted in golden letters on an arch of triumph: *Marsilio Ficino, the Hero Who Restored Our Dignity*. The Pope himself will shower you with blessings.'

"The stranger laughed.

" 'You always exaggerate, dear Leonardo!'

" 'You think so?'

" 'The merit belongs entirely to Pythagoras, to Socrates and Plato, even to Aristotle, not to me. I've merely translated them into Latin for all to have access to their wisdom.'

" 'Well then, Marsilio, what can possibly worry you?'

" 'The Pope worries me, Master. There are plenty of reasons to believe that the assassination attempt on Lorenzo de' Medici in the Cathedral was carried out under his orders. And I'm certain that his reasons were not only political but also religious.'

"Leonardo arched his thick eyebrows, not daring to interrupt.

" 'It's been months now that we suffer from that damned curfew in the city. Since the attempt against the Medici, the situation has become unbearable. The churches are forbidden to celebrate the sacraments or acts of worship, and the worst is that all this will continue until I throw up my hands—'

" 'You?' Leonardo snorted angrily. 'And how are you concerned with all this?'

" 'The Pope wants the Academy to relinquish possession of a series of texts and ancient documents in which are written things contrary to the doctrine of Rome. The plot against Lorenzo sought, among other things, to lay hands on them by force. In Rome, they're especially keen on snatching from us the apocryphal writings of John, which, as you know, have been in our possession for some time now.'

" 'I understand.'

"Leonardo stroked his beard, as he did whenever he was deep in thought.

" 'What information are you afraid of losing, Marsilio?'

" 'In those writings, which are copies of copies of lines written by the Beloved Disciple, John, is an account of what happened to the Twelve after Jesus' death. According to them, the head of the early Church, the original one, was never Peter but James the Less. James! Can you imagine! The legitimacy of the Pope would dissolve into thin air!'

" 'And you believe that in Rome they know about these papers and want to get hold of them by whatever means . . .'

"The stranger nodded, and then added:

" 'John's texts don't stop there.'

" 'They don't?'

" 'They say that besides the Church of James, another church broke off from among the disciples, this one headed by Mary Magdalene and supported by John himself.'

"Leonardo grimaced while the man in black continued.

" 'According to John, Mary Magdalene had always been very close to Jesus. So much so, that many believed that she was the one to carry on His teachings, and not the pack of cowardly disciples who denied Him in His moment of greatest danger—'

" 'Why do you tell me all this now?'

" 'Because you, Leonardo, have been chosen as the repository of all this knowledge.'

"The stranger took a deep breath and said:

" 'I know how dangerous it is to keep these texts. Their possession might lead one to the flames. However, before destroying them, I ask you to study them carefully, to learn all you can about this Church of Mary Magdalene and John. And that whenever you have the chance, you leave some of the essence of these new Gospels in your work. Then the old biblical saying will come true: "He who hath eyes to see—" '

" 'Shalt see.'

"Leonardo smiled. He didn't hesitate long. That very afternoon, he promised his visitor that he'd take charge of the legacy. I know that they met again and that the man in black handed over to the Master books and papers which he afterward studied with great care. Later, with the new developments, when Savonarola ascended to power and the House of the Medici collapsed, we moved to Milan in the service of the duke and began work on a series of different projects. From painting we passed on to the design and construction of war machinery and flying engines. But that secret, that strange revelation that I witnessed in Leonardo's *bottega*, never vanished from my mind.

"I'll tell you something else that will surprise you.

"Even though the Master never spoke of this with any of his disciples, I believe that he's now fulfilling the promise he made to Marsilio Ficino in Florence. I'm telling you this with an open heart: there's not a single time when I visit his work in the Dominican refectory that I don't recall Leonardo's last words to his visitor on that winter afternoon so long ago . . .

" 'When you see in the very same painting the face of John and your own, dear friend Marsilio, you'll know that there, and nowhere else, have I hidden the secret with which you've entrusted me.'

"And, Elena, I've discovered Marsilio's cherubic face among the faces in *The Last Supper*."

27

We buried the father librarian in the Cloister of the Dead shortly before vespers on Tuesday the seventeenth of January. Since it was feared that his remains might begin to decompose during his wake in the chapel, it was decided that the burial should take place as soon as possible. Two novices wrapped his body in a white shroud to which straps were attached, by means of which he was lowered into a deep grave that soon was covered with earth and snow. It was a brief ceremony, with no great formalities, a hurried farewell scarcely justified by our monastic obligation to eat before sunset. And while the brethren spoke in whispers about the rice and vegetables or the honey cakes left over from Christmas, I was overcome by a strange feeling of despondency. Why had the Father Prior and his acolytes—the bursar, the cook, the one-eyed Benedetto and the monk responsible for the scriptorium—presided over the second funeral at Santa Maria in less than a week, with such equanimity? Why did they seem to care so little for Father Alessandro? Would no one spill a tear for his sake?

Only the Father Prior showed, in the end, a glimmer of human compassion for the poor soul who lay now below ground. In his brief sermon, he had already alluded to the fact that he possessed proof that the librarian had been the victim of a madman recently arrived in Milan. "Therefore, no one is more deserving of a Christian burial place. But," he had added, lifting his eyes from the body as it was lowered into the bottom of the grave, "do not believe the false rumors afoot in the city. Father Alessandro Trivulzio, may God have mercy on his soul, died a martyr at the hands of an abominable criminal who sooner or later will receive due punishment. I myself will see that it is so."

Murder or suicide, however hard I tried to stifle my suspicions, it was not easy to believe that two burials in such a short space of time were normal in Santa Maria. The last words that Master Leonardo spoke to me before returning to his workshop echoed in my mind like thunder before a storm. "In this city, nothing happens just by chance. Don't ever forget it."

That evening I took no supper.

I felt utterly incapable.

The other monks, less fastidious than this poor servant of God, ran to fill their bellies in a nearby hall turned into a dining room for the occasion, where they devoured the remains of the meal offered by the duke on the day of his wife's funeral. Since the refectory was put out of use thanks to the scaffolding and the painting equipment, the monks had grown used to having their customs upset and their eating place moved.

Amidst such precariousness, I discovered a personal advantage: while the work continued, I knew that the room in which *The Last Supper* progressed was the perfect hiding place into which I could retire to reflect during mealtimes. No brother would come into this room to disturb my meditations, and no one from outside the monastery would want to wander through a place as cold and dusty as this.

Therefore, with my mind on the days we shared trying to solve the mysterious riddle, I headed toward the refectory in order to pray in peace for the soul of Father Alessandro.

As I had expected, the room was empty. The last rays of the sun barely lit the lower part of Leonardo's composition, illuminating Our Lord's feet, which seemed crossed one over the other. Was this a foretelling of what Christ was to suffer on Calvary? Or had Leonardo depicted His feet in this position for another, obscure reason? I made the sign of the Cross. The thin light, filtered through the irregular line of columns in the neighboring courtyard, lent the scene a ghostly atmosphere.

Only then, observing the guests at the Holy Supper, did I see that what Leonardo had told me was true.

Judas indeed had the features of Father Alessandro.

How had I not realized it earlier?

The wicked apostle was sitting at Jesus' right hand, silently gazing on His serene beauty. In fact, not counting the surprised gesture of James the Elder and the animated conversation between Matthew, Judas Thaddeus and Simon at the other end of the table, all the other apostles seemed to keep their mouths shut. It was ironic to think that at this very moment, Father Alessandro's soul might be truly looking upon the face of Our Father in Heaven. However, if, like Judas, the librarian had decided to take his own life and the Father Prior was deceiving himself as to his innocence, his fate now was not that of Holy Glory but that of the eternal torments of Hell.

Letting my eyes wander over the mural, another detail caught my attention. Judas and Our Lord seemed to be sharing a single piece of bread (or was it a fruit?) that neither of them actually touched. The traitor, holding in his right hand the infamous money bag, was stretching his left hand toward the edge of the table, as if about to grab hold of something there, while Our Lord, oblivious to Judas's gesture, stretched His right hand in the same direction. What was there that might interest the One as well as the other? What might Judas want to steal from Christ at the very moment in which the Son of God announces that He has been betrayed and that His lot is cast?

These were my thoughts when suddenly an unexpected visitor interrupted my reflections.

"I'd wager ten to one that you can't make a thing out of it, can you?"

I started. A figure that I could not quite make out, dressed in a scarlet cape, crossed the room and stopped a few feet away from me.

"You are Father Agostino Leyre, are you not?"

With astonishment, I realized that the intruder was a woman. What I could see of her face, under a purple hat, was soft and rounded. She was dressed up as a man, something both illegal and dangerous, and she was observing me with curiosity. She was of more or less my height and her feminine features were well disguised under the large cape. Her gloved hands rested on the hilt of a shining rapier.

I must have stammered my answer.

"Don't be afraid, Father." She smiled. "The blade is for your protection. It will not harm you. I've come because your many questions deserve an answer. And because my master believes you deserve to live."

I was speechless.

"I need you to accompany me to a more discreet place. An urgent matter requires your presence in another part of the city."

Her invitation did not sound threatening, merely a courteous invitation. Under her cape and hat, the woman radiated an extraordinary sense of power. Her look was keen and feline, and her attitude made it clear that she would not take no for an answer. In the now gloomy light, the stranger led me across the refectory, through a corridor and into the church, a path with which only the monks were familiar. How was it that she knew these rooms so well? Once we had exited into the street without having met a single monk, the stranger bid me quicken my step.

It took us some ten minutes to reach the Church of Santo Stefano some four or five streets farther down. By then, night had fallen. We went around the building to the right and down a narrow passageway that would have been difficult to discover without a guide. The façade of an imposing two-story-high brick palazzo, lit by a couple of torches, glittered at the end of the narrow passage. The stranger, who had not breathed a word since we had entered the street, pointed in its direction.

"Are we there?" I asked.

A footman in a tight woolen waistcoat and a hood came forward to meet us.

"If you'll allow me, Father," he said very formally, "I'll lead you to my master. He's eager to see you."

"Your master?"

"Indeed," he answered with a low bow, at which my companion's features broke into a smile.

The palazzo was decorated with pieces of extraordinary value. Old Roman marble columns, statues rescued from the earth only recently, paintings and tapestries crowded the walls and the floor. The venerable building was disposed around a central courtyard with a topiary maze in the middle, toward which we were led. The deep silence intrigued me. When we reached the center, I suddenly saw rows of serious faces lining the labyrinth, gazing ahead as if a catastrophe were soon expected.

At length, I understood what was happening. A row of worried servants was watching two men on a low platform, angrily facing each other. Both were in shirtsleeves, holding unsheathed swords, and, in spite of the cold, both were sweating copiously. My companion pushed her hat off and attended to the scene with delighted anticipation.

"It's begun," she said, sounding somewhat disappointed. "My master wanted you to see this."

"This? What is this?" I asked in alarm. "A duel?"

Before she could answer, the elder of the two contestants, a well-built, tall, broad-shouldered, balding man, threw himself against his opponent, putting all his weight onto his weapon.

"Domine Jesu Christe!" shouted the younger one in terror, stopping the blow by holding his sword across his chest.

"Rex Gloriae!" his attacker shouted back.

This was no training session. The bald man's fury grew with every passing moment, and the blades clashed relentlessly with quick, sharp thrusts.

"Mario Forzetta," my companion explained, pointing at the young man who had just stopped to catch his breath, "is a painter's apprentice from Ferrara. He tried to deceive my master in an agreement. Now their duel is to first drawn blood, as in Spain. The first one to wound his adversary wins."

The fight became wilder. Three, four new blows resounded in the courtyard. The sparks from the metal reached the balconies.

"Not your youth but my mercy will spare your life!" shouted the bald man.

"Keep your mercy where it better suits you!" answered the other.

But young Forzetta's pride did not last long. Three violent thrusts forced him to his knees, his hand on the ground to hold his balance. The bald man smiled victoriously and a loud cheer rang throughout the palazzo. The Master's enemy had lost his sword. Only the ritual needed to be fulfilled. With a surgeon's deft hand, the victor's sword whipped through the air, touching with its tip the young man's cheek, which began to bleed immediately.

First drawn blood.

"Do you see?" he roared. "God has dealt justly with

your lies. Never again will you try to deceive me by trying to pass off fake antiques. Never, do you hear?"

Then, turning toward me, gratified to see my white habit and black hood among the crowd of servants, he made a bow in my direction and spoke out loud so that all could hear him.

"This ruffian has been dealt with justly," he said. "But the same cannot be said in your case, with someone as notable as yourself. Isn't that true, Father Leyre?"

I was lost for words. There was a demonic glint in this man's eyes. Who was he and how did he know my name? What justice was he referring to?

"Preachers are always welcome in my palazzo," he said. "But I sent for you in particular because I hope that together we'll be able to rehabilitate a certain common friend."

"A common friend?" I stammered.

"A common friend we once had," he explained. "Are you not among those who believe that something strange lies behind the death of our own Alessandro Trivulzio?"

The victor (whose name, I soon learned, was Oliverio Jacaranda) approached me and gave me a friendly tap on the shoulder. Then he vanished inside the palazzo. My companion asked me to wait. As I did, the small army of servants went into action. In barely ten minutes, they had dismantled the platform set up for the duel and had carried Forzetta away, wounded and bound, into the palazzo. As they passed me, I saw that the defeated man was no more than a child. Green, plaintive eyes fixed themselves upon mine, begging for help.

"Spaniards are men of honor," said my companion in a kind tone, letting loose her blond hair as she resheathed her rapier. "Oliverio Jacaranda is from Valencia, like the Pope. And His Holiness's favorite provider."

"Provider?"

"He's an antiquarian dealer, Father. A new profession, very profitable, that consists in rescuing from the past the buried treasures of those who've preceded us. You can't imagine what can be found in Rome by just scratching the surface of its seven hills!"

"And you? Who are you, if I may ask?"

"I'm his daughter, Maria Jacaranda, your servant."

"And why did your father want me to see him fight this Forzetta? What has all this to do with the death of Father Alessandro?"

"He'll explain it all very soon," she answered. "It's the fault of his dealings in old books. You must know that there are upon this Earth volumes more precious than gold, and there are petty crooks like Forzetta who buy and sell them or, worse, try to pass new books for old, demanding disproportionate sums of money for them."

"And do you really think this subject concerns me?"

"It will," was her enigmatic promise.

28

Indeed, the master of the house was not long in returning. His servants had cleared away all traces of the duel
and the dwelling had recovered its comfortable and
untidy look.

Oliverio Jacaranda could not hide his satisfaction. He
had washed and perfumed himself, and was dressed in a
new woolen garment that reached his feet. He greeted
his daughter and invited me to pass into his study, to talk
in private.

"I know that my work doesn't please men of the cloth
like yourself, Father Agostino."

His first words disconcerted me: Jacaranda spoke a
mixture of Spanish and Milanese dialect that lent his
speech a peculiar tone. In fact, everything about the
man was peculiar, even his study, full of curious musical
instruments, strange paintings and the remains of
ancient masonry.

"Are you surprised by what you see?" His question
interrupted my perusal of the place. "Let me explain: my
work consists of rescuing from oblivion those things that
our ancestors left beneath the earth. Sometimes there
are coins, sometimes nothing but bones, often the effigies of pagan gods that, according to such men as you,

should never be allowed to resurface. I love those statues that date back to Imperial Rome. They are beautiful, well proportioned . . . perfect. And expensive. Very expensive. My business, why deny it, is better than ever."

Jacaranda poured out some wine in silver goblets and offered me one, before continuing proudly:

"Maria must have informed you that the Holy Father gives his blessing to my activities. In fact, years ago, when he was still a cardinal, he reserved for himself the privilege of seeing my pieces before anyone else. He chooses what he wants and pays generously."

"She did mention it," I said. "But I doubt if you've sent for me merely to inform me of your business."

The master of the house let escape a small cynical laugh.

"I know well who you are, Father Agostino. A few days ago you presented yourself as an inquisitor to the duke's officials and asked to pay your respects before the funeral of Donna Beatrice. You come from Rome. You're lodging in the monastery of Santa Maria and you spend your time trying to solve Latin conundrums. As you can see, you can keep no secrets from me, Father."

Jacaranda drank a sip of wine and corrected himself:

"Hardly any."

"I don't understand," I said.

"I'll come to the point. You seem like an intelligent man and perhaps you can help me solve a problem we have in common. I mean Father Alessandro's death, Father."

At last he had mentioned the dead librarian.

"Long before you arrived in Milan, he and I were the

best of friends. I might even say that we were associates. Father Alessandro acted as intermediary between some of the most important families in Milan and my business. Through him, I would inform them of my antiquarian offerings without raising suspicions among the clergy, and Father Alessandro would then receive a certain payment for the service."

The antiquarian's words took me aback.

"Does it surprise you, Father? Other priests in Bologna, Ferrara and Siena assist me in similar tasks. We harm no one; we only circumvent absurd prohibitions and scruples that, I'm sure, will one day be remembered as something laughable, worthy only of old-fashioned minds. What wrong is there in recuperating fragments of our past and offering them for the delectation of the rich? Is there not an Egyptian obelisk displayed in Saint Peter's Square in Rome?"

"You're digging your own grave, sir," I replied in all seriousness. "You forget that I'm part of that clergy that you say you circumvent."

"Yes, indeed, but allow me to continue. Unfortunately, it is not only the strict clergy that creates obstacles in our work. As you might suppose, I sell artworks and antiques to rich court ladies, sometimes behind their husbands' backs, since the gentlemen often don't approve of these kinds of transactions. Father Alessandro was an essential part in some of my most important operations. He had the exquisite ability of getting himself invited into any Milanese household of his choice, with the pretext of a confession or a lofty conversation, where he would then close a deal under the very noses of these noblemen."

"And what did he receive in exchange? Money? I doubt it—"

"Books, Father Agostino. He received manuscripts or printed volumes, according to the value of the sale. Texts delicately copied out or imported from presses in France or the Germanic empire. His whole obsession was to collect more and more books for the library of Santa Maria. But I suppose that you knew that already."

"I still don't understand why you're informing me of this. If Father Alessandro was your friend, why are you sullying his memory with your confessions?"

"Nothing would be further from my intentions." He laughed nervously. "Let me explain something else: shortly before dying, your librarian friend participated in a very special affair. He was familiar with one my best clients, so I put the matter in his hands without hesitating for a second. The truth is, this was the first time that someone of nobility wasn't asking for the statue of some faun or the like to decorate a villa. Her request was so strange that it filled us both with enthusiasm."

I looked at Jacaranda curiously.

"My client needed us to solve a small problem, something of an almost domestic nature. As I was an expert in antiquities, she wondered whether I could identify a certain precious object that she was able to describe with some precision."

"Was it a jewel?"

"No, not at all. It was a book."

"A book? Like the ones you would give as payment—?"

"This one had never been printed. She only gave me a few details of what it looked like: a volume of only a few pages with gilded edges, bound in blue and adorned with four gold clasps. A work of art resembling a breviary, no doubt imported from the Orient—"

"So you applied yourself to identifying it, with the help of Father Alessandro," I interrupted.

"We had two valuable clues to follow. First, the man whom my client had first heard speak of the book: Master Leonardo da Vinci. Fortunately, your librarian knew him well, and it would not be difficult for him to find out whether he had the book in his possession."

"And the second?"

"She gave me an exact drawing of the book I was to obtain."

"Your client had a drawing of the book?"

"Exactly. It appeared in a deck of cards of which she was extremely fond. On one of the cards depicting a large woman there was also a drawing of the book. It wasn't much, true, but many times I'd begun negotiations with far less information than that. We identified the woman as a nun or someone wearing a religious costume. But the book she was holding was closed and displayed no title nor any such identifying sign."

A book depicted in a deck of cards? I grew alarmed. Hadn't the Father Prior spoken to me of something similar?

"May I enquire the name of your client?" I asked.

"Of course. That is exactly why I've asked you here. Her name was Beatrice d'Este."

I opened wide my eyes in astonishment.

"Beatrice d'Este? Ludovico il Moro's wife? Do you mean to say that Father Alessandro and Donna Beatrice knew one another?"

"Very well. And now, you see, they are both dead."

"What are you suggesting?"

Jacaranda sat down at his desk, satisfied at having captured my full attention.

"I see that you begin to understand my concern, Father Agostino. Tell me. How well have you gotten to know Master Leonardo?"

"I've only spoken with him once. This very morning."

"You should know then that he's an odd bird, the strangest, most extravagant bird ever to land in this place. He employs every God-given minute of the day to work, read, draw and reflect on the most absurd subjects you might imagine. He invents cooking recipes with which he delights the duke, as well as modeling extravagant war machines out of almond paste for his banquets. He's also a very suspicious man, very jealous of his things, of all his property. He never allows anyone to go through his notes, and even less into his library which, as you can imagine, is very large and valuable. He even writes from right to left, like the Jews!"

"Does he?"

"I wouldn't lie to you about something like that. To read one of his notebooks, you'd need a mirror: only through a reflection can you understand what he's written. Isn't that a devilish device? Who do you know who's capable of writing like that, without an effort? That man, believe me, hides many terrible secrets."

"I still cannot comprehend why you're telling me all this."

"Because—" And here he made a theatrical pause. "I believe that Father Alessandro was murdered by order of Leonardo da Vinci. And I believe that the cause is that damned book, the same one the duchess desired and which ended up costing her her life."

I grew pale.

"That's a very serious accusation!"

"Prove it yourself," he replied. "You are the only one who can. You live in Santa Maria delle Grazie, but you are not sold to the duke, like all the others. The Father Prior wants the monastery to be finished with Ludovico's money, and I doubt if he would dare attack his favorite artist and risk losing the subsidies. I'm inviting you to solve this puzzle, the two of us working together. Find the book and not only will you shed light on the deaths of the duchess and Father Alessandro but you will also arm yourself with proof enough to accuse Leonardo of murder."

"I dislike your methods, Signor Jacaranda."

"My methods?" He laughed. "Did you have a good look at the man defeated in the duel?"

"Forzetta?"

"The same. Well, I'll tell you something about my methods. I ordered him to get for me the 'blue book' from Leonardo's *bottega*. You see, Forzetta had been one of Leonardo's old apprentices and knew all the possible hiding places."

"You ordered him to rob Leonardo da Vinci?"

"I wanted the matter resolved, Father Agostino. But

I'll admit my failure. That useless fool took from the *bottega* a different book, the *Divini Platonis Opera Omnia*, a book printed in Venice years ago, of very little value. And then he tried selling it to me as if it were the precious volume I was looking for."

"*Divini Platonis . . .* ," I repeated. "I know the work."

"You do?"

I nodded.

"It's the famous translation of Plato's complete works that Marsilio Ficino made for Cosimo de' Medici of Florence."

"Well, the scoundrel says that Leonardo held it in great esteem, and that he spent many days using it to shape one of the apostles in his *Cenacolo*. And what do I care about that! I've lost a friend, thanks to Leonardo, and I want to know why. Now: Will you help me?"

29

Porta Romana was the city's most elegant quarter. Crossed day and night by the most splendid carriages in Lombardy, it boasted of being the only monumental entrance into Milan. Its porticos were always crowded with well-attired gentlefolk, and the ladies enjoyed wandering under them in order to feel the city's daily pulse. Papal nuncios, foreign ambassadors and noblemen of every kind let themselves be seen there, hoping to be admired. It stood next to the city's main canal and was an unparalleled gallery of vanities.

In the very center of the road stood the Palazzo Vecchio. This was a public building much beloved by the Milanese, the habitual meeting place of fraternities, guilds and even the law courts. It was two stories high, possessed six vast halls and a maze of offices that changed ownership frequently.

On the night that I spent at Oliverio Jacaranda's house, all the rooms in the Palazzo Vecchio were bursting with expectation. More than three hundred people were lining up in the street to admire the latest masterpiece of Leonardo; many of the notables of the city had made an appointment here, using as a pretext the wish to comment on the latest court events. There was not a single citizen who did not long for an invitation to the event.

Leonardo had organized the exhibition in a hurry, perhaps at the suggestion of the duke, who, barely forty-eight hours after his wife's burial, was already thinking of reanimating public life in Milan.

Master Bernardino Luini arrived in the company of a radiant Elena Crivelli, who had insisted so ardently on coming with him that the painter had agreed. He still blushed at the thought of what had taken place between them barely a few days ago, and his mind was still in torment. To make matters more difficult for him, Donna Lucrezia's daughter had chosen a dazzling outfit for the occasion: a blue dress trimmed in fur with a low-cut bodice embroidered in gold. With her hair done up in a net of precious stones and her lips painted scarlet, she looked like a young goddess. Luini tried hard to keep his distance and not even touch her.

"Master Luini!" Leonardo's loud voice stopped them on the second floor of the Palazzo Vecchio. "I'm pleased to see you. And in such fine company! Whom have you brought with you?"

Luini bowed ceremoniously, surprised at his teacher's undisguised curiosity.

"This is Elena Crivelli, Master," he said, introducing her. "A young lady who admires you and has insisted in accompanying me to your exhibition."

"Crivelli? What a delightful surprise! Are you by chance related to the painter Crivelli?"

"I'm his niece, sir."

Elena's pale eyes stirred certain old memories in Leonardo.

"Then you're the daughter of—"

"Of Lucrezia Crivelli, whom you know well."

"Donna Lucrezia! Of course!" he said, turning his eyes toward Luini. "And you've come with Master Luini, for whom you've sat! You're the new Mary Magdalene!"

"Yes, sir."

"Wonderful! You've come at a very opportune moment."

Leonardo examined the girl once more, looking for the features that had so impressed him in her mother. A quick glance allowed him to see the same forehead, the same nose, the same cheekbones and chin. The geometrical marvel of Donna Lucrezia's face now had a double in that of her daughter.

The Master pointed to a small room, next to the gigantic landing, which had been lovingly decorated. Each of its walls had been covered in black cloth, displaying in the room's center a small painting framed in polished pinewood.

"You see," Leonardo said. "I thought this would be the best moment to show it. Donna Beatrice's death has saddened us so deeply that we need as much beauty as possible to gladden our spirits once again. Perhaps Master Luini has told you that I need to have happiness around me. I need life. And since every time I show one of the paintings from my studio it receives such acclaim—"

"—You thought that showing a new work of yours might bring people out into the streets again," Luini concluded, approvingly.

"Exactly. And in spite of the cold weather, it seems that I've succeeded." Leonardo now changed his tone, pointing toward his new work. "Well? What do you think of it?"

They looked carefully at the painting. It was a thing of splendor. A young woman attired in a red dress, to which Leonardo had managed to lend not only the quality of velvet but also the stitches in the brocade collar, watched them serenely at eye's level. Her hair was gathered in a long tress and a fine diadem crowned her forehead with infinite delicacy. It was an extraordinary portrait, one of Leonardo's masterpieces. If instead of a frame she were surrounded by a window, no one would have said that she was not truly there, watching them.

Elena and Luini stared at each other, at a loss for words.

"We thought—" Luini stammered, "we thought you'd show us a portrait of Donna Beatrice, Master."

"And why should I, tell me?" He smiled. "The Duchess d'Este never found a single moment to sit for me."

Elena's eyes grew moist with emotion.

"But she's—she's—"

"She's your mother, Donna Lucrezia. Yes," said Leonardo, wrinkling his large nose, "no doubt one of the most beautiful women I've ever known. Beauty and harmony: Isn't that what we need right now, in these times of mourning?"

Elena could not take her eyes away from the portrait.

"I would never have shown this in public if it hadn't been necessary. Believe me."

"Is it—" Elena hesitated. "Is it because of your theory of light? Master Luini told me how important it was for you."

"Did he, now?"

A curious glint shone in Leonardo's eyes.

"For you, light is the essence of what is divine. Its presence or absence in a painting reveals everything about the artist's final purpose. Am I right?"

"Well . . . You surprise me, Elena. And tell me: what secret purpose can you guess is in this picture?"

The young countess examined the painting once again. Her mother's radiant face lacked only speech.

"It's like a sign, Master Leonardo."

"A sign?"

"Yes, a sign. As if you were sending signs of light in the midst of the darkness. Like a lighthouse in the night. You're sending signals to those of faith. To those who choose light over the shadows."

The Master was taken aback.

Suddenly, his astonishment turned to concern. And Elena noticed the change. The Master looked around to see that no one was listening and then begged the little countess to allow him a moment with Luini. Elena withdrew to one of the windows overlooking the Porta Romana.

"What have you done, Master Luini?"

Leonardo's whisper was sharp and cold. Luini winced.

"Master, I—"

"You've spoken about the light! To a child!"

"But I—"

"No buts. Does she know that light is one of her

family's attributes? What else have you told her, you madman!"

Luini was horrified, unable to move. All of a sudden he realized the terrible mistake he had made in allowing Elena to accompany him here. He lowered his head in shame and said nothing.

"I see," Leonardo said. "Now I understand."

"What do you understand, Master?" Luini asked with a knot in his throat.

"You've slept with her, haven't you?"

"Slept?"

"Answer me!"

"I—I'm sorry, Master."

"You're sorry? Don't you realize what you've done?"

Leonardo choked his words down so as not to startle the young woman.

"You've slept with a Magdalene! You! A devotee to the cause of John!"

Leonardo swallowed hard. He needed time to think. His mind tried to fit in this piece of the puzzle just as it tried to fit the cogs in his machines. What could he do? He would consider it yet another sign of Providence. Another proof that times were changing fast and that soon the great secret would escape from his hands.

How could he have been so innocent, he who had willingly rejected carnal love? How could he not have foreseen the possibility that this young apprentice, charged with watching over Donna Lucrezia's daughter, might himself fall into her tempting arms? Now he needed to hurry. He would have to initiate Elena into the mysteries of her apostolate before other lovers steered her away from her rightful path. Yes. He would call the little countess to his side and do what no one had seen him do before: he would speak to her of his concerns.

He called her back.

"Forgive me," he said, addressing himself to both of them. "I want to tell you how well-timed your visit has been. I needed someone to speak to in confidence. I believe I'm being spied on. I believe my movements, and those of my helpers, are being watched."

"You, Master?" Luini said, aghast.

"Yes," Leonardo continued. "I've been suspecting it for years. You know well, Bernardino, that I've long been wary of people in general. For a long time now I've been writing all my correspondence in code, and I jot down my notes so that very few can read them. And I distrust anyone who comes near me only to sniff around my things. On Sunday, when we buried the duchess, those old fears were suddenly rekindled. Within a day of each other, two holy men died in very strange circumstances."

Luini and Elena looked incredulous. Neither of them had heard of this before.

"One was found hanged in the Piazza Mercanti. He was carrying a card that you, Master Luini, know as well as I do. It belongs to a deck designed for the Visconti family almost half a century ago, and depicts a nun of the Order of Saint Francis carrying the cross of John the Baptist in one hand and the book of John the Evangelist in the other."

"Mary Magdalene!"

"Indeed, that is one of the many ways in which she's represented. The knots on the cord around her swollen belly tell us as much. But few, very few are those who know the code."

"Please, tell us more," Luini insisted.

"As you can well imagine, Master Luini, I interpreted the card as a signal. A warning from someone trying to approach me. I tried to convince the duke's men that the priest had committed suicide. I wanted to gain some time to investigate, but the second death confirmed my fears."

"What fears?" asked Elena dauntlessly.

"You see, Elena, the second murdered man was also a friend of mine."

The little countess drew in her breath.

"You—you knew them both?"

"Indeed. Both. Giulio, the second victim, died bleeding in front of my *Maestà*. Someone pierced his heart with a sword. The murderer didn't rob him of any money, of any belongings—except—"

"Except?"

"Except the Franciscan card that was later found next to the priest. I have the disagreeable impression that the murderer wanted me to be fully aware of his crimes. After all, the *Maestà* is a work of mine and the priest belonged to the community of Santa Maria."

Uneasy about interrupting again, Elena nevertheless felt the need to speak up.

"Master, is this related to your showing me now the portrait of my mother? Is it linked at all with this terrible news?"

"You'll soon understand, my child," Leonardo answered. "This was not the only time your mother sat for me. In her younger days, she served as the model for the Virgin in the *Maestà*. Then, just a few months ago, I made another version of the *Maestà* with your mother again as the model. When I delivered this second version, ten days ago, the Franciscans exchanged it for the first. It was all so fast that I had no time to warn the Brotherhood of the substitution."

"The Brotherhood?"

"I see that Master Luini has not told you everything yet," Leonardo said, lowering his voice. "The *Maestà* is like a gospel to them. It was a spiritual balm, especially after the Inquisition took their holy books away. They would come to worship it by the dozen. But when the Franciscans realized what was happening and started quarreling with me, I was forced to produce a new version, stripping it of the symbols that made it so special. I waited ten years before fulfilling their new request, and I wasn't able to delay it any longer. Unfortunately, I didn't warn the Brotherhood so that they would cease coming to San Francesco in search of illumination, and my dear Giulio paid for my mistake with his life. Someone was waiting for him."

"Have you any idea of who that might be?"

"No, Bernardino. But his motive was the same as always, the same one that led Saint Dominic to create the Inquisition: to do away with the last pure Christians. They are trying to extinguish by force what they didn't manage to extinguish in Montségur when they crushed the last of the Cathars."

"But, Master, where will the Brotherhood go now to satisfy its faith?"

"To the *Cenacolo*, of course. But not till it's finished.

Why do you think I'm painting it on a wall and not on a canvas? Because of the size? Not at all." He lifted a warning finger. "It's so that no one may unhook it or force me to redo it. This is the only way for the Brotherhood to find long-lasting consolation. No one will think of looking under the very noses of the inquisitors themselves."

"That's very ingenious, Master . . . but very dangerous as well."

Leonardo smiled.

"Between the Roman Christians and us there's a great difference, Bernardino. They need tangible sacraments to feel that they're blessed by God. They eat bread, anoint themselves with oil, are sprinkled with consecrated water. Our sacraments, on the other hand, are invisible. Their strength lies in that they are abstract sacraments. Whoever perceives them from within feels a blow in the chest and an all-invading joy. You know you're saved when you feel that force inside you. My Last Supper will bestow such privileges upon them. Why do you think that my Christ does not display the Roman host? Because His sacrament is another—"

"Master," Luini broke in. "You speak to Elena as if she already knew all about your faith. But she hasn't heard the full story."

"Yes . . ."

"I hope you'll grant me a favor. Give me permission to take her to see the *Cenacolo* and initiate her in your secret. In your symbols. Perhaps then—" Luini hesitated, weighing his words. "Perhaps then we might both cleanse ourselves and merit a place in your presence. This is what she wants."

Leonardo did not seem surprised.

"Is that so, Elena?"

The young woman nodded.

"Then you must know that the only way of getting to know my work is to take part in it. And you know that better than anyone else, Bernardino. I am the only Omega toward which you must wend your way from now on."

"If your intention is to guide her toward you, Master, then why not take her as your model? The mother sat for your 'painted gospel' in the *Maestà*. Why should not the daughter sit for the mural you are completing?"

Leonardo hesitated.

"For the *Cenacolo*?"

"Why not?" Luini answered. "Don't you need a model for the Beloved Apostle? Where will you find a more angelic face to finish your Saint John?"

Elena lowered her eyes, delighted. Leonardo caressed his blond beard thoughtfully, carefully observing the young Crivelli. Then he let out a peal of laughter that echoed through the room.

"Yes!" he thundered. "Why not? After all, I can't imagine anyone better suited for the task at hand."

30

"Oliverio Jacaranda?"

A look of disgust came over the Father Prior's face as he spoke the name.

He had summoned me as soon as he knew that I had returned to the monastery. It seems that the brethren had spent hours on alert because of my unexpected absence and that several of the monks, armed with clubs and torches, had gone out to look for me shortly after nightfall. Therefore, when Maria Jacaranda delivered me to the doors of Santa Maria, unharmed but with a troubled mind, the Father Prior called me at once to his side.

"And you tell me, Father Agostino, that you spent the night in the company of Oliverio Jacaranda, in his own house?"

His tone of voice betrayed his deep concern.

"I see that you know him, Father Prior."

"Of course I do," he answered. "All of Milan knows the scoundrel. He deals in liturgical objects, as well as buying and selling pictures of saints or naked Venuses, and he handles more money and securities than many a nobleman in the duke's court. What I can't understand," he said half-shutting his eyes, "is what he might want from you."

"He wanted to talk to me about the father librarian."

"About Father Alessandro?"

I nodded. The Father Prior seemed disconcerted.

"Apparently, both of them maintained a sort of commercial relationship. They were, so to speak, associates."

"That's nonsense! What could Father Alessandro, may he rest in peace, want with an immoral and depraved man such as Jacaranda?"

"If what Signor Jacaranda said to me is true, then Father Alessandro Trivulzio led a double life. On the one hand, he appeared as a man fearful of God, a lover of letters and of study; but on the other hand, far from your protecting eyes, he had become a dealer in antiquities."

The Father Prior seemed to consider this revelation carefully.

"I'm at pains to believe it," he muttered. "And yet, perhaps this might explain certain things . . ."

"Certain things? What do you mean, Father Prior?"

"I've spoken to the duke's police about the circumstances of Father Alessandro's death. There's an obscure point that none of us can explain. A great contradiction that has us all baffled."

"Pray tell."

"You see, the police found no signs of violence or resistance on the body of Father Alessandro. However, it seems that he did not hang himself on his own. Someone else was with him at the time, someone who left a strange card at the naked feet of our librarian."

The Father Prior dug into his pockets and produced a well-worn piece of parchment full of scribbles and incomprehensible lines.

"Look," he said, handing me the card.

I must have shown my astonishment, because the Father Prior looked at me strangely. How else could I have reacted? Because a section of the scribbles corresponded to the riddle that had brought me here in the first place. Indeed, *Oculos ejus dinumera*, the Soothsayer's peculiar signature, could be read in the very center. Its seven verses had been copied out in a trembling hand and they appeared to have been studied carefully, since the notes on the margins looked like the efforts of someone trying to make sense of the whole.

"This is my riddle!" I exclaimed.

" 'Count its eyes but look not on its face / The number of my name / you shall find on its side . . .' Yes. I know. You told me some time before Father Alessandro's death, as you surely remember. But these"—and here he drew a circle on the card with his finger—"are not my notes, Father Agostino."

His eyes sparkled.

"And that's not all. Look here."

The Father Prior turned the card over. The unmistakable figure of the Franciscan nun holding in her right hand a cross and in her left a book left me stunned.

"Dear God!" I cried out. "The card—your card!"

"No. Leonardo's card," the Father Prior corrected me. "No one knows who placed this card at the feet of Father Alessandro's body after his death, but obviously it's supposed to have a meaning. I'll remind you that the Tuscan challenged us over this same picture. And now it appears, together with your own riddle, next to our dead librarian. What do you make of it?"

I drew a deep breath.

"There's something I haven't told you, Father Prior."

My host wrinkled his brow.

"I don't know how to interpret this following your revelations, but Signor Jacaranda and I were talking precisely about this very same card. Or rather, about the book this woman is holding in her hand."

"The book?"

"It isn't just any book, Father Prior. Jacaranda wished to get hold of it for an important client and entrusted the job to Father Alessandro. Apparently, it seems that the owner of this valuable book is Master Leonardo himself, and so he thought that it would be easier for our librarian than for any other messenger to get in touch with him and make him an offer. A simple commercial transaction that has already cost two lives."

"Two, you say, Father Agostino?"

"I haven't told you this yet, Father Prior, but the client who desired to buy the book was Beatrice d'Este, may God have mercy on her soul."

"Dear Heaven!"

The Father Prior invited me to continue.

"Jacaranda doesn't know why the duchess contracted his services to obtain the book and didn't ask Leonardo himself for it. But he's convinced that, in one way or another, Leonardo is implicated in these deaths."

"And what do you think, Father Agostino?"

"I have difficulty believing it. Leonardo is an artist, not a soldier."

The Father Prior looked down with troubled eyes.

"I too am of that opinion, but from what I can see, death appears to be an everyday event where Master Leonardo is concerned."

"What do you mean?"

"Yesterday a strange thing happened, not far from here. The Church of San Francesco was desecrated with the murder of a pilgrim within its walls."

"A murder?" I was aghast. "On consecrated ground?"

"That is so. The unfortunate soul had his heart pierced by a blade just behind the main altar, under Leonardo's new painting. It must have happened only a few hours before the death of Father Alessandro. And there is something else."

The Father Prior took a deep breath before continuing.

"The police found among his things the deck to which this card belongs. Whoever killed that man stole it from him, scribbled your riddle on the back and left it by the body of our librarian. You must help me find him. Unless I am much mistaken, our murderer, whoever he might be, is also after that damned book of Leonardo's."

31

"I want you to hand over your prisoner."

Maria Jacaranda looked at me in astonishment. She was no longer wearing the man's costume from the previous night, but had changed into a dress with a loose waist, blue and white sleeves and a striped bodice. Her blond hair was gathered in a fetching net, and her whole aspect was radiant.

It was obvious that the young woman had not expected to see me again so soon, especially not bearing such an odd request. Little did she know my reasons. Mario Forzetta, the swordsman whom her father had defeated in the duel, was, as far as I knew, the last person who had tried to obtain the "blue book" of Leonardo's card. And the only one still alive. It was obvious that I needed to speak with him.

"I don't think my father will be keen on the idea," she said when she heard my clumsy explanations.

"You're wrong in assuming that, Maria. You were present when Signor Oliverio asked me to help him obtain Leonardo's book. And that is why I've come."

"And what will you do with Mario?"

"First of all, place him in my custody, that is to say,

the Holy Office's. Then take him with me for questioning."

The mention of the Holy Inquisition undermined the
young woman's objections. Impressed by my severity, she
decided to agree to my demands and accompanied me to
the cellars of the palazzo. No doubt she did not wish to
upset the Dominicans in her father's absence. She told
me that he had left shortly after our meeting and that he
was not likely to return to Milan for another week.
While he was away, it was her responsibility to oversee
the running of the household and guard his possessions,
among them the young Forzetta.

"Is he violent?" I asked.

"Oh no, not at all. I think he'd be incapable of harming a fly. But he's cunning. Be careful with him."

"Cunning?"

"That's a quality he learned from Leonardo," she
added. "All of his disciples have it."

The young man had been imprisoned in a section of
the palazzo that had long ago functioned as a jail. Thick
walls and deep stairwells enclosed a strange underground
world impossible to imagine from the rooms and gardens
on the surface. Jacaranda, in a magnanimous mood, had
allowed his impertinent servant one of the cells *murus
strictus*, that is to say, one whose dimensions barely
allowed him to lie down, stand up and walk a few steps
from one wall to the other. With no windows, in the
midst of an impenetrable darkness, Mario Forzetta could
consider himself nevertheless fortunate. Next to his com-
partment, Maria held up her lantern to show me another
cell, *murus strictissimus*, in which a man could neither

stand upright nor lie full length, and from which no prisoner emerged except stark raving mad or in a coffin.

By the door of Mario's cell I felt short of breath, but I didn't want Jacaranda's daughter to see me falter. I hated visiting prisons. Closed spaces made me sick. In fact, the only inquisitorial tasks I never turned down were the administrative ones. I preferred the heavy weight of files and papers to the stench of damp and the drip of water pipes on the stone. Left alone, with a second lantern in my hand and a ring of iron keys in the other, it took me a moment before I could speak.

"Mario Forzetta?"

No answer.

Behind the bars consumed by rust, the prisoner seemed to be waiting for nothing except death. I put one of the keys in the lock and entered. Forzetta was standing against one of the walls, both hands manacled, his eyes lost in vacancy. As soon as I shone my lantern on him, he tried to cover his face. His shirt still bore signs of blood and the wound on his cheek seemed to be festering. His hair was covered in a coat of dust and his whole aspect, in spite of the short time spent in seclusion, was terrible.

"I know you're from Ferrara, like Donna Beatrice," I said as I sat down on his cot, giving him time to get accustomed to the light. He nodded in some confusion. He had never heard my voice before and did not know who I was.

"How old are you, my son?"

"Seventeen."

Seventeen, I thought. He's not yet a man!

Mario wouldn't take his eyes off my black and white

habit, wondering about the reason for my visit. I must be truthful: a certain sympathy established itself between us. I decided to take advantage of it.

"All right, Mario Forzetta. I'll tell you why I've come. I've been authorized to take you out of here and set you free, as long as we can reach an agreement," I lied. "All you have to do is answer a few questions. If you tell me the truth, I'll let you go."

"I always tell the truth, Father."

The young man moved forward from the wall and sat by my side. Seen from close by, he certainly did not look dangerous. Somewhat lanky and round-shouldered, he was obviously ill-suited for physical exertions. No wonder Jacaranda had beaten him so easily.

"I know you were an apprentice with Leonardo. Is that right?"

"Yes, it is."

"What happened? Why did you leave his workshop?"

"I wasn't worthy. The Master is very demanding with his own."

"What do you mean?"

"I didn't pass the tests he put to me. Just that."

"Tests? What kind of tests?"

Mario took a deep breath while he stared at his manacled hands. My lantern allowed him to see the bruises on his wrists.

"They were intelligence tests. For the Master, it isn't enough that his apprentices should know how to mix colors or draw a profile. He demands that their minds be alert—"

"And the tests?" I insisted.

"One day he took me to see several of his paintings and asked me to interpret them. We went to see his *Cenacolo* when he had barely started work on it, and also several of his portraits in the duke's palace. I suppose I performed badly, because a short time later he asked me to leave the *bottega*."

"I understand. And that's why you decided to take your revenge and rob him. Isn't that so?"

"No! Not at all!" He became very agitated. "I'd never steal from the Master! He was like a father to me. He took us everywhere to teach us how to work and he even fed us. When the money wasn't enough, I remember that he'd assemble us in your refectory, the one of the Dominicans in Santa Maria, and he'd seat us around a large table, like the apostles, and would watch us from a distance while we ate—"

"So you witnessed the evolution of the *Cenacolo*—"

"Of course. It's the Master's greatest work. He's been studying for years, in order to complete it."

"Studying from books like the one you stole?"

Mario protested once more.

"I didn't steal anything, Father! It was Signor Oliverio who insisted that I go to the *bottega* and fetch from Master Leonardo's library an old book with blue covers."

"That is stealing."

"No, no, it isn't. The last time I was in the *bottega*, I asked Master Leonardo to let me have it. When I told him what I wanted it for, and that it was to please my new master, he gave me the book, which I later placed in the hands of Signor Oliverio. It was like a gift. For old times' sake. He said he no longer needed it."

"And you tried to sell it to Signor Jacaranda."

"It was Master Leonardo who taught me to ask for gold from those who live by gold. That was all. But Signor Oliverio wouldn't listen to me. He became furious and put a sword in my hands and told me to defend my honor in a duel. Then he locked me up here."

I thought the boy was being honest, certainly more than Jacaranda, a despicable creature, capable of trafficking with monks and adolescents just to obtain something with which to make a fair bagful of ducats. And what if I took Mario into my service? What if I took advantage of the knowledge of this ex-disciple of Leonardo, master of secret codes, and used him to solve my riddle?

I decided to try my luck.

"What do you know about a deck of cards, one of which shows a Franciscan woman with a book on her lap?"

Mario stared at me in surprise.

"Do you know what I'm talking about?" I insisted.

"Signor Oliverio showed me that card before sending me after the Master's book."

"Continue."

"When I went with my request to Master Leonardo, I showed him the card and he burst out laughing. He told me it held a great secret and that unless I were able to decipher it all by myself, he would never discuss it with me. He's always like that. He never discusses anything unless you unravel it first."

"And did he tell you how?"

"The Master trains all his disciples in the art of reading the secrets of all things. He taught us the *Ars Memoriae* of the Greeks, the number codes of the Jews, the letters that outline figures of the Arabs, the occult mathematics of Pythagoras. But I was a slow student and didn't get too much from his teachings."

"Would you work on a problem for me, if I asked you to?"

Mario hesitated for a second and then nodded vigorously.

"It's a problem worthy of your old master," I explained while I rummaged in my pockets for the piece of paper, to help him understand. "It holds the name of a person I'm looking for. Study the text carefully," I said, reaching it over to him. "Do it for me. In thanks for my kindness to you today."

The boy brought it close to my lantern, in order to see it more clearly.

" 'Oculos ejus dinumera' . . . It's in Latin."

"Yes, it is."

"And will you free me if I help?"

"Only after asking one last question, Mario. You told Signor Jacaranda that Master Leonardo had used the book he gave you to shape one of the disciples in the *Cenacolo.*"

"Yes, he did."

"Which disciple was that, Mario?"

"The Apostle Matthew."

"And do you know how he used that book to shape his Matthew?"

"I think so. Matthew was the author of the most popular of all four Gospels, and Leonardo wanted the man who had lent his face to his Matthew to have achieved at least the same dignity as the Apostle."

"What man was that? Plato?"

"No, not Plato." Mario smiled. "It's someone who's alive today. Perhaps you've heard of him. He translated the *Divini Platonis Opera Omnia* and they call him Marsilio Ficino. I once heard the Master say that when the moment came for painting him in one of his works, that would be the awaited sign."

"Sign? What sign?"

Mario waited a moment before answering.

"It's been a while since I've spoken with the Master, Father. But if you keep your promise and set me free, I'll find out for you. I swear. As well as solving the riddle you gave me. I won't fail you."

"You must know that you're giving your word to an inquisitor."

"And I'll keep it. Give me my freedom and I'll be faithful."

What could I risk? That very same afternoon, just before nones, Mario and I left the Jacaranda Palazzo together, watched by the wary eyes of Maria. On the street, the dark-haired boy with the scar on his face kissed my hand, rubbed his freed wrists and ran off toward the center of the city. Curiously, I never asked myself if I would see him again. I hardly cared. I already knew more about the *Cenacolo* than most of the other monks whose house I was sharing.

32

Early on the morning of Thursday the nineteenth of January, Brother Matteo Bandello, the Father Prior's adolescent nephew, burst into the refectory of Santa Maria. His eyes had a startled, frightened look, and he could barely breathe. He needed to talk to his uncle, and seeing him there, standing by Leonardo's mysterious mural, made him feel both comforted and uneasy. If what they had told him at the Piazza Mercanti was true, then to stay here, watching the progress of this diabolical machinery, might lead them all to their graves.

Matteo approached cautiously, trying not to interrupt the conversation between the Father Prior and his inseparable secretary, Brother Benedetto.

"Tell me, Father Prior," he heard, "when Master Leonardo painted the portraits of Saint Simon and Saint Judas Thaddeus, did you notice anything strange in his behavior?"

"Strange? What do you mean by strange?"

"Come, Father! You know exactly what I mean! Did you see him consult any note or sketch to give these disciples their characteristic features? Or maybe you can recall if someone visited him at the time, someone from whom he might have received instructions about how to complete these portraits?"

"That's an odd question, Brother Benedetto. I fail to see what you're trying to get at."

"Well . . ." The one-eyed monk cleared his throat. "You asked me to find out as much as I could about the riddle Fathers Alessandro and Agostino had brought to us. The truth is that, lacking any clues, I spent my time trying to find out what it was that they did on the days previous to the librarian's death."

Matteo trembled: they were discussing the very subject that had brought him here.

"And?" asked his uncle, unaware of his nephew's terrified presence.

"Father Agostino spent all of his free time here, thanks to the key you gave him. Which was normal."

"And Father Alessandro?"

"This is what's so strange, Father Prior. The sexton surprised him several times speaking with Marco d'Oggiono and Andrea Salaino, Leonardo's favorite disciples. They'd meet in the Cloister of the Dead and converse for hours. Those who saw them there say that they were talking about the Tuscan's deep concern over Saint Simon's portrait."

"And this astonished you?" growled his uncle, frowning, as Matteo had seen him do so many times. "Master Leonardo is a stickler for details, for the slightest minor point, the tiniest question. You should know that. I don't know any other artist who revises his work as many times as he does."

"It's as you say, Father Prior. And yet, at the time,

Father Alessandro obeyed Leonardo's whims with more determination than ever before. He sought out books and engravings that might be of use to him. He worked all hours at the library. He even went up to the duke's castle to supervise the transport of a very heavy box of which I've not been able to discover anything at all."

The Father Prior shrugged.

"Maybe it's not as strange as it seems, Brother Benedetto. Didn't Father Alessandro sit for him? Didn't he choose him among many others to lend a face to Judas? Of course, they'd have become friends, and of course Leonardo would have asked for his help."

"So you think it was by chance? Father Agostino has spoken to you of his suspicions, hasn't he?"

"Father Agostino, Father Agostino!" the Father Prior muttered. "That man is keeping something from us. I can see it in his face every time we talk!"

Matteo hesitated as to whether to interrupt them or not, and the more he listened to them discuss the *Cenacolo* and its secrets, the more impatient he grew. He knew something vital about Leonardo's mural!

"But he believes that Leonardo may have had a hand in Father Alessandro's murder, isn't that right?"

"You're mistaken. That's what Oliverio Jacaranda believes, and he's an old enemy of Leonardo's. The Tuscan is an extravagant man, of unusual tastes, and the fact that we don't see him often at Mass or that he says he's locked a secret inside this mural doesn't make him a murderer."

"Well," Brother Benedetto admitted, "that's true enough. It makes him a heretic. Who but a man of his colossal vanity would paint himself present at the Last Supper? And especially as Judas Thaddeus!"

"That is an interesting point. He paints himself as Saint Jude, the 'good' Judas, and Father Alessandro as the 'bad' one."

"Respectfully, Father Prior: have you noticed in what pose he's painted himself in the mural?"

"Of course," the Father Prior answered, searching for the figure among those depicted on the wall. "He's turning his back on Our Lord."

"Exactly! Leonardo—or Thaddeus, if you like—is talking to Saint Simon instead of paying attention to Christ's announcement of the betrayal. And why? Why is Simon more important than Our Lord to Leonardo? And taking this further: if we know that each apostle represents someone special for Leonardo, then who in fact is this Simon?"

"I don't see where all this is leading."

"Let me explain," answered Benedetto. "If the people in *The Last Supper* are not who they seem, and Master Leonardo shows more esteem for Saint Simon than for the Messiah, then this Simon has to be someone of great importance to him. And Father Alessandro knew this."

"Saint Simon . . . Saint Simon the Cananaean . . ."

The Father Prior rubbed his forehead, trying to fit into the picture the piece Brother Benedetto had offered him. Matteo, still trying to keep silent, was growing impatient. His message, he knew, was urgent.

"Since you insist, Brother Benedetto, I do remember that something odd happened as Leonardo was completing that section of the *Cenacolo*," the Father Prior said at last, still unaware of his nephew's presence.

"Tell me."

Brother Benedetto's single eye lit up.

"It was something quite peculiar. For the past three years, Leonardo had been interviewing candidates to sit for his apostles. We all were examined, remember? Then he summoned the duke's guards, the gardeners, the goldsmiths, the pages. He drew something from each one: a gesture, a profile, the outline of a finger or an arm. But when it came time to paint the right-hand corner, Leonardo interrupted his interviews and stopped seeking inspiration in models of flesh and blood."

Brother Benedetto cocked his head inquisitively.

"What I'm trying to tell you, Brother Benedetto, is that in order to paint Saint Simon, Master Leonardo didn't make use of any living subject."

"He made it up, then?"

"No. He used a bust. A sculpted bust that he ordered to be brought over from the duke's castle."

"There you have it! Father Alessandro's box!"

"I remember perfectly the summer day on which they brought that marble bust to the monastery," the Father Prior proceeded, unperturbed. "The sun was shining fiercely and the two-horse cart had to make an extraordinary effort to bring the box up the hill. I couldn't understand why all the trouble. But as they were unloading it, Donna Beatrice arrived."

"Donna Beatrice?"

"Yes. She looked radiant, her cheeks glowing in the heat. She was wearing one of those elaborate headdresses of which she was so fond. She was accompanied by the duke's guards, as usual, but she broke away from them to speak to the workmen who were handling the bust. And then, all of a sudden, she lost her temper. She started shouting at the poor men."

"You mean she shouted orders at them?"

"More than that, Brother Benedetto. She lost all composure. She railed at them. She bombarded them with profanities and threatened to hang them if they as much as made a scratch on the bust of her philosopher."

"Her . . . philosopher? But wasn't it a bust of Saint Simon?"

"You asked me if I remembered something odd. Well, this is the oddest thing I remember."

"Forgive me, Father Prior. Pray continue."

"Leonardo set up the bust close to the refectory entrance, on a heap of bags of earth. It was a very old bust, an antique. He moved it around from time to time to see how the various lights of day affected it. And once he'd learned its features by heart, he drew them on the wall. His technique was prodigious."

"And where had he found that bust?"

"That's what's so curious about it. Donna Beatrice had ordered it from Florence at the Master's request."

Matteo was bursting to speak, but still he did not dare interrupt the conversation.

"Was Donna Beatrice always as willing to please the Master?" asked Brother Benedetto.

"Certainly. Leonardo was her favorite artist."

"And do you know why Leonardo was interested in a Saint Simon from Florence?"

"I too thought it strange. To send for a Saint John the Baptist from Florence would have made sense, since he's the city's patron. But a Saint Simon—"

"It's not Simon, Uncle! It's not Simon!"

Matteo, red in the face, had shouted out at the two men. He knew that he should not have interrupted, but he could not hold himself back any longer.

"Matteo!" The Father Prior was astonished. All of a sudden, his twelve-year-old nephew stood there in front of him, eyes wide open and tears streaming down his face. "What's happened to you?"

"I know who that apostle is, Uncle, I know! But we must abandon this place at once!" Matteo tried to hide the trembling that shook his entire body. Then he fell senseless to the floor.

33

The Father Prior and his assistant spent a long moment trying to restore the boy. Matteo opened his eyes nervously. He tried to speak, but his body shivered with fear and cold. All he wanted was to leave the refectory as soon as possible. "It's the work of Satan," he sobbed, to the great astonishment of both men. Since it was impossible to calm him down, they agreed to his demand and sought refuge in the library. In the warmth of the room, the boy slowly regained his composure.

At first he would not speak. He clung to his uncle's arm and shook his head every time they addressed him. He did not seem to have any wounds or blows; in spite of the dirt and mud on his clothes, he did not seem to have been hurt. Why then was he afraid? Brother Benedetto went down to the kitchen to get him some warm milk and a piece of Siena almond paste that he kept for special occasions. His stomach full and his body warm again, Matteo broke his silence.

The story he told left them amazed.

As was his wont, Matteo had gone that morning to the Piazza Mercanti to buy some food for the monastery's pantry. Since Thursdays were the best days to purchase grain and vegetables, the boy took a few coins from

Brother Guglielmo's purse and went off to fulfill his task as quickly as possible. Outside the Palazzo della Ragione, that solemn three-story stone and brick building above the piazza, he ran into a large group of people who seemed to be in a sort of trance. They were listening without blinking an eye to a speaker who had set himself up on a platform just under the portico of the palace. At first, he paid little attention to the scene. And yet, as he was about to walk away, something seemed to draw him back. Matteo felt he knew the preacher.

"Here, in this very same place, a true believer gave up his life for God's sake! A good man, who sacrificed himself for you and for his faith! Like Jesus Christ Himself! And what for? For nothing! You are not at all moved by his memory! Can't you see that more and more we're becoming like the beasts in the field! Can't you see that with your cursed passivity you're turning your back on God?"

The Father Prior and his assistant listened in astonishment. The portico Matteo was describing was the same one under which Father Alessandro had been found hanged. Sipping his milk, the boy continued with his story. When he came to the identity of the preacher, their astonishment increased even further: the man who accused the passers-by of having lost their souls for not having recognized God's envoy was, apparently, Brother Giberto. The Germanic sexton with his red hair, the keeper of Santa Maria's gates, had seemingly abandoned his functions that very morning and set himself up to preach in the same place where the librarian had met his end. But why?

However, the strangest part of the story was yet to come.

"You'll all be condemned unless you renounce the Church of Satan and return to the true religion!" the sexton had howled as if possessed. "Eat nothing that proceeds from copulation! Reject the flesh of animals! Abominate eggs and milk! Keep away from false sacraments! Do not take communion from nor be christened by false hands! Disobey Rome and revise your faith, if you wish to be saved!"

Brother Benedetto shook his head. "Brother Giberto said these things?"

Edged on by the Father Prior, Matteo, a little calmer, continued. When the sexton had seen him among the people below, he had jumped down from his improvised pulpit and, grabbing him by the scruff of the neck, had held him up to the crowd.

"Do you see this wretch?" he had said, shaking him as if he were a sack of stones. "He's the nephew of the Prior of Santa Maria delle Grazie. If now, when he's still a child, no one teaches him the true faith, what will become of him? I'll tell you what!" he had shouted. "He'll become a servant of Satan, just like his uncle! A damned renegade from God! And he'll drag hundreds of fools like you to eternal damnation!"

The Father Prior's face became creased with angry lines.

"He said that? Are you certain, my boy?"

Matteo nodded.

"And then he stripped me naked."

"He stripped you?"

"And lifted me up in the air for everyone to see."

"But why, Matteo? Why?"

The boy's eyes filled with tears as he recalled the scene.

"I don't know, Uncle; I don't know. I—I only heard him tell the people not to believe that a child is pure just because he hasn't lost his innocence. That we all come into the world to expiate our sins and that, if we don't accomplish it in this life, we'll return to that vale of tears, to a life worse than the first."

"Reincarnation is not a Christian doctrine!" Brother Benedetto protested.

"But it's a Cathar belief," the Father Prior interrupted. "Let him continue."

Matteo dried his eyes and carried on.

"Then—then he said that, even though the monks of this monastery worship in the Church of Satan and follow a Pope who venerates ancient gods, he promised it would not be long before this house would become a beacon that would guide the world to its salvation."

Brother Benedetto grimaced. "And did he say why?"

"Don't hurry him, Brother."

The adolescent grabbed hold of his uncle once again.

"It isn't true, is it?" he whimpered. "We're not the Church of Satan, are we?"

"Of course not, Matteo." The Father Prior patted him on the head.

"It's that—Brother Giberto got very angry when I told him it wasn't true. He slapped me in the face and shouted that only when we've been hounded out of the *Cenacolo*'s presence and the painting is open to contemplation by the entire world, will the true Church shine again."

A growing feeling of rage filled the Father Prior.

"How dare he slap you!"

Matteo seemed not to hear and continued his story.

"Brother Giberto said that the more we studied the *Cenacolo*, the closer we'd be to his Church. That Master Leonardo's mural contained the secret of eternal salvation. That this was the reason why he and Father Alessandro accepted being portrayed next to Christ."

"He said that?"

"Yes." He sniffled. "Painted on that wall they had already earned their place in Heaven."

The boy looked up inquisitively at the stern faces of his elders.

It was Brother Benedetto who explained: not only had the father librarian sat for Judas but other brothers as well had served as models for the apostles. Brother Giberto was Philip; and Bartholomew, the two Jameses and Andrew all had features lent by the monks of Santa Maria. Even Benedetto himself had allowed himself to be portrayed as Thomas. "I'm shown from the side, so that the eye I lost is not apparent," he explained.

Brother Benedetto patted the boy in a kindly gesture.

"You're a brave young man," he said. "You did well in urging us to leave that place. Evil can cause us to lose our wits, as the serpent did with Eve."

Suddenly, Brother Benedetto asked Matteo a question that surprised even the Father Prior.

"A while ago you said that you knew who the model for the Apostle Simon really was. Did you hear the sexton say so?"

The boy looked away toward the empty desks of the *scriptorium* and nodded.

"While he had me there, hanging naked for everyone to see, he told the story of a man who had lived before Christ and who had preached the immortality of the soul."

"Is that so?"

"He said that this man had studied with the ancient wise men of the world. He also said that he preached things concerning fasting and prayer and cold."

"What exactly did he say?"

"That these three things help us leave the body behind, since in the body reside all the sins and all the weaknesses, and then we can identify only with our soul. And he also said that, in the *Cenacolo*, all dressed in white, that man keeps offering his teaching to us."

"Only one of the thirteen is dressed all in white in the mural," observed the Father Prior. "And that is Simon."

"And did he give a name to that great man?" Brother Benedetto insisted.

"Yes. He called him Plato."

Benedetto leaped up in excitement. "Of course! Donna Beatrice's philosopher! The bust she ordered to be brought from Florence was of him!"

The Father Prior scratched his head.

"And why would Leonardo want to portray himself attending to Plato instead of to Our Lord?"

"What! Don't you understand, Father Prior? It's all so clear! Leonardo is telling us, in his mural, the source of his knowledge. Leonardo, like Brother Giberto and the late Father Alessandro, is a Cathar. You said it before. And you were right. Plato, like the Cathars later on, defended the thesis that true human knowledge is obtained directly from the spiritual world, without mediators, without the Church, without Masses. He called this knowledge *gnosis*, which is the worst of all possible heresies."

"How can you be so sure? What you're saying will not be enough to accuse him of heresy."

"Won't it? Don't you see that Leonardo always dresses in white, like Simon in the *Cenacolo*? Don't you know that he refuses to eat meat and that he practices celibacy? Have you ever known him to have had a woman?"

"We too wear white habits and we fast, Brother Benedetto. Also, it is said that Leonardo fancies men, which would make him not as celibate as you assert," the Father Prior added, while Matteo looked at him, somewhat bewildered.

"It is said!—And who says so, Father Prior? Those are nothing but rumors. Leonardo is a solitary soul. He steers away from the idea of forming a couple as if it were the plague. I am willing to wager that he's as celibate as the *parfaits* of the Cathar heresy! Everything fits!"

The Father Prior looked distraught.

"Let us suppose you are right. What then should we do?"

"First of all," Brother Benedetto continued, "we must convince Father Agostino that Leonardo is a heretic. He is the inquisitor, and he's here by God's grace. No doubt he'll know more about the Cathars than we do."

"And then?"

"We must arrest Brother Giberto and interrogate him, of course," was the answer.

"That will not be possible . . ."

Matteo whispered these words as if fearing to interrupt. He was feeling comforted and more at peace, but he had not finished telling what he had seen in the Piazza Mercanti.

"What did you say?"

"I said that you won't be able to arrest him."

"And why not, Matteo?"

"Because . . . ," he said haltingly. "Because after finishing the sermon, Brother Giberto set fire to his habit and burned to death before everyone's eyes."

"My God!" Brother Benedetto covered his mouth in horror. "You see, Father Prior? There's no doubt about it. The sexton preferred submitting to the *endura* than to our judgment—"

"The *endura*?"

Matteo's question was left to float off in the rarefied atmosphere of the library while Brother Benedetto begged leave to retire and meditate on the problem, and having been granted it, went out of the room in a hurry. That very morning, overwhelmed by Matteo's revelations, he came to tell me that in Santa Maria delle Grazie there were at least two *bonshommes*, the name the ancient Cathars gave themselves. As an inquisitor, he thought I should know about it.

But Brother Benedetto insisted on a second point that, he felt, concerned me more deeply. He had identified the sitter for the apostle with whom Leonardo was conversing in *The Last Supper*; he knew the name of the man in the white robe who distracts the attention of at least two of Christ's disciples: the philosopher Plato.

His revelation provided an answer to a question left unresolved since my meeting with Oliverio Jacaranda. Now, the presence of the philosopher made it clear why Leonardo had in his library the complete works of Plato, a volume that was now collecting dust in a corner of Jacaranda's palazzo, without anyone paying it the attention it deserved.

The circle was closing in.

34

Three days later, in Rome, an officer of the Papal Guard firmly pointed the way for the Dominican Master General. Father Torriani, whom the guards knew full well, thought the security measures extreme. But their orders had been strict: three cardinals had died of a stomach ailment during the past six months, and the Holy Father, whom many held responsible for these sudden deaths, had ordered the pretense of an investigation which included the rigorous control of all entrances leading to the Papal Palace.

The atmosphere was vitiated. Rome had reason enough to tremble when Alexander VI named as cardinal one of the notables of the city. Everyone knew that if His Holiness coveted someone's possessions, all he had to do was make him cardinal first and do away with him discreetly afterward. The law was on his side: the Pope was the sole legitimate heir of all property in his realm. And in the case of His Eminence Cardinal Michieli, the very rich patriarch of Venice whose body was now growing cold in the pontifical morgue, the law had been fulfilled with absolute precision.

Father Torriani submitted without protest to the new

regulations granting access to the Borgia chambers. After a few minutes, leaving behind him the golden door of the Chapel of the Holy Sacrament, he saw them clearly: they were in the third room, eyes glued to the ceiling and a strange look of triumph on their faces. There, close to the windows of the eastern wing, protected from the rigors of the Roman winter, were Annio de Viterbo and His Holiness engaged in an animated discussion beneath freshly painted frescoes that still emanated the odor of resin and varnish.

Alexander VI, his round face shaven, his auburn hair turning white, tried to conceal his paunch under a wine-colored cassock that enveloped him from head to foot. In comparison, Annio—or Nanni, as he was known— looked like a slim weasel, his pointed nose spouting a brush of straight black hairs and his long, bony hands, like those of a scarecrow, making grand gestures toward the painted ceiling.

Nanni's fiery words thundered through the room.

"Art is the most essential of your weapons, Holy Father! Have it always at your service and you'll dominate all of Christendom! Lose it, and your entire pastoral mission will fall to pieces."

Torriani, with rising bitterness in his throat, saw His Holiness assent without a word. He had heard this speech many times. This idea had traveled far and wide, invading Rome, and along with it, the flower of the Florentine arts. The Pope himself had snatched away from Lorenzo de' Medici a whole army of artists, merely to satisfy the secret desires of Nanni. And, at the same time, Torriani had watched in agony the unstoppable rise of sculptors and painters, privileged always to the detriment of cardinals and priests. Upset, and jealous of the influence that this pernicious monk from Viterbo had on His Holiness, Father Torriani pretended not to notice them and addressed himself to the Head of the Guards, instructing him to announce his arrival. The Master General of the Dominican Order was here, obeying the summons of His Holiness.

The Pope smiled.

"We're delighted to see you at last, dear Gioacchino!" he exclaimed, offering his ring to be kissed. "You arrive at an opportune time. Just a moment ago, Nanni and I were discussing the matter that weighs so heavily on your mind."

The Dominican raised his eyes from the pontifical ring.

"What—what matter is that, Your Holiness?"

"Come, come, Father Torriani! No need to be discreet with us! We know practically everything, even that you've sent a spy to Milan in our name, to verify certain rumors concerning a heresy that is gathering strength in Ludovico's court."

"I—" The old man hesitated. "I've come to inform you of what our envoy has discovered."

"We're delighted!" His Holiness laughed. "We're anxious to hear."

Annio de Viterbo and the Holy Father abandoned the contemplation of the frescoes and sat down in a pair of leather armchairs that two servants set out for them. Torriani, too nervous to relax, preferred to remain standing. He carried a folder under his arm with the long letter that I myself had written concerning the discovery of a Cathar infestation in the heart of Milan.

"For the past several months," Torriani began to explain, still under the shock of my revelations, "we have been receiving information suggesting that the Duke of Milan was employing the celebrated Florentine artist Leonardo da Vinci to divulge heretical ideas in a magnificent painting he's completing on the subject of the Last Supper."

"Leonardo, you say?"

The Pope looked toward Nanni, awaiting his learned comment.

"Leonardo, Your Holiness. Doesn't Your Holiness remember him?"

"Vaguely."

"Of course," said the Weasel soothingly. "His name was not on the list of artists recommended to Your Holiness by the House of Medici, to work in Rome during the cardinalship of Your Holiness. He is known to be a proud, irascible man, not well disposed toward Our Holy Mother the Church. The Medici knew this and wisely avoided recommending him to Your Holiness."

The Pope sighed.

"Another problematic soul."

"No doubt, Your Holiness. Leonardo felt snubbed for not having been recommended, and so, in 1482, left Florence, turned his back on the Medici and settled in Milan to work there as inventor, cook and, if possible, not at all as an artist."

"In Milan? And why in the world did they welcome a man like that?" The Pope's tone turned cynical as he continued. "Aha! I understand. That is why you say that the duke is unfaithful to me, Nanni—"

"Your Holiness must ask that question to our Dominican Father," Nanni answered dryly. "It seems that he's brought proofs of what he says."

Torriani protested.

"Not proofs, only suggestions for the time being, Holy Father. Leonardo, guided and protected by the duke, has been working on a painting of colossal proportions and a Christian theme, but full of irregularities that deeply worry the Father Prior of Santa Maria delle Grazie."

"Irregularities?"

"Yes, Your Holiness. In *The Last Supper*."

"And what might be irregular in a work like that?"

"I'll explain, Your Holiness, if I may. We know that the Twelve Apostles represented in the mural are not what they seem, but portraits of pagan characters, or characters of questionable faith, whose disposition in the piece intends to transmit teachings that are not truly Christian."

The Pope and Nanni exchanged glances. Then, when the latter demanded more details, Torriani opened his folder.

"We have just received the first report from our envoy in Milan," he said, brandishing my letter. "He is a scholar from Bethany, an expert in ciphers and secret codes, who is now scrutinizing both the painting and Master Leonardo himself. He's examined one by one the portraits in *The Last Supper* and has looked for relationships between them. Our expert has tried almost everything: from matching each apostle with a sign of the zodiac to looking for correspondences between the position of the hands and the notes on a musical scale. His conclusions will not be long in reaching us, and what today are mere indications, tomorrow may be proofs."

Nanni became impatient.

"But has he discovered anything concrete or hasn't he?"

"Of course, Father Annio. The true identity of three of the apostles has been uncovered beyond doubt. We know that the face of Judas Iscariot, for instance, corresponds to that of a certain Father Alessandro Trivulzio, a Dominican who died shortly after Twelfth Night, hanged in the center of Milan—"

"Like Judas himself—" whispered the Pope.

"That is so, Your Holiness. We have not yet established if he took his own life or if he was murdered, but our informant believes that he belonged to a Cathar community infiltrated into the monastery."

"Cathars?"

The Holy Father looked astonished.

"Cathars, Your Holiness. They believe themselves to be the true Church. They employ only the Our Father in prayer and reject both the clergy and the authority of the vicar of Christ as God's only representative on Earth—"

"We are well aware of the Cathars, Father Torriani!" the Pope interrupted angrily. "But we thought that the last ones were burnt at the stake in Carcassonne and Toulouse in 1325. Did not the Bishop of Pamiers put an end to the lot?"

Torriani knew the story well. Not all Cathars died then. After the victory of the crusade against the

Cathars of southern France and the fall of Montségur in 1244, the heretic families fled to Aragon, Lombardy and the Germanic countries. Those who crossed the Alps settled in the neighborhood of Milan where the more temperate political forces, such as those of the Visconti, allowed them to live in peace. Their heterodox ideas, however, fell slowly into disuse and ended up disappearing along with their tenets and their rituals.

"This may be a serious situation, Your Holiness," Torriani continued sternly. "Father Alessandro Trivulzio wasn't the only one we suspected of practicing Cathar rites in our Milanese monastery. Three days ago, another friar declared himself openly a member of the heresy and then took his own life."

"*Endura?*"

"Exactly."

"In the name of all that's holy!" cried Nanni. "*Endura* was one of the most extreme of all Cathar practices. It's been two hundred years since someone has had recourse to it."

Nanni cast a surreptitious glance at the Pope, who seemed not to have grasped the meaning of the term. Diplomatically, Nanni explained.

"In its 'passive' version," he said, "*endura* consisted of the solemn oath of not ingesting anything, whether food or otherwise, that might contaminate the body of a Cathar aspiring to perfection. If he died in a state of purity, the deluded fool believed that his soul would be saved and would become one with God. But there was also an 'active' version—suicide by fire—which took place only during the siege of Montségur. The inhabitants of that last Cathar bastion preferred to throw themselves into a huge blazing pyre rather than fall into the hands of the papal troops."

"The friar I mentioned died by setting fire to himself, Father."

"I'm at pains to believe that someone would have resurrected the old formula, Father Torriani," Nanni said dubiously. "I imagine you have other facts to justify your alarm."

"Unfortunately, I do. We have reason to think that proofs of the existence of a full-fledged Cathar community in Milan are encrypted in *The Last Supper,* on which Leonardo is now still engaged. He has portrayed himself conversing with an apostle who is really the philosopher Plato, who, as you know, was the ancient master of these damned heretics."

The Weasel jumped from his chair.

"Plato? Are you sure of what you're saying?"

"Entirely. The worst, Father Annio, is that the link is not exempt of a perverted logic. As you know, Leonardo studied in Florence under the guidance of Andrea del Verrocchio and in close contact with the Academy that Cosimo placed under the direction of a certain Marsilio Ficino. And, as you also know, that Academy was founded in imitation of that of Plato in Athens."

"Well?" The Pope's assistant made a gesture of disdain, as if wary of so much erudition.

"Our conclusion cannot be more obvious, Father. If the Cathars drew from Plato many of their more injurious doctrines, and if the Academy in Florence continues certain Cathar practices such as not eating meat, what then forbids us from concluding that Leonardo is using his work to transmit doctrines contrary to the faith of Rome?"

"What do you want from us then? That we excommunicate him?"

"Not yet. We need to prove beyond all doubt that Leonardo has introduced these ideas in his mural. Our envoy in Milan is working hard to gather this evidence. After that, we shall act."

"But, Father Torriani," Nanni interrupted. "Many artists such as Botticelli and Pinturicchio were formed at the Academy and are nevertheless excellent Christians."

"They only appear to be, Father Annio. You should be wary of them."

"Dominicans are always too suspicious! Look around you. Pinturicchio has painted those marvelous frescoes for His Holiness," he said, pointing to the ceiling. "Do you see in them even the inkling of a heresy? Come now. Do you see one?"

Father Torriani knew the frescoes well. Bethany had opened a secret file on them, a file that never grew as much as had been expected.

"Do not upset yourself, Father Annio. Above all because, in spite of yourself, you're agreeing with me. Indeed, do look at that work by Pinturicchio. What do you see? Pagan gods, nymphs, exotic beasts, scenes you will never find in the Bible. Only a follower of Plato, imbued in the old pagan doctrines, would think of painting something like it."

"It's the story of Isis and Osiris!" the Weasel objected, on the verge of losing his temper. "Osiris, if you don't know it, resurrected from among the dead just like Our Lord. And his memory, though in a pagan guise, renews our hope in the salvation of the flesh. Osiris appears here in the shape of an ox as our own Holy Father is represented by an ox. Have you never seen the Borgia coat of arms? Isn't it obvious, the relationship between this mythological figure, a symbol of courage and strength, and the beast that appears on the shield of His Holiness? Symbols are not heresies, Father Torriani!"

As the Master General was about to answer, the smooth but tired voice of the Pope intervened.

"What we don't understand," he said, dragging the words as if intensely bored by the whole discussion, "is where you see the duke's sinful conduct in all this business."

"That's only because you haven't examined with close attention the work of Leonardo, Your Holiness!" Father Torriani answered excitedly. "The Duke of Milan is paying for it in its entirety, and he protects Leonardo from the criticism of our brethren. The Father Prior of Santa Maria has spent months attempting to divert the course of the painting toward a more pious aesthetic, but with no success. Ludovico il Moro has allowed Leonardo to portray himself with his back turned toward Christ and engaged in a conversation with Plato."

"Yes, yes . . ." The Pope stifled a yawn. "And you've also mentioned Ficino."

Father Torriani nodded.

"Is that not the man you've spoken of a number of times, my dear Nanni?"

"Indeed it is, Holy Father." The assistant bowed his

head with an obsequious smile. "Ficino is an extraordinary character. Quite unique. I doubt very much that he's a heretic such as Father Torriani has portrayed for us. He's now in his midseventies and the canon of the Florence Cathedral. His bright spirit would enchant you."

"Bright spirit?" The Pope coughed discreetly. "Not another Savonarola, is he? Are they not both canons in the same church?"

The Pope winked at Torriani, who had started at the mention of the name of the exalted Dominican who preached the end of the "wealthy Church."

"It is true that they share the same roof, Your Holiness," the Weasel said apologetically, "but they are men of distinctly opposed personalities. Ficino is a scholar who deserves all our respect, a learned man who has translated into Latin innumerable ancient texts, such as the Egyptian treatises that helped Pinturicchio decorate this ceiling."

"Indeed?"

"Before working on your frescoes, Pinturicchio studied the books of Hermes that Ficino had just finished translating from the Greek. In them are the stories that tell of the love between Isis and Osiris—"

"And Leonardo?" the Pope said gruffly. "Has he too read Ficino?"

"And shared his friendship, Holy Father. Pinturicchio was well aware of their relationship. Both were his students in Verrocchio's workshop and both followed his classes on Plato and the immortality of the soul. Is there any idea more profoundly Christian than that?"

Nanni pronounced these last words as a challenge to

Father Torriani. He knew well that most Dominicans followed the teachings of Saint Thomas Aquinas, inspired in turn by Aristotle and much opposed to rescuing Plato from oblivion. The Master General felt that he was at a disadvantage before Father Annio and bowed his head meekly before taking his leave.

"Your Holiness, Reverend Annio," he courteously saluted them. "It is useless to continue to speculate on the sources of inspiration for Leonardo's *Last Supper* in Milan until our investigation is at an end. With your blessing, we'll continue our research and try to determine what exactly is Leonardo's sin against our doctrine."

"If sin there be," commented Nanni.

The Pope returned Father Torriani's salutation and, drawing the sign of the Cross in the air, added:

"A piece of advice before you leave, Father Torriani. From now onward, watch where you tread."

35

I never saw such long faces as those of the brethren at Santa Maria on that Sunday morning. Sometime before matins, the Father Prior had gone through the entire monastery, cell by cell, rousing us from our sleep. He shouted at us to make our ablutions as quickly as possible and to prepare our conscience for what is known in the Church as a "chapter extraordinary."

Of course, no one dared object. The brothers all knew that sooner or later they would be asked to account for the sexton's death. Perhaps that is why they had begun to eye one another suspiciously and, for a stranger such as myself, the situation was untenable. The monks began gathering in small groups according to their places of origin. Those from south of Milan would not speak to those from the north who in turn would not mix with those from the lakes, as if the others had had a hand in the ignominious death of Brother Giberto. Santa Maria was divided. And I still had no solution to offer them.

That morning, as I washed and dressed in the dark, I pondered the gravity of the crisis. Though it was true that every one of the brothers seemed to be muttering against the others, it was also true that they all agreed on one thing: to keep me at a distance from their troubles. Because what terrified them more than anything else was that I, in my capacity as inquisitor, might begin procedures against their community. The rumor that Brother Giberto had died preaching the Cathar gospel filled them with fear though none, of course, dared say so openly. They looked at me accusingly, as if I had forced Father Alessandro to hang himself and Brother Giberto to lose his mind. They seemed to think that I possessed some kind of diabolical powers.

What impressed me most, however, was to see how the Father Prior took advantage of their fears.

After waking us, the Father Prior led us to a large empty table that he himself had set up in a room close to the stables. The room was cold and even more badly lit than the cells, and in that frozen gloom the Father Prior informed us of what was in store for us. From matins to compline, we would examine our sins, perform acts of contrition and publicly confess our misdemeanors. And when the day was over, a group of brothers chosen by himself would go to the Cloister of the Dead and exhume Father Alessandro's body. Not only would his remains be taken from the earth but they would be carried beyond the city walls where they would be exorcised, burnt and cast into the wind. The same would be done with the bones of Brother Giberto.

The Father Prior wanted his monastery clean from heresy before sunset. He, who had believed in the innocence of the father librarian and had even suggested that there was a plot afoot against his life, now knew with certainty that Father Alessandro had lived with his back turned to the True Christ, placing the monastery's moral integrity in serious danger.

I noticed the brother grave digger, Mauro Sforza, cross himself nervously at one end of the table.

We found the Father Prior more stern and taciturn than ever. He had not slept well. The bags under his eyes lent his face a ravaged aspect. I knew that I was partly to blame for his deplorable state. On the previous afternoon, while Master General Torriani and Pope Alexander were meeting in Rome, the Father Prior and this humble servant of God were discussing the implications of having two Cathar heretics infiltrate our community. Milan, I explained to the Father Prior, was under siege by the forces of evil as never before in the past hundred years. All my sources confirmed it. At first, the Father Prior looked doubtful, as if he did not believe that a stranger only recently arrived might understand the problems of his diocese, but as I lay my arguments before him, he gradually changed his mind.

I contended that the strange sequence of deaths that we had endured did not obey simple laws of chance. I explained how they were linked to the murdered pilgrims in the church of San Francesco. Even the duke's police had agreed with me, concluding that those poor unfortunates had died without offering resistance, just like Father Alessandro. Furthermore, the site at which the crimes had taken place was by the main altar, under the painting by Leonardo known as the Maestà. That fact, together with the discovery that the pilgrims had with them nothing but a piece of bread and a handful of painted cards, made me suspicious. All of them carried the same objects, as if these were part of some obscure ritual. Perhaps of some Cathar ceremony, unknown until now.

It was all so strange. Leonardo, as I suggested to the Father Prior, was a singular source of problems. Father Alessandro had died after sitting for him as Judas Iscariot, and I knew that, among the brethren, he was the one closest to Leonardo. And Donna Beatrice, of course: dead after having granted him her protection. How could one ignore the subtle thread linking both occurrences? Was it not evident that Leonardo was surrounded by powerful enemies, as much opposed to his heterodoxy as we were, but capable of taking up arms against him and his friends?

These victims, and the impending threat that there might be more, obliged me to speak to the Father Prior about the Soothsayer. I believe I was right in doing so.

At first he stared at me in disbelief when I explained to him that Rome had already been informed about this spate of misfortunes. In fact, highly placed officials in the service of the Pope had long been receiving communications from a mysterious correspondent who had announced what would happen if the work on the *Cenacolo* was not stopped. The profile of this emissary (I explained) was that of a cunning individual, intelligent, probably a Dominican, who was hiding his identity for fear of the duke's revenge. A man who, no doubt, was acting out of hatred toward Leonardo and whose only obsession seemed to be to lead him to his discredit and ruin. Someone, therefore, whom we needed to track down immediately if we wanted to stop the incessant trickle of deaths and lay our hands on the clear incriminatory proofs against Leonardo that he said he possessed.

"If I'm not mistaken, Father Prior, the passivity of Rome has obliged him to take justice into his own hands."

"And why, Father Agostino? What can this man possibly have against our painter?" asked the Father Prior.

"I thought about it carefully and, believe me, there's only one answer that I find plausible."

The Father Prior looked at me inquisitively, inviting me to proceed.

"My theory is that in the recent past, the Soothsayer was Leonardo's accomplice and even shared his heterodox beliefs. Then, for some obscure reason that we must still determine, this man felt himself disappointed in the painter and made up his mind to betray him. First, he wrote relentless letters to Rome, informing us of Leonardo's crimes against the Catholic faith and of the evil he was hiding inside his *Cenacolo*, but in view of our skepticism, he lost all hope and decided to act."

"I don't understand."

"I can't blame you, Father Prior. I myself don't yet have all the clues. But my theory makes sense if we assume that the Soothsayer was a Cathar, just like Father Alessandro and Brother Giberto. For a time, he too must have thought himself the heir of the true apostles of Christ and, like them, he decided to await patiently the Messiah's Second Coming. That is the dream of every *bonhomme*. They believe that on that day, their 'True Faith' will be confirmed in the eyes of the whole of Christendom. What I believe is that, after a long and fruitless wait, upset by some serious mishap, the Soothsayer lost his senses, reneged on his vows of not committing violence and demanded to be paid back in blood for the time he had lost among the 'pure men.' "

"That is a ghastly accusation, Father Agostino."

"Let us study the facts, Father Prior," I suggested. "The Cathars' sourcebook is the New Testament. When the Soothsayer killed Father Alessandro, he set up the crime so that it would look like suicide. Leonardo realized this at once and, even though he tried to divert the attention of the police, he unwittingly gave me a fundamental clue: Father Alessandro had died in the same manner as Judas Iscariot after betraying Christ."

"And what importance do you attribute to this fact?"

"A great deal of importance, Father Prior. The Cathar universe proceeds along a path of symbols. If the Soothsayer managed to have the community of *bonhommes* believe that they were reenacting the events that led up to the death of Christ, he might convince them that the Second Coming was at hand. Don't you see? The librarian's 'suicide' was announcing to them that the prophecies of old were coming to pass, that Christ would soon walk the Earth again and that His faith would once again reappear from among the shadows."

"The Second Coming of Christ—"

"Indeed. Because of this, Brother Giberto, impressed by the revelation, abandoned his fears and went out to preach the Cathar way, giving up his life unafraid, certain that when His Lord had returned, he'd be raised from among the dead. The Soothsayer was taking his revenge with fiendish cleverness."

"You seem very certain of your theory."

"I am," I agreed. "I've already told you that our informant has a complex personality. He's a brilliant man who has left nothing to chance, not even the place he chose to hang Father Alessandro."

"You mean—?"

"I thought you'd have realized." I smiled somewhat cynically. "When I went to scrutinize the portico of the Palazzo della Ragione and in particular the beam from which our librarian was hanged, I saw a curious bas-relief. It is inscribed to a certain Orlando da Tressano with the words *'Spada e Tutore della fede per aver fatto bruciare come si doveva i Catari.'* That is to say, 'Sword and Master of the Faith for having burnt to death the Cathars as they well deserved.' A curious mockery, don't you think?"

The Father Prior was astonished. The plague of heresy had infected his monastery far beyond what he might have imagined.

"Tell me, Father Agostino," he asked, his voice full of concern. "How far do you suppose that the Soothsayer has gone in deceiving his own comrades?"

"Enough to have convinced those pilgrims murdered in San Francesco to abandon their hiding places in the mountains and travel to the city in search of salvation. They've offered their lives meekly in expectation of the Second Coming. The Soothsayer has managed to force the Cathars to make themselves visible. And, I'm sure, he believes that it's only a question of time before Leonardo too takes a wrong step."

"Then . . ." The Father Prior hesitated. "You think that the Soothsayer is still among us."

"I'm convinced of that. And he remains hidden because he knows it's too late for him to obtain your pardon. Not only has he sinned against the doctrine of the Church but he has also broken the fifth commandment: 'Thou shalt not kill.' "

"How are we to know who he is?"

"Fortunately, he's made a small mistake."

"A mistake?"

"In his early letters, when he was still hopeful that Rome would intervene, he gave us a clue to help us find him."

The Father Prior looked astonished. His quick mind, trained to sift through information and solve problems, hit at once on the solution.

"Of course!" He hit his forehead with his hand. "That is your riddle! The Soothsayer's signature! That's why it was written on the card we found next to the librarian!"

"Father Alessandro attempted to solve the mystery on his own. Rashly, I gave him the text of the riddle, and his own curiosity may have led him to his death."

"In that case, Father Agostino, we already have him. All we need to do is solve the conundrum to know his name."

"Alas, Father Prior, I wish it were that easy."

36

The good prior must have been unable to close an eye all night. Seeing him standing in front of his monks, his eyes red and his face haggard, I guessed that he had spent the night turning in his head the miserable *Oculos ejus dinumera*. I almost felt sorry for having burdened him with this new responsibility. To the obligation of having to unmask those among the brethren who professed heretical beliefs, and determining what kind of subversive message was being concealed in the decoration of his own refectory, I had added that of finding the friar who had been the cause of several deaths while convinced of acting in the name of a just cause.

The monks looked at their prior uneasily. The chapter was about to begin.

"Brothers," the Father Prior started off in all solemnity, in a stern tone of voice and with both fists on the table. "We have been living between these walls for thirty years now, and never before have we had to face a situation like this one. Our Lord God has put our endurance to the test, making us witnesses to the death of two of our most beloved brothers, while at the same time revealing to us that their souls had been corrupted with the stench of heresy. How do you think He must feel seeing our weakness? How can we pray to Him now, we, who for our part have been blind to their errors and have allowed them to die in sin? The dead men whom we repudiate today ate our bread and drank our wine. Does that not make us accomplices of their faults?"

The Father Prior took a deep breath.

"But Our Lord, dear brothers, has not abandoned us in these terrible times. In His infinite mercy, He has allowed that there come among us one of his wisest doctors."

A whisper ran through the community as the Father Prior pointed at me with his finger.

"That is why he's here. I've asked our eminent Father Agostino Leyre, from the Holy Office in Rome, to help us understand the tortuous ways through which we must pass in these moments of pain."

I rose so that all could see me and gave a slight nod of acknowledgment. In a more conciliatory tone, the Father Prior now continued with his sermon, trying hard not to intimidate the brethren.

"You all lived with Brother Giberto and Father Alessandro. You knew them well. And yet none of you denounced the irregularities in their conduct, nor their fatal allegiance to the Cathar faith. We slept peacefully, in the belief that this doctrine had been extinguished more than fifty years ago, and we were guilty of the sin of pride for believing that never again would we be forced to face it. And we were proven wrong. Evil, my brethren, is hard to dissolve. It profits from our ignorance. It feeds on our blindness. That is why, in order to try and prevent any new onslaughts, I've asked Father Agostino to illuminate for us that most perfidious of all Christian deviations. It's probable that in his words you will recognize manners and customs that you yourselves may have practiced without knowing their origin. Fear not: many of you come from Lombard families whose ancestors may have had some form of commerce with these heretics. My firm purpose is that, before the setting of the sun, before you all leave this room, you forswear all these abominations and you reconcile yourselves with the Church of Rome. Listen carefully to our brother, meditate on his words, repent and ask for confession. I wish to know if our dead brothers were or were not the only ones infected by the Cathar plague, and to take measures accordingly."

The Father Prior then called upon me to speak, gesturing toward the head of the table. No one moved an eyelid. The eldest of the monks, Brothers Luca, Giorgio and Stefano, too old to undertake any active work in the monastery, leaned forward to hear me better. The others followed my progress with palpable fear. I could tell, merely by looking at their eyes.

"Dear brethren, *laudetur Jesus Christus*."

"Amen," they all answered in one voice.

"I am unaware, dear brothers, to what extent you recall the details of the life of Saint Dominic de Guzmán." A murmur spread through the assembly. "No matter. Today provides an excellent occasion for reviving his memory and reviewing his work."

A sigh of relief rose from the table.

"Allow me to tell you a story. In the first months of the year 1200, the first Cathars had settled in most of the

Western Mediterranean. They preached poverty, the return to the customs of the early Christians, and they vaunted the merits of a simple religion that didn't require churches, tithes or privileges for the ministers of the Lord. Their followers rejected the worship of saints and of the Virgin Mary, as if these had been savages or, worse still, Mohammedans. They renounced the sacrament of baptism. And these vermin even preached that the Creator of the world had been not God but Satan. What a perversion of the Christian doctrine! Can you imagine? For them, Jehovah, God the Father according to the Old Testament, was in reality a diabolical spirit who was capable both of expelling Adam and Eve from Paradise and of destroying the armies that threatened Moses' exodus. In his hands, men were but puppets incapable of discerning good from evil. The common people accepted these lies with enthusiasm, recognizing a faith that excused them from sin and that allowed them facilely to believe that all the suffering in the world was created by the Evil One. Anathema! They placed God and the Devil, good and evil, on an equal plane, with identical powers and fields of action!

"The Church tried to correct these miscreants, from the pulpit, but failed. The heresy's increasingly numerous sympathizers realized how uneven the battle was. Many of the common people ended up taking pity on the heretics, considering them to be, for the most part, exemplary neighbors. They argued that the Cathars preached by example, showing themselves to be humble and poor, while the clerics dressed in ornate chasubles and frippery, condemning them from altars decked in costly ornaments. So, instead of banishing the heresy, what the Church succeeded in doing was spreading it far and wide, like a great sickness. Saint Dominic was the only one to see the mistake and decided to descend to the level of these Cathars or 'pure men,' which is what *katharos* means in Greek, in order to preach to them from that very same apostolic poverty they so admired. The Holy Spirit made him strong. It gave him the courage to penetrate the heretic bastions of France, where the Cathars were legion and where he countered their objections one by one. Saint Dominic dismantled their absurd propositions and proclaimed that God alone was the Lord of Creation. But even an effort such as his proved futile. The evil was far too extended."

The Father Prior interrupted at this point. He had studied their history in his years of theological training and knew that the Cathars had won followers not only among the peasants and craftspeople but also among kings and noblemen who recognized in their tenets a perfect recipe for not paying taxes and not conceding privileges to the clergy.

"That's very true," I agreed. "Not to pay the tithes that the Bible prescribed for priests was to scorn the laws of God. Rome could not remain impassive. Our beloved Saint Dominic was so concerned with this straying from the rightful path that he decided to act. He assembled a group of preachers with whom he would evangelize vast territories, such as that of French Languedoc. We, today, are the children of that group and the heirs of its divine mission. However, at Saint Dominic's death, seeing that it had become impossible to fight against evil with words alone, the Pope and the kings faithful to Rome decided to organize a military repression on an immense scale to finish with these devils once and for all. Blood, death, entire towns wiped out with fire and sword, persecution and suffering—for many years that was the lot of God's people. When the papal troops would enter a city in which the heretics had taken root, they killed all men, women and children, making no distinction between Cathars and Christians. When they reached Heaven, the soldiers said, God would distinguish His own."

I lifted my eyes and observed my audience. No one broke the silence. I continued.

"Brothers, that was our first crusade. It seems incredible that it should have taken place barely two hundred years ago and so near to where we are now. In those days we didn't hesitate to raise our swords against our own families. The armies made justice by the sword, broke up the groups of 'pure men,' exterminated many of their leaders and forced hundreds of heretics into exile, far from the lands that once were theirs."

"And so it was that, fleeing the Holy Father's hosts, the last of the Cathars reached Lombardy," the Father Prior added.

"They arrived in these lands much weakened. And even though everything seemed to indicate that they were on the point of extinction, luck was on their side: the political situation favored the heretics' reorganization. Remember that this was the time of war between Guelphs and Ghibellines. The former argued that the Pope was invested with an authority superior to that of any monarch. For them, the Holy Father was the representative of God on Earth and, therefore, had the right to His own army and to great material resources. The Ghibellines, on the other hand, with Captain Matteo Visconti at the head, rejected this notion and proposed instead a separation between the temporal and the divine powers. Rome, they said, should busy itself only with things of the spirit. Everything else was the task of kings. Therefore, it was to nobody's surprise that the Ghibellines welcomed to Lombardy the last of the Cathars. It was yet another way of defying the Pope. The Visconti lent them their support, secretly, and later the Sforza continued the same policy. It is almost certain that Ludovico il Moro pursues these same directives, and that is why today this house, which lies under his protection, has become a sanctuary for this vermin."

Nicolo di Piadena stood up and begged leave to speak.

"Father Agostino, are you accusing our duke of being a Ghibelline?"

"I can't do so officially, Brother," I answered, avoiding his invidious question. "Not without proof. However, if I were to believe that one of you harbors these proofs, I'll not hesitate to set up a Holy Tribunal, and even resort to torment if necessary, in order to obtain them. I'm determined to reach the bottom of this matter at whatever cost and by whatever method."

"And how do you intend to demonstrate that there are 'pure men' in this community, Father Agostino?" Brother Giorgio exclaimed, relying on his fourscore years for protection. "Will you torture all these brothers yourself, one by one?"

"Allow me to explain exactly what I'll do."

I made a gesture to Matteo, the Father Prior's nephew, to bring forth a wicker cage in which I'd placed a barnyard hen that I had requested minutes before the chapter. The startled fowl was cocking its head in all directions.

"As you know, Cathars don't eat meat and refuse to kill any living thing. If you were a *bonhomme* yourself, and I gave you a chicken like this one and asked you to kill it, you'd most certainly refuse."

Brother Giorgio's face flushed when he saw me raise my knife over the bird.

"If one of you refuses to kill it, I'll know who you really are. The Cathars believe that animals are inhabited by human souls who died in sin and who must return to this Earth to purge it. They fear that by sacrificing the animal they'll be taking the life of one of their own kind."

I held the bird firmly on the table and stretched its neck for all to see. Then I handed over the knife to Brother Giuseppe Boltraffio, the monk closest to me. At my command, the blade cut through the chicken's neck, splattering us with blood in the process.

"So you see: Brother Giuseppe is free from suspicion," I said with a smile.

"And is there not a more subtle way of detecting a Cathar?" asked Brother Giorgio, horrified by the spectacle.

"Of course there is, Brother. There are many ways of identifying them, but they are all less conclusive. For example, if you set a crucifix in front of them, they'll refuse to kiss it. They believe that only a satanic church like ours can adore the instrument of torture on which Our Lord was killed. Nor will you see them worship relics, nor lie, nor fear death. Though this, of course, is only characteristic of the *parfaits*."

"The *parfaits?*" Several of the monks repeated the French term inquisitively.

"The 'perfect men,' " I explained. "They are the men who govern the spiritual life of the Cathars. They believe that they follow the apostolic life as none of us can. They refuse all property, because neither Christ nor his disciples had any. They are in charge of initiating all those aspiring to join them, into the *melioramentum*, a genuflexion that must be performed every time the novice meets a *parfait*. They are the only ones entitled to lead an *apparellamentum*, public confessions during which the sins of the heretics are brought to light, are debated and publicly absolved. And, as if all this were not enough, they are the only ones allowed to administer the only sacrament accepted by the Cathars: the *consolamentum*."

"The *consolamentum?*" the group asked once again.

"It served as baptism, communion and extreme unction all in one," I explained. "It was administered by placing a sacred book on the head of the neophyte. But never the Bible. This act was considered by them to be a 'baptism of the spirit' and whoever was worthy of receiving it became a 'true' Christian. One of the 'consoled.' "

"And what has led you to believe that the sexton and the librarian were both members of these 'consoled'?" asked Brother Stefano Petri, the jovial bursar, always proud of having well in hand the material life of the community. "If I may say so, I've never seen them abjure the Holy Cross, nor do I believe that they were baptized by having a book placed on their heads."

Several of the brothers nodded in assent.

"However, Brother Stefano, you must have seen them perform extreme feats of fasting, have you not?"

"We all saw them do that. Fasting lifts the spirit."

"Not in their case. For a Cathar, extreme fasts are one of the ways by which to reach the *consolamentum*. And as far as the Cross is concerned, we must not confuse matters. For a Cathar, to wear a Latin crucifix around the neck with no compunctions, it's enough to file down the ends and make them blunt. And if the crucifix is *patté* or Greek, then they'll tolerate it as well. And I'm sure, Brother Stefano, that you've seen them recite the Our Father with us all. It is in fact the only prayer they'll accept."

"These are only circumstantial proofs, Father Agostino," said Brother Stefano before sitting down again.

"It's possible. I'm willing to admit that Father Alessandro and Brother Giberto were merely sympathizers waiting for their baptism. However, that does not exempt them from sin. I'm not forgetting either that our librarian wholeheartedly collaborated with Leonardo da Vinci in his *Last Supper*. He wished to be portrayed as Judas in the middle of a suspicious work, and I think I know why."

"Tell us," the brethren asked.

"Because, for the Cathars, Judas Iscariot was a pawn

in God's plan. They believe that he acted well, that he betrayed Jesus in order to fulfill the prophecies, so that Our Lord might give His life for our salvation."

"Are you suggesting that Leonardo too is a heretic?"

Brother Nicolò di Piadena's question made Brother Benedetto smile. A moment later, the one-eyed monk left his seat and went out into the courtyard to empty his bladder.

"Judge for yourself, Brother Nicola. Leonardo dresses all in white, eats no meat, would never harm a fly, has had no carnal knowledge as far as we can tell and furthermore, he has omitted the bread of the Eucharist in your *Cenacolo*, placing a dagger in the hand of Saint Peter, the representative of what the Cathars consider to be the Church of Satan. For a Cathar, only a servant of the Evil One would hold a dagger at the Last Supper."

"And yet, Leonardo has depicted the wine," the Father Prior observed.

"Because the Cathars do drink wine! But observe, Father Prior: instead of the Passover lamb that, according to the Gospels, was eaten on that night, Master Leonardo has painted a fish. And do you know why?"

The Father Prior shook his head. I addressed myself to him directly.

"Remember what your nephew heard from the lips of the sexton before his death: that the Cathars don't accept any nourishment that is born from copulation. In their eyes, fish do not copulate; therefore they can be eaten."

A murmur of admiration ran through the room. The monks were following my explanations with rapt attention, astonished at not having detected earlier the heresies depicted on their refectory wall.

"Now, my brothers, I need you to answer my questions, one by one," I said, changing my tone to a more serious one. "Examine your conscience and speak out in front of your brethren: Has any one of you followed, whether by his own will or by that of another, any of the actions that I have described?"

I saw the monks hold their breath.

"Holy Mother Church will be merciful with whoever forswears these practices before leaving the assembly. But after that time, the full weight of the law shall fall upon him."

37

The Soothsayer acted with spectacular precision.

Someone having the misfortune of crossing his path would have concluded that he moved about the monastery like someone familiar with its innermost reaches. Wrapped in a black cape from head to foot, he moved along the empty rows of pews inside the church, turning left toward the chapel of the Madonna delle Grazie to enter the adjacent sacristy. No one intercepted him. The monks were attending the chapter extraordinary, far from the intruder's movements.

Satisfied, the Soothsayer left the chapel through the archway leading to the small priory courtyard, which he swiftly crossed. Once in the Cloister of the Dead he left the refectory and ascended the stairs leading to the library, three steps at a time.

The Soothsayer—man or ghost, angel or demon, it hardly mattered—moved nimbly. After inspecting the *scriptorium* with a professional eye, he walked up to the desk of Father Alessandro. There was no time to lose. He knew that Marco d'Oggiono and Bernardino Luini had just left Leonardo's house across from Santa Maria and would be in the refectory in just a few moments. He was ignorant of why they were coming, nor did he know that, following the Tuscan's wishes, they were bringing with them a certain young woman.

Very carefully, the Soothsayer took off his cape and placed it on the dead librarian's desk. Trying not to make any noise, he felt the tiles on the floor. He tapped them: only two moved ever so slightly. He had found what he was looking for. He bent over to examine them and saw that they were not fixed with mortar, and that their edges were clean and polished, a clear indication that they were handled frequently. He lifted them and recognized, beneath them, the heating vents. He felt satisfied. The Soothsayer knew that this thin layer of masonry ran from wall to wall across the refectory ceiling and that a well-trained ear would be able to hear the slightest word spoken there.

With great precaution, he lay down the full length of his body and placed his ear to the floor, closing his eyes for better concentration.

A minute later, he heard a loud creaking. The bolt of the refectory door was being drawn. Leonardo's guests were about to enter the room of *The Last Supper*.

"What do you think that the Master meant when he said that he was the Omega?"

Elena's question rose to the floor above. The Soothsayer was surprised to hear a woman's voice.

"The first time I heard him speak of it was in the presence of Sister Veronica, the day of her death," Marco d'Oggiono answered. The Soothsayer recognized his voice immediately.

"Were you then with Sister Veronica the day her prophecy came to pass?"

Elena spoke admiringly.

The little countess had spent the night awake, listening to the explanations of Leonardo and to the jokes of his apprentices, preparing herself for her sitting. Leonardo had said that he would agree to portray her as John, the Beloved Disciple, if she could show, with the help of her two companions, that she was capable of understanding the importance of the mural.

Leonardo, seduced by Elena's beauty, had not been able to forget her since coming across her at the Palazzo Vecchio. She was certainly a perfect "John." But he did not want to make any hasty decisions. He had invited her on a couple of occasions, always accompanied by Master Luini, to his celebrated musical evenings, during which troubadours and poets entertained his guests. He wanted to inspect closely the progress of this unforeseen couple.

The young woman felt under a spell. To see herself in a circle that she knew only through her mother was like entering a world of dreams from which she did not want to be woken. Ever since Lucrezia Crivelli had charmed her nights as a girl with stories of princes and troubadours, knightly combats and wizards' gatherings, Elena had longed to be there.

"Sister Veronica? Goodness! That nun would fly into a temper at the slightest provocation," Marco recalled, blowing on his cold hands.

"Truly?"

"Oh, yes. She would always criticize the Master's eccentric tastes and the fact that he was more familiar with the works of the Greek philosophers than with the

Holy Scriptures. The truth is that they didn't discuss art much, and even less the work of the Master, but on the day she died, Sister Veronica asked him about the work in the refectory."

"And what has that to do with the Omega?" asked Elena.

"Let me tell you. That day, Leonardo felt offended. Sister Veronica had accused him of having minimized the importance of Christ in the *Cenacolo*. And the Master lost his temper. He told her that Christ was the only Alpha in the composition."

"He said that? That Christ was the Alpha of the mural?"

"Christ, he said, was the beginning. The center. The axis of the work."

"In fact," Luini observed, trying to make out the figure of Christ in the gloom, "it is true that Christ occupies the dominant position. Moreover, we know that the vanishing point of the whole composition is exactly above His left ear, under His hair. That is where Leonardo placed his compass on the very first day. And from that sacred point he drew the rest."

The Soothsayer was surprised to hear Luini speak. It was the first time he heard the painter's voice, though he knew well that Luini shared Leonardo's heretical subjects in his work, obsessively painting, like his master, scenes from the life of Saint John. John's encounter with Jesus on the flight to Egypt, the baptism in the Jordan, John's head on Salome's silver platter: all these were repeated again and again in painting after painting. All the pilgrims who worshiped Leonardo's *Maestà* knew him well. Wolves, he thought as he listened to Luini speak in Leonardo's refectory, run always in packs.

"Your observation is correct, Master Luini," said Marco, his eyes on their pretty companion, who was beginning to distinguish the outlines of the apostles illuminated by the faint light of dawn. "If you look at His body, with His arms stretched before Him, you can see that He has the shape of an enormous letter A. He's the Alpha that rises in the midst of the chosen twelve. Can you make it out?"

"Of course I can. But what about the Omega?" Elena insisted.

"Well, I think the Master said that because he considers himself the last of Christ's disciples."

"Who? Leonardo?"

"Yes, Elena. Alpha and Omega. The beginning and the end. It makes sense, doesn't it?"

Luini and the little countess shrugged their shoulders. The young painter intuited, like Marco, that the mural hid a profound message of initiation. It was evident that if the Master had allowed them to reach this point in their quest, without giving them the key to read the whole, then he was in some obscure manner putting them to the test. They were standing alone in front of the largest riddle ever designed by Leonardo, and their ability to decipher it held the promise of their access to greater secrets. And, above all, the salvation of their souls.

"Perhaps Marco is right and the whole *Cenacolo* hides a sort of visual alphabet."

At these words, the Soothsayer started.

"A visual alphabet?"

"I know that the Master studied with the Dominicans in Florence the art of memory. His teacher, Verrocchio, practiced it as well and taught it to Leonardo when he was only a child."

"He never mentioned it," said Marco, somewhat disappointed.

"Maybe he didn't consider it essential for your education. After all, it is only a question of mental exercises, designed to retain a great deal of information or place it according to the characteristics of certain buildings or works of art. The information is open to everyone, but it remains invisible to the uninitiated."

"And where do you see that alphabet?" said Marco.

"You've said that the body of Jesus is in the shape of an A, which, for Leonardo, is the Alpha of the composition. If he said that he himself is the Omega, we should look in the portrait of Judas Thaddeus for something resembling an O."

The three glanced at one another and approached the mural in silence. The figure of Thaddeus was easily recognizable, turning his back upon the scene where the action was unfolding. Leaning forward, both his arms crossed in an X, palms lifted toward Heaven, he was dressed in a red tunic, with no clasp. Unfortunately, there was nothing in the figure to allow one to imagine an Omega.

"Alpha and Omega may also be related in some way to Saint John and Mary Magdalene," Luini murmured, trying to mask his disappointment.

"What do you mean?"

"That's easy, Marco. You and I know that the mural is secretly dedicated to Mary Magdalene."

"The knot!" Marco recalled. "Of course! The knot at the end of the table!"

"I think Leonardo has wanted to send us off on a wrong track. For some time now, the Master has been spreading the rumor that the knot is his own way of signing his work. In the Romance tongue, Vinci comes from the Latin word *vinculum*, that is to say, knot or link. However, its hidden meaning can't be all that obvious. Necessarily it must relate to Jesus' favorite companion."

The Soothsayer stirred uncomfortably in his hiding place.

"Not so fast!" Elena complained. "What has this to do with the Alpha and the Omega?"

"It's in the Scriptures. If you read the Gospels, you will see that John the Baptist had a fundamental role to play at the beginning of the Messiah's public life. John baptized Jesus in the river Jordan. John was His starting point, His Alpha, in His mission on Earth. Mary Magdalene, however, belongs to His end. She was present when He emerged from His tomb. And, in her own way, she also baptized Him, anointing Him with scented oil, only a few days before the Last Supper, in the presence of the disciples. Don't you remember Mary of Bethany, in the episode of the washing of Christ's feet? She acted then like a true Omega."

"Magdalene, Omega—"

The explanation did not fully convince the young

girl. John and Thaddeus did not, as far as she could see, have much in common, except that neither of them was looking at Christ. She spent a long moment trying to find an alternative interpretation for the mysterious O, casting her eyes from left to right over the mural, attempting to disentangle the riddle. It would soon be light, and they had to hurry if they wanted to fulfill the test before the monks arrived. If there was something to be "read" in the *Cenacolo*, they had better discover it quickly.

"I think the solutions you propose are too far-fetched," she said at last. "And the Master, from the little I know him, is a great lover of simplicity."

Marco and Luini turned toward the little countess.

"If he has so obviously knotted one of the ends of the cloth, leaving the other smooth, it's because he wishes to draw the viewer's attention to that particular side of the table. There must be something there, in that section where he's portrayed himself, that he wants us to see."

Luini raised a hand toward the knot and caressed it with his fingertips. The cloth was painted with great mastery, and each fold in the fabric lent it an uncanny illusion of reality.

"I believe that Elena is right," he admitted.

"Right? How is she right?"

"Look carefully, Marco. The area around the knot is that in which the light is most intense. Observe here the shadows on the apostles' faces. See? They're stronger, more pronounced than the rest."

Marco's eyes swept across the wall, comparing the

wide range of chiaroscuros in the clothing and faces of the Twelve.

"Perhaps it makes sense," Luini continued, as if he were thinking out loud. "This area appears to be better lit than the rest because, for Leonardo, Plato represents the light of reason. He's the sun shining upon our rationality. And therefore, the most brilliantly lit of the disciples is Saint Simon, with his Greek profile and the only white robes in the scene—"

Suddenly Luini remembered.

"And Matthew, the disciple at Leonardo's elbow, is none other than Marsilio Ficino. Of course!" Luini raised his voice. "Ficino entrusted John's texts to Leonardo before we left Florence. That's the key!"

Elena stared at him, uncomprehending.

"What key?"

"Now I understand. The Cathars initiated novices by placing a secret Gospel of John on their heads. They thought that by doing this, they would transmit by contact the spiritual essence of the work straight to the heart and mind of the candidate. That book of John's contained great revelations about Christ's mission on Earth and showed the path we should take to secure a place in Heaven. Leonardo . . ." Luini paused to take a deep breath. "For that text, Leonardo has substituted a painting that contains all the fundamental symbols. That is why he's sent us here to initiate you, Elena! Because he believes that his painting will invest you with John's mystical secret!"

"And can you initiate me without knowing *exactly* what the Master has inscribed here?"

Elena sounded incredulous.

"Since we have no more clues, we must. In the olden days, the novices never even opened the lost book of John. Many certainly didn't even know how to read. Why then would this mural not perform the same service for us? Furthermore, look at Christ. He's at a height that will allow you to stand beneath Him and receive the mystical imposition from His own hands, one palm protecting your head and the other invoking Heaven above."

The little countess lifted her eyes toward the Alpha. Luini was right. The supper scene was set at a sufficient height to allow someone of normal proportions to stand beneath the tablecloth's rim. It was a perfect place to position oneself to receive the spirit of the work, and yet Elena's pragmatic mind sought a more rational explanation. Leonardo was a practical man, not much inclined to mystical lucubration.

"I think I know how we might read the message of the *Cenacolo*—"

Elena broke off. A sudden intuition had revealed itself to her, shortly after standing under the protection of the Alpha.

"Do you remember the attributes that the Master had you memorize for when the time came to portray one of the Twelve?"

Luini nodded without understanding. The memory of the day when the little countess had snatched the paper away from him was still vivid in his mind. He blushed.

"Can you then tell me what virtue was attributed to Judas Thaddeus?" she asked.

"Thaddeus?"

"Yes, Thaddeus," insisted Elena, while Luini sought for the answer in his memory.

"*Occultation*. He who conceals."

"Exactly." She smiled. "An O, don't you see? There we have our Omega again. And that certainly can't be by chance."

38

"By all that's holy!"

Bernardino Luini's joy resounded within the four walls of the refectory.

"It can't be that easy!"

Delighted with Elena's discovery, Luini began to analyze the arrangement of the Apostles. He stepped back to enjoy a full view and discovered that a few steps from the northern wall was the best place to see them all, from Bartholomew to John and from Thomas to Simon. They were grouped in threes, all with their faces turned toward their master, except the beloved disciples John, Matthew and Thaddeus, all of whom either had their eyes closed or were looking elsewhere.

Luini tore a piece off one of the cartoons that Leonardo had left scattered about the floor and, on the back, with a piece of charcoal, began sketching out the figures. Marco and Elena were following his every move while, up above, the Soothsayer was becoming uneasy at not hearing them make a sound.

"I know now how to read the message of the *Cenacolo*," he finally announced. "All this time we've had it in front of our eyes and we haven't been capable of seeing it."

Beginning with the left end of the mural, Luini reminded them that Bartholomew was *Mirabilis*, "He Who Is Miraculous." Leonardo had portrayed him with curly red hair, according to what Jacobus de Voragine had written in *The Golden Legend*: that he was Syrian and of a fiery nature, as befits men with red hair. Luini wrote M on the piece of paper, beneath the outline. Then he did the same with James the Less, *Venustus*, or "Full of Grace," the apostle often confused with Christ and who, because of his inspired deeds, received that particular epithet. A letter V was added to the list. Now came Andrew, *Temperator*, "He Who Prevents," portrayed with his hands spread in front of him, as is called for by his attribute, who soon became reduced to a simple *T*.

"Do you follow?"

The three young people smiled. It all was beginning to make sense. "M-V-T" seemed like the beginning of a Latin word, since *U* was written V in Latin. But the enthusiasm faded upon discovering that the next group of apostles gave rise to an unpronounceable syllable. Judas Iscariot was *Nefandus*, "The Abominable One" who betrayed Christ. His position, however, was somewhat ambiguous. Even though Judas was the fourth head from the left, Saint Peter's peculiar position, with his dagger held behind the traitor's back, might lead to an error in the counting. In any case, Luini pointed out, the N might still be the correct letter, since Simon Peter was the only one among the Twelve who three times denied Christ, and therefore one could imagine an N for *Negatio*, even though it did not appear in Leonardo's list.

Elena protested. The most logical procedure was to be

guided by the order of the heads and by the attributes that Leonardo had taught them. And nothing else.

Following that order then, the apostle who came next was indeed Peter. Leaning toward the center of the scene, he had been given the epithet *Exosus*, "He Who Hates," as reflected in the white-haired man with the threatening look, about to carry out his revenge with a fierce-looking dagger. Then John, asleep, his head inclined and his hands folded like the ladies in Leonardo's portraits, did honor to his M for *Mysticus*, "He Who Knows the Mystery." "N-E-M" was therefore the disconcerting result of those three.

"Jesus, as we know, is the A," said Elena, as they reached the middle of the painting. "Let's proceed."

Thomas with his lifted finger, as if indicating who among those present would be the first to receive the privilege of eternal life, was inscribed on Luini's paper as L for *Litator*, "He Who Placates the Gods." His attribute led to a brief discussion. According to the Gospel of John, Thomas inserted a finger in Christ's wound to see whether He had indeed risen from the dead. And he also fell on his knees crying, "My Lord and my God!" tempering Christ's possible anger at not having been immediately acknowledged.

"Also," Luini insisted for the sake of his theory, "this is the only portrait in which the corresponding letter is copied in the profile."

"You forget Jesus' Alpha," pointed out the little countess.

"Except that here the letter is not in the body of Thomas but in that finger pointing toward Heaven. See?

The finger, together with the thumb, clearly has the shape of a capital letter *L*."

His two companions agreed. Next, they scrutinized the figure of James the Elder but were incapable of finding any feature that might reproduce the corresponding O of his attribute, *Oboediens*.

"And yet," said Luini, "whoever has studied the apostle's life will conclude that *Oboediens*, 'He Who Obeys,' fits him perfectly."

Indeed. Jacobus de Voragine wrote that James the Elder was John's blood brother and that "both wished to occupy in the Kingdom of Heaven the positions closest to the Lord, one seated to His right and the other to His left." Leonardo, therefore, had re-created in his *Cenacolo* a heavenly table, set in the realm of perfection inhabited by pure souls. In that realm, John and James occupied the places Christ had promised them.

Finally came Philip, the *Sapiens* among the Twelve, or "He Who Loves High Matters," the only one pointing at himself, to the only place where we must seek salvation. With Philip, Luini composed a third mysterious syllable: "L-O-S."

The remaining group of apostles was disentangled with equal swiftness. Matthew, the disciple whose name, according to de Voragine, meant "He Who Is Diligent," promised a speedy end. Luini smiled, remembering that Leonardo had nicknamed him *Navus* because of his promptitude. His secret letter plus the Omega of Thaddeus formed a legible syllable, "N-O," to which Luini added the C of Simon's *Confector*, "He Who Fulfills," resulting in "N-O-C." The ensemble consisted now of four groups of three letters each, with always a vowel in the middle and an enormous A presiding over the scene. It read like a strange and forgotten magical formula.

MUT NEM A LOS NOC

Bartholomew	*Mirabilis*	He Who Is Miraculous
James the Less	*Venustus*	He Who Is Full of Grace
Andrew	*Temperator*	He Who Prevents
Judas Iscariot	*Nefandus*	The Abominable One
Peter	*Exosus*	He Who Hates
John	*Mysticus*	He Who Knows the Mystery
Thomas	*Litator*	He Who Placates the Gods
James the Elder	*Oboediens*	He Who Obeys
Philip	*Sapiens*	He Who Loves High Matters
Matthew	*Navus*	He Who Is Diligent
Judas Thaddeus	*Occultator*	He Who Conceals
Simon	*Confector*	He Who Fulfills

"And now what?" asked Elena. "Does that mean anything to you?"

The two men read over the line once again without finding any meaning to it: just a series of monosyllables that resembled an ancient litany of some sort. But they were not surprised. It was typical of the Master to invent one riddle that led to another riddle. Leonardo amused himself making up this sort of entertainment.

"*Mut, Nem, A, Los, Noc . . .*"

Not far above their heads, the Soothsayer pronounced the formula out loud. He muttered the syllables a number of times and finally, euphoric, he left his hiding place. "What a clever little trick!" he said to himself.

And smiling with satisfaction, he began to think about how to deliver his discovery into the hands of Rome.

39

A few days later, in Rome, Annio de Viterbo was urging on his coachman.

"We must hurry. The clocks will soon strike twelve."

Alexander VI's foremost advisor never left his palazzo on the west bank of the Tiber without his coach and his faithful secretary, Fabio Ponte. It was one of the many privileges that the Weasel had been granted by His Holiness Alexander VI. So much pomp, however, clouded his judgment and made him incapable of remembering that young Fabio, besides being cultured and refined, was also the nephew of Father Torriani. Nor did he realize that it was through Fabio that Bethany would be informed about the activities of one of the most deceitful and treacherous characters in history.

"Twelve!" he repeated. "Are you listening? Twelve o'clock!"

"You have nothing to be concerned about," Fabio answered politely. "We'll be there on time. Your coachman is very fast."

He had never seen the Weasel so nervous. Haste was uncommon in someone of his nature. Since he had settled in the vicinity of the Borgia dwellings by express command of His Holiness, Annio moved through Rome as if the city were his, not owing explanations to anybody. His hours of arrival and departure obeyed no protocol whatsoever; his every move was deemed appropriate. Rumor had it that he owed these advantages to the Pope's desire to embellish his ancient, noble and divine family history with stories that would justify such grandeur. And it was true that Annio had known how to tell them like no other. He had managed to concoct fabulous tales about Alexander: that he was the descendant of the god Osiris who had visited Italy in the dawn of time to teach its inhabitants to plow the land, make beer and trim the trees. He always supported his fabulations with classical texts, and he often would quote long passages of Diodorus Siculus to justify his strange obsession with the mythology of the pharaohs.

Neither Bethany nor the Holy Office was able to stop such fantasies. The Pope adored the charlatan and shared with him a visceral hatred of the splendor of the cultured courts of Florence and Milan, in whose libraries the Weasel saw a serious threat to his fabrications. He knew that Marsilio Ficino's translations of the texts attributed to the great Egyptian god Hermes Trismegistus, also known as Toth, God of Wisdom, undermined most of his stories. These texts made no mention of Osiris's visit to Italy, nor did they link the Apennines to the Alps, nor did they mention the city of Osiricella, near Treviso, as the stopping place for the god.

Until now, Fabio had thought that Ficino's memory was incapable of upsetting Father Annio. But he had obviously been mistaken.

"Have you seen the decorations in the apartments of His Holiness?"

Fabio shook his head. He was concentrating on the tapping of the horses' hoofs on the cobblestones, wondering what the reason was for the Weasel's great hurry.

"I'll show you," he said with enthusiasm. "Today, Fabio, you'll meet the Master responsible for them."

"Indeed?"

"Have I ever lied to you? If you'd seen the paintings I'm talking about, you'd understand how important they are. They depict the god Apis, the sacred ox of the Egyptians, as the prophetic icon of the times we live in. Haven't you noticed that on the papal coat of arms there's also an ox?"

"You mean a bull."

"What's the difference? What matters is the symbol, my dear Fabio! Next to Apis you'll see the goddess Isis. She's as solemn as the Catholic Queen of Spain, and she appears seated on a celestial throne with an open book on her lap, teaching Hermes and Moses law and science. Can you imagine?"

Fabio closed his eyes, as if concentrating on his master's words.

"What these frescoes are saying, dear Fabio, is that Moses received all his wisdom from Egypt, and through him, we Christians have inherited it all. Do you now understand the genius of this art? Do you grasp the sublime lesson that I'm telling you? Our faith, my dear Fabio, proceeds from there, from faraway Egypt. The same as our Holy Father's family. Even the Gospels say that there is where Jesus fled to escape from Herod. Do you realize it? Everything has its source in the Nile!"

"Even the man you're going to see, Master?"

"No, not him. But he knows much about that land. He's obtained many things for me from that paradise of knowledge."

Annio fell silent. To speak of the Egyptian roots of Christianity stirred in him contradictory feelings. On the one hand, it comforted him to know that day after day there were more wise men who, like Leonardo in Milan, knew the secret and imagined works such as the *Maestà*, depicting a plausible encounter between John and Jesus during their flight to the land of the pharaohs. On the other, an imprudent spreading of these truths might endanger the moral stability of the Church and condemn it to lose some of its precious privileges. How would the common folk react when they discovered that Christ was not the only man-god who returned from among the dead? Would they not ask uncomfortable questions when aware of the enormous parallels between His life and that of Osiris? Would they not question the Pope with uncomfortable accusations, branding the Church Fathers as mere copyists of a sacred story that did not belong to them in the first place?

Nanni stirred in his seat.

"You know something, Fabio? All the knowledge locked in those frescoes is nothing compared to that which I expect to receive today."

Fabio lowered his eyes, fearful that his master might discover the eagerness with which he received this information.

"If he gives me what I hope for, then I'll have the key

to everything I've been telling you about. I'll know it all . . ."

Noticing that the coach was slowing down, he fell silent and looked through the curtains. They were outside Rome and close to their destination.

"I believe we're almost there," his assistant said.

"Excellent! Can you see if anyone is waiting for us?"

Fabio stuck his head out of the window and saw the enormous whitewashed façade of the Old Giant, an inn on the outskirts of Rome, famous for being the meeting place of both religious pilgrims and fugitives from justice. A solitary man wrapped in a brown cloak was making signs at them from the door of the establishment.

"There's a man who seems to have recognized your coach, Master," he said.

"That must be him. Oliverio Jacaranda. It's been a long time since we last met."

The young man hesitated. "You know Jacaranda, Master?"

"Oh yes. He's an old friend. There's nothing to worry about."

"Respectfully, Master, this is not a safe place for someone in your position. If you were recognized, you might be robbed or even kidnapped . . ."

Annio smiled, much amused. Fabio did not know how many times he had concluded transactions in this place. Long before his appointment as papal advisor to Alexander VI, the Old Giant had been one of his favorite "offices." The owners knew and respected him well. He had nothing to fear. Within its confines he had

received statues, paintings, ancient gravestones, manuscripts, vestments, perfume, and even complete funeral
costumes in exchange for heavy bags of gold from the
pontifical treasury. Jacaranda was one of his most reliable
providers. The pieces he had bought from him had
helped him ascend more than one rung in his career. So
when the Spaniard had returned to Rome and asked to
see him urgently, it could only mean he surely had something important to offer him.

Annio trembled in anticipation. Had Jacaranda
obtained for him the ancient treasure at last? Had he
brought with him the final piece that he so much longed
to possess?

His fertile imagination carried him away. As Fabio
opened the door of the coach for his master to descend,
Nanni rejoiced to think how close he was to his greatest
triumph. Why else would his faithful procurer have had
him travel all this way?

Jacaranda's appeal had come at a fortunate moment.
The previous afternoon, Nanni had met again with the
head of the Dominicans, the temperamental Torriani, to
hear from his lips the latest news regarding Leonardo's
Last Supper. In private audience with His Holiness, Torriani explained that he had discovered the secret message
hidden in the mural.

"Leonardo," he said, "has concealed among his figures
a phrase, a sort of invocation, written in a strange language that we are now trying to decipher. A letter from
Milan has unveiled the mystery."

The Master General then recited the sentence in the
presence of himself and the Holy Father. Neither under-

stood the meaning. To Nanni's ears, however, it sounded undoubtedly Egyptian.

"*Mut, Nem, A, Los, Noc*," he murmured.

Was not the origin crystal clear? Did it not contain the name of the goddess Mut, wife of the god Ammon and Queen of Thebes? Was it not providential that Oliverio Jacaranda, a true expert in Egyptian hieroglyphs, had arrived almost at the same time as Torriani's revelation? Had not God Himself sent him to help Nanni solve the riddle and earn the Pope's eternal respect?

Yes. Providence, he thought, was certainly on his side.

In front of the Old Giant's stables, Jacaranda kissed Nanni's ring and invited him to step inside. There they would discuss the ancient treasure and the mysterious hieroglyphs.

Led into the interior of the inn, the Weasel sat down in one of the small booths. In the meantime, Fabio thanked the stars for his luck, to be able to witness the conversation that he would later transmit to Bethany.

"My dear Father Annio," said the Spaniard, making himself snug on his seat and helping himself to a generous jug of beer. "I trust I've not alarmed you with this sudden visit."

"On the contrary. You know I always await your visits with great impatience. It's a pity you don't appear more often around here, where you are much esteemed."

"It's more prudent that way."

"More prudent?"

Oliverio decided to go straight to the point.

"This time, I bring news that won't be to your liking."

"Your visit alone is a pleasure. What more can I ask for?"

"For the ancient treasure, of course."

"What about it?"

"It refuses to fall into my hands."

Annio grimaced. He knew full well that it would not be easy to obtain what he wanted. After all, the treasure had arrived in Italy more than two hundred years ago, and it had passed through many hands, vanishing suddenly at the most unexpected moments. It was not a piece of jewelry, nor a venerable relic, nor anything that might satisfy the costly appetite of a king. His treasure was a book. An ancient Oriental treatise, bound in morocco leather and secured with leather straps, in which he hoped to find the truth about the Messiah's resurrection and His ties with the powerful and ancestral Egyptian magic. Leonardo, they both knew, had been its latest owner. In fact, proof of this was in the mysterious phrase that Father Torriani had told them about. An Egyptian invocation could come from no other source.

"You disappoint me, Oliverio," the Weasel hissed. "If you haven't brought it with you, then why have you called me here?"

"I'll explain. You're not the only person in search of that treasure, Father Annio. Even the Donna Beatrice d'Este wanted it before losing her life."

"That's all water under the bridge!" Nanni exclaimed. "I know that the crafty woman appealed to you, but now she's dead. What's stopping you, then?"

"There's someone else, Father Annio."

"Another competitor?" The Weasel's cheeks flushed.

"What is it you want, Jacaranda? More money? Is that it? Has he offered you more money and now you've come to raise your price?"

The Spaniard shook his head, somewhat frightened at Nanni's tone. His dark eyes betrayed a rare gravity.

"No, it isn't a question of money."

"What is it then?"

"I need to know whom I'm up against. Whoever is seeking your treasure is willing to kill in order to obtain it."

"Kill?"

"Ten days ago he murdered one of my intermediaries, the librarian at Santa Maria delle Grazie in Milan. After that, the bastard has eliminated all those who've shown interest in your book. That is why I've come: to ask you to tell me the name of your competitor."

"An assassin . . ." The Weasel shuddered.

"Not a common criminal. He's a man who signs his crimes and mocks us all. In the Church of San Francesco he's done away with several pilgrims and has always left by the side of the corpse a tarot card."

"A card?"

"The Priestess. Do you understand now?"

Nanni said nothing.

"Yes, Father Annio. The same card that both you and Donna Beatrice gave me to find your treasured volume."

Oliverio took another gulp from his beer and then he continued.

"You know what I think? That the murderer knows of our interest in the book of the Priestess. I believe that he hasn't chosen that card merely by chance. He knows who we are and he'll do away with us too, if he thinks we're in his way."

"Yes, yes." The Weasel seemed very perturbed. "But tell me, Oliverio, those pilgrims in San Francesco, were they after my treasure as well?"

"I've done some questioning among the duke's police, and I can tell you that those were no ordinary pilgrims."

"No?"

"The latest one was identified as Brother Giulio, an ancient Cathar 'perfect.' I learned this just before coming to see you. The Milan police are at a loss. It seems that this Giulio was rehabilitated by the Holy Office a few years ago, after having been in charge of a community of *bonshommes* in Concorezzo."

"Concorezzo? Are you certain?"

Jacaranda nodded, not noticing how his old client had grown suddenly pale.

Annio saw that the merchant was unaware that this village on the outskirts of Milan, northeast of the capital, had been one of the principal Cathar sites in all of Lombardy and the place where, according to all the sources, the book that Nanni wanted had been kept for over two centuries. Everything fit: Father Torriani's suspicions regarding Leonardo's Cathar proclivities, the murdered "perfects" in Milan, the Egyptian phrase in the *Cenacolo*. Unless he was much mistaken, the root of everything had to be sought in that ancient treasure: a text of enormous theological and magical value, full of occult references to the teachings that Jesus Christ entrusted to Mary Magdalene after the Resurrection. A text that brought to light the parallels between Jesus and Osiris, the god who came back from the dead, thanks to the magic of Isis, the only one by his side at the moment of his return to Earth.

The Holy Office had spent decades trying to lay its hands on the treatise. The only fact they could uncover was that a copy, perhaps the only one ever made, had been smuggled out of Concorezzo and had come into the possession of Cosimo during the Council of Florence of 1439. It was never returned. In fact, only a casual indiscretion by Isabella d'Este, sister of Donna Beatrice, during the coronation festivities for Pope Alexander in 1492 had allowed the Holy Office to know that the book had been in Florence, in the hands of Marsilio Ficino, the Medici's official translator, and that he gave it as a gift to Leonardo da Vinci shortly before the latter's departure for Milan. It was therefore not impossible that someone from Concorezzo was also aware of this and wished to get the book back.

"Tell me, Father Annio," Jacaranda said, interrupting the prelate's musings, "why don't you explain what it is that makes this book so dangerous?"

Seeing the Spaniard's deep concern, Nanni decided to answer.

"It's an extraordinary book," he said at length. "It records the dialogue between Saint John and Jesus Christ in the heavens, concerning the origin of the world, the Fall of the angels, and the paths laid out for us mortals in order to attain the salvation of our soul. It was written just after the last vision the Beloved Disciple had before dying. They say it's a lucid, intense narration, depicting details of life in Heaven and the order of Creation, to which no other mortal ever had access."

"And why do you think that a book of this kind is of interest to Leonardo? He's not a man who's at all keen on theology—"

The Weasel lifted a finger to silence Jacaranda.

"The real title of this 'blue book,' my dear Oliverio, will answer your question. Listen. Two hundred years ago, Anselm of Alexandria mentioned it in one of his writings. He called it *Interrogatio Johannis*, or *The Secret Supper*. And according to the information available, Leonardo has made use of the information contained in the book's first pages to illustrate the wall of the Dominican refectory. Nothing less!"

"And that is the book that appears on the Priestess's card?"

Nanni nodded and then added:

"And its secret has been reduced by Leonardo to a single phrase that I want you to translate for me."

"One phrase?"

"In ancient Egyptian. It reads '*Mut, Nem, A, Los, Noc.*' Do you know it?"

Oliverio shook his head.

"No. But I'll find the translation for you. Leave it in my hands."

40

From sunrise to sunset.

That is how long they lasted, the interrogations of January twenty-second.

I remember that the Father Prior, Brother Benedetto and myself interviewed the brothers of Santa Maria delle Grazie one by one, struggling to find in their words clues to solve our riddles. We lived through astonishing moments. All had something to confess. Trembling, they begged for absolution from their faults and swore never again would they put in doubt the divine nature of Christ. Poor things. Most of their revelations were simply the fruit of a defective theological education. They took trivial deeds to be mortal sins, and vice versa. And yet, it was through these patient interrogations, little by little, that the intentions of Brother Giberto and Father Alessandro began to take shape, revealing their plans to take control, from inside the resting place of the *Cenacolo*. The four monks who, as it turned out, had been largely involved in the preparations confessed separately the powerful motive that had moved them: the colossal work of Leonardo concealed what all four defined as "a pictorial talisman." That is to say, a subtle geometrical design, imagined with the purpose of seducing the unaware and imprinting in their memory information that, unfortunately, none of them was able to articulate. "It is God's third revelation," one of them dared to assert.

This caught my attention.

Our four heretics came from small villages north of Milan, from the region of the lakes and even further, and they had joined the Dominicans shortly after the founding of the monastery, when they heard of Ludovico il Moro's intentions to turn it into the family mausoleum. Unlike their brethren, these four were men of some culture, admirers of Saint Bernard's famous maxim, "God is length, width, height and depth." They were familiar with the works of Pythagoras, had read Plato, whom they preferred to Aristotle, the inspiration for our system of theology. The most stubborn among the four was Brother Guglielmo Arno, the cook. Not only did he refuse to confess any sins to our tribunal but he also scorned us for belonging to the "False Church."

The little I knew about him until then was his great friendship with Leonardo. Father Alessandro had been the first to mention it. Both men were seduced by the same pleasures. They mocked and despised the duke's sumptuous meals, trading the huge roasted meats for cabbages, plums, sliced carrots and fermented pies. Leonardo and his friend achieved their moment of glory during Christmas 1495, when they invented a cake with a rounded top that mirrored Santa Maria's Bramante dome, and presented it at the duke's banquet. It was such a success that even Donna Beatrice begged them to reveal the secret ingredient that had made the dough rise in such a spectacular manner. Brother Guglielmo declined, the duchess insisted, and many still remember the cook's rude riposte that earned him five weeks' detention in his kitchen and a stern reprimand from the House of Sforza.

Brother Guglielmo's character had not changed. His temper and his stubbornness toward us showed clearly that he would rather die than retract his actions. The Father Prior ordered that he be locked up, muttering between his teeth what he really thought of the rebellious cook.

"He's incapable of reining in his feelings," he said. "There's nothing to be done about it. When he sat for the *Cenacolo* as James the Elder, Leonardo himself was incapable of soothing him."

I looked astonished.

"Oh! Has no one told you? Perhaps the apostle's long hair distracted you, Father Agostino, but if you look closely at the cook's features, you'll recognize him there on the wall. I myself gave the authorization. Leonardo asked me to suggest a fiery man who gestured with his arms much as James does now in the painting. Brother Guglielmo immediately came to mind."

"And why did Leonardo want to include someone of that nature among the Twelve?"

"That is exactly what I asked him, and you know what he answered? 'Geometry! Everything is geometry!' He told me that in a nude, his method for assessing its beauty was to measure the distance between the nipples and compare it to that between the middle of the breast and the navel, and then, to that between the navel and the legs: all three had to be the same. As far as anger was concerned, he said he could depict it simply by the merest outline of a glance. The next time you visit the *Cenacolo*, observe James's eyes. He's avoiding to look in Christ's face and lowers his eyes in wrath, as if he'd discovered there something monstrous."

"That one of his companions is about to betray the Messiah," I said.

"No!" Brother Benedetto, who had remained silent until then, suddenly spoke out. "That's what he wants us to believe. Have our brothers not told us that what we're seeing is a pictorial talisman? In a painting like that, the presence, or the absence, of symbols is essential for its effectiveness. And, in this case, what James is looking at in horrified anger is the shared gesture of Judas and Jesus competing for the same piece of bread . . . or perhaps the absence of Christ's chalice. The Holy Grail."

It was a pointed observation.

"And think of this: James, the wrathful, is in the section where the light is the brightest. He's on the side of the Just."

Brother Benedetto told us that he had attended some of the classes on the distribution of light and space given by Leonardo in the hospital cloister. His lectures were strange and spellbinding. He taught that inert matter, if distributed harmoniously, could come to life on its own. Often he would compare this miracle with the notes in a musical score: written on paper, they were nothing but a series of static squiggles with no other value than ideographic, depicting an idea rather than a sound. But filtered through the mind of a musician and transposed to the fingers or the lungs, the squiggles would vibrate, would fill the air with new sensations and would even manage to alter our spirits. Was there anything more alive than music? Leonardo did not think so.

The master painter saw his own work in similar terms. Apparently, they were still lifes, little more than canvases or pieces of wood covered with pigment and glue. And yet, interpreted by an initiated observer, they acquired an astonishing force.

"And how do you think Leonardo manages to lend life to that which does not have it?" I asked.

"Through astral magic. You know of course that this monstrous heretic studied the works of Ficino?"

Brother Benedetto's question sounded like a trap. The one-eyed monk must have been aware of my suspicions, thanks to the Father Prior; therefore, I prudently acquiesced with a nod.

"Well," he continued. "Ficino translated the *Asclepios* from the ancient Greek, a work attributed to Hermes Trismegistus, in which it is taught how the priests of the old pharaohs brought the temple statues to life."

"Is that so?"

"They excelled in the *spiritus*, an occult science by which they learned to draw on lifeless images cosmic signs that connected them to the stars. Astrological signs. And Leonardo has applied these techniques to his *Cenacolo*."

The Father Prior and I glanced at each other.

"Don't you see? Twelve Apostles, twelve signs of the zodiac. To each disciple corresponds a constellation, and Jesus, in the center, is the sun. A talisman indeed!"

"Calm down, Brother Benedetto. These are only suppositions—"

"Not at all! Study the *Cenacolo* closely! The worst thing about it is not that it's alive. From what we can tell, through our knowledge of Cathar doctrine, this work encloses the wildest of all heretic ideas. It's a Satanic Bible. And it sits in our refectory!"

"What idea do you mean?" I asked.

"I mean the idea of dualism, Father Agostino. If I didn't misunderstand your lecture this morning, the whole system of Cathar belief is based on a confrontation between a good God and an evil one."

"Exactly."

"Then, when you return to the refectory, see if this battle between good and evil is not clearly portrayed in the *Cenacolo*. Christ is in the center as the needle on a pair of scales, halfway between the realm of the spirit and that of the flesh. To His right, or your left, are the shadows, the realm of evil. Go and see: that section lies in the gloom, lacking light. Not by chance that is the place in which Judas Iscariot sits, but also Peter with his dagger. With the weapon which, according to you, lends him a diabolical character."

The irascible Brother Benedetto concluded:

"On the other hand, on the opposite side are those that Leonardo considers are the light. It's the side of the table that's illuminated, and in it he has depicted not only himself but also Plato, the ancient source of so many heretic Cathar doctrines."

Then I remembered:

"And also the brothers Guglielmo and Giberto, the

two avowed Cathars," I added. "You told me that Giberto sat for the portrait of the Apostle Philip."

He nodded.

"Of course," I argued, thinking of the geometrical placement of the apostles, "you too are in that section. Lending your features to Saint Thomas, yes?"

Brother Benedetto snorted.

"Let's stop all this chatter," he said. "Obviously we must try to interpret Leonardo's mural, but the real question is, what are we to do with this work? I'll only say it once: either we attack this matter at its roots and we brick up the painting, or the contents of this mural will act as a lighthouse for heretics and bring us nothing but sorrow."

41

"I don't understand. Are you going to do nothing, just wait for him to be condemned?"

Leonardo seemed unmoved by Bernardino Luini's question. He had been standing in his garden for some time now, concentrating on the development of his new machine, and had hardly noticed his apprentices' return. What was the point? Deep inside him, he held few hopes that Elena, Marco and Luini would come back from the *Cenacolo* enlightened by the knowledge he had so carefully implanted in the mural. The Master was tired, and bored with watching the coming and going of followers incapable of understanding his particular way of writing in charcoal and paint.

And, as usual, his apprentices brought only disheartening news from the monastery. They said that Santa Maria was ready for battle. That the Father Prior had decided to interrogate all the monks under his command in his search for heretics, and that he had ordered that Leonardo's beloved Brother Guglielmo, the cook, be put in solitary confinement, accused of conspiring against Holy Mother the Church.

Leonardo listened to all this in sorrow, without knowing what to say.

"Nor do I understand your attitude, Master," Marco rejoined. "You can't be pleased with what has happened. Are you not concerned by your friend's fate? Are you becoming insensitive to all?"

Leonardo lifted his blue eyes from the gardening box and fixed them on his dear Marco.

"Brother Guglielmo will stand up to them," he said at last. "No one will be able to break the circle he stands for."

"Enough of these allegories! Don't you see the danger? Don't you see that they'll soon be coming for you?"

"All I see, Marco, is that you're not listening to me," he replied brusquely. "No one does."

"Just a minute!" Young Elena, who up to then had not said a word, stepped forward and stood among the three men. "I know now what you've been trying to teach us, Master! Now I understand! Everything is stated in the *Cenacolo*!"

Leonardo's eyebrows rose in surprise. The little countess proceeded.

"You used Brother Guglielmo to represent James the Elder. Of that, there's no doubt. And in the *Cenacolo* he represents the letter *O*. Just like you do."

Luini shrugged, blushing as he looked at Leonardo. After all, he himself had taught Elena as much.

"That can mean only one thing," she added. "That Brother Guglielmo and you are the only ones holding the secret that you want us to find. And also, that you're as certain of his discretion as of your own. Both of you are responsible for the same plan."

"Admirable!" Leonardo applauded. "I see you're as clever as your mother. And do you also know why I chose the letter *O*?"

"Yes . . . At least, I think I do."

Leonardo stared at her inquisitively. So did her two companions.

"Because Omega is the end, the opposite of Alpha, the beginning," she said. "In this way, you place yourself at the final point of a project that began with Jesus, who is the only A in the mural."

"Admirable," repeated Leonardo. "Admirable."

"Of course! Brother Guglielmo and you are the ones who will bring us the Church of John!" Luini cried. "That's the secret!"

Leonardo bent once again over the strange machine he had designed for his garden, shaking his head.

"There's more to it than that, Luini."

The device Leonardo was working on consisted of an extraordinary apparatus. He had begun to concentrate on it shortly after failing in his intent to automate the kitchens of the Sforza castle. His automatic roasting machines, his meat grinders, his bread slicers and his enormous bellows that blew on the fire to boil huge cauldrons of water had resulted in a number of wounded and proved useless to satisfy the colossal requirements of the duke. But his new machine, the giant turnip collector, would be different. If all went well, the duke would no longer make fun of his invention, proposing to use it as a weapon in his war against the French. It was true that in its first trial, at Porta Vercellina, the collector caused three fatalities, but after a few necessary adjustments, he was certain that the machine would no longer be lethal.

"Master," Luini insisted, seeing Leonardo so distracted. "We've advanced hugely in the decipherment of your *Cenacolo*. But you don't seem to be at all interested in our progress. Don't you see that the time has come to let us into your secret? Tomorrow they might come and take you to be interrogated. If they do, your entire project will be lost."

"I've listened to you, Bernardino. Very attentively," he said without lifting his eyes from his machine. "And even though I much appreciate the fact that you've discovered the letters I hid in the *Cenacolo*, I also see that you're not capable of interpreting them. And if you, who know where to look, are like children who cannot read, how much more lost will be those monks who you say are after me."

"A book. The whole clue is there, isn't it, Master? In a book in which you yourself learned everything."

Luini's words sounded like a challenge.

"What do you mean?"

"Come now, Master. The time for guessing games is over. And you know it. I've recognized in the *Cenacolo* the face of your old friend Ficino, the translator. Was it not with him that you agreed that the execution of such a portrait would announce the arrival of the Church of John? Did he himself not give you a book destined to be the Bible of this new Church?"

Leonardo let fall his tools next to the turnip collector, raising a cloud of dust.

"What can you know about all that?" he sighed.

"I know everything you taught me: that, ever since the time of Jesus, both churches are fighting for control over our souls. One, the Church of Peter, was imagined as the temporal Church, useful to teach men the road to the awakening of their conscience. But it is only the forerunner of another, more glorious Church that will nourish our spirit once we become open to receive it. Peter is the Church of the past, the one that forged the road toward the one to come, the Church of John. Your Church."

Leonardo was about to say something, but his apprentice had not finished.

"The man you painted as Matthew in the *Cenacolo*, the man Ficino, gave you a book with writings by John for you to study. I remember it well. I was there the day it happened. I was only a boy then. And if now you've placed him in your mural, perhaps to allow others such as us the possibility of reading your work, then it's because you believe that the time has come to replace the old guard. Isn't that true? That is what your *Cenacolo* means. Admit it. The arrival of your new Church."

Marco and Elena stood quietly by. Leonardo indicated silence with a gesture he often used: his finger extended toward Heaven as if asking God for leave to speak.

"My dear Bernardino," he said, in a conciliatory tone. "It is true that Ficino entrusted me with certain very valuable texts shortly before moving to Milan. And your appreciation of the two Churches is also true. I will not deny any of it. I've been painting John the Baptist for years in my work, hoping for a time like the present. A time that I believe has come at last."

"What makes you think so, Master?" said Elena.

Leonardo spoke to Elena in a much quieter voice.

"Doesn't everyone see it? The Pope has led the temporal Church into a state of depravity hard to equal. Even his own clerics, like Savonarola in Florence, have turned against him. The time has come for John's Church, the Church of the spirit, to replace the Church of Peter and lead us to true salvation."

"But John the Baptist is not in the *Cenacolo*, Master," said Marco.

"The Baptist isn't, no." Leonardo smiled at Marco, always attentive to details. "But John is."

"I don't understand."

"Almost everything is in the Scriptures. If you read the Gospels attentively, you will see that Jesus didn't begin His public life until John baptized Him in the waters of the Jordan. The four evangelists needed to justify Christ's mission by referring to John as part of the Messiah's preparations. That is why I always paint him with a finger pointing toward Heaven. It is my way of saying that he, John the Baptist, arrived first."

"Then why do we worship Jesus and not John?"

"It was all part of a carefully calculated plan. John was incapable of transmitting to that group of rough and uncultured men his spiritual teachings. How could he have made a handful of fishermen understand that God is within us all and not inside a temple? Jesus would help him educate these savages. They designed a temporal Church in imitation of the Jewish one, and another secret one, a spiritual one, such as had never been seen on Earth before. And these teachings were entrusted to a very intelligent woman, to Mary Magdalene, and to a keen-spirited young man whose name was also John. And that John, my dear Marco, is indeed in the *Cenacolo*."

"And so is Mary Magdalene!"

Leonardo was not able to hide his admiration for the tempestuous young woman. Luini, blushing, was forced to clarify the source of her response. It was he, Luini, who had taught her that, there where she saw a large, visible knot, she would know that it was a work linked somehow to Mary Magdalene. There was such a knot depicted in *The Last Supper*.

"Let me tell you something else," Leonardo added. A note of fatigue had crept into his voice. "John is much more than a name. It was the name of both the Baptist and of the Evangelist. But John is also a title. It is the *nomen mysticum*, or 'mystical name,' carried by all depositaries of the spiritual Church. Just like Pope Joan, who appears on the Visconti cards."

"Pope Joan? Was that not a myth? A fable for credulous folk?"

"And what fable doesn't mask real facts, Bernardino?"

"That means—"

"You should know that the man who painted those cards was Bonifacio Bembo, of Cremona. One of the 'perfect men.' Seeing that the fate of our brothers was in danger, he decided to conceal in this pack of cards for the Visconti family some of the basic symbols of our faith. Like the belief that we are the mystical offspring of

Jesus. What better symbol of this belief than to paint a pregnant Pope, holding in her hand the Cross of the Baptist, making clear to all who can read it that the New Church is about to be born? That card," Leonardo said in a reverential voice, "is the precise prophecy of that which is to come . . ."

42

I cannot tell for what strange reason the Father Prior sent me on such a mission. Had he been gifted with foresight and been able to see what was to befall me, I am certain that he would have kept me by his side. But fate is unpredictable, and God, on that January day, had cast the die of my future, moving, as always, in His mysterious ways.

At first, I must confess, the business turned my stomach.

To exhume the funeral remains of Father Alessandro—in the presence of Brother Benedetto, Mauro the grave digger and Brother Giorgio—made me utterly sick. Fifty years had passed since the Holy Office had last dug up the body of a criminal in order to burn it, and even though I begged the Father Prior to leave the dead in peace, I could do nothing to prevent the disinterment of Father Alessandro. His corpse, waxy and pale, gave off an unbearable stench. However carefully my companions and I took the precaution of wrapping him up in a clean winding sheet and tying him up like a roast, his pestilential odor accompanied us throughout our excursion. Fortunately, not all was so unpleasant. I was surprised to notice that, though it was almost impossible to breathe close to the body of Father Alessandro, the same could not be said about Brother Giberto's. Brother Giberto had no smell at all. The grave digger attributed this phenomenon to the fact that the fire that had consumed him in the Piazza Mercanti had put an end to his corruptible parts, conferring on his remains this singular quality. Brother Benedetto, on the other hand, defended a different theory. According to him, the fact of having stayed out in the open, in the courtyard of the Dominican hospital, in a temperature several degrees below freezing, had sucked into the air the sexton's worst effluvia. I never knew which of the two was right.

"If you notice, the same happens with animals," Brother Benedetto attempted to convince me. "Does the corpse of an abandoned horse on a frozen road smell of anything?"

We arrived at the Campo Santo Stefano without having concluded our discussion. It was still an hour and a half before vespers. We had crossed the military control at Porta della Corte all'Arcivescovado and left behind us the offices of the Capitano di Giustizia, without having had to answer too many questions from the guards. The police knew of our labors and approved of our decision to take the heretics far away from the city. Our carriage, laden with ropes and other trappings, passed all the inspections. And so we arrived at Santo Stefano, a clearing in the woods, lonely and silent, with a firm rocky ground on which it would not be difficult to pile up the wood we had brought in order to set fire to our dead.

Most affably, Brother Giorgio directed the proceedings.

He gave instructions as to how to best build the mountain of logs and to render it solid, so that it would burn appropriately. For someone such as myself, who had witnessed so many autos-da-fé without lifting a single log, this was an entirely new experience. Giorgio taught us to pile them up in inverse order of their size. He had attended the procedure many times. He explained that we must place the thinnest branches at the base, so that, as they burned, the thicker logs would catch fire more easily. Once the pile was finished, he made us throw a rope over the lot, tighten it, and then heave the bodies of our brothers to the top. In this way, we would fulfill the Father Prior's instructions and return to Milan before nightfall, when the duke's soldiers would bar the city's several entrances.

"You know what's best about this undertaking?" Brother Benedetto panted, after succeeding in lifting Brother Giberto's body onto the pyre. He had climbed to the top with the grave digger in order to pull up the corpses and put them into place.

"So you think there's something good in what we're doing?" the grave digger asked.

"What's good about it, Brother Mauro," I heard Brother Benedetto say, "is that with a bit of luck the ashes of these infidels will fall on the Cathars still hiding in those mountains."

"Cathars here?" Brother Mauro snorted. "You see them everywhere, Brother."

"And you lend them too much cunning," I added,

from the ground, securing the rope around Father Alessandro. "Do you think them capable of distinguishing these ashes from those of their own bonfires? Allow me to doubt it."

This time, the one-eyed monk did not answer. I waited a moment for the rope to tighten and begin pulling on the librarian's corpse, but nothing at all seemed to be happening. Mauro Sforza made no reply to Brother Benedetto's comments, and I noticed that a long and uncomfortable silence had settled suddenly on the clearing.

Puzzled, I stepped back to see what was happening. High up on the pile of logs, Brother Benedetto was standing still as a statue, his face turned and his eye lost in the distance. He had let go of the rope. Mauro seemed to be trembling and breathing heavily, like a mystic in an ecstatic vision, silent and almost incapable of movement. I understood that they were trying to point out something, gesturing toward a point behind my back. I turned and looked, and almost fainted.

By the edge of the woods, a short distance from where we found ourselves, a group of some fifteen hooded men were observing our movements in silence. None of us had noticed them earlier. They were dressed in black from head to foot, with their hands tucked inside their sleeves, and they appeared to have been there for a long while, watching us. They did not look hostile, since they carried no weapons of any kind with which to attack us, but neither was their attitude reassuring. They simply stared at us through the slits in their hoods without speaking a word or making any attempt to draw near us. Where had they come from? As far as we knew, there was no monastery or convent near, nor was this a holy festivity that would explain the presence of a group of monks in the open field.

What then did they want? Had they come to attend the post mortem execution of our heretics?

Mauro Sforza was the first to descend from the pyre and head toward the hooded men with his arms held high, but his gesture was received with utter indifference. None of the visitors moved a muscle.

"Good Lord!" Brother Benedetto exclaimed at last. "The heretics!"

"What do you mean?"

"Don't you see, Father Agostino?" he spluttered, half in surprise and half in anger. "I told you. Dressed in black. No belts or ornaments. Like the Cathars seeking perfection."

"Cathars?"

"They're not armed," he added. "Their religion forbids it."

Mauro, hearing what Brother Benedetto had said, advanced one step further toward the group.

"Go on, Brother," the one-eyed monk encouraged him. "You'll not risk anything by touching them. If they're not capable of harming a chicken, how do you think they'd hurt you?"

"*Laudetur Jesus Christus!* They're here for their dead!" cried Giorgio, who had stuck to my side as soon as he had seen them. "They want them returned!"

"And why does that frighten you? Haven't you heard what Brother Benedetto just said?" I attempted to calm him down. "These people are incapable of using violence against us."

I never knew if Brother Giorgio managed to mouth an answer, because at that moment the intruders launched into a moving Our Father that filled the clearing with their voices. Their deep notes echoed through Santo Stefano, leaving us speechless. Giorgio was mistaken. The *bonshommes* had not come to collect the bodies of their brethren. They would never have thought of it: they loathed the very thought of the flesh, which they considered the prison of the soul, a diabolical obstacle to the purity of the spirit. If they had come here, risking detention, it was because they wished to pray for the souls of their dead brothers.

"Cursed be you all!" cried Brother Benedetto, raising his fists at the top of the pyre. "A thousand times cursed!"

We were all taken aback by his reaction. Brothers Giorgio and Mauro stood back as he jumped down from the pile of wood and ran toward the hooded men as if possessed. He was red in the face with wrath, his veins gorged to the point of bursting. Brother Benedetto charged against the first man he met, throwing him to the ground. Then he knelt on his victim and pulled out a knife.

"You should be dead! All of you should be dead! You have no right to be here!" he shouted.

Before we could stop him, Brother Benedetto had plunged his knife to the hilt into the hooded man's back. A cry of pain rang through the clearing.

"To Hell with you all!" he shouted.

The next few minutes are blurred in my memory.

The hooded men looked at one another before falling on Brother Benedetto. They tore him off their wounded brother, who was bleeding copiously, and held him against a pine tree. He kept spurting curses at them, his only eye bloody with wrath.

As to the others, I think that Giorgio ran toward the city gates, as far as his eighty years allowed him. I lost sight of Mauro when one of the men threw a sack over my head and tied it around my neck with a rope. The sack must have been soaked in some narcotic, because shortly afterward, I felt that I was fainting. Seconds later, I heard no more the cries of the wounded man and an extraordinary feeling of lightness spread through my arms and legs.

Before losing consciousness, I still had time to hear a voice whispering a few words whose meaning was lost to me.

"Now, Father, I'll be able to answer all your doubts."

Stunned and perplexed, I fell into a deep stupor.

43

I awoke with a feeling of nausea and a powerful headache, not knowing how long I had remained unconscious. Everything kept turning around me and my thoughts were more confused than ever. There was a constant pressure against my temples that provoked a cyclical, circular pain. Every so often it ran through my skull from left to right, troubling my senses. Its poundings were so hard that for a long while I did not even try to open my eyes. I remember I felt my head, trying to find a wound. I found nothing. The wound was no doubt interior.

"Don't worry, Father Agostino. You're all in one piece. Rest. Soon you'll feel better."

A gentle voice, the same one that spoke to me before I lost consciousness, surprised me before I managed to stand up. It spoke to me again, in a familiar, soft tone, as if it had known me for long.

"The effects of our oil will last only a few hours more. Then you'll feel yourself again."

"Your . . . oil?"

Disoriented and weak, with my arms and legs stiff, lying on an uneven surface of some kind, I gathered strength to speak. I realized that I'd been taken to some kind of shelter, since my clothes felt dry and the cold was not as bitter as in the Santo Stefano clearing.

"The cloth in which we wrapped you was soaked in a dream-provoking oil. It's an old recipe from the sorcerers of this area."

"Poison . . . ," I murmured.

"Not exactly," the voice answered. "It's a balm extracted from bearded darnel, henbane, hemlock and poppies. It never fails. A small dose absorbed through the skin suffices for its lethargic effect to work. But it will soon be over. Don't worry."

"Where am I?"

"Somewhere safe."

"Give me something to drink, I beg you."

"At once, Father."

I groped for the mug that the unknown placed between my hands. A pungent broth helped my weary body to restore itself. I gripped at the mug until I felt strong enough to glance around and inspect my prison.

I had intuited correctly. I was no longer in Santo Stefano. And indeed, my captors had separated me from Giorgio, Mauro and Benedetto and placed me in a closed, windowless room, probably an improvised cell in a remote country house. I realized that I must have spent a fairly long time stretched on this straw matting. My beard had grown and someone had dared strip me of my Dominican habit, replacing it with a rough woolen outfit. But exactly how long had I been here? Impossible to tell. And where had my brothers been taken to? Who was responsible for bringing me to this place? And why?

Anguish gripped my throat.

"Where . . . am I?" I repeated.

"In a safe place, a village called Concorezzo, Father Agostino. And I'm glad to see that you've recovered. We have much to talk about. Do you remember me?"

"Who . . . ? " I hesitated.

I tried to turn toward my captor, but a new pounding forced me to stop.

"Come now, Father! Our oil put you to sleep but didn't blot out your memory. I'm the man who always tells the truth, don't you recall? The one who swore to solve the riddle that was troubling you."

A memory flashed through my brain. It was true. Dear God! I had certainly heard that voice before. But where? I made a great effort to turn around and look at my captor. And I saw him at last, as red in the face as ever, his emerald eyes as clear and as intelligent. It was Mario Forzetta, the former apprentice who had fought a duel with Jacaranda.

"Remember me?"

I nodded.

"I'm sorry to have had to resort to these methods to bring you here, Father. But, believe me, it was our only chance. You would not have come with us willingly."

He smiled.

The plural intrigued me.

"With *us*, Mario?"

Forzetta's face lit up when he heard me say his name.

"The 'pure men' of Concorezzo, Father. Our faith forbids us from doing violence, but not from using cunning."

"You are a . . . *bonhomme?*"

"You are horrified, I know. You freed a heretic from the prison he deserved. But before you judge me too harshly, I beg you to listen to me. I have much to tell you."

"And my brothers?"

"We left them asleep in Santo Stefano. By this time, if they're not frozen stiff, they'll be back in Milan, suffering from your same headache."

Mario was looking reasonably well. The wound that had cut his face several days ago was still noticeable, but he had let his beard grow and his skin was dark from the sun. He was no longer the pale specter who had spoken with me in the prison of Oliverio Jacaranda. He had gained weight and he looked happy. The knowledge that he was safe from Jacaranda's clutches had no doubt agreed with him. What I could not understand was why he wished to detain me. Why precisely me, the man who had granted him his freedom?

"My brothers and I hesitated for a long time before taking this step," Mario explained, sitting down on the floor, by my side. "I know that you, Father, are an inquisitor, and that your order has, for over two hundred years, persecuted families such as ours, simply because we have a different way of approaching God."

"But—"

"But seeing you in Santo Stefano, I understood that you were a sign sent by Our Lord. You appeared just at the moment when I had found all the answers I promised to give you. Do you remember? Isn't that a true miracle? I convinced our 'perfect' to bring you here, so that I might pay back my debt to you."

"No such debt exists."

"It does, Father. God has intertwined our paths for a reason He alone can fathom. Perhaps it is not so that I can solve your riddles, but to face an enemy we have in common."

His words took me aback.

"What enemy?"

"Do you recall the riddle you put in my hands the day you set me free?"

I nodded. This *Oculos ejus dinumera* kept outsmarting my wits. I had almost forgotten that I had entrusted Forzetta with a copy.

"After leaving you, Father, I sought refuge in Leonardo's workshop. I knew that his house would be the only one in Milan that would shelter me. And obviously, I spoke with the Master. I told him of our meeting, and of your great generosity, and I asked him to help me. Not only did I want him to protect me from Signor Jacaranda's temper but I also wanted him to assist me in giving you thanks for having delivered me from jail."

"But you were no longer Leonardo's apprentice—"

"No. And yet, once you've been his apprentice, you never cease to be one. Leonardo treats his apprentices as if they were his children and, though many of us are not talented enough to become painters, he still shows us his affection. After all, his teachings go well beyond the mere business of being an artist."

"I see. So you went to seek protection under Master Leonardo's wing. And what did he say?"

"I gave him your riddle. I told him it concealed the

name of a person you were looking for, and the Master solved it for me."

This seemed to me a great irony. Leonardo had deciphered the name of the one who had written to Bethany seeking the Master's ruin? Full of curiosity, I tried to overcome my dizziness and took Mario's hands in mine to emphasize my question.

"He succeeded, then?"

"He did, Father. I can tell you the hidden name."

Mario laid down the Priestess's card on the floor, between our feet.

"Master Leonardo was much surprised when I asked him about your riddle," he continued. "In fact, he told me he knew it well. That a monk from Santa Maria had brought it to him some time earlier, and that he'd solved it for him."

"Father Alessandro!"

The memory of the *Oculos ejus dinumera* written on the reverse of a card like the one found next to the librarian's body came back to me. Suddenly everything made sense: the Soothsayer must have murdered Father Alessandro after having been unmasked and must have thought up a plan to discredit Leonardo. To kill an obscure Dominican must have been easy for him, but not to do away with the duke's favorite court painter. So he decided to incriminate him in the heresy. By writing letters to Bethany.

Breaking into my wild thoughts, Mario continued.

"Yes. It was Father Alessandro. I remember the Master's words perfectly: that both riddles, the verses and the card, were intimately linked. Your verses were incompre-

hensible without the card, and the card makes no sense
without the verses. They are like both sides of the same
coin."

I begged Mario to make himself clearer. The young
man took the Latin words written in the paper I'd given
him in Milan, and placed it next to the Visconti-Sforza
card. Once more, those cursed seven lines lay before me:

> *Oculos ėjus dinumera,*
> *šed noli voltum ádspicere.*
> *In latere nominis*
> *mei notam rinvenies.*
> *Contemplari et contemplata*
> *aliis tradere.*

> *Veritas*

"In fact, it's a simple three-leveled riddle," he said. "The
first seeks to identify the card that will help you solve
the problem. 'Count its eyes but look not on its face.' It
has a very simple meaning. If you observe carefully, you'll
see there's only one other kind of eye possible, other
than those on the woman's face."

"Another eye? Where?"

Mario seemed amused.

"In the belt, Father. Don't you see? It's the eye of the
knot through which passes the cord that binds the
woman's waist. It's a metaphor, cleverly used by the man
you seek.'

"But that's not all," he continued. " 'The number of
my name, you shall find on its side' is an open question. If
you look closely, you see that you can't tell on what side to

look. Is it the right side or the left that holds 'the number of my name'? I'll tell you: it's the woman's right side."

"How can you be so sure?"

"Master Leonardo stumbled upon the solution thanks to a steganographic detail."

"A what?"

"Steganographic. The Greeks, Father, were masters in the art of concealing secret messages in writings or in paintings visible to all. In their tongue, *steganos* means hidden or occult writing, as in the obvious case of your riddle. A spelling mistake gives us the clue: *rinvenies* should be spelled without an *R*. A man as meticulous as the sender of this message would not have overlooked such a detail. After finding this extra *R*, I examined all of your verses carefully and discovered that certain letters were marked with a dot. You might have overlooked them, but they're there, in the words *ejus*, *dinumera*, *sed*, *adspicere* and *tradere*. I'm surprised that no one has noticed them."

I leaned down to read the Soothsayer's message to see what Mario was pointing at, and I discovered that, indeed, the letters *E*, *D*, *S*, *A* and *T* carried dots just above them.

"You see?" he insisted. "With these, plus the mis-

placed R, you can read the word *destra*, meaning 'right.'
That is the clue we needed."

It was impressive. Leonardo had done that which
none of us had thought of doing: relating the Priestess's
card with the riddle of the Soothsayer's letters. Intuition
or genius, the truth is that I felt a sort of vertigo, knowing that we were so close to the solution of the enigma.

"The rest is quite easy, Father. According to the lessons of the *Ars Memoriae*, the hands are the parts of the
body that always carry the number in any given composition. On this card, as you can see, there are two hands,
each showing a different number of fingers. If your man
tells us that we must choose the right, it's because the
number of his name is five."

"So you know the *Ars Memoriae* as well?"

"It was one of Leonardo's favorite assignments."

"So now I suppose I should look for a monk whose
name consists of letters that add up to five, isn't that
right?"

"Not necessarily," said Mario more proudly than ever.
"Master Leonardo found it. The name is Benedetto: his is
the only name in Santa Maria with that numerical value."

Mario explained. According to the *Ars Memoriae*,
the number of any given name is obtained by summing
up the value attributed to each of its letters. Taking
into account that the Latin alphabet lacked the letters
J, *U*, *W*, *Y* and *Z*, the table of correspondences read as
follows:

A	B	C	D	E	F	G	H	I	K	L	M	N	O	P	Q	R	S	T	V	X
1	2	3	4	5	6	7	8	9	10	11	12	13	14	15	16	17	18	19	20	21

"Benedetto" adds up to 86, a number which is then reduced to 14 by adding up 8 plus 6, and further to 5 by adding 1 plus 4. As Mario pointed out to me, there is also a second 14 (therefore a second 5) in the Priestess's card: the 14 coils of the woman's belt. Mario added that Leonardo had thought this an unexpected number, since the logical one would have been 13, corresponding to the 13 wounds Christ received on the Cross.

But I was only half listening.

Benedetto?

I suppose that I blanched, because Mario stopped talking and looked at me closely.

Benedetto? The monk with a single eye, like the knot in the priestess's belt?

The irony of the situation struck me in full.

How had I not seen it earlier? How had I not realized that the one-eyed monk, the Father Prior's confidant, had been granted access to all the monastery's secrets and was the only one sufficiently wrathful to attack Leonardo da Vinci? The revelation fitted like a glove the profile I had already drawn of the Soothsayer who, I had guessed, was a renegade disciple of the Master. Was not his face depicted in the *Cenacolo* under the guise of the Apostle Thomas, an irrefutable proof of his old allegiance to Leonardo's organization?

As I embraced Mario I wondered whom I would pursue first: Father Alessandro's murderer, or the members of this lost community of heretical Christians.

44

Brother Benedetto spat another gob of blood into the basin.

He looked terribly ill.

Ever since he had lain for hours under the open sky in the clearing of Santo Stefano, unconscious and barefooted, the one-eyed monk had not regained his normal breathing. He coughed painfully, and his clogged lungs made it difficult for him even to move.

The Father Prior ordered that he be taken to the hospital. There he was put to bed, isolated from the other patients and treated with aromatic vapors, daily bleedings and prayers for his speedy recovery. But Brother Benedetto was unable to sleep. His temperature rose inexorably and everyone feared for his life.

The last day of the month of January, as he lay there exhausted, the most wrathful of the monks of Santa Maria begged to be given Extreme Unction. He had spent the afternoon delirious, muttering unintelligible phrases in foreign tongues and haranguing his brethren to set fire to the refectory if they wanted to save their souls.

Father Nicola Zessati, a dean with half a century of service to the community and an old friend of Benedetto's, anointed him with the holy oil. First, he asked the dying man for his confession, but Brother Benedetto refused to say a single word about the events at Santo Stefano. All efforts to dissuade him failed. Neither Father Zessati nor the Father Prior succeeded in convincing him to reveal my whereabouts or the names of the men who had assaulted us.

Those were days of deep confusion. As strange as it might seem, neither was Brother Giorgio of much use. The old man, his hands bitten by the cold and suffering from congestion, barely remembered the mysterious black monks that had come out to meet us. He was nearsighted and his age betrayed him, so that when he told the Father Prior that Benedetto had attacked someone with a knife, he was deemed to be suffering from delusions and was put to bed in the same wing of the hospital as the one-eyed brother, where he quickly recovered.

My third companion, Brother Mauro, was left speechless for several days. His youth had protected him from the cold, but since his return to Santa Maria no one had seen him leave his cell. Those who paid him a visit were horrified by his demented look. Mauro barely ate anything and seemed unable to follow a conversation. He appeared to have simply lost his mind.

It was Brother Giorgio who warned the Father Prior that Brother Benedetto was quickly fading. This was on Tuesday, January thirty-first. The old man found the Father Prior in the refectory with Master Leonardo, going over the latest progress in the *Cenacolo*.

After the burial of Donna Beatrice and my own disappearance, Leonardo had gone back to his work with renewed energy. Suddenly, it was as if he felt a pressing urge to finish his work. That very day he had given the last touches to the youthful face of Saint John, and was proudly showing it off to the Father Prior, who was scrutinizing it warily.

The apostle looked magnificent. A long blond mane fell over his shoulders, his half-closed eyes had a languid look, and his head was leaning to his right in an attitude of submission. Light poured from his face: a supernatural, magical radiance that suggested to the viewer a state of contemplation and a mystical life.

"I've been told that you used a young girl as your model."

The Father Prior's reproach was the first thing Brother Giorgio heard upon entering. He did not, however, see the Master smile.

"Rumors are rife," he said ironically.

"And reach further than your wooden birds."

"All right, Father Prior. I won't deny it. But before you become annoyed with me, you must know that I only used the girl to give certain touches to the Beloved Disciple."

Brother Giorgio recognized Leonardo's acid humor.

"So it's true."

"John was a sweet creature, Father Prior. You know he was the youngest of the disciples and Jesus loved him like a brother. Or even more, like a son. And you know I haven't been able to find among your friars one who would evoke to me the innocence with which he is described in the Gospels. What does it matter if I used an innocent young girl to complete his portrait? What evil can you see in it, since this is the result?"

"And who is the girl, if I may know?"

"Of course, you may know." Leonardo bowed toward his patron. "But I doubt that you've met her. Her name is Elena Crivelli, and she's from a noble Lombard family. She visited my *bottega* accompanied by Master Luini not many days ago. As soon as I saw her, I knew God had sent her to me to finish my *Cenacolo*."

The Father Prior gave him a sideways glance.

"If you could only see her!" Leonardo continued. "Her beauty is enchanting, pure, perfect for John's face. She gave me that air of beatitude that is now apparent in John's features."

"But there were no women at the Last Supper, Master Leonardo."

"And who can be certain of that, Father Prior? Anyway, I only took her hands, her look, the twist of the lips and her cheeks. Only her most innocent attributes."

"Reverend Father—"

Brother Giorgio had been waiting impatiently for a break in the conversation, and his interruption did not allow the Father Prior to answer. After a quick genuflection, the monk whispered the bad news about Brother Benedetto's health.

"You must come with me," he told the Father Prior. "The doctors say that he's not got long to live."

"What is the matter with him?"

"He can barely breathe and his skin grows paler by the minute, Father Prior."

Leonardo, observing the old brother's bandaged hands, deduced that this must be one of the monks who had been assaulted outside the city walls.

"If you care for my opinion," he said, "I believe that what ails your brother is tuberculosis. If you wish, I can put my medical knowledge at your disposal to alleviate his suffering. I know enough about the human body to suggest an efficacious treatment."

"You?" the Father Prior interjected. "I thought you hated him—"

"Come, Father Prior. How could I wish ill to someone in whose debt I am? Remember that Brother Benedetto sat for my Saint Thomas. Could I hate Elena, who helped me to paint John? Or the librarian whose face inspired my Judas? No. I owe your brother one of the most important faces in my *Cenacolo*."

The Father Prior thanked him with a bow, not detecting the irony in Leonardo's words. Certainly Saint Thomas had all the characteristics of a rejuvenated Brother Benedetto, and Leonardo had taken the trouble to paint him in profile, so as to hide his missing eye. But it was also true that for a long time now, Leonardo and Brother Benedetto had not been on friendly terms.

With the Father Prior's blessing, Leonardo quickly gathered his brushes, closed his various jars of paint and headed toward the hospital. On the way, they were joined by Father Zessati, who was carrying in a small bundle a flask with holy water, a jar with consecrated oil and a silver sprinkler.

They found Brother Benedetto lying alone on a cot on the second floor, in one of the few independent buildings. A large linen cloth hung from the ceiling. At the threshold, Leonardo bade the two monks to wait for a

moment in the garden. He explained that the first stage
of his treatment required a certain privacy, and that
there were few men like himself, impervious to the fatal
effluvia of the disease.

When Leonardo found himself alone by the bedside,
he drew aside the linen curtain and observed his wrathful patient. Why had he not yet invented a machine to
free him of his enemies? he wondered. Gathering his
courage, Leonardo gently shook the one-eyed man to
wake him.

"You!"

The surprise made the old man sit up in his cot.

"What the Devil are you doing here?"

Leonardo observed the dying man with professional
curiosity. His aspect was worse than he had expected.
The bluish hue spreading over his cheeks was an ominous sign.

"I was told that you were attacked in Santo Stefano,
Brother. I'm truly sorry."

"Don't speak like a Pharisee, Master Leonardo!" He
coughed, spitting out more bloody phlegm. "You know as
well as I do what really happened."

"If that is what you believe—"

"It was your brethren from Concorezzo, wasn't it?
Those bastards deny God and reject the divine nature of
the Son of Man . . . Out of here! Let me die in peace!"

"I decided to come and speak to you as soon as I
learned about your illness. You're making a rash judgment, as you always do. Those people you refer to do not
deny God. They are pure Christians, who venerate the
Savior just as the first Apostles did."

"Enough! I won't listen to you! Don't say anything more! Leave!"

The one-eyed monk became livid with rage.

"If you think about it for a minute, Brother, by pardoning your life these 'bastards' have shown infinite mercy toward you. Especially since they know that you've killed several of their brothers in cold blood."

The friar's anger turned suddenly to astonishment.

"How dare you say that!"

"Because I know what you've become. And I also know that you've done everything possible to banish me from here, so that the faith of all these people would be left in the dark. First you killed Father Alessandro. Then you pierced the heart of Brother Giulio. You clouded the spirit of your brothers who were on the path to purity—"

"To heresy, rather," the old man answered, his single eye wide open now.

"And you sent apocalyptical messages to Rome, anonymous letters signed *Augur dixit*, merely to instigate a secret investigation against me, leaving you in the shadows. Am I not right?"

"Damn you, Leonardo!" The monk's chest heaved with a new fit of coughing. "Damn you forever!"

Leonardo, impassive, undid from his belt the white linen pouch that never left his side and deposited it on the cot. It seemed larger than usual. Leonardo pulled it apart ceremoniously and extracted from it a small book with blue covers which he placed by the old man's pillow.

"Do you recognize it?" he asked with a knowing smile. "Even if you curse me now, I'm here to forgive you. And to offer you salvation. We are all God's children and deserve to be saved."

The monk's eye glittered as he saw the volume so near his grasp.

"This is what you were looking for, isn't it?"

"*Inter . . . rogatio . . . Johan . . . nis . . .*"   Brother Benedetto deciphered the title on the spine. "John's final testament! The book with the answers that the Lord gave to his Beloved Disciple at the Secret Supper, in the Kingdom of Heaven!"

"Exactly. *The Secret Supper*. The book I've decided to open to the eyes of the world."

Benedetto stretched out a thin hand to touch the cover.

"You will annihilate Christendom if you do," he said, trying to catch his breath. "This book is cursed. No one in this world deserves to read it . . . And in the other, at the feet of the Eternal Father, no one has need of it. Burn it!"

"And yet there was a time when you wanted to make it yours."

"There was a time, yes," he rasped. "But I realized that I was falling into the sin of pride. That is why I abandoned your project. That is why I ceased to work for you. You filled my head with mad ideas, as you did with Father Alessandro and Brother Giberto. But I caught on to your stratagems in time—" He gasped for breath. "And I managed to free myself from you."

The one-eyed monk pressed a hand against his breast before continuing in a broken voice.

"I know what you're after, Leonardo. You came to

Catholic Milan full of extravagant notions. Your friends
Botticelli, Raphael, Ficino filled your head with vainglo-
rious ideas about God. And now you want to give the
world the formula for speaking directly to Him, without
intermediaries and without the Church."

"As John did."

"If the people believed in this book, if they knew that
John spoke to the Lord in the Kingdom of Heaven, and
that he returned to Earth to write of it, why then would
anyone need the ministers of Peter?"

"I see that you've understood."

"And I also understand that Ludovico has supported
you all this time because—" He coughed. "Because by
weakening Rome he himself will become stronger. You
wish to change the faith of all good Christians with your
work. You are a demon, a son of Lucifer."

Leonardo smiled. The dying monk could barely
begin to imagine his meticulous plan. For many months,
he had been inviting artists from France and Italy to
come see the *Cenacolo* in order to copy it. Marveled by
his technique and by the novel disposition of his figures,
masters such as Andrea Solario, Giampietrino, Bon-
signori, Buganza and many others had duplicated his
design and were beginning to spread it throughout
Europe. Also, his debatable painting technique *a secco*,
never intended to be long-lasting, lent urgency to the
copying project. The marvel that was the *Cenacolo* was
destined to disappear by express wish of the Master, and
only a continuous, meticulous and carefully planned
effort to reproduce it and make it known would save it.
And in this way, he would disseminate the secret further

and wider than any other work of art in the whole of history.

Leonardo made no reply. What need was there?

His hands still reeked of varnish and solvent, the same that he had used on the brushes with which he had finished the face of John, the man who had written the Gospel that now lay by the dying man's side. The same book that the Visconti Sforza, Dukes of Milan, had caused to be pictured enclosed in the hand of the Priestess on the card, the same one that appears on the lap of the Virgin above the door of Santa Maria dei Fiore in Florence. The same heretic book that Leonardo now intended to reveal to the world.

Without a word, Leonardo took the book and opened it to the first page. He asked Benedetto to recall the scene of the Supper in the refectory, in order to begin to understand his plan. Then, very solemnly, he placed the volume before his eyes and read:

> I, John, who am your brother and share in the affliction so as to be allowed into the Kingdom of Heaven, as I rested on the bosom of Our Lord Jesus Christ, I said unto him: "Lord, who shall betray Thee?" And He answered thus: "He that dippeth his hand with me in the dish, the same shall betray me. For Satan hath entered him, and he seeketh the manner to betray me."

Benedetto shuddered.

"That is what you have painted in the Cenacolo— dear God!"

Leonardo nodded his assent.

"Cursed serpent!" Benedetto coughed furiously.

"Do not deceive yourself, Brother. My work is much more than a scene taken from this Gospel. John asked the Lord nine questions. Two were about Satan, three about the creation of body and spirit, three on John's baptism and the last one on the signs that will precede the Second Coming of Christ. Questions about light and shadow, good and evil, the two opposing forces that hold sway over the world—"

"And all that conceals a secret charm. I know."

"You know?"

Leonardo's face registered his surprise. This old man, fighting against death, still had his wits about him.

"Yes—" he gasped. *"Mut, Nem, A, Los, Noc* . . . And also in Rome they know. I told them. Soon, very soon, Leonardo, they will fall upon you and destroy all that you have so patiently constructed. On that day, Master Leonardo, I will die a satisfied man."

45

Milan, the twenty-second day of February, of the year 1497.

"*Mut, Nem, A, Los, Noc . . .*"

I heard that strange phrase for the first time on the feast day of Holy See. Almost two weeks had gone by since Brother Benedetto's soul had been called to God's Judgment in the hospital of Santa Maria, while he was in the midst of a violent coughing fit. God had punished his pride. The Soothsayer had not lived to witness the wrath of Rome falling on Master Leonardo and shattering his project. His decline was swift. The doctors who attended him night and day gave up the fight when they saw that he had lost his voice and that pustules began to cover his body.

Brother Benedetto died on the afternoon of Ash Wednesday, feverish and muttering my name obsessively in a desperate attempt to bring me before him to fire me against Leonardo. Unfortunately for him, it was many days before I was released from my captivity among the "pure."

Now I believe that Mario Forzetta waited for that precise moment to return me to Milan. Never, during the weeks I stayed in Concorezzo, did Mario speak to me of

Brother Benedetto's illness, nor did he predispose me against him, or insist that I inform the Holy Office of Benedetto's breaking of the fifth commandment; much less induce me to hate him. Mario's attitude astonished me. His training in the secrets of occult writings had helped us unmask the old man and his complex signature, but his strange moral standing prevented him from seeking revenge for the murder of his companions. Mario's was indeed an odd faith.

I came to believe that the men of Concorezzo would hold me there forever. I realized that their extreme respect for life did not permit them to kill me, but I was equally aware that everyone in the town knew full well that, if they set me free, their own lives would be in danger.

I toyed with the question for many days, during which I lived among them and learned their customs. I was surprised to discover that they never entered a church to pray. They preferred to do so in a cave or in the open air. I also confirmed many of the things I already knew, such as their rejection of the Cross and the repudiation of holy relics, since they considered them memories of the impure, and therefore satanic bodies, which, one day, had been home to the souls of great saints. I noticed many things that made me marvel. For example, their rejoicing in death. Every passing day was celebrated because it brought them closer to the moment in which they would shed their mortal coil and ascend to the luminous spirit of God. They, who called themselves "True Christians," looked at me full of pity, and made great efforts to have me join their rituals.

One day, Mario came into my room in a very agitated state and woke me. He asked me to dress in a hurry and then led me down the mountain, to the cobbled road that led to Porta Vercellina. I was intrigued: the young man had made a decision that compromised all his brethren. He would return to the world an inquisitor who had witnessed from within a Cathar community, had been present at their prayers and knew intimately the weaknesses of these last "pure men" of Christendom. And in spite of all this, he was taking the risk of setting me free. Why? And why on this day? And why in such a hurry?

It would not be long before I found out.

As we approached the road that would take us into the duke's domains, Mario changed the tone of the conversation for the first and last time. He had dressed immaculately in white, with a robe that reached his knees and a ribbon in his curly hair. I felt that he was conducting me to a strange and final rite.

"Father Agostino," he said in all solemnity, "now you have met the true disciples of Christ. You have seen, with your own eyes, that we don't carry weapons or offend anything in Nature. For that reason, and because the original followers of Christ would never have accepted that we take away your freedom, we can detain you no longer. You belong to a different world from ours, a world of iron and gold in which men live with their backs turned to God . . ."

I was about to answer, but Mario did not permit me. He looked at me sadly, as if taking leave of a friend.

"From now on," he continued, "our destiny is in

your hands. Your crusaders had the right words: *Deus lo volt!* God has willed it! Either you exempt us and join our ranks, becoming yourself a *parfait,* or you betray us and seek our death and the ruin of our children. But it will be you on your own, a free man, who will choose. We, alas, are accustomed to being persecuted. It's our fate."

"You set me free?"

"In truth, Father, you were never a prisoner."

I looked at him without knowing what to say.

"I only ask you to reflect on one thing before denouncing us to the Holy Office. Remember that Jesus too was a fugitive from justice."

Mario opened his arms and embraced me. Then, in the faint light before dawn, he gave me a small bag with bread and fruit, and left me on my own on the road to Milan.

"Go back to the refectory," he said before losing himself in the wooded slopes. "To your refectory. In the time you've been away, many things have happened that concern you. Meditate on them and then decide what path to choose. I hope that one day we'll meet again and that we'll be able to look into each other's eyes, like brothers of the same faith."

I walked for several hours before glimpsing on the horizon the fortified city of Milan. What was this strange test to which Divine Providence submitted me? Was Mario returning me to the duke's court to eliminate his enemy, Brother Benedetto, or for some other obscure reason?

It was on approaching the sentinel's box that I realized how much the sojourn at Concorezzo had changed me. In the sentinel's eyes, I was no longer the respectable Dominican that had vanished into the woods of Santo Stefano a fortnight earlier. I could not blame him. The city believed that Father Agostino Leyre had died in an ambush. No one expected me to return. My aspect was that of a vulgar, dirty peasant, dressed in black pantaloons and a shepherd's sheepskin coat. My face was covered by a thick black beard and even my tonsure had grown back, hiding my priestly condition.

I passed the box without catching anyone's eye and I headed down the streets that would lead me to the monastery of Santa Maria. In spite of it being a cloudy Saturday, the atmosphere around me seemed extraordinarily festive. The surroundings of the monastery had been decorated with flags, flowers and ribbons, and there were many groups of people on the streets, chatting. Apparently, the duke had passed by on his way to an important celebration.

It was then that I heard a woman give the reason for so much commotion: Leonardo had finished his *Cenacolo*, and His Grace, Duke Ludovico il Moro, had hurried to visit it and admire it in all its splendor.

"The *Cenacolo*?"

The woman looked at me, laughing.

"In what world are you living? The whole city is on its way to see it! Everyone! They say it's a miracle. That it seems as real as life. The monks are opening their monastery for a month, so that everyone can come and admire it."

I was gripped by a feeling of unease. Leonardo had finished a masterpiece on which he spent three years of hard labor, but had he also completed the terrible iconographic program that the Soothsayer had tried to stop at all costs? And the Father Prior? Had he too succumbed to the charm of the work? Should I not reveal to him at once the true identity of his personal assistant? And how was I to face him? What was I to say about my captors?

When I reached the top of Corso Magenta and managed to circumvent the long line that surrounded the monastery, I stood aghast. Ludovico had ordered the erection of an enormous platform on which the duke himself, dressed in black velvet and with a hat with a golden band, stood conversing with several of the city's dignitaries. Among them, I saw Luca Pacioli, the mathematician, very much at his ease. Someone told me that, barely a few days earlier, he had given the duke his book *De Divina Proportione*, in which he unveiled the mathematical secrets of Creation. Also Antonio Billi, the court chronicler, who seemed dazzled by what he had just seen.

I also saw Master Leonardo, away in a corner with a small group of admirers. They were all splendidly dressed, but they seemed nervous, casting glances from side to side, as if expecting the arrival of someone or as if aware that something in the ceremony was not going as planned.

So absorbed was I in trying to understand what was happening in that group, that I did not notice that

The Secret Supper   361

someone had made his way through the crowd and was advancing in my direction.

"Heavens above!" he cried out when he reached me, touching me on the shoulder. "Father Agostino! We all thought you were dead!"

Oliverio Jacaranda, sporting a purple beret embellished with a goose feather, his sword dangling from his belt and riding boots, addressed me in his foreign accent.

"I never forget a face. And far less one like yours!"

"Don Oliverio . . ."

The Spaniard inspected me from head to foot, wondering what had become of my black and white Dominican habit. He had come to Santa Maria, like everyone else, to see Leonardo's work. As a merchant in precious objects he had been granted privileged access to the refectory and he proposed to be at the very center of the city's major social event since Donna Beatrice's funeral.

"Father . . . ," he began. "Will you tell me what happened to you? You look ill. What are you doing dressed like that?"

I tried to invent a credible excuse that would not betray my singular situation. I could not tell him that I had spent over two weeks under the roof of the man who was once his prisoner. He would have considered it disloyal and God knows how the Spaniard would react to such an admission.

"Do you recall my fondness for solving Latin conundrums?" I asked him.

Jacaranda nodded.

"I came to Milan to solve one, by order of my superiors. And to succeed, I was obliged to disappear for some time. Now I'm returning under cover to proceed with my investigations. Therefore I ask you to be discreet."

"Ah, you priests! Always with intrigues and secrets!" He smiled. "So you pretended to disappear in order to investigate the murders at San Francesco il Grande?"

"Whatever makes you think that?" I asked in astonishment.

"The way you look, of course. I told you there are few things in this city that escape my notice. Your clothing reminds me of the poor unfortunates who met their death under the Francescan *Maestà*."

"But—"

"No buts!" He stopped me. "I admire your method, Father. I never would have thought to dress up as a victim in order to discover the murderer."

I said nothing.

I had imagined so many times that, should we meet again, our conversation would not be pleasant, that now I was surprised to see him concerned about me. After all, I had meddled in his business, I had freed one of his prisoners and I had not paid much attention to his efforts to incriminate Leonardo in the murder of Father Alessandro. It was obvious that Signor Oliverio had other, more important things to concern him. And he did seem worried. He hardly mentioned Forzetta's escape and merely said that he imagined it had been part of my strategy to investigate the murders. It was as if my *parfait* costume had obliterated his interest in all the rest.

"Have you been back long in Milan?" I asked to change the subject.

"Some ten days ago. And, to tell the truth, I've been looking for you ever since. They told me you'd been killed in an ambush—"

"I'm glad to say it isn't so."

"So am I, Father."

"Tell me then. What did you require me for?"

"For your help," he said with a sigh. "Do you recall what I said about Leonardo the day we met?"

I turned around, toward where I had last seen the Tuscan. I would not have wanted him to hear a false accusation of murder, such as Jacaranda was surely about to make.

"You know I was in Rome. Well, when I was there, a person close to the Holy Father delivered into my hands the final secret that Master Leonardo wished to conceal in his Last Supper."

"Final secret?"

Jacaranda frowned.

"The same one that your librarian carried to his grave, Father Agostino. The one he must have taken from the 'blue book' that Donna Beatrice ordered me to obtain for her, and that I was never able to deliver. Do you remember now?"

"Yes."

"That secret, Father, is now in my hands. And it's another one of those damned conundrums of Leonardo's. As you're an expert in deciphering riddles and also, because of your position—you're above suspicion of being anyone's accomplice—I thought you might be willing to help me solve it."

Oliverio said this with barely contained anger. I could

guess his desire to avenge his friend Father Alessandro. And, even though he was wrong about his target, I was intrigued by the revelation he might have received from his informer. I could not know then that Bethany too possessed this riddle and had been trying for days to deliver it into my hands.

"Will you show it to me, then?"

"Only in front of the *Cenacolo*, Father Agostino."

46

What a strange sensation.

Dressed in the rags Mario Forzetta had given me before setting me on the road to Milan, I crossed the threshold of Santa Maria without being recognized by any of the brothers. The smell of incense gave me misgivings. I felt as if I were setting foot in a church for the first time. The profusion of floral motifs, red and blue tiles and geometrical designs adorning the ceiling seemed to me improper in the House of the Lord. Never until that day had I paid attention to them, but now, suddenly, they offended me.

Oliverio did not notice my discomfort and pulled me toward the apse, forcing me to turn left and overtake the enormous line of the faithful who were praying and singing as they waited to be allowed into the refectory.

Brother Adriano de Treviglio, whom I had not met more than twice during my stay at the monastery, greeted the Spaniard and with a satisfied gesture pocketed the coin that was placed in his hand. He threw me a supercilious glance, but he did not recognize me. It was better that way.

The refectory that I remembered as cold and still was now swarming with people. It was still empty of furniture, but the monks had made it look presentable, airing it and cleaning it thoroughly. No trace of paint fumes was left, and the recently finished mural shone brightly in all its splendor.

"The Secret Supper," I murmured.

Oliverio did not hear me. He pushed me toward the center of the room and, making his way through the crowd, said something, half in Spanish and half in Lombard, that I did not then fully grasp.

"The mystery of this place is linked to the ancient Egyptians. The disciples are distributed in triads, like the gods of the Nile. Can you see? But the real secret is that each of these characters represents a specific letter."

"A letter?" The old lessons of the *Ars Memoriae* returned to me. "What kind of letter?"

"Only one letter stands out clearly, Father. Look at the great A formed by the body of Our Lord. That is the first clue. Together with the rest, concealed in the attributes that Jacobus de Voragine gave to each of the Twelve, it forms a curious hymn, written in ancient Egyptian, that I hope you can translate—"

"A hymn?"

Oliverio nodded, pleased with my surprise.

"Exactly. Gathering the letters that Leonardo attributed to each disciple, you obtain a phrase which was read to me in Rome: *Mut, Nem, A, Los, Noc*—"

Mut.

Nem.

A.

Los.

Noc.

I repeated the syllables one by one to myself, trying to commit them to memory.

"You say the text is Egyptian?"

"Why, yes! Mut is an Egyptian divinity, the wife of Ammon, 'the Hidden One,' the great god of the pharaohs. No doubt Leonardo heard Marsilio Ficino speak of her. Master Leonardo had all his books in his *bottega*, remember?"

How could I forget? Ficino, Plato, Father Alessandro, the one-eyed monk—they were all there, right in front of my eyes! Staring at one another, as if plotting among themselves to preserve the mystery from those who were not worthy to decipher it. They were all depicted as the true disciples of Christ. As *bonshommes*, in fact.

"And if the language of the phrase were not Egyptian?"

My doubts exasperated the Spaniard. He put his lips to my ear and, trying to make himself heard above the chatter of the curious and the chants of the faithful, he tried to tell me all he had learned from Annio de Viterbo about these men, here reduced to simple letters. I observed them one by one. They seemed so alive! Bartholomew, his hands on the table, watching over the scene like a sentinel. James the Less was trying to calm Peter's fiery temper. Andrew, aghast at the revelation that there was a traitor among them, extended his palms to show his innocence. And Judas. And John. And Thomas pointing toward Heaven. Christ's brother, James the Elder, his arms in the shape of a cross, announcing the Messiah's approaching Passion. Philip. Matthew. Thaddeus turning his back on Christ. And Simon, at his corner of the table, hands extended, as if inviting us to contemplate the scene once again.

To contemplate it once again.

Dear Lord!

It was like a flash of lightning in the night.

As if, suddenly, one of the tongues of fire that illuminated the disciples on Pentecost had descended on me.

Dear Lord! There was no riddle here. Leonardo had not concealed anything in his *Cenacolo*. Nothing at all.

A singular emotion, such as I had never felt in all my years in Bethany, overcame me all at once.

"Do you remember what you told me one day about Leonardo's peculiar writing habits?"

Oliverio looked at me, wondering what my question had to do with the revelation he had just made.

"Do you mean his custom of writing everything in reverse? That's another of his eccentricities. His disciples require a looking glass to read what their master writes. He does that with everything: his notes, his inventories, his receipts, his personal letters. Even his shopping lists! He's a madman."

"Perhaps."

Oliverio's artlessness made me smile. Neither he nor Annio de Viterbo had realized anything, in spite of having held the answer in their hands.

"Tell me, Oliverio. From where did you begin to read your Egyptian phrase?"

"From the left, of course. M for Bartholomew, U for James the Less, T—"

Suddenly he stopped.

He turned his head to the far right of the mural and saw Simon, who, with his arms stretched out, seemed to be inviting him to enter the scene. There also was the

Afterword

Father Agostino Leyre's Final Note

The revelation changed my life.

It was not sudden, but rather a gradual, unstoppable alteration, like that of a forest as spring approaches. At first, I barely noticed it, and when I tried to react, it was too late. I imagine that my peaceful discussions in Concorezzo and the confusion of my first days back in Milan were what had produced the miracle.

I waited for the open-door days at Santa Maria delle Grazie to be over, and then I returned to the *Cenacolo* and placed myself under the hands of Christ. I wanted to receive the benediction of that living, breathing work, which I had seen grow almost imperceptibly. I still do not know quite well why I did it. Nor why I decided not to present myself before the Father Prior and tell him where I had been and what I had discovered during my absence. But, as I have said, something changed within me. Something that would put an end forever to the Agostino Leyre that I had been, preacher and brother at the Secretariat of Keys of the Papal States, theologian and official of the Holy Office.

Illumination? Divine flame? Madness, perhaps? It is probable that I will die among the rocks of Yabal al-Tarif without knowing what name to give to my transformation.

It matters not.

The truth is that the discovery of the Cathar sacrament exposed to the contemplation and veneration of all, in the very heart of the House of the Dominicans, those patrons of the Inquisition and guardians of orthodoxy, had a cleansing effect on my soul. I discovered that evangelical truth had cleaved its way through the darkness of our Order, streaming from the refectory like the beam of a lighthouse in the night. It was a much different truth from the one I had believed in for forty-five years: Jesus had never instituted the Eucharist as the only means of reaching Him. Rather the contrary was true. His teachings to John and to Mary Magdalene were aimed at showing us how to find God within ourselves, without having recourse to exterior artifices. Jesus was a Jew. He saw how the priests exercised their control over God by shutting Him up in the Tabernacle. And he fought against it. Fifteen centuries later, Leonardo became the secret carrier of the revelation, which he entrusted to his *Cenacolo*.

Perhaps it was then that I lost my mind. I admit it. But everything took place exactly in the way I have related.

Three decades have elapsed since those events and Abdul, who has now brought my food up to my cave as usual, has also brought me strange news. A group of hermits, followers of Saint Anthony, have arrived in his village with the intention of staying in the vicinity. I have searched the banks of the Nile trying to find them, but my weak eyes have not been able to discover their location. I am aware that they might be my last chance. If someone were worthy of receiving my confidences in this last stretch of my life, I would deposit these pages in his hands and I would explain the importance of keeping them in a safe place until the time comes to reveal them. But my strength ebbs and I am not certain of being able to climb down these cliffs to reach them.

Also, even if I managed to do it, it would not be easy to make myself understood.

Oliverio Jacaranda, for example, never understood the secret of the *Cenacolo*, even though it was before his eyes. The fact that the thirteen protagonists carried the thirteen letters of *Consolamentum*, the only sacrament admitted by the *parfaits* of Concorezzo (a spiritual, invisible, intimate sacrament), meant nothing to him. He ignored how linked this symbol was to the "blue book" that he was destined never to hold in his hands. And of course, he never suspected that his servant, Mario Forzetta, had betrayed him for the sake of that volume. A volume that, for generations, had been used in Cathar ceremonies to receive the neophytes into the Church of the Spirit, the Church of John, and initiate them on their individual quest for the Father.

I know that Oliverio returned to Spain and settled near the ruins of Tarraco, and that he went on doing business with Pope Alexander. Around that time, Leonardo entrusted his book, his precious *Secret Supper*, to his disciple Bernardino Luini, who in turn gave it to

an artist of the Languedoc who took it with him to
Carcassonne. There it was intercepted by the French
Holy Office, which never succeeded in interpreting
it correctly. Luini never painted the Eucharist, nor
did Marco d'Oggiono. Neither did any of Leonardo's
beloved disciples.

Elena's destiny was a curious one. I never met her in
person. After sitting for the Master, the little countess
realized that perhaps John's Church would never be
instituted. She left Leonardo's *bottega*, stopped pursuing
poor Luini, and entered a convent of Clares near the
French border. Leonardo, having discovered her sharp
intelligence, revealed to her the great secret of her line:
that her remote ancestor was Mary Magdalene, who had
seen Christ resurrected outside the tomb that Joseph of
Arimathea had prepared for Him. For centuries, the
Church had refused to hear her full story. Leonardo, on
the other hand, had listened carefully, learning how, fifteen hundred years ago, Mary Magdalene saw the living
Christ not as a mortal body but as pure light. His cold,
dead body lay still in the tomb when she was met by His
"body of light." Moved by the experience, she decided
to steal His physical remains and hide them in her
house, where she carefully embalmed them and took
them with her to France when the persecutions began.

That was the secret and no other. Christ did not resurrect as a mortal body. He resurrected as light, showing
us the path of our own transmutation when the final
hour comes.

I learned that Elena stayed with the Clares for only
five years. One day, she simply disappeared from her cell,

and no one saw her again. It is told that she accompanied Leonardo during his exile in France and settled at the court of François I as one of the queen's ladies-in-waiting, and that, on occasion, she still sat for the Master. It seems that Leonardo called her on his deathbed and asked her to lend him her face and hands so that he could retouch the unfinished portrait of a woman known as the *Mona Lisa*. Those who have seen it say that the similarities between the John of the *Cenacolo* and the woman in the portrait speak for themselves. I, unfortunately, cannot judge.

If Elena was in fact granted further access to secrets of the Church of John and Mary Magdalene that Leonardo had planned to set up, she took them with her to the grave. Shortly before I decided to travel to Egypt to spend my last years here, Elena died of the fever.

All that is left now is for me to explain why I came here, to Egypt, to write these pages, and why I never denounced the existence of a community of *parfaits* in Concorezzo, linked to Master Leonardo.

The fault, once again, is his, the blue-eyed giant in white garments.

After the opening of the *Cenacolo*, I did not see him again. After discovering its secret meaning, I returned to Rome and knocked on the doors of the House of Truth in Bethany. I resumed my work there without anybody asking too many questions. The following year, however, I learned that Leonardo had fled Milan as soon as the French troops breached the duke's defenses and captured the city. He took refuge in Mantua, then in Venice, and finally he arrived in Rome. There he was given employment by Cesare Borgia, son of Pope Alexander. He became *architecto e ingegnere generale*, architect and principal engineer, wasting his other talents. But while this new occupation did not last long, it was long enough for him to meet the official responsible for the Palazzo Sacro, Father Annio de Viterbo.

Annio was much affected by their meeting. His secretary, Fabio Ponte, informed Bethany of the encounter in the spring of 1502. They spoke of the supreme function of art, of its uses to preserve memory and of its all-powerful influence on the minds of the people. According to Fabio, there were two of Leonardo's opinions that greatly affected Father Annio.

"All I have found out regarding Jesus' true message is nothing compared to that which is still to be revealed," he answered to one of the Weasel's questions. "And just as, for the sake of my art, I've drunk at the Egyptian sources and studied the secrets of their geometry translated by Ficino and Pacioli, I tell you that the Church has still much to drink from the Gospels that lie buried under the sands of the Nile."

Annio de Viterbo died five days later, probably poisoned by Cesare Borgia.

A month after that, fearing that I would soon suffer reprisals from those who feared the return of the Church of John, I left Bethany forever in search of those ancient lost Gospels.

I know they are somewhere near yet still I have not found them. But I have sworn that I will continue to search for them until the end of my days.

*

In 1945, in a region close to the Egyptian village of Nag Hammadi, in the Upper Nile, thirteen volumes of lost gospels were unearthed, bound in leather. They were written in Coptic and contained teachings of Christ unknown to the Western world. Their discovery, of far greater importance than that of the famous Dead Sea Scrolls of Qumran, proves the existence of a considerable community of primitive Christians who believed in the coming of a new Church based on spiritual values and a direct communication with God. These are known today as the Gnostic Gospels, and it is certain that copies arrived in Europe toward the end of the Middle Ages, greatly influencing certain intellectual circles.

The cave in Yabal el-Tarif where Father Agostino Leyre died in August of 1526 was less than one hundred feet away from the niche where these books were found.

AUTHOR'S NOTES

- In 1208, Pope Innocent III ordered the eradication of the Cathar heresy, creating a military force to exterminate the heterodox rebels from the French Languedoc. Even though it is generally accepted that by 1244 the last heretics had died out in Montségur, many historians point out that entire families of "good men," or *bonshommes*, had sought refuge in Lombardy, close to the Milan of today, where they lived for many years safe from the persecution of Rome, keeping their original faith.

- Luini refers to the famous "conspiracy of the Pazzi" that made an attempt against the life of Lorenzo the Magnificent in the Cathedral of Florence. Lorenzo managed to escape unharmed, but his brother Giuliano was stabbed twenty-seven times. The resulting repression was one of the most bloody of the fifteenth century.

- Until the nineteenth century, the Catholic Church identified Mary of Bethany, sister of Lazarus and of Martha, with Mary Magdalene.

- The most recent and complete study relating the signs of the zodiac to the Twelve Apostles is by Nicola Sementovsky-Kurilo. According to him, the disciples in the *Cenacolo* are distributed in four groups of three to represent the four elements of Nature: earth, fire, air and water. Sementovsky assigns to each disciple a specific astrological sign. To Simon, at one end of the table, corresponds Aries; to Thaddeus, Taurus; Matthew, Gemini; Philip, Cancer; James the Elder, Leo; Thomas, Virgo; John, Libra (an important symbolic reading since, according to Sementovsky, the young John lends equilibrium to the future Church); Judas, Scorpio; Peter, Sagittarius; Andrew, Capricorn; James the Less, Aquarius; Bartholomew, Pisces.

Regarding Leonardo da Vinci's paintings mentioned in the novel:

Cenacolo is the colloquial term by which *The Last Supper* was known in Milan. *Maestà,* or "Majesty," was the name given to *The Virgin of the Rocks.* The portrait of Lucrezia Crivelli became celebrated under the title *La Belle Ferronnière.* Both these paintings now hang in the Louvre.

Regarding the bust that Leonardo supposedly used to portray the Apostle Simon, it can be seen today in the Uffizi, in Florence. It is a bust of Plato attributed to the Greek sculptor Silanion, who was, as far as we know, the only artist to portray the philosopher during his lifetime, by order of King Mithridates, in 325 B.C.

TRANSLATOR'S NOTE

In Leonardo's time, the Bible most commonly read was St. Jerome's translation into Latin, known as the Vulgate. The version here quoted is the English translation called the King James Bible, produced more than a century after the events of the novel, the virtue of familiarity overriding, in this translator's opinion, the sin of anachronism.

ACKNOWLEDGMENTS

My unraveling of an enigma locked away for five centuries could not have been possible without the help of a great many people from different parts of the world. The three years of investigation that preceded the writing of *The Secret Supper* allowed me to meet with experts in art, literature and history, many of whom eventually became my dear friends. Interestingly enough, the most decisive contributions to this undertaking were made by women. Their input was crucial at key moments, and for this reason I wish to offer my special thanks to all of them, starting with my agent, Antonia Kerrigan, who believed in my project and got behind it with absolute devotion. Her enthusiasm promptly infected Elaine and Tom Colchie, my new agents in the States, who knew how to open the best of all possible doors for my book: Atria Books. There, my editors Judith Curr and Johanna Castillo nurtured Leonardo da Vinci's secret with uncommon zeal. As did Deborah Blackman at Plaza & Janés, in Spain, the first European publisher of the novel.

I lack the words to thank the extraordinary editorial team at Simon & Schuster in the United States for all their help. During the months preceding the publication of *The Secret Supper*, I grew to understand what it means to have a top editorial team and how much determination can emanate from really believing in an idea. My sincere appreciation goes to Carolyn Reidy, president of Adult Publishing, for her visionary publishing. And also to Justin Loeber and Melissa Quiñones in publicity; to Michael Selleck, Sue Fleming, Karen Louie-Joyce and Christine Duplessis in marketing; to Sybil Pincus, Isolde Sauer and Nancy Inglis in production; to Nancy Clements, Karen Mender and Orly Sigal; and to Amy Tannenbaum, who always kept me in the loop regarding day-to-day developments.

Obviously, I cannot forget my first Spanish readers, who contributed so much to improving the original manuscript: above all, Eva, my wife, to whom this book is deservedly dedicated. She read absolutely everything, including those pages that did not survive. Also, Juan Eslava Galán, a contemporary master of Spanish letters, who taught me a great deal about the craft of writing; Antonio Piñero, Professor of New Testament Philology at the Universidad Complutense in Madrid, who read and corrected me, profligate with his wisdom; and Juan Sol, Gloria Abad, Ángeles Carmona and Roser Castellvi, who regaled me with their astute observations.

Among these names should also figure that of David Gombau, who from the beginning oversaw my webpage with tireless energy; María Ángeles Puche, my lawyer, for her generous and invaluable advice; and the jury that selected this novel as finalist for the Premio Internacional de Novela Ciudad Torrevieja, in Spain, in September 2004, judging its literary quality—an attribute that my English-language readers will now be able to judge for themselves, certainly, through the superb translation by Alberto Manguel.

But there's more.

During my research work in Milan, the hospitality of Brother Venturino Alce, of the Dominican monastery of Santa Maria delle Grazie, was decisive; he allowed me to consult both the archive and the library of the same premises to which Leonardo da Vinci himself had had access five centuries ago. Not to mention the assistance—and the obstacles—presented to me by the Soprintendenza dei Beni Culturali, which luckily never suspected what I already understood about *The Last Supper* prior to my admission there. That knowledge, for certain, owed much to the work of Dr. Pinin Brambilla and Professor Pietro Marani, who for twenty years had worked on the restoration of Leonardo's masterpiece.

Finally, I'll never forget that the first coffee I had after I'd just seen *The Last Supper* for the very first time was with my Italian publisher, Marco Tropea, who wanted to read this book from the moment I told him what it was to be about. Nor will I forget the writer Robert Bauval, who was the first person that I'd heard talk about the *Ars Memoriae*, when I was in Cairo at the spring equinox of 2000. But, above all, I cannot fail to mention my parents, who not only forgave my absences during three long years but who also made me feel the extent of their love when they finally read the result.

Their smiles, upon learning my secret, are what actually made this whole project worth the while.

CAST OF CHARACTERS

The novel's main characters are described below. Those whose names are followed by dates of birth and death are actual historical figures who also appear as characters in *The Secret Supper*.

Alberti, Father Leon Battista (1404–1472). Besides being a priest, he was a painter, architect, poet, antiquarian, philosopher and inventor. But he was also famous in the art of encrypting messages, designing the first cryptograph in history: a "coding disk" that facilitated the encrypting and deciphering of secret messages.

Alexander VI, Pope (1431–1503). Of Spanish origin, he was one of the most complex figures of his time. He purchased his accession to the throne of Peter, and his corrupt and dissolute life earned him numerous enemies. He had five sons. And surprisingly, he believed himself a descendant of the Egyptian god Osiris.

Amadeo of Portugal (1430–1482). This Franciscan, whose lay name was João Mendes da Silva, was born in Ceuta, Spain, the brother of Saint Beatriz da Silva, and died under suspicion of heresy. He wrote *Apocalipsis Nova*, a treatise that inspired Leonardo for his *Virgin of* *the Rocks*. Amadeo's text also prophesied the coming of an angelic pope.

Arno, Brother Guglielmo. Responsible for the meals served at the monastery of Santa Maria delle Grazie; "infected" with the Cathar heresy.

Bacon, Brother Roger (1214–1294). A member of the Franciscan order, an inventor, theologian and philosopher. Author of the treatise *De Secretis Artis et Naturae Operibus*, which elaborates twelve distinct forms of hiding a message in a work of art. In effect, this was the first European book that described the use of cryptography. Many consider Bacon a kind of "Leonardo" of the thirteenth century.

Bandello, Brother Matteo (1484–1561). He was only twelve years old when Leonardo painted *The Last Supper*. He was a cousin of Father Prior Vicenzo Bandello and became the most celebrated novelist of the Italian Renaissance. In his writings he spoke of his childhood in the company of Leonardo.

Bandello, Father Prior Vicenzo (1435–1506). Prior of the monastery of Santa Maria delle Grazie in Milan between 1495 and 1501. After his term in that office and the death of Master General Gioacchino Torriani, he was named Master General of the Order of Saint Dominic.

Benedetto, Brother. A Dominican at Santa Maria delle Grazie, confessor and secretary to Father Prior Bandello. He lost an eye at seventeen years of age from an assault at the monastery of Castelnuovo. After this event he was transferred to the convent of Santa Maria delle Grazie.

Botticelli, Sandro (1444–1510). He was, like Leonardo, a disciple of Verrocchio, although also of Fra Filippo Lippi. He is considered one of the great geniuses of the Italian Renaissance. Thanks to the Medici, he studied pagan themes and applied this knowledge to works like *Spring* and *The Birth of Venus*. For a time, he used his painting as an instrument of magic on behalf of his protector. Under the influence of the heretical monk Savonarola he abandoned painting.

Cosimo the Elder (1389–1464), also known as Cosimo de' Medici. Governor of Florence and famous merchant, he was the great patron of intellectuals and artists of his time. After the Council of Florence, in 1431, which attempted to unite Eastern and Western Christianity, he founded the Platonic Academy, which he promptly entrusted to the then extremely young Marsilio Ficino.

Crivelli, Elena. Daughter of Lucrezia Crivelli and niece of Carlo Crivelli, the celebrated Italian painter of the fifteenth century. In the novel she is presented as the descendant of a sect of women initiated in the secrets of Mary Magdalene.

Crivelli, Lucrezia (1452–1519). She was the model Leonardo used for *La Belle Ferronnière* (today in the Louvre, in Paris). As one of the mistresses of Ludovico Sforza, she bore him at least one daughter out of wedlock.

da Benasco, Sister Veronica (1445–1497). Augustinian nun from the Milanese convent of Santa Marta; later beatified. Her life was filled with visions and ecstasies, and her divinations caused a sensation during her epoch. She actually admonished Pope Alexander for his profligate ways. She correctly predicted she would die on Friday, January 13, 1497.

d'Este, Beatrice (1475–1497). Duchess of Milan, daughter of the Duke of Ferrara and wife of the Milanese Ludovico Sforza. Her lifelong obsession was to convert Milan into a new Athens that would restore humanity to the "Golden Age" about which the ancient philosophers had spoken. She lived surrounded by luxury and fashion until her death during childbirth, in January 1497. She incarnated the Italian ideal of the Renaissance princess.

de Viterbo, Annio (1432–1502). A Dominican friar, professor of theology and expert in Oriental languages. Alexander VI named him Master of the Holy Palace and he died probably from poisoning. Author of various books, he was the first "archaeologist" of history, although he was also one of the great falsifiers of his time. He fabricated Egyptian pieces to which he added spurious inscriptions to justify his theories. Today he is practically forgotten.

d'Oggiono, Marco (1470–1549). He became one of Leonardo da Vinci's favorite students, remarkable for his talent at painting frescoes. After witnessing the completion of *The Last Supper*, at Santa Maria delle Grazie, he was one of the artists to copy it most.

della Mirandola, Pico (1463–1494). He was one of the most fervent disciples of Plato in the Renaissance. His teacher was Marsilio Ficino, by whose hand he learned Hebrew and was introduced to the Kabbalah. Although the Pope banned the reading of his books, the Pope absolved him in 1493.

Ficino, Marsilio (1433–1499). Outstanding intellectual, doctor, musician and preacher of his time. He translated into Latin for the first time the works of Plato and the treatises on magic of the Egyptians known as the *Corpus Hermeticum*. He founded the Academy of Florence, from which the Renaissance was "born."

Forzetta, Mario. Painter's apprentice, born (like Beatrice d'Este) in Ferrara. At seventeen, he traveled to Milan to work in the *bottega* of Leonardo da Vinci. However, he soon ended up trafficking in ancient manuscripts in the service of Oliverio Jacaranda. It was in his native Ferrara that he entered into contact with the Cathar heresy.

Giberto, Brother. Sacristan at Santa Maria delle Grazie. He was born on the frontier of the Germanic empire. His pumpkin-colored hair made him the butt of not a few gibes in his community.

Jacaranda, Oliverio. Antiquarian, originally from Valencia, Spain, as was Pope Alexander VI. He was one of the first antiquarians to furnish the pontifical palaces, as well as the Sforza family, with ancient works of art.

Leonardo da Vinci (1452–1519). Embodied the ideal of the Renaissance man. Painter, sculptor, scientist, engineer, cook and musician, he bequeathed to posterity more than thirteen thousand pages of notes, a few paintings and an enigmatic, finished mural known as *The Last Supper*. His contemporaries considered him a bad Christian, and the Pope never called upon him to decorate any Vatican building. However, until the publication of this novel, no one seems to have understood very well what exactly Leonardo's beliefs were.

Leyre, Father Agostino. Inquisitor from Rome and important member of the Secretariat of Keys of the Papal States. Expert in cryptography and theology. He narrates the story as an old man, from his retreat in Egypt, the place to which he fled following the discoveries he made in Milan during his mission to spy on Leonardo da Vinci in the winter of 1497.

Lorenzo the Magnificent (1449–1492), also known as Lorenzo de' Medici. Grandson of Cosimo the Elder, he was an impassioned patron of the arts. He maintained Marsilio Ficino as head of the Platonic Academy and was also Michelangelo's benefactor. He was particularly interested in ancient manuscripts, numismatics and stone engravings.

Luini, Bernardino (1470–1532). Important disciple of Leonardo da Vinci whose works may be seen in various important European museums. Little biographical information about him survives, but he seems never to have left the area of Italian Lombardy.

Pinturicchio (1454–1513). His real name was Bernardino di Betto. His intellectual formation took place at the Academy of Marsilio Ficino. In 1493 he was called to Rome to decorate the Borgia apartments, by order of Pope Alexander VI. Under instructions from Annio de Viterbo, Pinturicchio re-created the myth of the Egyptian gods Osiris, Isis and Apis, depicting for the first time sacred oxen, pyramids and pagan divinities in the heart of the papacy.

Plato (428–347 B.C.). This father of Western philosophy lay forgotten until the fifteenth century, when his works were translated by Marsilio Ficino and printed for the first time in Italy in 1483. To impart his knowledge, Plato founded the Academy, an institution that Ficino would try to imitate nineteen centuries later with the assistance of the Medici family.

Ponte, Fabio. Personal secretary to Annio de Viterbo and nephew of the Master General of the Dominicans, Gioacchino Torriani.

Savonarola, Girolamo (1452–1498). This Dominican, born in Ferrara, was one of the most polemical figures of his time. He preached against the wealth of the papacy and managed even to convince artists like Botticelli to burn their works that employed pagan motifs. His influential enemies eventually had him hanged and burned at the stake for heresy.

Sforza, Brother Mauro. Cousin to the Duke of Milan, he entered the monastery of Santa Maria delle Grazie after the death of his uncle Gian Galeazzo Sforza, in 1494. He worked as a sexton.

Sforza, Ludovico (1452–1508), also known as Ludovico il Moro (i.e., the Moor) because of his dark skin. Duke of Milan, patron of Leonardo da Vinci and responsible for the project of *The Last Supper* in the monastery of Santa Maria delle Grazie. He commissioned this painting as part of his plan to convert the monastery into his family mausoleum.

Torriani, Master General Gioacchino (1417–1500). Highest authority of the Order of Saint Dominic, he was a man of great culture and one of the first humanists of the Renaissance. He spoke five languages.

Toscanelli, Paolo (1398–1482). Italian scientist, cartographer and geographer who inspired the voyages of Columbus to America. His studies contributed to the knowledge of astronomy in his time, and he constructed a sundial for the Cathedral of Florence, described in the novel.

Trivulzio, Father Alessandro. Native of Riccio, he was the librarian at Santa Maria delle Grazie. Devoted to the study of ancient manuscripts, he assembled an important collection for the monastery.

Also:

For more information about this book, please visit

www.thesecretsupper.com

An excerpt from
Javier Sierra's
upcoming novel

THE LADY IN BLUE

"The man is a bloody eccentric," Baldi thought to himself, only to regret the thought a short while later.

Giuseppe Baldi walked through the gate designed by the architect Filarete in 1477, whose doors opened onto the *loggia della benedizione*, the portico of blessings, and into the most famous basilica in Christianity. Baldi headed toward the spot where tourists line up to climb to the dome of Saint Peter's.

After a quick look at the confessionals along the south wall, he sought out number nineteen. The identifying numbers were only barely legible near the top of the tall wooden boxes but looking closely, a keen observer could discern what were, once upon a time, resplendent Roman numerals hand-painted in gold, with the designation "Heavenly Listening Room" in the upper right-hand corner. XIX was the booth farthest to the right and the one closest to Adrian VI's extravagant tomb. Visible on the entrance to the booth was a plaque, laden with years of grime, which announced CONFESSIONS WILL BE HEARD IN POLISH BY THE PRIEST IN CHARGE, PADRE CZESTOCOWA.

Baldi felt like a fool. Just thinking about it made him turn red. It must have been more than a hundred years since members of the clergy used the confession booths for clandestine meetings, much less in these times when the Vatican had entire auditoriums wired with illegal listening devices. Although he admitted that it was unlikely that the sophisticated listening devices favored by the Sant'Uffizio's secret service and other "agencies" had been installed here.

The Benedictine had no other choice. He had the correct time for the appointment. And what's more, it wasn't a mistake: the message in the mailbox at the residence where he was lodging made it perfectly clear.

Very well then, he would do as he was told. Giuseppe Baldi, Benedictine priest, professor of music and a resident of Venice, entered booth nineteen on the right-hand side and bent down on his knees. As he might have guessed, there were no Polish Catholics on line at that hour to receive absolution. The faithful who came from the same part of the world as the Holy Father generally preferred to use that time of day for a quick nap or a bit of television.

"Hail Mary full of grace," he whispered.

"Conceived without sin, Padre Baldi."

The voice on the other side of the latticework made it clear he had made the right choice. The "evangelist" tried to camouflage his enthusiasm.

"Monsignor?"

"I'm glad you could make it, Giuseppe," he said. "I have important news for you, and I have good reason to believe that even my office is no longer secure."

Stanislaw Zsidiv's unmistakably nasal voice bore a certain funereal air which disturbed the "penitent." His heart began to beat faster.

"Have you learned something new about the death of Padre Corso?"

"Analysis of the adrenaline content of his blood indicates that 'Saint Matthew,' our own dear brother Corso, had some sort of grave confrontation before he died. Something that so overwhelmed him, he made the decision to take his own life."

"What could it be, Your Eminence?"

"I don't know, my son, but doubtless something terrible. Now, as Doctor Ferrell will tell you, every effort centers on finding out who the last person to see Corso alive was and what their influence was on his decision, if any."

"I understand."

"But I didn't ask you to come here for that, my son."

"No?"

"Do you remember when we spoke of Benavides' *Memorial* in my office?"

The Monsignor was testing Baldi's ability to retain information.

"If I remember correctly, it was a report assembled by a Franciscan in the seventeenth century concerning the apparitions of the Lady in Blue who appeared somewhere in the southern United States."

"Bull's eye." His Eminence nodded with satisfaction. "That document, as I already told you, fascinated Corso at the very end of his life, because he believed that he had discovered in it a description of how a cloistered nun was physically carried from Spain to the New World in order to preach to the Indians. In 1629!"

"I see."

"What you may not know is that Corso was in the process of requesting an unpublished manuscript by the same Padre Benavides, in which he identified the Lady in Blue as a nun by the name of Sor María Jesus de Ágreda, and that he had learned the method she used to send herself, by bilocation, to America."

"The formula for bilocation . . . ?"

"Just so."

"And he discovered it? It's in the manuscript?"

"This is where things get murky, my son. We're talking about a text to which no one has paid the slightest attention until now. Corso searched for it in the Pontiff's Archives the very day before his death, without success. Nevertheless, that same day someone entered the National Library in Madrid and stole a manuscript belonging to King Philip IV."

The Cardinal took a deep breath before the Benedictine had a chance to react.

"Yes, Giuseppe. It was the very same *Memorial* that 'Saint Matthew' was looking for."

Baldi struggled desperately to find some sort of logical connection between the disparate events.

"According to what we learned this morning," Zsidiv went on, "the Spanish police have not as yet detained any suspects, but everything points to the robbery being the work of professionals. Perhaps the same criminals who stole Padre Corso's files."

"What makes you suspect that, Your Eminence?"

"It's my impression that someone wants to make every scrap of information relevant to the Lady in Blue disappear. Someone on the inside. Someone who wants to block the development of our Chronovision, and who doesn't seem inclined to take half measures to do so."

"But why go to so much trouble?"

"The only thing that makes sense to me," Zsidiv whispered, "is that this 'someone' has developed an investigation parallel to ours, has obtained successful results, and is presently erasing each and every clue that led them to their accomplishment."

Baldi protested. "That's nothing more than conjecture."

"Which is why I asked you to come here today. I don't feel safe in Saint Peter's, my son. The walls have ears. The Holy Office has called a meeting to take a look at the latest developments on the project. A meeting at the very highest level."

"Are you saying that the enemy resides in the very heart of the Church, Your Eminence?"

"And what do you propose, Giuseppe?"

"Nothing. Perhaps if we knew what that purloined document contained, we would know where to start looking. . . ."

Zsidiv made an effort to stretch his legs inside the sort of vertical coffin that is a confessional. And then he added laconically, "But we know what's in it."

"Really?"

"Certainly, my son. Benavides wrote his *Memorial of New Mexico* here, in Rome. He made two copies of the document: one for Urban VIII and a second for Philip IV. The second is the copy that was stolen."

"Which means, we still have it!"

"Yes and no . . ." he clarified. "You see, Fray Alonso de Benavides was governor for the New Mexico region until 1629. After interrogating the missionaries who had collected data on the Lady in Blue, he went off to Mexico, from where his superior, the Basque Archbishop

Manso y Zúñiga, sent him to Spain to bring a certain investigation to a close."

"Which investigation, Your Eminence?"

On the other side of the latticework, 'Saint John,' the coordinator of the Chronovision project, let out a short laugh. "Benavides left New Mexico convinced that the Lady in Blue was a nun famous in Europe as a miracle worker, a woman by the name of María Luisa de Carrión. The only problem with that theory is that the Indians described a woman who was young and attractive, and at that point Carrión was well over sixty years old. Even so, that wasn't enough to convince Benavides. And instead of believing that the Lady in Blue could possibly be a new apparition of the Virgin of Guadalupe, he preferred to believe that her 'voyage through the air' had brought new life to Carrión's appearance."

"What tripe!"

"It was the seventeenth century, my son. Nobody knew what the implications were for someone who flew through the air."

"Of course, but . . ."

"Let me tell you something else, my son," the Monsignor cut in. "Something I learned this morning in the Secret Archive."

Giuseppe Baldi's ears opened all the way.

"In Mexico City, the archbishop showed Benavides a letter from a certain Franciscan friar by the name of Sebastián Marcilla, in which he spoke of another nun, younger, with mystical powers, who also suffered all sorts of supernatural ecstasies."

"She was able to bilocate?"

"That was, in fact, one of her graces. Her name was

Sor María Jesús de Ágreda. Manso y Zúñiga, unnerved by the letter, sent the very same Benavides to Spain to investigate. He crossed the Atlantic at the beginning of 1630, disembarked at Sevilla and from there traveled to Madrid and Ágreda to investigate. He personally interrogated the supposed Lady in Blue, and afterward took up residence in Rome, where he wrote his *Memorial*."

"Then, why did you say that the copy of *Memorial* he made for the Pope isn't useful to us?"

"Because the copy in the King of Spain's possession and the one in the Pope's library weren't exactly identical. To begin with, the copy given to the Pope was dated incorrectly in 1630. And it is still listed under that date in the Archive. Which is why Corso didn't find it. Second, in the copy that Benavides sent to the King, the Portuguese wrote notes in the margins, with full details as to how he believed the nun was able to transport herself physically, taking with her liturgical objects which she gave to the Indians."

"Liturgical objects?"

"Rosaries, votive cups . . . The Franciscans found them when they arrived in New Mexico. The Indians preserved them, regarding them as gifts from the Lady in Blue. Benavides took a rosary with him. He asked to be buried with it."

"And how could this lady . . ."

"It seems, my son, that at the same time that the nun in the monastery in Ágreda plunged into a trance that left her in a sleeplike state, her 'essence' materialized in a different location. It became flesh."

"Exactly like Ferrell's 'dreamers'!"

"What's that?"

Baldi imagined Cardinal Zsidiv's gesture of surprise on the other side of the confession booth's latticework.

"I thought you already knew about that, Your Eminence."

"Knew what?"

"That the final experiment undertaken by Corso, in conjunction with the doctor, was an attempt to project a woman whom they called the 'dreamer' back to the Lady in Blue's time. They hoped she would discover the secret of the voyages, and they would then serve it to INSCOM, an organization within the CIA, on a silver platter."

"And did they pull it off?"

"Well, the experiment they tried on the woman was very hush-hush, but they said she became distraught and broke off all connection with them. She returned to the United States but I have not, as of yet, been able to verify her whereabouts."

"Find her!" Zsidiv ordered in a very serious tone. "She has the key! I'm sure of it!"

"But how will I do it?"

The Cardinal leaned in so closely to the partition that Baldi could feel the other man's breath on his face.

"Let the signs show you the way," the Cardinal said.

Before Giuseppe Baldi could respond, an unexpected event forever changed the course of their conversation.

Three loud explosions went off at exactly the same moment in St. Peter's, deafening detonations that released clouds of smoke and whose echoes reverberated inside the confession booth where Zsidiv and Baldi were sitting. The two men sat there, frozen. What was happening? It was almost as if the colossal statue of San Longino, Bernini's masterpiece, had tumbled from its pedestal and all of its forty-five feet had shattered on the floor. Had it been destroyed? The blasts sounded as if they came from very nearby. Baldi instinctively shifted position in the booth, leaning away from the latticework to try to ascertain where the sound had come from. The bursts of noise emanated from the no-less-gigantic statue of Saint Veronica. From his position in the confessional, all he could make out was a cloud of billowing smoke rising toward the roof of the nave.

"An attack!" he muttered fearfully.

"What did you say?" Zsidiv was paralyzed.

"It looks as if someone tried to blow up the statue of Veronica," Baldi said to make himself clear.

"It can't be. Santa Veronica?"

There wasn't time to react. Two seconds later, a woman with an athletic build, swathed in black, emerged from the cloud of smoke and dust. Moving like a cat, she eluded the crowd watching the unfolding events and ran straight toward Padre Baldi and the door leading to the dome.

"One minute, thirty seconds," she said, breathing heavily.

The Benedictine tumbled down, falling back on his heels, while the fugitive seized the moment—and took a deep breath—before delivering a cryptic message.

"Ask the second, Giuseppe. Pay attention to the signs."

Baldi nearly lost his balance again. Did she say his name? And what was that about signs? Hadn't Zsidiv just said the same thing?

"The second?" Baldi quickly went to the heart of the message. As he turned around to look in the direction of the fugitive, he raised his voice and shouted, "Who'd you say that to? Listen to me! Was that for me?"

"The second," she repeated.

It was the last thing he saw.